Woman on the Run

Prologue
September 30th
Boston

"Your new name is Sally Anderson," the U.S. Marshal said.

"That's ridiculous," Julia Devaux snapped testily. "Do I look like a Sally?"

"Well, to be perfectly truthful..." The Marshal looked her up and down with compassion. "What you look like right now is a mess."

"Thanks a lot." Julia pulled the smelly, worn hotel blanket closer around her shoulders, sure that generations of traveling salesmen had jerked off on it. But it was warm. For three days now, she'd felt chilled to the bone. Of course, for three days now someone had been trying to kill her, which would be enough to chill anyone.

The man sat down next to her on the dingy hotel bed in the dingy hotel room and took her hand. As U.S. Marshals went, Herbert Davis was no Gary Cooper. Not much taller than she was, he looked more like a CPA than a U.S. Marshal.

Had Julia worked for Central Casting, she would have chosen someone else to play the role of a U.S. Marshal. Had anyone asked Julia, she would have said that Herbert Davis simply didn't have *le physique du role*. Marshals were supposed to be tall, athletic, steely eyed, a six-shooter strapped to lean hips. Not short, roundish and nearsighted, with a cellular phone in the holster. But no one had asked her opinion and she had to go with what she had.

"Listen, Sally —"

"Sally?"

"From now on, you are Sally Anderson." Herbert Davis pulled some papers from his rumpled suit jacket. "Your full name is Sally May Anderson. You were born on August 19th, 1977, in Bend, Oregon, to Bob and Laverne Anderson, bookkeeper and homemaker. You have lived your entire life in the Pacific Northwest and have never been abroad, not even to Canada. You graduated from the local teacher's college in 1999 and have been teaching school and living at home in Bend ever since. You wanted to get away from your parents, so you have just accepted a job in Simpson, Idaho as a second-grade teacher."

A grade school teacher? *Ewww.*

"No way," Julia said firmly, standing. The tiny mud-colored carpet with coffee stains and cigarette burns was too small to pace so she quivered instead.

"This isn't going to work. I've never been to Oregon and I've never been to Idaho. I've never been further west than Chicago, actually. I couldn't possibly pretend to be a grade school teacher. I'm an only child. I've never been around kids, I'm not interested in kids, I don't know anything about them. I'm an editor—a good one—not a teacher. My father and my mother are both dead. They were definitely not a...a Bob and Laverne. I was born abroad and have never in my life been without a passport. And I am definitely not...a...Sally. And most certainly not a Sally May." She stopped to drum her fingers on the cracked plastic shelf holding the few personal effects Davis had picked up for her in a drugstore, then dropped back onto the bed, hugging the scratchy blanket. "So, you see, you'll just have to come up with something better."

Herbert Davis listened to her rant with his head bent to one side, looking at her soberly, letting her have her say. "Well." He rubbed his hands on his knees and pursed his lips. "I suppose all of this is not really necessary."

Julia blinked. It wasn't?

Davis sighed. "I guess you could always decide not to testify against Santana and we'll just go ahead with the evidence we've got. The law says we have the power to restrain you as a material witness, but we don't often enforce it. Nobody can force you to do your duty as a citizen to put the scum of the earth away behind bars. If you really want to, you can simply walk out of this room, go home and pick up your life where it was before you saw Dominic Santana shoot Joey Capruzzo through the head last Saturday."

Hope thrilled through her. *Yesss!!* It was all a nightmare, and now it was going to fade away. Julia started to feel warm again for the first time in three days. The sharp three day-old pain in her chest started to abate.

It hadn't occurred to her that there might be a way out. Of course, it was her duty as a citizen to see justice done. For about two seconds, Julia weighed good citizenry against getting her life back.

It wasn't even a contest. Her life won hands down.

She threw the reeking blanket down on the bed. "Well, if that's the case, then I guess—"

"Of course," Davis mused, picking at the lint on the blanket, "you wouldn't last more than fifteen minutes out there. Santana's put out a contract for you and our word from the street is that the first person to bring him your head—and I'm not being poetic here, lady, he wants your head, cut from your shoulders—gets a cool million. One million buckaroos, Sally—"

"Julia," she whispered as she slumped back onto the lumpy bed. She could feel the blood draining from her head.

"Sally," Davis said firmly. "As I was saying, the first person to bag you gets one million dollars. Cash. Lotta people out there would do a lot worse than murder and decapitation for a lot less. It's hunting season, Sally. And you're the game."

She made a noise in her throat, and Davis nodded.

"Now." Davis consulted his notebook again. "Let me tell you about yourself. You were born in London on March 6th, 1977, an only child of elderly parents. Your father was an IBM executive and you grew up all over the world, attending American schools. Your parents are both dead and you have no other living relatives. After graduating from high school, you came back to the States for college and got a degree in English at Columbia. You've been working as an editor for a prestigious publishing house in Boston since 2001. You earn $38,000 a year with benefits. You bought a small apartment in Boston with what your parents left you. You live alone in that apartment with your cat, Federico Fellini. You love films, the older the better. You love books and spend most of your free time in secondhand bookshops. Your best friend's name is Dora. You like spicy food. You occasionally date a man named Mason Hewitt." He looked up, face bland. "How am I batting so far?"

Julia gaped at him, wordless.

"Everything I've told you is a matter of public record and your neighbors and colleagues were more than happy to tell us your habits. Believe me, anyone could find out what we know. A million dollars is a great incentive. So here we've got a portrait of a very sophisticated and well-traveled young woman who loves cities, books and art films and has always lived on the East Coast. Now do you see why we have to put you out West in a town so small it doesn't have a bookshop and turn you into a grade school teacher who doesn't have a passport?"

Davis put on his old-fashioned tweed jacket and headed for the door.

"Please," Julia whispered. "I can't do this." Her voice was a shaken whisper.

Davis regarded her somberly out of basset hound eyes. "Welcome to the food chain, Sally," he said quietly, turned the tarnished greasy doorknob and let himself out.

* * * * *

A million dollars.

The professional stared at the computer screen. Not that many years had gone by since the professional had been an ace hacker and cracker at Stanford. The power was still there. Information was power.

Most people thought contract killers were thickheaded goons, barely smart enough to point a gun. They were wrong. It was a wonderful profession for the upwardly mobile and ambitious. You made your own hours, the money was fabulous and — above all — it was tax-free. The final act, pulling the trigger, was the easiest part. A few hours a week on a firing range took care of that.

No, finding the victim, the hunt — that was the hard part. That was what distinguished the million dollar professional from the hundred dollar thug. This John — the professional smiled — or rather this *Joan* was a perfect target. Once found, a single shot would do it.

Hell, probably a simple cyanide capsule slipped into a cup of coffee would do it. It wouldn't be hard to coax her into a cup of coffee. Everyone agreed that Julia Devaux was a friendly soul. Likeable, hard worker, bookworm, film buff. Grew up abroad, spoke three languages, degree in English, job doing book editing, loved cats, hated dogs. Her cat's name was Federico Fellini.

It hadn't been hard to come up with information on her. It was amazing what people would say to a well-tailored suit flashing a ten dollar fake FBI badge.

A million dollars. A tidy sum. With the money from the other jobs already completed, it was enough to retire on in that beachfront villa in St. Lucia, with the Swiss francs arriving every month, steady and sure, and the IRS far, far away. Retirement at thirty, in a luxury villa in the sun. What a wonderful job.

Julia Devaux had to die.

Bit of a pity, that. Everyone spoke so highly of her. And she seemed pretty, judging from the only photograph the professional could find — a smudged print in the company newsletter. Still...a million dollars was a million dollars.

Santana's goons would be fanning out now, beating the bushes, making fools of themselves, leaving trails even the blind could follow.

No, the professional thought, tapping steadily on the keyboard. There were other, more intelligent ways to find Julia Devaux.

Chapter One
One month later
Halloween
Simpson, Idaho

"Hey, Sally," a breathless voice called out. "Wait up!"

Julia Devaux kept on walking down the school corridor, then suddenly froze. Sally. She was *Sally* now. Would she ever get used to that name? She didn't feel like a Sally, though glancing down at herself, she just possibly looked like one.

Dark brown skirt, dull brown sweater, sensible flat-heeled brown shoes. All of which matched the blah brown Herbert Davis had insisted she color her hair, covering the glossy red Julia had been so proud of. Idiotically, it was when she'd had to color her hair that her predicament had truly come home to her. She had read the instructions on the box through streaming eyes—which might explain the lifeless, light-absorbing mass on top of her head. She'd cut it herself. She looked like a female George Clooney.

Herbert Davis hadn't let her bring any of her own clothes. She had found two suitcases full of clothes waiting for her at the airport--stodgy, dull, shapeless, and unfashionable—things she wouldn't ordinarily have been caught dead in.

At the time she hadn't cared. That's why God invented shopping. She hadn't counted on the fact that the best-stocked store in town would be Kellogg's Hardware Emporium.

One thing for sure—she did fit right in. Fashion was not a major priority in Simpson, Idaho. Julia shivered, and pulled her sweater closer about her slender frame. Survival and warmth were.

"Hi, Jerry." She tried to drum up some enthusiasm for the school administrator. He was nice enough and mainly harmless except for trying to rope her into his endless rounds of amazingly pointless good works. His last triumph had been to ship four hundred pounds of ham and woolens off to an earthquake-shattered Islamic country where the median winter temperature was ninety degrees.

"Hi, Sally." Jerry Johnson smiled and pushed his glasses up his pug nose. He had dark, narrow polyester trousers that ended at his anklebone, a short-sleeved polyester shirt though it was sleeting outside and cheap plastic horn-rimmed glasses. *Who dresses this guy?* Julia thought, clenching her teeth. *Elmer Fudd?*

"How ya doing?" Jerry asked, a puppylike smile on his face.

People were trying to kill her. She had been banished to Simpson, Siberia. Federico Fellini, her beloved finicky cat, was in a foster home. Would his foster parents remember to feed him only the choicest cuts of meat and take him to the homeopathic vet? She had lost a job she loved and was living in a house where not only the roof, but now the walls were leaking.

She smiled thinly. "Great, Jerry. Just great. What can I do for you?"

He smiled back, showing acres of white teeth. His wife's brother was studying to be a dental hygienist and practiced on Jerry. A lot.

"Elsa and I are having some people over for dinner tomorrow night and we'd like to know if you can make it." He leaned close and Julia caught a lethal whiff of mint. He'd had his teeth cleaned again. "Elsa's making her macaroni special. You wouldn't want to miss it."

Julia perked up.

Pasta.

Visions of her favorite *trattorias* in Italy swam before her eyes and she almost wept. Gorgonzola and penne. Amatriciana. Pesto. She would give her soul for a taste of real food.

"I didn't know Elsa cooked Italian," she sighed.

"Oh sure." Jerry beamed proudly. "Great recipe. We have it all the time. She just cooks the noodles for about an hour until they're nice and soft, then adds ketchup and cheddar and shoves it in the oven." He grinned, big brown eyes gleaming behind the oversized lenses. "Yummy."

Julia closed her eyes and sent up a silent prayer to that Great Director in the Sky to get her out of this terrible cheesy B movie she was trapped in. She wanted a new script—a nice sophisticated romantic comedy, starring, say, Cary Grant. *Charade*, or *Bringing up Baby*. Not *American Pie*.

"You can bring someone along, if you like," Jerry added. "A date. Elsa always makes extra."

A date. Was that something soft and cylindrical that grew on trees? In her month in Simpson, all the males she'd met had either been married since they were twelve or lacked a faculty or two. Not a Cary Grant in sight. Heaven knew what the single female population of western Idaho did for sex. Emigrated to the Yukon, maybe.

Then she remembered that she wasn't supposed to date, wasn't even supposed to fraternize with the locals and grew even more depressed at the thought of maybe never ever having sex again in this lifetime.

"Thanks, Jerry. That's kind of you, but I've got a lot to do." File my nails, alphabetize my spice rack, rinse out my stockings. "I'm really behind on my grading. But thank Elsa anyway. Maybe I can take a rain check."

"Okay." His cheerfulness grated on her already sensitive nerves. "You're missing a fun evening, though."

Julia smiled weakly then screamed. "Damn it! Er—darn it! Can't you do something about that bell, Jerry?" Her ears were still ringing and she slapped the side of her head. "Where on earth did you get it? From a decommissioned submarine?"

"It gets the kids' attention," he replied mildly. "Well, gotta go. Sorry you can't make it tomorrow."

Julia dredged up a smile. "Another time, Jerry." She braced herself and tried not to flinch as the second bell sounded — the one the kids called the "or else" bell, because the teachers shouted for them to settle down in their room — or else.

Her own kids were remarkably well-behaved. She clearly remembered walking gingerly into the class of twelve second-graders expecting...what?

It was hard now to remember the trepidation bordering on fear she had felt a month ago. Visions of black-jacketed hoodlums with knives and machine guns, driven crazy by whatever street drugs were currently popular, had flashed through her head. They would carve her up and dump her body on the outskirts of town and the law wouldn't even be able to touch them because they were underage.

As it happened, she had walked into her classroom, introduced herself as the new teacher, taking over from Miss Johanssen who had to move suddenly to California to take care of her ailing mother. She'd taken roll-call, opened the reader's primer to page one and that had been that. The kids were shockingly well-behaved, had only minor scuffles amongst themselves and she soon grew to think of herself as "ma'am", they said it so often.

Actually, in the beginning, the kids were so nice she had had the crazy notion that she had walked straight into a remake of *The Body Snatchers*; the kids really aliens grown in tiny little pods down in the basement of the school. Gradually, she realized that they lived in such a harsh environment-- and grew up doing chores as soon as they could walk-- that they were used to unquestioning obedience.

She walked into the classroom, then stopped as a small brown cannonball barreled straight into her stomach. She let out a whoosh of air, then laid her hands on two narrow shoulders. The small bones felt as fragile as a bird's under her hands.

"Rafael." She smiled and hunkered down. Rafael Martinez was her favorite pupil. Small, shy, with a sweet nut-brown face, he had hovered around her the past month, bringing her fistfuls of late-blooming daisies, a piece of filthy tea-colored bone he assured her was a dinosaur fossil and—her favorite—a tiny spring green turtle.

Julia had been worried to see him growing sadder and sadder over the last two weeks. Something was happening at home. She could have resisted the temptation to interfere if Rafael had become aggressive and violent, like kids did in the movies. But he had simply turned quiet, then morose, waves of unhappiness palpably quivering in the air around his little round, dark-haired head.

"Hey, buddy," Julia said gently. She reached out a finger to casually wipe away a tear. "What's the matter?"

He mumbled something at the floor. She thought she heard "Missy" and "mother" and glanced sharply at Missy Jensen, her cropped straw-colored hair and overalls making her look more like a little boy than a little girl.

Julia was puzzled. Ordinarily Missy and Rafael were best friends and swapped baseball cards and tadpoles.

"Baffroom," Rafael mumbled into her waist, head down. He needed to cry in private. Julia opened her arms and the small boy snaked around her and rushed off to the bathroom across the hall.

She walked over to where Missy was staring after Rafael, a stricken look in her eyes.

"What was that about, Missy?" she asked quietly.

"I don't know, ma'am." The little girl's lower lip quivered. "I didn't mean nothin'. All I asked was whether Rafael's momma would take him trick-or-treating with me." Missy raised troubled cornflower blue eyes. "Then he just runned away."

Uh-oh. Julia thought. *Trouble. Right here in River City.*

"Ran," she corrected automatically. "Well, then, just let him be. We have to get to work if we want everything ready for this evening." Julia stepped away and clapped her hands. "Okay, class, let's get going. We've got Mr. Big to get ready."

All the kids had brought their own pumpkins to prepare for Halloween that evening. Fourteen small pumpkins with crazed, skewed grins were lined up on the shelf. Now it was time to tackle Mr. Big. One of the local farmers had dropped by that morning and without a word—the inhabitants of Simpson were definitely not talkers—had deposited a forty-pound whopper of a pumpkin for the kids to carve up.

Carving the enormous pumpkin was going to be a class project and that evening the finished product would be put out on the steps of the school with a candle inside.

Like most expatriate Americans, Julia and her family had observed American holidays religiously, no matter where they were posted. Julia's mother had managed to find a turkey for Thanksgiving in Dubai, pumpkins for Halloween in Lima and a Christmas tree in Singapore. Julia had felt cheated when she found out in New York and Boston that kids no longer trick-or-treated because it was too dangerous.

Luckily, about the only danger to children in Simpson was getting gored by an elk. She was happy to note that her kids had been excited all week at the thought of dressing up and going trick-or-treating.

"Henry, Mike, I want you to get the big plastic sack. That's where we'll put the seeds and pulp. Sharon, get the felt tip pen so we can draw the face. Who's got the candle?"

"Me." Reuben Jorgensen gave a gap-toothed grin and held up an industrial-size candle.

"Great. Okay, gang, let's get going. We've got half an hour to put the biggest, meanest jack-o'-lantern this town has ever seen on the school's steps."

"Yeah! Oh boy!" In a tangle of limbs and with a maximum of fuss and mess, Mr. Big began to take shape. Oddly, the noise and confusion soothed Julia, who was used to the clamor and bustle of a big city. Simpson was silent and deserted even at noon and it creeped her out.

She watched the kids try to wrestle the seeds out of the enormous pumpkin, interfering only to pick up most of what slopped out onto the floor so the kids wouldn't skid and fall down. Jim, the janitor, would take care of the rest.

After about a quarter of an hour, Rafael slipped inside the classroom, eyes dry but red-rimmed. Julia hoped he would join in the fun, but he stayed on the outskirts of the whirl of activity. Julia sighed, and penned another note to his parents, asking to meet with them, and slipped that one, too, into the little boy's lunch pail. It was the fifth note in two weeks. Much as she hated the thought, if she got no response this time, she would ask Jerry for Rafael's home number and call his parents up on Monday.

"Miss Anderson, lookee."

Julia was thinking what kind of parents could be so indifferent to the sadness of such a sweet little boy. It took her a minute to respond to the excited request. She turned to find twelve shiny faces turned up to her, so many buds to her sun. If they only knew that she was winging it, she thought wryly.

"Look what we done." Reuben stood proudly, one hand on the enormous pumpkin.

"Did," Julia corrected. But she was smiling as she walked around the desk, raising an eyebrow at Mr. Big's ferocious stare. Pressed for time, the kids had left a lot of pulp and seeds in, but the outside had been carved into a horror movie fan's fondest dream.

Tongue in cheek, Julia tilted her head. "He's real scary. Looks like something carved by Freddy Kruger." Something sharp and painful tugged in her chest at the sighs of satisfaction. Her smile faded. They were so young. Being scared was fun at that age — things that go bump in the night, ghosts leaping out of closets, and mommy and daddy ready to make them go away with a hug and a smile.

Who would make her ghosts go away?

A wild clanging noise erupted. Julia jumped at the bell and cursed Jerry. Jumping and cursing Jerry was becoming an automatic reflex.

"Bye, Miss Anderson. Bye." In the space of a second or two, the room was emptied. Nature knew nothing faster than small children leaving the classroom at the end of the school day. In an amazingly short time, the whole school was deserted. It was Friday and the teachers left as soon as possible, too.

She would see most of these children that evening, decked out in their costumes. A bag full of candy was waiting on the scarred and scuffed occasional table next to the front door.

A couple of times a week, Julia stayed on after hours with one excuse or another. Herbert Davis had asked her to call collect from a public phone every two or three days since cell phone reception was spotty in the boonies and he didn't want. Her to use the land line from her house.

Davis obviously had no idea what Simpson was like. There were three public phones in the town, one outside the school, one in Carly's Diner and one in the grocery store. Julia had to rotate her calls among the phones to avoid attracting suspicion.

Julia's footsteps echoed hollowly in the corridor as she walked to the exit. The janitor would be coming soon, but for now she was alone in the deserted building. The cheery confusion created by the children hid how old and dilapidated the building was. She walked on cracked tiles, shuddering at the crumbling plasterwork and yellow waterstains of the walls.

Julia stopped for a moment at the entrance to the building and looked up and down Main Street. The only street, really, in Simpson, Idaho, population 1,475. Almost two thousand souls, actually, if you counted Greater Metropolitan Simpson, which included the inhabitants of the ranches scattered over the wide, empty countryside.

It had stopped sleeting for the moment, but the bruised-looking clouds over Flattop Ridge heralded a possible flurry later in the evening. She knew the kids would brave the weather to go trick-or-treating, no matter how frigid. They were tough little survivors. They had to be, in such a harsh country.

Davis was wrong, Julia thought bleakly. *I need a passport to be here.*

The wind lifted and she pulled her sweater more tightly around her. For a moment, just a moment, she felt as if the wind were pushing her until she stood poised on the edge of the world. One more step and she'd fall off...

She remembered a medieval map she'd seen once. The earth was flat and at the outer rims was wilderness, where the mapmaker had penned in "Here be lions". The end of civilization. It was like that now, the only difference being— "Here be cougars".

Santana can never find me, she thought. *How can he, when I can't find myself?*

Simpson was like the old joke: you either wanted to be there or you were lost. It didn't lead to anywhere, it wasn't on the way to anywhere. Thirty miles back down the potholed road was a turnoff that led either to Rupert, a buzzing metropolis of 4,000, or to Dead Horse, a smudge on a crossroad as sophisticated as its name.

A single tiny snowflake drifted by. It melted before it hit the ground, but one quick glance at the sky told her that there was more up there where that came from. And her boiler had chosen *now* of all times to go temperamental on her.

A huge lump of homesickness lay heavy and sodden in her chest. Back home, if anything went wrong with her heating system, she would have called the super, Joe, from work and it would have been fixed by the time she got home. Back home, on a cold, dank day like this, she'd have made a point of doing something special. Maybe rent a movie classic, buy herself a new book or arrange to meet a friend for dinner. Dora, say. Dora liked hot spicy meals on cold, sleety days, too. They could go to The Iron Maiden, that funky new Ukrainian restaurant on Charles, or maybe try for some Szechuan...or even order in some Mexican...

Or she could call Mason Hewitt. They'd track down some standup comic, have dim sum at Lo's and late night coffee at Latte & More. Lately she'd been thinking seriously about letting Mason seduce her. It had been a long, long time since she'd had sex. Since her parents' deaths, as a matter of fact. She hadn't planned it that way but that's the way it had turned out.

Mason might be a good person for her to dip her toe back into the waters of sexuality. Though he wasn't sexy, he was funny and if it went badly, they could always have a good laugh about it.

A flurry of ice needles hitting the side of her face pulled Julia out of her reverie. She wouldn't be going anywhere with Dora this evening. She wouldn't be renting a movie or buying herself a book. She definitely wouldn't be getting any sex. She probably wouldn't even have heating at home.

What am I doing here? Julia thought bleakly, *fifty miles from the nearest Estée Lauder outlet, where the only fast food is deer?*

The irony of it was that Dora, Mason and everyone else thought she was in Florida. Davis had had her call the office on an untraceable phone line and ask for unpaid compassionate leave to tend a sick grandfather in St. Petersburg. At irregular but frequent intervals, postcards signed by her were mailed from Florida to her office colleagues and to a list of friends Davis had had Julia draw up. Probably Dora and Mason were envying her right now, getting to spend time down in Florida, basking in the sunshine, doing well by doing good.

The unfairness of it ate like acid into Julia's soul.

A wave of despair so strong it almost brought her to her knees swept through Julia. What on earth had she done to deserve this? She was being punished for a crime she hadn't committed. She'd accidentally witnessed a murder and her life had been snatched away from her in the space of a few hours.

She slowly crossed the street and walked the half-block to the public phone with its intact shell. Unlike the public phones she'd seen in New York and Boston, it wasn't vandalized. But it was in a state of woeful disrepair, on the blink more often than not, as if the phone company hadn't bothered to swing round for repairs since Edison.

The phone stood outside the ramshackle, two-story clapboard house of Ramona Simpson, the last descendant of Casper Simpson, the town's immortal founder. Rumor had it that Ramona Simpson was crazy. Julia fervently believed the rumor. She glanced at the ROOMS TO LET sign in the front window of Mrs. Simpson's home and shuddered. Except for the fact that it wasn't on a hill, the house looked exactly like Norman Bates' hotel in *Psycho*.

Julia stopped at the phone and looked up and down the street. She needn't have bothered. Main was deserted. It would be nice to think that Main Street was deserted because it was 4 p.m. on a freezing Friday afternoon, but that wasn't it. Main Street was deserted all the time.

She pushed a coin in the slot and asked the operator for the collect connection to be made.

"Davis."

Julia slumped against the hard plastic shell in relief at hearing his voice. "Hi, it's me." Davis had given her strict rules never to state her name. When he wasn't in, she was supposed to say that cousin Edwina had called. *Where does he get these names?* she wondered for the thousandth time. *From the family Bible?*

"How are you doing?" Davis' voice was even, almost bored. It enraged Julia to think that he was in his warm office in one of the great cities of the world and she was in this freezing dump. He had Louisburg Square and she had Main. He had access to great food and she had access to soggy macaroni and ketchup.

"How am I doing?" Julia pursed her lips and looked to the livid sky for inspiration. She drew in a deep breath, then let it out slowly, waiting to make sure her voice wouldn't tremble. "Well, let's see. It's about forty below and the temperature's dropping. The town looks like Tombstone during a gunfight. Missy Jensen made Rafael Martinez cry and I feel like joining him. I'm a thousand miles from nowhere. How the *hell* do you think I'm doing?"

It was a little routine they had, like old married couples who'd stayed together for the sake of the kids first and then for the sake of the dogs. She complained and he listened and sympathized. Julia waited for Davis to issue soft, comforting sounds, but they weren't forthcoming.

"How long?" Julia sighed, and rubbed her free hand up the arm holding the phone. She huddled further into the shell, hoping to escape the icy tendrils of wind.

How long? It was the question she always asked.

"Looks like after Easter, now."

"After *Easter*?" Julia straightened and sucked in an outraged breath. "What do you mean after Easter? How on earth do you suppose I can stand being here for another six months, Mr. —"

"No names," he warned quickly.

"Arghh —" If there was anything Julia hated, even more than Simpson, Idaho, it was having to watch what she said. "You were supposed to get me out of here as fast as possible, remember? What's happened?"

"What's happened is that our friend, Fritz —" their code name for Santana " —has engaged the services of S. T. Akers."

"Who?" Julia asked blankly.

"S. T. Akers. Jesus, I keep forgetting you weren't brought up in the States. He's America's most famous criminal attorney. All his clients are very, very rich and very, very guilty. His slogan is he always gets his man...off."

Julia's breath clogged in her throat. "And does he?"

She heard a heavy sigh. "Yeah, he does. So far he's batted a thousand. He's just snowed the District Attorney's office with so many motions for reprieval that it looks like a Russian winter over there. It will take them a month just to process everything.

The DA told me privately yesterday that they'll be lucky to come to trial before summer."

"And..." Julia swallowed around a heavy lump, "...and me?"

"Well, you...you're our trump card. All the other evidence is meaningless. Akers could get Hitler off on a technicality. It looks like you're going to have to stay put for a while longer."

Julia hoped that the wet sting in her eyes was the chilly arctic wind and not tears. Another six months — maybe longer — in Stalag Simpson. Her chest burned.

"What?" she asked. Davis had said something, but it sounded as if a snowstorm had hit the telephone wires. "The connection's bad. What did you say?"

She heard static, then "...strange?"

"I can't hear you," she shouted. "What did you say?"

The connection was suddenly clear and she heard Herbert Davis as if he were speaking directly in her ear. "I said...have you noticed anything strange lately?"

"Strange?" Julia ruthlessly repressed the urge to cackle like a crazed witch. "You want *strange*?"

She looked around. The dark clouds had built up until they covered the horizon in muddy layers, so that the fading light of day came up under the sky. The light mercilessly showed the shabbiness of the town.

Main Street was, as always, deserted. Every building on Main Street needed a coat of paint. Every other shop was boarded up. She wasn't so surprised at the failed businesses, but at those which managed to hold on. Simpson was a town that had died, but the news hadn't reached the corpse yet. She turned back to the phone.

"This whole place is strange. Did you have anything specifically strange in mind?"

"Well..." To her surprise, Herbert Davis sounded embarrassed. Maybe it was the faulty connection. "I mean, have you noticed anyone different--out of place...around? Someone...odd?"

Julia stamped her feet and blew a breath of frustration, which came out in a white plume. The temperature was dropping quickly. "Everyone here is odd, they've all been marrying their cousins forever and the gene pool is shallow. No one here is normal. Otherwise they wouldn't be here at all; they'd have left years ago. What are you talking about?"

White noise buzzed in her ears so loudly she had to hold the phone away from her ear. "What?"

Herbert Davis' voice was faint. "Computer...encrypted...confidential." Then, alarmingly, "...files lost...your data..." Then static.

"Hey!" Just in time, Julia swallowed Davis' name. "Run that by me again."

Abruptly the static stopped. "...telling you we lost a section of our computer files. We were converting our files to CD-ROM." Julia could hear the enthusiasm in Davis' voice. "We've got a new data-compression program in, it's great, and we've been able to convert..."

Julia huddled into her sweater and watched the black roiling clouds cover more of the sky. A flash of sheet lightning briefly lit the horizon.

"Come on, cut to the chase." The tough-guy line was out of her mouth before she could stop herself and she winced. The chase. Bad choice of words. "Why are you telling me this? What does it have to do with me?"

"Oh." Julia could almost see Davis at the other end of the line, blinking and stumped because she wasn't showing enthusiasm for his new computer toy. She heard him draw in a breath. "Now, I don't really think this affects you, and I don't want to alarm you, but we...misplaced some files for a while and part of the files we lost...misplaced—just for a while, you understand—covered your case."

"What?" she shrieked, then lowered her voice just in case there were any living human beings in the vicinity. Her heart thumped high and wild in her chest. "My case? You mean information on where I am now? In files? That you lost?"

"Well...lost is too strong a term. I prefer to think of them as misplaced. Temporarily. But..." Davis lowered his voice to what he probably assumed was soothing, but only had Julia more terrified than ever. "...don't worry. All of the information was in code and our encryption programs are very tight. And our Witness Security files are double-encoded. It would take a genius or array computers more than a month to crack the code and, believe me, Fritz doesn't have access to either. The files are programmed to self-destruct unless a special code is entered every half hour, so you're safe. We've found the files and they've been downloaded in a new encryption program."

Julia clutched the receiver and listened to his computer gobbledygook, trying to breathe, wondering what to do to calm herself down. There wasn't even a drugstore in Simpson. No Prozac. No Xanax. Whisky gave her heartburn. Not even bad sex was available.

"I just asked whether you'd seen someone suspicious out of a sense of duty, but believe me," Davis continued, "no one knows who or where you are."

Well, that makes sense. I don't know who or where I am, either, Julia thought. She stamped her frozen feet. The telephone receiver once again filled with static.

A sudden noise made Julia whip around, heart thumping. It was only an old, faded Coca-Cola poster, wildly flapping in the gelid wind against a cracked concrete wall and Julia slumped back against the shell in relief. The force of the wind ripped the poster from the wall. It tumbled crazily down the empty street, buffeted by forces beyond its control.

I know just how you feel, she thought.

"Connection's bad again," she yelled, hand cupped around the receiver, and hung up. She'd had too much bad news already. It wasn't enough that she would be stuck here for months to come—someone had apparently come close to finding out where she was.

Julia stopped for a moment, frozen more by a chilling thought than by the cold. Davis had seemed terribly certain than no one could crack the Justice Department's files, but she'd read the newspaper stories about pimply twelve-year-old hackers breaking into corporate and military computer networks.

What if Dominic Santana was a computer expert? Her mind raced back to that terrible, terrible day one month earlier. Usually, she tried to wipe the images out of her mind, particularly at 2 a.m., when the nightmares threatened to swamp her sanity, but now she deliberately conjured up the scene, imprinted on her mind forever.

It had been hot then. A muggy day on an unusually hot Indian summer afternoon.

In slow motion, she ran through the scene...the scrawny man on his knees, the sweat of fear dripping on the oil-stained pavement, another man holding a gun to his head, finger slowly tightening on the trigger, the report, the scrawny man's head exploding...this was where she always shut off the film in her head, but now she continued, concentrating on the man holding the gun. He'd been tall. Heavy-set. She zoomed in on his face. There had been a feral coldness stamped on his features, violence, brutality—but not intelligence. Julia started breathing again. No, she thought, that man could not crack a computer code. A safe, maybe, but not a code.

Besides, Julia thought, as she walked back into the empty school building, she'd been around Simpson long enough to recognize everyone by sight. She hadn't seen any new faces lately.

The sky rumbled as she made her way down the corridor, and the lights flickered once. *Great*, she thought. *Just great.* She really had to hurry home now. Something in her house was leaking and she didn't want to have to try locating the source by flashlight.

She entered the classroom, with its familiar smell of chalk dust. Mr. Big leered at her from his corner perch. She'd have to remember to tell Jim to leave it on the school steps when he finished cleaning.

The lights flickered again in the shadowed room. Heavy footsteps sounded in the corridor outside the classroom, loud in the silence of the school. Someone was striding quickly, then stopping, then walking quickly again, as if—her heart started racing—as if looking for something...or someone.

Don't be silly, she told herself, but her heart continued its wild thumping, anyway. She pushed papers into her briefcase with shaking hands, cursing as one slipped to the floor. She could hear herself panting and made a conscious effort to slow her breathing. The footsteps stopped, then started again. Each teacher had his or her name taped to the door. If someone was looking for Sally Anderson...

Stop, start...

She grabbed her coat, trying to calm her trembling. Davis had spooked her, that was all. It was probably Jim...

...except that Jim was an old man and shuffled...

...or one of the teachers...

...except that all the other teachers had gone home...

Closer, closer...

The footsteps stopped at her door and her gaze froze on the glass pane that covered the upper half of the door. She had to see who was out there, reassure herself that it was just one of the harmless citizens of Simpson and not...and not...

A face pressed against the window. A man. He reached inside his jacket to pull something out.

The lights went out.

Julia whimpered and tried to think around the icy ball of fear that had formed in her mind. What could she use as a weapon? There was nothing in her purse but a pocket diary, keys and makeup. The kids' desks were too heavy to lift, and the chairs were of lightweight plastic. Her hand brushed something hard and round. *Mr. Big!*

Panting wildly, she angled her chair next to the door, climbed up on it and hoisted the enormous pumpkin in her arms. She stood, trembling, at the side of the door, ready to smash the man out there over the head. Her body tensed, going into fight and flight mode.

The knob rattled.

Julia closed her eyes and saw again the face that had been revealed in the bright fluorescent lights of the corridor.

Overlong, straight black hair, framing a series of slabs angling harshly together to form cheeks and chin, a straight slash of a mouth, black eyes.

An unfamiliar face.

An unforgettable face.

A killer's face.

Chapter Two

Sam Cooper felt like killing someone. Preferably his foreman and best friend, Bernaldo Martinez. Or, failing that, Bernie's faithless, two-timing wife, Carmelita. Either one would do nicely.

They should be the ones here, ready to talk to little Rafael's teacher, not him. He'd rather walk across hot coals than have to deal with all this emotional shit. He had enough problems, what with rising feed prices and falling roofs.

He hadn't the faintest idea what he could possibly say to Rafael's teacher. He only knew that Bernie was in no condition to talk to anyone right now.

Cooper reached into his jacket to touch the notes the teacher, a Miss Anderson, had sent home with the little boy. He knew them all by heart, having reread them a dozen times since coming home after a business trip to Boise and finding Bernie passed out, clutching an empty bottle of cheap bourbon in one fist and the notes in another.

He'd pried the notes out of Bernie's hand, hoisted him over one shoulder and put him, fully dressed, in the shower stall and turned on the cold water tap.

Bernie had come out of his stupor long enough to curse him weakly, then had fallen onto his bed, which hadn't been made in a long, long while. Cooper had been tempted to leave Bernie as he was, in his sodden clothes on the unmade bed, but he'd given in with a sigh, undressed him and heaped blankets on him.

Bernie would be feeling bad enough when he faced his hangover without tossing in pneumonia.

But Bernie would owe him. Big-time. Playing nursemaid and facing grade school teachers were not high on Cooper's list of favorite pastimes.

Cooper stood outside the door of the schoolroom. He didn't have any more reason to wait. The little plaque outside the door confirmed that this was Miss S. Anderson's classroom. He pressed his face against the glass pane of the door, hoping the room would be empty, but the lights in the corridor were so bright all he could see was his own face reflected back at him.

He looked as annoyed as he felt.

Fuck. I don't want to do this, he thought, pressing his lips together. He moved forward anyway, wondering if he should knock on the door. Then he thought…what the hell…turned the knob and pushed the door open. A thousand tons of bricks fell on his head.

"Wha…?" Cooper found himself against the classroom wall, legs splayed out. He raised his hand to his head and felt a large sore area he was certain would start turning into a whopper of a goose egg very soon. His hand came away wet and for a panicky moment he thought it was blood, then he saw it was orange glop and big white seeds.

Pumpkin? He stared for a moment at his hand, covered with pumpkin pulp and seeds. He'd been brained with a *pumpkin*?

"Don't move," a high tight voice warned him. A small, slender, beautiful woman faced him, panting and shaking.

She was terrified, Cooper realized.

She should have been a redhead. Though her hair was a dull shade of brown, she had the pale skin and deep turquoise eyes of a redhead. She reminded him of a fox cub he had once come across, paw caught in a trap. The cub was mortally wounded and he wanted to free it from the trap but the cub had hissed and growled and tried to bite him with baby milk teeth.

So he sat in the puddle of pumpkin glop and stared at her while she hyperventilated and trembled.

She held a small spray can aimed at him, held in unsteady hands. It was a replica of the breath freshener he had in his bathroom. "This is Mace," she lied. "If you make a move…just one move, I'll spray you."

He'd already brushed his teeth, so he stayed put.

* * * * *

Now what?

Julia kept her finger on the spray nozzle, hoping the can wouldn't just squirt out of her sweaty, trembling hands. Sweat fell into her eyes but she didn't dare wipe it away. She could barely breathe. Oxygen deprivation was shooting colored sparks in front of her eyes. Trying to knock this terrifying man out was the bravest thing she'd ever done in her life, but it was useless pulling a Xena, Warrior Princess act if she fell into a dead faint right after.

Footsteps sounded in the corridor. Keeping wide eyes on the terrifying man sitting against the wall, she edged towards the door.

"Jim!" she yelled. "Call the sheriff! Tell him I've got a dangerous criminal here. Tell him to get over here *now!*" Julia shifted her gaze slightly and saw Jim drop his mop and hustle out the door. Her eyes flickered back to the man sitting against the wall.

Even sitting down, he was scary as hell. Braining him with Mr. Big hadn't knocked him out. Long, massively built with shoulders a yard wide, dressed in a black turtleneck sweater, black bomber jacket and jeans, with hard dark features and dark glittering hyperaware eyes, he looked every inch a killer. Her hand trembled. Thank God she had thought of the little spray can of breath freshener in her purse.

"Don't move," Julia said again, breathlessly, trying to crouch in a gun stance. She was so frightened it felt as if her chest were being squeezed in a giant's grasp. The terror of the past month came rushing back tenfold, all wrapped up in one long, lean, broad-shouldered package. Obsidian-black eyes fixed on her, and she knew that the man was calculating his next move. This man was a professional killer. How long could she hope to keep him at breath spray point?

The door to the school opened and running footsteps sounded in the corridor. The classroom door was yanked open and Sheriff Chuck Pedersen filled the doorway, a pistol in his hand.

He skidded to a stop, taking in the killer sprawled on the floor and Julia holding him at bay.

"Officer." Julia's voice came out a squeak. She coughed to clear her tight throat and began again. "Officer, arrest that man! He's a dangerous criminal!"

Sheriff Pedersen holstered his pistol and leaned against the doorframe. "Hey, Coop."

"Chuck."

Julia locked her knees because she could feel that they were about to give way. She looked at the sheriff and took in a huge gulp of air into her starved lungs. "You know this man?"

Sheriff Pedersen shifted his considerable weight and transferred his chewing gum from one cheek to another. "Know?" he asked philosophically. "What does it mean to 'know' someone? You can spend years with a man and never really understand..."

"Chuck," the man on the floor said again, his deep low voice a growl.

Pedersen shrugged. "Yeah," he said, turning to Julia. "I know Sam Cooper. Known him all his life. Knew his dad. Hell, knew his grandpappy."

"Oh, God," Julia whimpered. She couldn't get her insides to stop. They felt as if they were racing at a thousand miles an hour. Gallons of adrenaline were still pumping through her bloodstream and she couldn't connect her thoughts.

She had fully expected to die, she had bravely defended herself against a vicious contract killer and then had knocked out a good citizen of Simpson.

The man was still sitting on the floor, glaring up at her.

Julia tried to think of something reasonable to say. How on earth could she apologize? *Excuse me for having attacked you, but I thought that you were a hired killer,* sounded insane.

Still, it hadn't been such a wild leap of the imagination. The man—this Sam Cooper—certainly looked dangerous. Exactly the way a hired gun would look. There wasn't a thing about him that wasn't frightening as hell. Dark coiled power emanated from him and, even sitting down, he gave the impression of a tiger ready to leap to destroy its prey. His face was like something that should have been carved on Mount Rushmore, all harsh angles. Everything about him was dark, which was why she'd instinctively assumed he wasn't from Simpson.

After about a week in the town, Julia realized why Herbert Davis had given her the assumed name of Sally Anderson. It seemed as if everyone in Simpson was a Jensen or a Jorgensen or a Pedersen. She was sure that sometime in the last century a bedraggled group of Scandinavian settlers aiming for the Pacific Ocean had just given up the ghost by the time they reached western Idaho. Everyone in Simpson seemed to share the same gene pool. Bland, pale faces and bland, pale hair.

Not the man she'd had a little round of assault and battery with, though. Nothing pale and bland about him.

He had jet-black hair and jet-black eyes, matching his jet-black bomber jacket and the black stubble covering his cheeks. About the only light-colored thing about him was the pumpkin pulp.

Julia swallowed around a lump of guilt in her throat. She surreptitiously slipped the breath freshener back in her purse. "Er...how do you do? My name's Ju...Sally Anderson." She tried to keep the waver out of her voice, but it was touch and go.

"Sam Cooper," he said. He braced a large hand on the ground and stood up in one lithe, powerful movement so sudden she found herself stepping back in fright. He started brushing off seeds and Julia had another guilt attack.

"Most people call him Coop," the Sheriff offered.

Julia wondered what her stickler of a mother would have thought about the etiquette of the situation. Could you use a nickname for someone you'd done your best to knock senseless?

Probably not.

"Mr. Cooper."

"Miss Anderson." She had a momentary pang of doubt. His voice sounded like a killer's voice...deep, low and raspy. She sneaked another look at him.

He still looked dangerous.

"You're sure you know this man, Sheriff?"

"Yes, ma'am." Sheriff Pedersen grinned. "Breeds and trains horses on a big spread between here and Rupert. All kinds of horses, but mostly thoroughbreds and Arabians."

"I...ahm...I guess I owe you an apology, Mr. Cooper." Julia tried to think of something logical to say. "I...I mistook you for someone else."

An embarrassing silence fell over the room.

"Can't believe you let someone get the drop on you, Coop." The Sheriff chuckled. "'Specially a girl."

"Woman," Julia murmured, refraining from rolling her eyes.

"What? Oh, yeah, can't call girls *girls* any more." The Sheriff shook his head in sorrow at the ways of the modern world. He looked Julia up and down and cackled at Cooper. "I'll bet you have a foot and ninety pounds on her, Coop. You must be getting soft." He turned to Julia. "Coop used to be a SEAL, you know."

A seal?

For a moment, Julia wondered whether a month of terror had shorted out her brain. What on earth did the Sheriff mean? A seal...?

Oh. He meant a SEAL. A commando. Trained killer.

So she hadn't been so off the mark, after all.

Julia absorbed this information as she looked at Sam Cooper, brainee. Splayed on the floor, he had looked dangerous. On his feet, he was terrifying, huge and menacing. Prime commando material, if she ever saw it. She observed him carefully, paying particular attention to his alarmingly large hands, and turned to the sheriff.

"That may be," she said politely. "But his flippers are gone now."

The Sheriff stared at her for a moment. He wheezed heavily once, then twice. It was only when he bent double, shoulders shaking, that Julia realized he was laughing.

It was the last straw. The whole miserable day came crashing in on her. Herbert Davis and his less than reassuring news that killers might have come close to discovering where she was; the terror when she thought one of Santana's hired killers had found her; her heroic last stand at the Alamo; the overwhelming relief when she'd discovered that she might live, after all.

Then the Sheriff running to her rescue, only he didn't rescue her at all. Actually, he could probably have her arrested for...for what? Assault with a deadly vegetable?

And to top it all off, the Sheriff was doing this lousy imitation of Walter Brennan in *Rio Bravo*, except he had all his teeth and didn't limp. Julia had hated *Rio Bravo*.

Come to think of it, she'd hated *The Alamo*, too.

"If you don't *mind*, Sheriff," she said coldly.

Chuck Pedersen wheezed once more and wiped his eyes. "Flippers," he said and wheezed again. He shook his head. "No, Miss..."

Devaux, she thought. "Anderson," she said.

"Anderson, that's right. Sorry. You just moved here, right?"

"A little less than a month ago." Twenty-seven days and twelve hours, but who's counting?

"So you don't know everyone in the area yet. But old Coop, here, he used to be in the Navy, a SEAL, like I said. Crack troops. Coop did damned well, too, got hisself a medal, he did. Then his daddy died and he came back to run the Cooper spread."

Oh, God. Julia closed her eyes in pain for a moment. This was worse than she thought. It wasn't bad enough that she'd assaulted one of the good citizens of Simpson. No, she'd clobbered a *war hero*. She opened her eyes and stole a look at Sam Cooper again.

He still looked hard and dangerous.

Gathering the few tattered shreds of dignity left, and pumping up her courage, she held out her hand to Sam Cooper, horse breeder/SEAL.

She stared straight into black, expressionless eyes and shivered. "Please accept my apologies, Mr. Cooper."

After a moment, Sam Cooper took her hand. His was huge and hard and calloused. Julia held his hand and he held her eyes. Julia stared, then slipped her hand from his grasp and turned away, feeling as if she'd just escaped a force field. He made a sound, and she decided to take it as acceptance of her apology, remembering that SEALs didn't talk. They just grunted.

Julia turned to the Sheriff and tried to smile. "I guess I owe you my apologies as well, Sheriff."

"Chuck." The sheriff grinned. "We don't stand much on ceremony around here."

"Chuck, then. I'm really sorry I caused all this commotion."

He rocked back on his heels. "Well, I won't say anytime, because you gave me a fright there, Miss Anderson…"

"Sally," Julia said, hating the name.

"Sally. As I was saying, I thought I'd caught myself a criminal. Mostly what I do is break up a few fights on Saturday night and arrest speeders. Not many of those, either."

"No, I imagine not," Julia murmured. "Simpson seems like such a nice little town." After all she'd been through that afternoon, what was a little lie? All right, a big lie. "Friendly and quiet."

Years of living abroad made it easy to say the pleasant, untrue thing. Julia remembered her mother saying kind things about the landscape around Reykjavik—a sere, treeless, lifeless expanse—to a delighted Icelander.

The Sheriff beamed. "That it is. Glad you like it here. We're always happy to welcome newcomers to Simpson. We need new blood. The youngsters keep leaving us, right after high school. I keep telling 'em it's a nasty world out there, but nobody listens. Can't imagine what they think they're gonna find out there."

Oh, I don't know, Julia thought. *Bookshops, cinema, theater, art galleries. Good food, good conversation, shops. Sidewalks. Humans.* Then, because she'd always been told her face was an open book, she smiled and tried to think of something else. "You know what kids are like. I guess they feel they have to go and find out for themselves."

Out of politeness Julia turned to the man she'd brained. "Isn't that right, Mr. Cooper?"

* * * * *

Cooper started. He'd been thinking how easy this Sally Anderson was finding it to talk to Chuck even after five minutes' acquaintance. He'd found it enormously difficult to tell Chuck how sorry he'd been when Carly, Chuck's wife, had passed away.

And then Chuck had just stood around morosely, patting him awkwardly on the back when Cooper's own wife, Melissa, had left. Looked like beautiful grade school teachers didn't have the kind of problems men did. Particularly not beautiful schoolteachers with red, no—he checked again while she wasn't looking—*brown* hair.

He could have sworn it was red. She looked like a redhead. He was real partial to redheads. Though truth be told, he'd never seen a redhead outside the movies as gorgeous as this one was.

She was still scared. Her hand had trembled in his. It had been soft and small and icy cold. The temptation to keep holding it just to warm it up had been overwhelming. He'd let her go because she looked terrorized by him. It was hard to forget the look of sheer terror on her face as she'd held him at bay. The last time he'd seen anyone look like that had been under gunfire.

She was hiding her fear well now, with a polite expression on that lovely face, but he remembered her trembling hand.

There was a sudden silence, and Chuck and the teacher were both looking at him in expectation. The echo of Miss Anderson's question hovered in the air.

"Er...that's right." It must have been an appropriate response, because the teacher gathered her things and slipped out the door, Chuck patted him on the back and followed her and he was left alone in the school, except for Jim, out swabbing the corridor.

He listened to the sounds of Jim whistling "Be My Baby" out of tune but in time with the sweep of the mop. Cooper moved towards the door and heard something crackle. The notes. The notes Sally Anderson had written. He'd come here to talk about Rafael.

Fuck. He'd forgotten all about it.

* * * * *

The opening strains of *Tosca* filled the airy, light-filled room. The room was a treasure trove of beautiful, rare objects. The casual onlooker would never see the state of the art security system and the collection of handguns and rifles hidden in the false bottom of an oak Renaissance chest.

A computer sat on a Hepplewhite console. Next to it, an 18th century Wedgwood canister held pencils and pens.

The professional opened the file and started entering the custom-made decryption program that was a personal triumph.

Sold on the software market, the program could easily have fetched over $100,000. If it were for sale—which it was not. A hundred thousand was a long way from a million and the Stanford Business program had been very clear on the fact that you had to spend money to make it.

The last of the commands to start the program had been entered and the computer beeped. Immediately, letters started scrolling down.

alkdjfpiwe cmòkjèqruepijfkmcx,vnsakjfqpoiurpi

alksdjpoiurekcnòlskjfpieujfnòlkdjfpawieurhmadnf

ncjdnemvkjfjruthdsgsrwvcjfkginbjdmslkcjhfgjkdk

Decryption 60%...70%...80%...90%...

Decryption completed.

The computer beeped softly and the professional sat up.

File: 248

Witness Placed under Witness Security Program: Richard M. Abt

Born: New York City, 03/05/65

Last domicile: 6839 Sugarmaple Lane, New York City, NY.

Case: Accountant for group of attorneys Ledbetter, Duncan, and Terrance. All three attorneys indicted for laundering money for the mafia. Abt only person willing to testify. Testimony to be given 11/14/05.

Placed under Witness Security Program: 09/09/04

Richard Abt relocated as: Robert Littlewood

Area 248, Code 7fn609jz5y

Current domicile: 120 Crescent Drive, Rockville, Idaho

Right church. Wrong pew.

The data starting spewing forth and the professional sat for a moment, swallowing the disappointment, then got up and poured some chilled *Veuve Clicquot* into a Baccarat flute, easing off the kidskin shoes ordered specially from an English cobbler, James & Sons. This would take a while.

The *Veuve Clicquot* was dry and went down like a dream. The light of the Murano chandelier glanced off the crystal of the flute, making a thousand little rainbows. Sipping, the professional watched the rainbows dance in the light.

It was easy, so easy to get used to the good things in life. Fine clothes, fine furnishings, a penthouse suite.

It was a long, long way up from the trailer park and waiting for the old man to come home, drunk more often than not. That was all over with. Forever. No more swinging belts, no more sympathetic teachers gently enquiring about the black eye, no more collecting food stamps.

No more. Not ever again.

kdsjcnemowjsiwexnjskllspwieuhdksmclsldjkjhfd
kdiejduenbkclsjdjeudowjdiejdocmdksdldkjdjeiel
mpnwjcmsmwkcxosapewkrjhvgebsjckgfnghgdsj
Decryption 60%...70%...80%...90%...
Decryption completed.

The computer beeped again. After a moment, in which it seemed to pause to consider, the computer screen filled with words.

File: 248

Witness placed in Witness Security Program: Sydney L. Davidson

Born: Frederick, Virginia, 07/27/56

Last domicile: 308 South Hampton Drive, Apt 3B, Frederick, VA

Case: Chemist for Sunshine Pharmaceuticals. All top company executives indicted for providing designer drugs to friends and other business associates. Davidson turned State's witness in exchange for reduced or waived sentence. Due to testify against employers on 11/23/05.

Placed in Witness Security Program: 8/25/04

Sydney Davidson relocated as: Grant Patterson

Area 248, Code 7gj668jx4r

Current domicile: 90 Juniper Street, Ellis, Idaho

The professional immediately lost interest.

Nobody said this would be easy.

It was certainly taking enough time. Enough time to make serious inroads on a contraband jar of Iranian caviar and to listen to the second act of *Tosca*. The *Veuve Clicquot* was running at half-mast. Tosca noisily plunged her knife into Scarpia's treacherous chest and the orchestra swelled as the computer hummed.

This was getting boring. Still, on the plus side, it looked like the fools in the Department of Justice had actually organized the file containing Julia Devaux's data in alphabetical order. If that was the case, then Julia Devaux should be coming up soon. The professional contemplated opening another bottle of champagne, then decided against it. Certain triumphs were to be savored with a clear head. The computer beeped.

The professional sat up, eyes narrowing.

kdsjcnemowjsiwexnjskllspwieuhdksmclsldjkjhfd

kdiejduenbkclsjdjeudowjdiejdocmdksdldkjdjeiel

mpnwjcmsmwkcxosapewkrjhvgebsjckgfnghgdsj

Decryption 60%...70%...80%...90%...

Decryption completed.

File: 248:

Witness placed in Witness Security Program: Julia Devaux

Born: London, England, 03/06/77

Come on, come on. The professional leaned forward, eyes riveted to the screen. *I know all that. Tell me something I don't know.*

Last domicile: 4677 Larchmont Street, Boston, MA.

Ah. The thrill of the chase was nothing in comparison to the intellectual thrill of knowing that you were smarter than everyone else.

Lisa Marie Rice

Now for the rest of it. The professional gently kept time to the music with an Italian breadstick dipped in the last of the caviar. The letters moved across the screen.

Case: Homicide, Joey Capruzzo, 09/30/04. Last known address: Sitwell Hotel, Boston, MA.

Proximate cause of death: massive hemorrhaging from .38 caliber bullet wound in left anterior lobe of brain.

Accused: Dominic Santana.

Current address: Warwick Correctional Facility. Warwick, Massachusetts.

Placed in Witness Security Program: 10/03/04

Julia Devaux relocated as:

Yes, that's it.

The cursor stopped, blinking on and off, as if patiently waiting for some signal from within the depths of the machine. Tosca fought with the police officer and cursed Scarpia's name while slowly, very slowly, the letters started blanking out, one by one, until the screen was empty.

The professional sat, stunned. It was clear what had happened. The files had a time bomb built in. If a code wasn't entered at predetermined intervals—the professional checked the gold Rolex Oyster that represented the first down payment on the first job—probably every half hour, the files would self-destruct.

The crystal flute shattered against the far wall, champagne spilling down the wall like bubbly tears. The caviar followed, the eggs leaving a greasy, gray-black trail behind them.

So close. So *damned* close.

After five minutes of enraged pacing, the professional calmed. A month of work down the drain. The Justice Department would change all the access codes and it could take another month to get back in.

Take a deep breath. Get yourself under control. Control is what took you out of the trailer park. Control.

File: 248. Julia Devaux's data was in a file called 248. Well, no one else hunting for Julia Devaux's head had as much to go on. A three digit code should be breakable within two weeks at the most. And with S. T. Akers on the case, it would be well into the new year before Santana went to trial, anyway.

There was still time. File 248…it wasn't much to go on, but it was something.

There was still hope, the professional reflected as Tosca threw herself off the parapet.

There was still hope.

* * * * *

It was a short walk from the school to Julia's home.

It was a short walk to *anywhere* in Simpson. Julia really didn't even need the clunky ancient lime green Ford Fairlane Davis had made available. It rattled, devoured gasoline and was old enough to vote.

She missed her classy Fiat.

She missed her classy life.

What was happening back in Boston? Dora had been thinking more and more about going freelance. She'd even hinted that she might welcome Julia on board. Had she made the leap? Andrew and Paul, her gay neighbors, had been spatting. Julia hoped they'd still be together when — if — she ever got back. Nobody made lasagna like Paul and Andrew could be counted on to accompany her to all the art shows.

An insanely cheery Halloween postcard was going to be sent to them from Florida, reminding them of the Halloween ball the three of them had attended the year before. If only they knew… Julia smiled as she had a sudden image of Andrew and Paul coming to her rescue.

And Federico Fellini, the world's most beautiful and most temperamental cat. Would his new owners realize that he liked his meat cooked medium rare and that he caught chills easily?

She wished her life were a movie and she could rewind it to a month ago and decide not to go on her little photographic safari in the wilds of the industrial area along the docks. Anything would have been preferable. Root canal work. Elective surgery. Even finally reading her ancient, unopened copy of *War and Peace*, cover to cover, including the footnotes.

Anything at all would have been better than what she actually did do—drive down to the docks for her try at gritty photographic realism, since her stab at a romantic nature shoot had simply netted her a wasted roll's worth of blurred butterfly wings and out-of-focus dandelions.

Well, she'd certainly gotten her share of gritty reality.

Julia made her way down the empty street, looking into shop windows as she went. Even though it was nearly dark, no one had turned on the lights yet and it was like walking through a ghost town. The street was eerie. The town was eerie. Her life was eerie.

She tried to cast the whole scene in her mind as a movie, an old trick of hers when she was scared or lonely or depressed. Right now she was all three so she dove inside her head and starred in her own film.

A '40s movie, she thought. Filmed in black and white. It fit. All color had been leached out by the gray sky edging towards night. The bad guy...oh, Humphrey Bogart. Or maybe...Jimmy Cagney.

And I'm the beautiful heiress tracking down a clue to the mysterious death of...of my uncle here in this ghost town...and I only have this statue of a falcon to go on...and this private eye I hired is handsome and suspicious...

Julia entertained herself with her fantasy that she spliced together from a number of classics until she reached the weather-beaten door of the small wooden A-frame house Herbert Davis had found her. Then the fantasy dissipated. No '40s movie heroine worth the name would have a house that let in gusts of gelid air, had a heating system that went on the fritz constantly and leaked.

Julia was forced to move back into cold, cold reality.

She walked up the steps of the wooden porch that was badly in need of repair and inserted her key. She stopped when she heard a scrabbling sound and sighed heavily. She'd been beating off a mangy, scrawny stray dog for two days now. He had tipped over her garbage can twice. No matter how loud she yelled, he always came scrounging back.

No wonder she preferred cats. Cats had too much dignity to behave like juvenile delinquents.

She spied a dusty yellow-brown shape at the edge of the porch. "Shoo!" she said angrily. Oddly enough, the dog didn't run yipping away, as it usually did. Julia sighed and decided to forego the rock-throwing. The way her luck was going today, she'd probably miss the stray and hit the mayor.

She turned the key and heard a low moan from the porch as she walked into the house.

A moan.

She threw her coat on a chair and rammed her hands into her skirt pockets, trying to blank out the memory of the sound. But the creature had definitely moaned.

Well, it wasn't any business of hers. Damn it, she didn't even like dogs. Julia walked into the kitchen to make herself a soothing cup of tea, then stopped, eyes narrowed, tapping her foot.

I'm a fool, she thought, turning around to walk back out the door.

The dog was huddled in the corner of the porch. Julia approached him gingerly. She knew zilch about dogs. For all she knew, the creature had some horrible disease, rabies or something, and would leap with a low growl for her throat. She tried to remember everything she knew about rabies, but it wasn't much and it wasn't pleasant. All she remembered was that the treatment was really nasty — shots in the stomach.

"Nice doggy," she said unconvincingly as she approached the matted, yellowish mass of fur. In the penumbra, she couldn't even tell which end was head and which end was tail. The dog took care of her uncertainty by lifting a pointed, stained muzzle and thumping the other end on the floorboards.

Julia edged closer, wondering what kind of vocabulary dogs understood. Federico Fellini, her cat, was an intellectual and she could talk about books and films to him, as long as it was after he'd been fed and fed well. She had a vague notion that dogs preferred football and politics.

This is a bad idea, Julia, she told herself. *It isn't enough to be in Simpson, Idaho under a death threat. You have to try to help a possibly rabid dog and get bitten for your pains.* She turned back.

The dog emitted a high-pitched whine.

Damn.

Julia walked back and squatted to look the dog over in the uncertain light from the lamppost on the sidewalk. At least the dog was breathing and she wouldn't have to give it mouth to muzzle resuscitation. She'd failed her CPR course.

The dog's tail thumped weakly on the boards as Julia reached out gingerly to pat it. She felt something wet and snatched her hand back, then realized that the dog was trying to lick her hand. The dog lifted its muzzle into her hand. Julia could swear that it was looking straight into her soul. The mutt looked lost and lonely.

"You, too, huh?" she murmured and with a sigh, snapped her fingers to shoo him in. The dog quivered and tried to stand, then collapsed, whining loudly.

"What's the matter? Are you hurt?" Julia gently ran her hands over the dull coat, trying not to think about ticks and fleas, stopping when she felt the right foreleg.

"Broken, huh?" she told the dog. He just looked at her and thumped his tail. "Or maybe sprained. I don't know. God knows if Simpson has a vet. Well." She took a deep breath and looked at him sternly. "You can come in tonight because it's cold and you're hurt, but just for the night and then you're out...is that clear?"

The tail swished again and he licked her hand.

"Okay, just as long as we understand each other." Julia lifted the surprisingly heavy dog in her arms, staggering a little. She remembered Federico's standards of cuisine. "And no home-cooked meals either. You'll get some bread and milk and that's it." The dog whined again as they crossed the threshold. Julia sighed. "Well, maybe if you're really good, you can have my leftover tuna salad."

She put some old towels on the floor in the corner of the little living room and stepped back. He was a big dog, but starved. His ribs were sticking out so clearly through the dull, matted coat that she could count each one of them.

Julia went into the kitchen, poured milk into a plastic bowl and put the remains of her tuna salad on a plastic plate. She knew that tomorrow she would stop by the grocery store to pick up some dog food and inquire about a vet.

You're a fool, Julia, she told herself again as she put the food in front of the dog, but she was pleased anyway as she watched the dog gulp the food down and slurp up the milk. He gazed at her through slitted eyes.

"Bad time, huh, big fellow?" Julia asked softly.

The dog yawned hugely, showing a mouthful of yellow teeth, put its nose on its forepaws and went out like a light.

Julia envied him. She hadn't had a decent night's sleep in over four weeks. It would take more than a blanket and some leftover tuna salad to repair her shattered life.

Julia shivered. Speaking of repairs...

Reluctantly, she walked into the pantry—actually a little cubbyhole just off the kitchen—where some joker with a sick sense of humor had installed something that was supposed to act like a hot water heater and had pretensions to heating the house. The only thing the big tank did was take the edge off the chill in the house and provide—with an inordinate amount of moaning and groaning—a reluctant trickle of tepid water.

Or had done, until this morning, when her shower had been icy cold and she had noticed a water stain on the wall. Something, somewhere had broken.

Her wall was a metaphor for her life.

The stain had spread. There was water on the floor and an alarming gurgling sound. Julia was sure that plumbers did something more than stare and wring their hands, but what?

The front doorbell rang.

With a last baffled look at the crisscrossing tangle of tubes and piping, she walked to the door and yanked it open.

Windblown gusts of ice streaked diagonally across the cone of light from the streetlamp. Julia shivered. The temperature had dropped another ten degrees.

Sam Cooper stood in her doorway, tall, dark, with a frighteningly grim expression on his face, dark eyes glittering. She stared at him for a long moment, then gathered her courage in both hands. If he was here, there could only be one reason for it. And it wasn't good.

"Are you going to press charges?" she asked, lifting her chin.

He blinked. Something, some unreadable expression, crossed his dark, hard face. "No."

Even his voice was dark, low and deep.

"Oh." Some of the battle-tension deserted her. "That's good."

"I came because—"

There was a loud crash and the sound of water splashing on the floor.

"Oh, no!" Julia groaned and ran to the pantry. Water was seeping from the wall, spreading out from where the water stain had been. Something popped and water cascaded out in an arc, taking great chunks of plaster with it.

"Where's the main distribution pipe valve?"

Julia turned at the sound of the deep harsh voice behind her. She stared helplessly up at Sam Cooper. He snorted, felt his way around the watery mess until he found something and wrenched his wrist to the right. Like magic, the water stopped spouting.

Then he knelt and started pulling out chunks of her wall. He stuck both hands into the innards of her house, eventually ending up on his side, his head stuck into the wall. Julia heard him grunt, then he pulled his head out.

"Lug," he said.

Right to her face.

Julia stiffened. *Lug?* He was calling her a *lug*? How dare he?

She hadn't the faintest idea what lug meant. Western dialect was still fairly new to her, but...but surely *lug* wasn't very complimentary. Lug rhymed with plug. And mug. And slug.

"I beg your pardon," she said huffily.

A faint smile crossed his austere features. "Need a lug wrench." He pulled some keys from his jeans pocket. "Keys to the pickup. Toolbox's on the front seat."

Julia took the set of keys from him, brushing his hand. It was harder than any hand she'd ever touched before. Hard and rough and warm.

She hesitated a moment, holding the keys in front of her as if they were some form of talisman. She stared down into his face, taking in the dark features and dark eyes glittering at her. She couldn't read what he was thinking at all. She opened her mouth to say something, then closed it again and walked to the door, looking in dismay at the sleet falling on her little front garden. She peered and sure enough, a battered pickup was parked outside.

It was black.

Figured.

She scampered, shivering, to the pickup. Through the passenger window Julia could see a steel toolbox, the kind handymen had. The third key she tried opened the pickup door and she pulled out the toolbox. It weighed a ton. Puffing, she carried it inside and shook off the mixture of rain and ice.

"Here." If he was going to be John Wayne-laconic, then by God so was she.

He rifled through the neatly arranged toolbox, picking up a wicked-looking implement Vlad the Impaler would have been proud to own.

"This." When she looked at him in bafflement, he sighed. "Lug wrench."

"Oh," Julia said and smiled.

* * * * *

Cooper would have been floored by the charm of that smile if he hadn't been stretched out on the floor already. It transformed Sally Anderson's face from beautiful to stunning. He'd seen her terrified and annoyed and baffled and now amused in the space of an hour. Each emotion had been so clearly visible it could have been written on her forehead. It was an ability he lacked. Melissa had called him stone-face so often he'd begun to believe he couldn't show an emotion if he tried.

Sally Anderson's smile faded and Cooper realized he was staring at her. He tried a smile himself, feeling unused cheek muscles crack. He couldn't hold the smile for much longer, so he bent back to the task of putting Sally Anderson's plumbing in order.

He had his work cut out for him. No one had changed the fittings in her house for forty years. The pipes were rusted and — more or less — all of the washers were ready to blow.

That was okay, his toolbox was top of the line. It had to be. Something was always breaking down at the Double C and he'd turned into a hell of a handyman since he'd come back to run it.

Concentrating on her washers kept him from staring at the gorgeous Miss Sally Anderson. She'd be a knockout even in a big city. In Simpson, she was a fucking miracle, like a rose in winter. It took all his concentration not to stare at her.

She was a beauty, a pocket Venus. The creamy ivory skin of a redhead, eyes the color of the sky over the Double C in summer, a smile that could give a man a heart attack at fifty paces.

Though she looked like a redhead, she wasn't. He'd never been able to resist redheads. If she had red hair instead of brown, he'd probably pick her up, throw her on her bed and jump on top of her. He was having enough trouble resisting her as it was, even with brown hair.

She was one of those women who caught the light and gave it back with a glow. It was impossible not to look at her when she was in the room. At least Cooper found it impossible...which was why he was trying to concentrate on rusty pipes and leaky gaskets. Left to his own devices, he'd simply stop and stare at her endlessly. Probably scare the shit out of her, too.

There was another reason to stay on the floor, curved in towards the wall.

He had a hard-on.

Just his luck. His cock chose *now*, of all times, to wake up.

His cock had been basically dead meat between his legs since Melissa left a year ago and for most of the year before that, while his marriage was slowly, painfully imploding. He hadn't had any sexual desire—none, nada, zilch—for what seemed like a lifetime. It was as if that part of his life had been switched off. He'd almost resigned himself to a nookie-less existence and here his dick was springing back to life, clamoring for what it had been missing all this time, at exactly the wrong moment. Now was definitely not the right time for a woodie.

A dead dick was not anything he thought he'd suffer from, ever. He'd always enjoyed sex and had had a lot in his time. The dead dick thing had taken him totally by surprise.

Part of it was the exhausting, back-breaking job of turning the Double C around from his father's neglect during the last years of his life. Cooper worked eighteen-hour days—hard, physical labor as intense as the PT he'd done daily in the Teams without the adrenaline-releasing highs of combat—and bed was a place where he slipped into sleep so deep it could have been a coma the instant his head touched the pillow.

Another part of it was the sheer hell he'd gone through during his marriage to a coldhearted woman, the memory of which made him wince even now. His marriage had been like living through a train wreck in slow motion.

That last year he'd as soon have put his cock between the jaws of a rattlesnake than between Melissa's thighs. He'd have found a warmer welcome with the rattlesnake, too.

But the biggest part of it was that attractive, single women didn't grow on trees in Simpson. Or Rupert or Dead Horse for that matter. It had been a long, long time since he'd seen anyone as beautiful as this woman. If ever.

The truth was, he'd fallen in instant lust with this Sally Anderson and now he had no idea what to do. He'd completely lost the knack of dealing with females. Human ones, at least.

If this was when he was in the Teams, and she was a girl in a bar next to a base, he could buy her a drink without having to worry about coaxing or courting or even making conversation. The music was too loud in bars and anyway, no one went there to talk. They went there to find someone to fuck. Sex while in the Navy hadn't been a problem at all, particularly in Coronado with its droves of SEAL groupies clamoring for a piece.

Then Melissa had set her sights on him and basically dragged him to the altar without Cooper having much to say about it. To her disgust, it turned out being an officer's wife wasn't as much fun as she thought it would be. And being a rancher's wife wasn't any fun at all. Melissa had not been a happy camper and she'd made sure, day and night, that Cooper knew all about it.

They'd been taught everything about Evade and Escape tactics in the Teams and he'd used that knowledge—a lot— during his marriage. He'd basically just shut his cock down and now that it had sprung to life he didn't have a tool in his toolbox that would help him win his way into this lady's bed.

Sally Anderson was clearly a lady. A gorgeous, well-educated lady with an easy charm. Cooper wasn't going to coax her into bed with his own charm. He didn't have any. He didn't have any smooth words or smooth moves.

Maybe fixing her plumbing would do the trick.

* * * * *

While Sam Cooper worked in silence, Julia mopped up the mess.

She had to step more than once around his long legs stretching out forever. Nice legs, she thought. Very, very nice legs. Then she was ashamed of herself for ogling the legs of a man who was helping her. Though they were supremely ogleable.

Julia stopped for a moment, studying those legs.

They were long and muscular with unusually strong thighs. The tight jeans showcased the long bands of muscles in his thighs, steel-hard and massive, swelling and bunching with his movements in a way Julia found utterly fascinating. She couldn't tear her eyes away from the play of those muscles. She'd rarely seen sheer male strength up close like that. She had to dig her fingernails into her palms to keep from reaching out and touching all that male power. Just for a second. Just to see what it felt like.

Julia had always chosen her men for their conversation and charm. And, of course, they had to be readers and love old films and get along with Federico — which wasn't easy. Federico was finicky about the company he kept.

Thigh muscles had never really entered into the equation.

It had never even occurred to her that she could be turned on by only the bottom half of a male body, as men were turned on by pneumatic breasts. This wasn't like her; she valued conversation and culture and charm. It was appalling to be fixated on a man's physical attributes. Stress and fear had turned her into this...this redneck *guy*.

She was absolutely certain that the man now repairing her plumbing had neither conversation nor charm, but apparently thigh muscles trumped charm out here, judging from the waves of intense heat prickling under her skin.

Danger and stress were driving her insane. That was the only possible explanation.

Cooper pulled himself further into the wall, doing something competent with the wrench, turning on his back for a moment and Julia got an eyeful of something else massive about Sam Cooper besides his thigh muscles.

Either the man had an enormous erection or he belonged in the *Guinness Book of Records*. Julia's internal temperature spiked in a flash of incandescent heat sapping her muscles of strength.

Oh, God. What was happening to her? Her legs were trembling and she couldn't take her eyes off Sam Cooper's jeans, old and white along the front and in the groin area where it was stressed by contact with his thigh muscles and his...

Oh, this wouldn't do.

On rubbery knees, Julia went into the kitchen to rub her wrists over ice cubes, since the water was turned off. She started cooling down. When she finally had herself under control, she went back to where Cooper was working.

He finally emerged from her wall. With an enormous *whump!*, her boiler came back on. As he had in the school after she'd brained him, Cooper stood in one smooth lithe powerful movement. He looked down at her. That dark, hard face was totally expressionless. He held his big hands up. They were covered in grease and she saw with dismay he'd nicked himself. Two of the knuckles were covered in blood.

"May I wash my hands?" His voice was deep and raspy, as if he didn't speak often.

"Of course. Thank you so much." The house was already beginning to heat up and Julia felt an enormous surge of gratitude towards him. Okay, so he didn't talk much, and his thighs and what was between them messed with her head, but he'd repaired her plumbing and she was really grateful. "The bathroom is the second door to the right. The towels are clean."

He nodded his head gravely and turned. With what she considered a heroic act of self-control, Julia did not check his buns out. The front of him was quite enough distraction. She headed back into the kitchen.

She'd make him a cup of tea—no, maybe cowboys preferred coffee. She was filling the filter when she heard a knock on the door.

The house was starting to resemble Grand Central Station. In the entire month she'd been here, no one had stopped by. Tonight was a circus. First the dog, then Cooper and now someone else.

Julia opened the door and her worst nightmare came out of the swirling darkness.

A pistol. Aimed straight at her head.

Chapter Three

Julia screamed and her heart tried to pound its way out of her chest. She scrabbled wildly for something to use as a weapon, though she knew it was too late. Crazily, she tried to brace herself for the shot.

"Trick or treat." The childish treble came from somewhere around her knees and she froze. A witch, a blond Harry Potter with fake round plastic glasses and a cowboy stared at her, frightened by her screams. The little cowboy dropped his plastic gun and the witch started crying.

Not killers. School kids wanting a treat.

The front door closed. Dimly, as if coming from a hundred miles away, Julia heard a deep male voice and the excited squeals of children from the porch. Then, a moment later, the front door opened again, letting in an arctic swirl of wind.

She stumbled into the little living room, her fingers clenching hard on the back of the garish flower-covered sofa. She ignored the heavy pounding in her chest and tried to control the trembling in her arms. For a moment, colored lights danced before her eyes and the edges of vision started to fade like a yellowing photograph. A hot tear dropped onto her white knuckles.

Terror, loneliness, despair all jostled sharply, painfully inside Julia's chest, as if there were knives in there fighting their way out, slicing her heart into shreds. She drew in a long sobbing breath as another tear squeezed out from behind her closed lids. Rough tremors shook her. In the instant before her knees gave way, she felt herself half-lifted and turned against a broad expanse of chest.

To Julia's intense horror, short, stuttering sobs racked through her. She swayed and was held tightly. Strong arms held her close and she let herself go limp.

It felt like a lifetime since she had been held and comforted by another human being. Since her parents' deaths, in fact. And now Julia found herself weeping out her fear and rage and loneliness in great, uncontrollable gasping sobs she couldn't have repressed had her life depended on it. She wept and wept and wept, knowing she was going to be flooded with remorse. Later. But not now. Now she needed the release like she needed air.

Finally the giant gulping sobs subsided into hiccups and she leaned against Cooper's chest, drained and spent. His sweater was wet from the water leaking from her rusty pipes and her eyes.

She breathed deeply, aware suddenly of whose chest she was leaning against, whose embrace she was in. One large hand held the back of her head, covering it. A hard arm was pressed against her waist, holding her tightly to him.

It was an erection. A very big one and, amazingly, it was still growing, pulsing and lengthening against her stomach. She could feel the heat of his penis through his jeans and her dress and wondered if he could feel the sudden flush of heat blooming inside her.

Julia instantly went from cold despair to a hot burst of lust. She morphed in a flash from distressed woman comforted by perfect stranger, to woman tightly held in the arms of an aroused man. It was enough to give a woman the bends.

She should step back. This was completely inappropriate. She knew nothing about this man except that he wasn't a talker and he knew how to fix plumbing.

Well, that was a lie.

She knew how big his penis was.

Enormous.

Julia stepped back immediately and tottered to her ugly couch. She collapsed on it, closing her eyes.

I can't deal with this, she thought. Any of it.

Being the object of a woman-hunt, exiled to Simpson, being terrorized by school kids trick-or-treating, lusting after an aroused non-talker with superb thighs. It was all too much.

The tears had dried up, but the hot hard tangle of pain in her chest still hurt.

She sensed Cooper's presence by her side.

"Here." He curled Julia's hand around a glass half full of liquid. Gratefully, she gulped it down then yelped as it burned its way to her stomach.

"What was that?" she gasped, looking up at him. Her eyes filled again with tears, but a better variety of tears.

"Whisky," Cooper said and took the glass from her numb hand. All of her was numb, except the parts that were hot.

"Where did you get whisky?" Julia gave one last cough then put a hand to her stomach, where a ball of warmth had settled. "I don't have any."

"I do."

"In your *toolbox*?" Julia blinked at Cooper in amazement.

"Nope." Cooper's mouth twitched, which she supposed was cowboy body language for amusement. "In the pickup. For emergencies."

For a second, Julia wanted to ask what kind of emergency, but one look at that angular, shuttered face had her biting her tongue.

Well, of course. In the movies, cowboys were always getting shot and pouring whisky over the wound. Just before digging the bullet out with a hunting knife by the light of the campfire.

The whisky was going to her head. Or the adrenaline deserted her body in a rush. Whatever the cause, Julia was completely drained. Cooper sat down on the matching armchair next to the couch, dangled large hands over his knees and watched her steadily.

Whoever had decorated her house had a taste in upholstery matching the taste in plumbing—terrible. The armchairs were covered with huge cabbage roses in unlikely shades of clashing pinks and reds. When Cooper sat down, with his black shirt and black hair, he seemed to absorb all the light like an eclipse of the sun. There was a man-shaped black hole in her armchair surrounded by a nimbus of fiery colors.

Silence fell over the room, broken only by the needle-sharp arrows of sleet hitting the windowpane. Julia hated silences and usually filled them with chatter. There was always something you could talk about to another human being. She'd often been in places where politics and religion were conversational no-nos, but the weather was usually good neutral ground.

Except in Saudi Arabia—where politics and religion had definitely been out—and where there had been no weather to speak of. There, she usually fell back on American films. Everybody in Saudi Arabia, from the lowliest camel driver on up, had a DVD player and was absolutely hooked on Hollywood's finest.

But now she had no idea how to talk to Sam Cooper. She had attacked him, been rescued from freezing to death by him, had sobbed all over him, had given him an erection, in return had felt incredibly intense stabs of lust for him and she still didn't have the faintest idea what to say to him.

She didn't have the energy to lie and the truth was too dangerous. There was a reason she was in such turmoil, jumping at shadows. A reason why her nerves were on a hair-trigger. A reason why she was so insane as to be able to fall in lust with a man she didn't know. But she couldn't say it. Davis had been quite clear on that point. Her life depended on no one knowing she was in the Witness Security Program.

Silence. Cooper watched her out of expressionless dark eyes. She had no idea at all what he was thinking. It couldn't be good, though.

"I can't talk about it," she blurted out when the silence began to be embarrassing. She lifted her chin.

Cooper nodded his head once, gravely, as if that were the most reasonable statement he'd ever heard and Julia slumped in relief.

She jumped when something cold and wet poked at her hand.

"Oh!" Julia bent over the arm of the chair and looked down into soulful brown eyes. It was crazy, probably induced by stress and alcohol, but she had the feeling that the dog understood everything she was going through. He gazed at her adoringly, then licked her hand. There wasn't a human being on earth who would have licked her hand in gratitude for leftover tuna salad and an old blanket.

"Do you repair animals as well as plumbing, Mr....ahm...Cooper?"

"Just Cooper'll do, ma'am."

He rose easily from the armchair, which was no mean feat. Julia knew the springs on that armchair were broken. She had struggled more than once to get out of it. Had she been a little less befuddled, she would have warned Cooper that he was sitting in a man-eating armchair. But Cooper rose out of it just as smoothly as if the chair had lifted itself up to tip him out, which meant that he had fantastic abdominals to go with the amazing thigh muscles. Actually, Julia thought abstractedly, as Cooper bent over the dog, he had fantastic everything.

He moved with an incredibly lithe, powerful grace. Long lean hard muscles showed through the black sweater. His hands moving gently over the dog were large, long-fingered, graceful. When he hunkered down to murmur softly to the dog, Julia was drawn again to those thighs. How did anyone develop thigh muscles like that? Well, he bred horses for a living, so he probably rode a lot.

Julia had a sudden searing vision of Cooper riding *her*, those incredible thighs flexing strongly as he...

Cooper looked up at her and Julia blushed furiously, the blood pumping hard and hot from her chest up into her face. Oh, *God*, she hoped he wasn't a mind reader.

His big hand was fondling the top of the stray dog's head and she grabbed the chance to focus on something other than this man's thighs. And worse...what was between them.

"The dog's not really mine, you know. I've seen him around for days. He's been scrounging food from the garbage bin for a few days and I've been shooing him off, but this evening when I came home after..." ...*after braining you with a pumpkin*...

Julia blinked and felt the blood pour back up into her face.

Cooper gave no notice. Those large, gorgeous male hands were running over the dog's body and stopped at the right foreleg.

"I noticed that too. Is it broken?" Julia peered over the couch's arm.

"Nope."

"What then?"

"Sprained. And someone's been mistreating him badly." Cooper made some reassuring sounds in a deep low voice to the dog that even had Julia lulled, then looked up again. "He have a name?"

"No. I told you. He just showed up this evening."

"Needs a name." Cooper gently ruffled the matted fur between the dog's ears.

"Ahm..." The mangy, yellow-haired dog was as far away from her sleek Siamese, Federico Fellini, as it was possible to be. Still...the mutt had four legs and a head, just like Federico. Close enough. "Fred. I want to call him Fred."

"Fred it is. Hey, Fred." Cooper let the dog sniff his fingers once again. "He'll be all right in a few days if he keeps his weight off that paw. Couple of good meals and a warm place to sleep is all he needs." Cooper picked out a burr then stood up suddenly. Julia craned her neck to look up at him.

"Are you going?" She had a sudden, unexplained panicky feeling.

"No." He looked down at her a moment, expressionless, and she found herself wishing she could read what he was thinking, though she probably wouldn't like it. His thoughts probably ran along the lines of how best to exit gracefully from a madwoman's house.

He opened the door and disappeared. It was night now, and Julia caught a glimpse of darkness and windborne needles of sleet slanting across the light thrown by the streetlamp. Before she had time to feel the cold from the door he was back, holding a first aid kit.

"Does that come from the magic pickup, too?"

Again, she had a fleeting impression of a smile. "Yup."

Cooper knelt down to Fred and started murmuring again, soothing, senseless noises. Julia was astonished to see that the dog made no protest, even when Cooper examined the forepaw carefully and wrapped an elastic bandage around it tightly. There was a deep scratch on the right haunch and though Fred whined when Cooper examined it carefully, he didn't move. Cooper cleaned the wound, but didn't bandage it.

Julia leaned over the arm of the sofa and watched Cooper with interest. He worked quickly, quietly and competently.

"What do you suppose happened to him?"

Cooper sat back on his heels, stretching the jeans. Julia carefully kept her eyes on his face. This sudden fascination with his lower body was embarrassing. Her life had become low-rent enough as it was. She was terrified of turning into the kind of woman who got horny and went to bars to proposition men.

"Car accident most likely," he said. "Either hit by a car or thrown out of one."

Julia sucked in her breath sharply in outrage. "Thrown out! You mean someone would deliberately throw an animal out of a moving car?"

"Yup. Happens all the time. Someone thought they wanted a pet, then changed their mind. Fred is definitely someone's dog, though. Or was. Got good clean lines, probably make a good hunter." Cooper's large hand brushed the top of Fred's head, thumb idly scratching behind his ears. Fred's bushy tail thumped heavily.

"If you say so." Julia looked doubtfully at Fred. The good lines, if they were there, were hidden beneath dirty, matted fur. "I'm not a dog person myself and I really have no intention of keeping him. I just felt sorry for him tonight."

Cooper stood up and stuck his hands in his back jeans pockets. "Might want to keep him for a while. Be company when you…" He stopped suddenly.

"When I fall apart?" Julia asked dryly. "I assure you, Mr. Cooper, I'm not in the habit of falling to pieces every evening."

"Didn't think you were, ma'am." He shifted his weight from one dusty boot to another, graceful even when embarrassed. "And the name's Cooper."

Julia tilted her head as she examined him. "Doesn't anyone call you by your first name? What is it? Sam?"

"Yup. But most everyone calls me Coop."

"Even when you were a child? What did your mother call you?"

"Don't know. She died when I was three. Hardly remember her."

"What did they call you at school?"

"Coop."

"And your wife?"

"Mostly she called me a son of a bitch, ma'am." His black eyes bored into hers. "'Specially just before she left me."

Well, *that* was a conversation stopper.

"Oh. I, ah…I'm sorry. I didn't mean to pry, it's just that…" Julia wound down with an embarrassed shrug, then watched curiously as Cooper pulled a note out of his jeans pocket and handed it to her.

Surprised, she unfolded it, only to find that it was one of the notes she had written and addressed to Rafael's parents and that she'd tucked into the little boy's Barney lunch pail. It didn't matter which note it was, they all said more or less the same thing.

Rafael is having serious problems at school and I would appreciate a chance to talk it over with you.

She looked at the tall, silent man before her, then back at the note. "I don't really see…"

Then, suddenly, she did.

Obviously, Sam Cooper was little Rafael's father. Julia's fertile imagination filled in the dots. Cooper's wife—the one who mostly called him a son of a bitch—must have left him very recently, which was why little Rafael was having so many problems.

No, that didn't work.

Rafael's last name was Martinez not Cooper, so she couldn't have been his wife…but he had said his wife had left him, so maybe Rafael was Cooper's wife's child from a first marriage—Cooper's ex-wife's child—it was hard to work it all out in her mind while those opaque black eyes were steadily watching her.

As always when at a loss, Julia talked.

"Look, I apologize for interfering, I usually don't, believe me, but Rafael is truly having problems coping at school. Why just today, he cried because Missy…"

"Tomorrow," Cooper interrupted. "Could you come out?"

She was starting to be able to decipher his code. Translated into human speech, Cooper was asking her if she would be willing to come out to the ranch tomorrow and talk over Rafael's problems.

Fred poked his nose into Cooper's hand and he idly scratched the matted fur, seeming to know just the spot to make Fred wriggle with delight. It looked like Sam Cooper was infinitely more gifted at communicating with animals than with human beings.

There wasn't much Julia had to do tomorrow afternoon, besides fret over her situation and whine to Fred. Even talking over a little boy's problems was preferable to that.

"Yes, of course," she said, and Fred swung his head around to her without leaving Cooper's side. "Where's your house...er, ranch?"

"Drive five miles west out the old McMurphy Road towards the Interstate, turn right at the intersection, then drive northeast for two miles, take the east fork, drive four hundred yards..."

Julia listened to him in rising panic, having a sudden image of herself zigging when she was supposed to zag, driving in frantic loops around the vast empty countryside until the gas ran out and wolves ate her.

Her face must have registered panicky despair because Cooper stopped. "I'm coming into town tomorrow morning," he said and she thought maybe she heard a slight sigh from him. "Could you be at Carly's Diner around ten?"

"Carly's Diner," Julia said, enormously relieved, delighted she wouldn't have to go out all by herself in this wild and lonely country, fodder for wolves. Five miles west...south fork...four hundred yards. He might as well have spoken Greek. "Ten o'clock. I'll be there."

"Fine." He dipped his head gravely. "Thank you."

"Don't mention it." Julia said softly. "It's the least I can do after..." She waved a hand awkwardly, fighting the urge to pantomime dropping a big pumpkin on Cooper's head.

Cooper was in the open doorway now. It was still sleeting and the temperature had dropped precipitously. His breath created a wreath around his head, making him look slightly unreal. Those strong, unhandsome, craggy features seemed chiseled from stone, as if he were a statue in the mist instead of a human being in the cold. Only his eyes glittered.

For some obscure reason, Julia found herself staring into those bottomless eyes. She was no longer frightened of him, not really, however forbidding he looked. He seemed so remote, so untouchable. Yet he'd shown her—and Fred—nothing but kindness. It was hard to square that kindness with a man who could make his little son so miserable.

They were so close and he was so tall, she was getting a crick in her neck looking up at him. Fred kept swinging his head back and forth between his new friends.

It was as if he held her in some kind of thrall. When Julia felt herself beginning to lean forward as if Cooper's eyes were a tractor beam in a science fiction film, she stepped back and tried to collect her scattered thoughts.

"Rafael," she said breathlessly. She found it impossible to tear her gaze from his. "He's such a nice little boy. I'm sure that with a little bit of help, things will straighten themselves out."

He was standing blocking her doorway and precious heat was dissipating into the gelid night. Wisps of steamy warm air curled around his legs. He turned and walked across the rickety porch. The second step down had a loose plank and it creaked. She watched him walk across her small garden. Halfway across he stopped and turned. "Miss Anderson…"

"Sally," she said.

"Sally. Rafael is…" Cooper hesitated.

"Yes, Cooper?" Her voice sounded soft in the snowy darkness. "Rafael is what?"

"Not my boy," Cooper said. He turned on his heel, climbed up into his pickup truck and drove away into the black, sleety night.

* * * * *

Cooper could drive the 27.2 miles from Simpson to the Double C blindfolded and handcuffed, using his toes, which was a damned good thing because all he could see was Sally Anderson's face in front of him and all he could think about was his steel hard-on, which fucking hurt.

It still hadn't gone down. Cooper was worried that his cock had somehow zeroed in on Sally Anderson and now had a serious jones for her and her alone. This probably meant he was never going to have sex again in this lifetime, considering how he'd behaved. He hadn't been able to get more than ten words out and had rubbed his hard-on against her when he held her after she'd been frightened by the trick-or-treaters.

She probably thought he was some kind of weirdo who couldn't talk to women, just rub up against them for his jollies.

Still, he couldn't fault his cock for its excellent taste. There was just something about Sally Anderson. Something about the quality of her skin, pale and so luminous it seemed to glow as if there were a light within. Or maybe it was the clear turquoise eyes, the color of the sea at Coronado at dusk. Whatever it was, he couldn't tear his eyes away from her.

She had a small dimple in her left cheek when she smiled and he suddenly wished he could have coaxed another smile out of her, just to see it. But he'd lost the art of making a woman smile, if he'd ever had it. He could rappel down from a hovering helicopter, scuba dive to 200 feet, make a two thousand yard shot, tame the wildest horse, but making a woman smile…that was another matter.

Cooper knew everything there was to know about soldiering and everything there was to know about livestock. But damned if he knew how to coax a beautiful woman into his bed.

* * * * *

"*Not my boy.*" Julia thought in bed later that night, as she read the same paragraph for the third time in a row.

Now what on earth did that mean? That Rafael was his wife's child? If so, not my boy seemed such a cold, cruel way of putting it. But Sam Cooper didn't strike her as cruel.

Granted, he wasn't the most articulate of men — though Julia felt that was due more to a defect of communication ability rather than of intelligence. She'd read somewhere that commandos or special forces or whatever they were called had to be above average in intelligence, though it was very likely that charm and the ability to chitchat weren't in the job description.

Sam Cooper certainly looked forbidding, but somehow she just couldn't bring herself to think of him as cruel.

She glanced at Fred, curled up on an old blanket in a corner of the room, watching her steadily out of soft brown eyes. Cooper had been gentle even in his handling of the mangy mutt who had adopted her. Surely a man who was kind to stray animals and stray women couldn't be cruel to such a small sweet boy. Could he?

But then again, what did she know? She wasn't sure of anything any more. Her whole world had been turned completely upside down in the past month.

She had been living a perfectly ordinary and satisfying existence and then *wham*! Her whole life had suddenly turned into a country and western song — one of those whiny, complaining ones. Julia started making up some lyrics in her head to a Nashville beat, tapping her foot under the blanket.

I Lost My Job and I Lost My House and I Lost My Car... Fred suddenly yipped and started biting angrily at his shoulder. *...And My Dog Has Fleas*, she finished despondently.

To top it all off, for the first time in her life she couldn't read her distress away. The greatest panacea in the world — becoming immersed in a good book — wasn't available. The only reading material in Simpson was *The Rupert Pioneer* and a few scandal sheets reporting weekly sightings of Elvis, available at

Loren Jensen's grocery store. So Julia had to make do with the few books she had with her.

She had had a hurried ten minutes at an airport bookshop during one of the many stopovers on the way to Boise and had basically just tipped the rack into the shopping bag. To her disgust, she had netted four books she had already read, a history of trade with Japan in the 20th century and a Spanish-English dictionary. The rest were the novels she'd been reading over and over again for the past month.

Julia's eyes fell on the book she was reading for the fifth time. Maybe that was why she couldn't concentrate on the murder mystery. She was reading it this time with her critical editor's eye. The book could have done with a good editor. The book could have done with her. She'd been a very good editor.

Before.

Who had taken her place at Turner & Lowe? The company had just been eaten up by a huge German publishing conglomerate when she had disappeared. The dust hadn't settled yet and there had been word that job cuts were in the offing. No doubt her request for indefinite unpaid compassionate leave had come in very handy. Had Dora taken over her job? No, Dora was known to have a keen editorial eye for nonfiction. Even the faceless businessmen on the other side of the Atlantic would want their editors to be working in their own area of expertise. It made good economic sense.

Maybe Donny had taken over her authors. Donny Moro had been her PA for a while and Julia had caught him more than once with a speculative gleam in his eye. He'd have leapt at the chance to take over from her. She could just hear him, the smarmy little brat. *Too bad Julia had to leave just now, when we're all so busy. What was she thinking? Never mind. I'll be happy to take up the slack.*

Who knew what she'd find when she got back?

If she got back.

Tears pricked her eyes, though she knew perfectly well a few tears weren't going to change her situation. Not one iota. She should know. She'd cried buckets over the past month, cried out her fear and her fury at what was happening. And her problems were still there at the end of the crying jag—looming over her life like Flattop Ridge loomed over Simpson.

Julia swiped at her eyes, then yawned. She had used up all her adrenaline today, what with Davis' phone call, braining a SEAL, then her plumbing threatening to flood the house, her terror when she thought one of Santana's killers had found her, lusting inappropriately after a non-talking soldier-rancher…it had been a big day. Her eyelids drooped. Time for sleep.

Her hand automatically reached out to the cheap alarm clock on the nightstand, then she stopped. Tomorrow was Saturday, so she didn't need the alarm.

And besides, she had been alarmed enough.

Chapter Four

"Freshen up your coffee?"

Julia glanced up from *The Rupert Pioneer* into the smiling, anxious face of a pretty young woman about Julia's age, holding a carafe of coffee.

Should she have more coffee? Maybe not, considering the fact that the closest hospital was probably two hundred miles away. The stuff was lethal.

Julia smiled at her. "No, thanks. One cup is plenty."

Julia tried to follow her normal routine as much as possible, which gave her the feeling of having some sort of control over her life. One of her most cherished routines was a long, leisurely cup of coffee in a favorite coffee shop after work, preferably with a girlfriend or two. And no Saturday would be complete without a morning coffee out while reading the paper.

If her life had been normal, right now she'd be having coffee at The Bookworm on State Street, a new supply of books at her feet, comfortably dissecting office gossip with Jean and Dora over a *mochaccino* in a bone china cup. Instead, she was reading *The Rupert Pioneer* over tepid river sludge in a chipped mug.

But her life was here now, like it or not, and she found herself being drawn into the life of Simpson, almost against her will. She had read every word of *The Pioneer*, including a breathless, blow-by-blow account of last week's local varsity basketball game — which the local team had lost — and obituaries of people she'd never heard of. A true Devaux, Julia thought wryly.

Making a home in the unlikeliest of places was in her blood. Her mother had been a diplomat's daughter and her father an

Army brat. Her father's job had kept them moving to a different country every two or three years. She'd learned the drill. You settle in and make do.

She was here in Simpson against her will, under a death threat. But like it or not, it was her home now.

"Sure you don't want any more?" The young waitress hovered eagerly. Julia could see how the waitress might want to please her. She was the only customer in the diner at the moment. "No, really. Thanks, anyway."

The young woman grimaced, set the pot down on the cracked linoleum table and slid into the seat opposite Julia. "I don't really blame you," she sighed. "Terrible stuff, isn't it?"

Julia's smile froze. There was absolutely nothing polite to be said about the coffee that wouldn't have a bolt of lightning immediately striking her dead. "Uhm, well…" Julia hedged.

"That's okay," the girl said cheerfully. "I know it's awful. I guess it's a family tradition. My mom's coffee was awful, too. Mom was Carly. Of Carly's Diner." She had an open expression, her pale blue eyes—a color Julia was beginning to think of as Simpson blue—sparkling with interest. She rested her chin on the heel of her hand and leaned forward. "You're Sally Anderson, aren't you? The new grade school teacher?"

"Yes," Julia sighed. She hated lying to such a sweet-faced woman. "I moved here a month ago."

"Yeah, I know," she replied, brushing back a shiny strand of taffy-colored hair. "I've seen you in here a couple of times. I wanted to introduce myself, but…I don't know." She shrugged, embarrassed. "I think it's been so long since I've met someone I haven't known all my life, I've kind of lost the knack for conversation. Like everyone else around here. Sometimes I think we're all dinosaurs, extinct and we don't even know it because we live in such a remote place."

It was so close to what Julia thought that she felt ashamed. "Well…" Julia said. The lie had passed her lips so often it didn't even feel like a lie. "I guess Simpson's not that bad, I mean compared to other places, er…"

"Alice," the young woman said eagerly and shot out a hand quickly, rocking the coffeepot. Julia steadied the pot with her left hand while grasping Alice's right with her own. Alice pumped Julia's hand energetically. "Alice Pedersen. Pleased to meet you. I don't often get a chance to meet new people. Especially not women close to my own age. This is great. Just great. I'm really glad you moved here. You married?"

Julia was gamely trying another sip of coffee and almost choked. "Pardon me?"

"Not supposed to ask that right away, are you?" Alice said glumly. "I forgot. Told you we're not used to dealing with outsiders. And lately, I've been spending way too much time with my little brother. He's seventeen and a handful, let me tell you. I love him, and he's had a bad time since Mom died, which is why I can forgive him for being such a megajerk, but he's not exactly gracious company, believe me. Ever been married?"

Alice's face was like an open book and Julia could see nothing but friendly curiosity in the light blue eyes. She stifled a sigh. "No, Alice. I'm not married, nor have I ever been married. I haven't even been engaged." *And the last thing on my mind is romance*, she thought. A picture of Sam Cooper of the fabulous thighs flashed across her mind. Lust, maybe, she corrected herself.

"That's strange." Alice blinked. "How come? You're sooo gorgeous. And you look—I don't know—big-city."

Julia put the cup down. "Er…thanks. I think." She cast about for a change of subject. "Alice Pedersen. Pedersen. By any chance are you related to the Sheriff?"

"Yup, and not by chance, either. He's my dad. I hear you and old Coop put on quite a show for him yesterday. He was still chuckling when he got home. I really owe you one for that. It's been a long time since I heard Dad laugh."

Julia gritted her teeth. "Well, I'm glad I was able to provide some light entertainment. I was actually quite scared at the time."

"Of *Coop*?" Alice's light blue eyes rounded. "Why Coop's the nicest guy in the world. I've known him all my life and he wouldn't hurt a fly." She thought for a moment. "Well, not an American. And certainly not a *woman*. Why even when Melissa—" Alice broke off and looked up, smiling. "Hi, Coop," she said.

Julia's head whipped around. Sure enough, there was Sam Cooper, tall and big as life. Still dressed in black, still looking dark and forbidding. How long had he been standing there? She hoped he hadn't got the impression that she idly gossiped about him, angling for more information.

"Alice," he said, then nodded at Julia. "Sally."

Julia surreptitiously placed a hand over her stomach. Sam Cooper's voice was so dark and deep it seemed to reverberate in her diaphragm.

Either that or the coffee was making her sick.

Cooper reached out and softly squeezed Alice's shoulder. "How are things going, Alice?" Julia was surprised at how gentle his deep voice sounded. "How's the diner coming along?" Cooper slid in next to Julia and she scooted over towards the window. His wide shoulders took up two thirds of the back.

Tears sparkled in Alice's eyes. "I don't know, Coop. I just can't seem to get it together." She stood up to fetch him a mug and poured him some coffee from the pot on the table, surreptitiously wiping her eyes. Julia saw that Cooper's mug had a chip, too, only his was on the right side of the handle and hers was on the left. *Cute*, she thought, *matching mugs*.

Alice sat down again and heaved a huge sigh. "I wonder if I'm doing the right thing." She waved a hand around the café, encompassing dirty, dingy walls and the cracked linoleum counter. There was no one in the café besides the three of them.

"Maybe I should just sell the place. Though I can't imagine anyone buying it."

Cooper sipped his coffee and grimaced. "Well, you're certainly keeping the traditions alive. Carly brewed a lousy cup of coffee and so do you. It's good to know some things don't ever change. Company's still good, though. Makes up for the coffee." His mouth curved slightly.

Julia stared at him. Was that Sam Cooper? Cracking a joke? And smiling? And yet, she thought distractedly, he had an extremely nice smile. It was probably a good thing he didn't unleash it all that often. It softened his hard features and made him look more human, more approachable. In the daylight, she could see that his eyes weren't obsidian black, just a very dark brown. He included her in his smile and her breath caught. *Uh-oh*, she thought.

Then Cooper turned back to Alice and Julia started breathing again. In. Out. In. Out. Easy, once you get the hang of it.

"How's Matt doing?" he asked.

Alice looked out the dirty window and bit her lip. "Not so good, Coop," she confessed. "He's not concentrating on his studies, and he answers back to Dad something fierce. He talks back to me, too, but that's different. He spends all his time in his room, listening to rap and banging away at his computer. He's starting to miss classes. He's really hurting."

"Give him some responsibility."

"What?" She swiveled her head and stared at him.

Cooper curled his big hands around the chipped mug. "Give Matt a few tasks here at the diner. Pay him if you have to. Keep him busy and ask his opinion on things. Get him involved in what you're doing."

"Oh, Coop," Alice wailed. "I don't know what I'm doing. What am I thinking of, trying to run this place? I mean, it was barely a paying proposition when Mom was running it, and you know how popular Mom was. People would stop by for a cup of coffee and a slice of pie just to say hello. But now nobody wants to stop by. And how can you blame them? I mean just look at the place." Alice waved her arm and Julia and Cooper obediently looked around.

It was no wonder people weren't thronging to Carly's Diner, Julia thought. Even if it was the only place for a drink and a meal in a forty-mile radius, you had to be awfully hungry, or awfully desperate, to risk a meal if the coffee was anything to go by. You'd probably be better off buying a chocolate bar and a couple of apples at Jensen's grocery store. The walls were dirty, the only decoration a few out of date calendars and a family portrait, with a younger, happier, thinner version of the Sheriff, a lovely, middle-aged woman with Alice's smile, a teenaged Alice and a sweet-faced little boy with a missing front tooth.

A soggy-looking apple pie lay on the counter under a water-speckled glass dish. A blackboard on the opposite wall advertised four-dollar hamburgers and an all-you-can-eat special for twelve dollars. Julia shuddered at the thought.

The whole place cried out for an interior decorator, but that didn't surprise her. The whole town cried out for an exterior decorator.

Something had to be done. So Julia did what any mature, compassionate woman in her position would have done. She hunched her shoulder and looked around with a furtive air. "Oh, I don't know," she cackled in her best Igor imitation. "It's not that bad. A little paint, a few throw pillows..." She cackled again and waited for the laughs. There was a long, embarrassing silence.

Alice was staring at her as if she had just lost all the dots off her dice. Cooper looked his usual, impassive self.

"That's from *Young Frankenstein*, isn't it?" he asked finally. He turned to Alice. "You're too young to remember. It's an old Gene Wilder movie. Actually—" Cooper turned back to Julia with a puzzled frown, "you're too young to remember it."

"No," she replied, straightening up with a sigh, "I have this rule. I only watch movies that are at least twenty years old. Saves me a lot of trouble. If it's good after twenty years, it's really good. Clothes and hairdos are sometimes a little funny though. And you have people talking into cordless phone handsets big as bricks."

Cooper was staring into his mug, so she did too, on the off-chance that an answer to Alice's problems could be found there. Heaven knew the answer to hers couldn't. But all there was in her mug was a muddy noxious brew. She stared deeply into it and then suddenly the answer stared back.

"Tea," Julia surprised herself by saying.

Alice lifted her head. "Tea?"

"Tea," Julia said firmly. "You need to offer tea to your customers. Black tea and...and herbal teas."

Alice looked blank. "Herbal teas?"

"Yes." Julia stole a glance at Cooper, only to find that he was watching her steadily out of opaque, dark-brown eyes. It was impossible to tell what he was thinking. "Lots of people drink tea, don't they, Cooper?" Feeling daring, she nudged his booted ankle under the table with her foot.

"Sure." Cooper's face gave nothing away, but again, she had a faint impression of a smile flickering briefly. Then it was gone. "Drink it all the time."

He was lying, of course, but Julia wanted to kiss him for it. Then she overheated at the thought of kissing Cooper.

"Coop? You do?" Alice looked skeptical.

Cooper nodded his head gravely and Alice's brow cleared. Clearly, anything Sam Cooper did was okay in Alice's book.

"I saw peppermint growing outside the diner." Julia suddenly had vivid memories of hot summer Moroccan days and cool mint tea. "Dry the leaves out and make an infusion of them. You can make herbal tea out of almost anything—rosemary, rosehip, verbena, sassafras, sage. The list is endless. Then you can add things like cinnamon or lemon peel to flavor black teas. I've got a great recipe for vanilla tea. You'd be surprised how good it tastes."

"Wait." Alice had pulled a pad and pencil out of her apron pocket and was scribbling madly. "...cinnamon, lemon peel, vanilla." She shook her head. "Hey, who knows? It just might work. Besides what have I got to lose?" She watched Cooper unfold himself from the seat and stand up. "Coop? What do you think?"

"Might work," Cooper answered, leaving some money on the table. "Why don't you try it?" He held out a large hand to Julia to help her out of the seat. "We should be going," he said to her.

Alice stared open-mouthed first at Cooper, then at Julia, then back to Cooper. Her thoughts might as well have been tattooed on her forehead. "Oh," she said, on a long drawn-out breath. "*Oh!*"

Julia was about ready to deny it, whatever it was Alice was thinking, but then Cooper took her elbow in a strong grip and started walking towards the door. Julia could either go with him or leave her arm behind. "I'll give you the recipes later," she called out hurriedly to Alice over her shoulder.

Just then the door opened and teenager walked in. The lower half of his skull was shaved clean of hair and the top half was gathered in a blond ponytail that hung down past his shoulders. He had a pierced ear, a pierced nose and a pierced eyebrow. He was wearing a ratty denim jacket over a hairless, bare chest, despite the chilly air, jeans torn at both knees and killer black boots with enough studs and cleats to rivet the roof of a stadium.

The youngster stopped and stared after Julia and Cooper as they passed by. "Hey, Sis," he called out, loud enough to be heard, "who's the bodacious babe?"

Julia winced. She could see how Matt Pedersen could be a real handful.

Outside, a gelid wind had sprung up. Julia stopped in the middle of the empty street and huddled in on herself, rubbing her arms. The day was much colder than she had anticipated, and her light jacket was no match for the icy wind. She felt cold and lost. *What am I doing here?* she thought suddenly.

She was almost paralyzed with depression and anxiety. Here she was, about to go out to an isolated ranch with a man she barely knew...however sexy she found his thighs...to discuss the psychological problems of a little boy, something she had absolutely no training for. And all on an empty stomach with just some bad coffee to fuel her. What was she doing?

Escaping a murderer, that was what.

Julia shivered again, then almost jumped when something heavy and warm was dropped around her shoulders. It was Cooper's black leather jacket, which hung to her knees. She put down her briefcase and slipped her arms into the sleeves, savoring the warmth for a moment. She looked up. Way, way up.

"Thanks." She tried to smile but her teeth were chattering. "I didn't think it would be this cold. But what about you?" She awkwardly waved the heavy leather sleeve at him. Only her fingertips showed.

"Don't mind the cold," he rumbled. He was probably lying but Julia wasn't about to relinquish that warm jacket. "Where's your car?"

Julia froze and tried to quell the sudden onset of panic. "My...my car?"

He wanted her to *drive* out? Memories of her botched trip to Rupert flooded her senses like jagged shards of ice. Not a good driver at the best of times, just the idea of getting behind the steering wheel and driving out into the wilderness had her heart thrumming in her chest, even though she knew she'd be following him.

But then when they'd finished talking about Rafael, she'd have to drive all the way back. Alone.

Of course, she couldn't show how horrified she felt at the thought. It would make her appear like a Martian. Kids out here learned to drive practically before they could walk. There was no other option in this enormous, empty land. Julia longed once more for the city. Any city. With trams and subways and buses. And taxis. And people. And not these endless stretches of emptiness.

Julia attempted a smile and licked dry lips. "I — I left my car behind the house. If you'll just wait a minute, I'll go get it — " She stopped suddenly at his hand on her arm.

"Just wanted to know where it was," Cooper said. "I'm coming back into town later," he said, though she was sure he was lying again. "I can drive you back." He bent to pick up her briefcase then walked off.

Julia stared after him for a moment then ran to catch up with his long strides, filled with relief.

* * * * *

"Er, how's Rafael?" she asked, more to hear the sound of a human being's voice than to hear the answer.

"Fine," Cooper replied. It was his third word in twenty minutes. The other two had been "yes", and "no", in answer to direct questions. Julia gave up and looked at the scenery. It was either that or look at Cooper and she found to her astonishment that looking at him was very disturbing so she tried to keep her eyes away.

He was a superb driver.

Julia really admired good driving, mainly because she was such a lousy driver herself. However much she tried to concentrate, after about five minutes there was always something much more interesting to think about than green lights, red lights and who had the right of way. But Cooper was concentrated and relaxed, playing the gearshift like a musical instrument. The Beethoven of Blazers, she thought wryly.

Maybe not much of a talker, but a real ace behind the wheel.

It was unusual for Julia to notice whether a man was a good driver or not, or whether he had strong hands or long legs. Yet she was stirringly aware of the tall dark silent—though certainly not handsome—man sitting next to her and, for the life of her, she couldn't figure out why.

Certainly not for his brilliant conversation, which was what usually attracted her in a man. Up to now, she would have sworn that all her sex hormones were in her head. Her three affairs had started because she'd found that the man shared her taste in literature or had interesting reasons why not, or because he was a witty conversationalist or because he made her laugh.

Definitely not because his large, strong hands, which had a light dusting of black hairs on the backs, rested with easy, elegant competence on the wheel, or because the muscles in his forearm did a fascinating dance every time he shifted gears or because when he popped the clutch, thick muscles played under the jeans from his knees to his groin... Julia whipped her head around and stared blindly out the window.

Something was definitely wrong with her. Stress was driving her crazy. Either that or the silence was driving her crazy. She wasn't used to silence. Maybe if she talked to him, this weird spell she was under would be broken.

"Is it far?"

Cooper's gaze flicked briefly over to her. "We're here."

Julia stared. "We are?" She took a good look around. She couldn't see anything but what had been there for the past half hour, trees, grass, trees, grass then more trees.

"We've been on Double C land for over ten minutes now," Cooper said. Sure enough, now that he mentioned it, she could see fences neatly laid out, running parallel to the road and in the far distance abutting a range of hills. The fencing enclosed land that looked exactly like the terrain they'd been traversing for half an hour. Julia couldn't see the difference between the fenced-in part and the free range part.

"Hey," she said suddenly, excitedly pressing her nose against the Blazer's window. "Horses!" She turned to Cooper, romantic visions dancing through her head. "Do you think they're mustangs?"

"No," Cooper said as he started to slow the vehicle. "They're mine."

"Oh." Julia watched the beautiful animals. There were at least forty of them, gracefully loping in the field and she felt an odd pang of disappointment. "I suppose mustangs only exist in the movies."

"Actually," Cooper said, turning into a wide driveway, "they mainly exist in Nevada and New Mexico. Here we are."

There was so much to see, and all of it foreign to her, that it took Julia a few moments to sort her impressions out. The fencing was white now and enclosed large, freshly painted buildings and circular areas full of sand. Julia had read enough Dick Francis novels to recognize stables and paddocks. Or were they corrals out West?

Ten or twelve men were working industriously, some raking the grounds, several leading horses by what looked like a single long rein, a few on horseback. The impression was of a busy, prosperous business.

Then Cooper slowed the Blazer and they drove by what Julia at first took for a geological formation. Then she looked again. No geological formation she knew of was rectangular and made of wood. "What's that?" she breathed and waved her hand at the...the thing they were driving by.

"The house." Cooper turned a corner and brought the Blazer to a halt in a carport as large as a normal building. The house itself must have been designed by NASA. Julia wondered if it was one of those buildings with its own weather.

"Who built the house?" She tore her eyes away from the huge building and looked at Cooper. "God?"

"My great-great-grandfather." He circled the truck and came to open Julia's door, cupping her elbow until she was safely on the cement floor of the carport.

Julia smiled up at him. "Looks like he had to fell a forest to build this thing."

His eyes were dark, fathomless. "My great-great-granddad believed in elbow room."

"No kidding. You can probably see it from outer space, like the Great Wall of China."

Julia stepped out from under the carport roof for a moment and looked around. She had to move her head to take the building all in since close up, it was bigger than her field of vision. "Good thing he built it before the EPA was around or they would have arrested him for destroying an ecosystem. Why'd he need so much room?"

Cooper shrugged. "When my great-great-grandfather emigrated from Ireland as a boy, he was dirt poor. He swore he would found a dynasty when he made his fortune. He was the twelfth of twelve and he wanted twelve children and each child to have twelve children of his or her own. And he wanted them all to live under the same roof."

"Why that would be 144 people in your grandfather's generation," Julia said, trying to do the calculations in her head. "And by your time, that would be, that would be..."

"Twenty thousand, seven hundred and thirty six."

"Well..." Julia looked at the house consideringly, "maybe a few of the distant cousins would have to stay in a hotel. Good thing they invented birth control before then. So, how many Coopers actually live here?"

"Just me," Cooper said.

"Just *you*?"

She saw him stifle a sigh. "Yeah."

"Not even an odd cousin or two lost somewhere in the house?"

"Nope." Cooper shifted his weight from one boot to another. That must be cowboy body language for embarrassment. "My great-great-grandfather had one child, a son, my great-grandfather had one child, a son, my grandfather had one child, a son, my father—"

"Wait," Julia said. "Let me guess. One child, a son. You."

"Bingo." He took her elbow. "Let's go."

They walked through a kitchen which was every bit as big as the baronial hall in the Errol Flynn version of *Robin Hood*.

It was a perfect example of the dictum that if something was worth doing, it was worth doing twice. There were two fireplaces big enough to roast whole oxen and two ovens that could roast entire kids. A trestle table long enough to rollerblade on ran the length of the kitchen. Julia barely had time to take it in because Cooper had her arm in an iron grip again and he seemed to want to march her through the house, through long, dark musty corridors where she caught glimpses of long, dark musty rooms. After a few miles, Cooper finally stopped to open a big oak door and put a hand to the small of her back.

Julia peeked around the door then walked into the big room warily, not too sure what to expect.

Like Carly's Diner, the room could have done with some major interior decorating. All the furniture was massive and dark and arranged around the walls, leaving an empty space in the middle that just sat there, doing nothing. Maybe Cooper held concerts there in the summer or something.

Then Julia's eyes slowly adjusted to the gloom and she felt herself relax.

Cooper was a reader.

In that instant she forgave him his communication problems and his crazy-making thighs and forearms.

Cooper belonged to her tribe. The tribe of readers.

Books lay everywhere, on every available surface and lining the walls. Real books, read books, not decorator ones. Julia's hands itched to go over and look at the covers, maybe rub her face in a few and inhale the smell. But then she might start crying and get Cooper's books all waterlogged, so she restrained herself.

The only note of warmth was a fire blazing in a huge hearth. Massive oak chairs were grouped around it. Julia could make out the forms of a man and a little boy. The man was black-haired and dressed in black, just like Cooper. Julia wondered if she had missed out on some new fad—ninja cowboys.

"Miss Anderson!" Rafael leapt out of his seat and came running to her. He lifted a small, anxious face. "Why are you here, Miss Anderson? I didn't do nothing wrong, did I?"

"No, honey," Julia said gently, ruffling his hair. "Of course you didn't do anything wrong. I just came for a visit and to let your daddy know what a good little boy you are." Some of Rafael's anxiety eased but Julia could still see tension on his face.

Cooper took her arm again and they walked over to the fireplace. "Sally Anderson, I'd like to introduce you to Bernaldo Martinez, Rafael's father and my foreman."

The man gave no sign that he heard the words. He sat slumped in the big chair, his head in his hands.

"Bernie…" Cooper's deep low voice was a threatening growl.

Slowly Bernaldo Martinez turned his head. He stood up as if he were a thousand years old.

Julia winced when she saw his eyes, the color of the many stoplights she'd distractedly run through in her life. She wondered if it hurt to look out of eyes that red.

The man was haggard, with a few days' worth of stubble on his lean, good-looking face. It wasn't designer stubble, achieved with the use of a special electric razor, but real stubble that came from not shaving for many days. Probably the same number of days he hadn't been sleeping.

"Bernie…" Cooper's voice was, if possible, lower and more threatening than before.

Martinez ran a hand through his black hair, and then nodded at Julia. "Miss Anderson." His voice was scratchy and rough.

"Mr. Martinez." Julia inclined her head.

"Listen, Sport." Cooper hunkered down until he was eye level with Rafael. His voice was gentle again. "Southern Star gave birth last night. Why don't you ask Sandy to take you to see the foal?"

"A foal?" Rafael's face filled with joy, all the tension clearing in an instant. "Yowee!" he screamed, punching the air. Remembering his manners, he murmured a hurried goodbye to Julia, then scrambled out the door.

Bernie Martinez's head slowly swung over to Cooper. It looked as if it hurt him to do it. "What was it? A filly?"

Cooper stood up and pinned Martinez with a hard look. "Colt."

"Colt." Martinez gave a harsh laugh. "Should have known. Not even female horses can stand it here. The Cooper Curse at work again—"

"That's just about enough, Bernie." Cooper's voice was deep and icy. Julia shivered. She wouldn't like to have him using that tone with her. It would have shut her up for the next century.

But Martinez wasn't impressed. "I'll bet if we hadn't moved here, my Carmelita would still be around. I'll bet—"

"I said that's enough!" Cooper's voice was, if anything deeper and frostier. He stepped towards Martinez with his big hands clenched into fists. Martinez angled his stubbled chin defiantly upwards, daring Cooper to take a crack.

There was a heavy, musky smell in the air. Julia wondered if it was from all those books or from the testosterone the two men were pumping out. Something had to be done and quickly. Martinez looked like he was barely going to survive his hangover, let alone a few rounds with Cooper. Julia looked again at Cooper's huge hands, now balled into fists. Probably not too many people would survive a few rounds with Cooper.

"Well," Julia said, and rubbed her hands together. "Well, here we are." She was getting no reaction from the two males in the room so she tried showing a few teeth in a smile.

Nothing.

They just stood there, glowering at each other as if she didn't exist.

She gave up. Maybe a few rounds would do them both good.

"Uh, Cooper?" Julia just managed to avoid tugging on his shirt sleeve to get his attention. But that wasn't necessary. Those fierce dark eyes were instantly focused on her. She shivered again, but not from fear.

"I…" Julia licked dry lips. "I left my briefcase in the Blazer and there's some of Rafael's homework I wanted to show Mr. Martinez. No…" she held up her hand as Cooper started forward. "I'll get it myself, if you'll just refresh my memory about how to get back to the kitchen. Or draw me a map."

Cooper's deep voice was gentle again. "Turn right outside the door then seven doors down turn left and follow the corridor to the end, then through the pantry and into the kitchen."

Julia was finding it hard to concentrate when he was looking at her so intently. The force field effect was working again. "Seven doors, left, pantry, kitchen," she said. "Got you." She turned and walked out the door and looked with dismay down the endless, enormous corridor.

Maybe she should have left a trail of bread crumbs.

* * * * *

When the door closed behind Julia, Bernie collapsed into the chair and scrubbed his face with his hands. He stared into the fire for a long time and Cooper just watched.

"She's gone, Coop," he said finally. "Gone for good."

"Yeah." Cooper shifted uncomfortably. This wasn't his scene, consoling men who'd been dumped.

Bernie looked like he'd been through hell. Cooper felt a pang of pity for his best friend. Carmelita's leaving had really punched a hole in Bernie's life. For a minute, Cooper almost envied Bernie the intensity of his feelings. When Melissa had finally left, all Cooper had felt was weary relief.

Bernie was really hurting. But that still didn't excuse his behavior with Sally Anderson.

"Listen, Bernie," Cooper said, "I understand how you feel, but you've got to pull yourself together. After all, Miss Anderson…"

"Forget it," Bernie said. "You don't stand a chance with her. You'd just lose her, anyway. All the women who come here leave." He raised red-rimmed eyes to Cooper. "You should have told me about the curse, Coop. How was I supposed to know that no female stays for long on Cooper soil?"

"That's a stupid legend." Cooper gritted his teeth. "I'm surprised you even thought twice about it."

"Thought twice about it? Damn you, I lost my wife because of it!" Bernie shouted, then winced and held his head.

"You didn't lose your wife become she was on Cooper land," Cooper said reasonably. "You lost her because— because…" Cooper stopped. He didn't know why Carmelita had left. Who knew why a woman did anything?

"Because we were on Cooper land," Bernie finished.

"No, dammit!"

"Well then—how come Melissa left?" Bernie's voice was hostile. "Answer me that, huh?"

"Because—because…"

"Because the two of you were living here." Bernie nodded his head sagely, as if he had just proved some difficult mathematical theorem.

"Because she didn't want to live with me anymore!" Cooper threw up his hands in exasperation. "Now stop this. It has nothing to do with the ranch."

"How come your momma left?" Bernie asked.

"She didn't." Bernie was hurting and Cooper could make allowances. But there were limits. "She died."

"Same thing." Bernie set his jaw mulishly. "And your great-grandma? Didn't she run off with the Singer sewing machine man? And your grandma? One kid and she was off."

"Bernie..." Cooper growled.

"And the mares they bring to us to be covered. How about them, huh? Huh? You have a 70-30 male female ratio. That's statistically impossible."

"A fluke."

"A fluke? Okay, how about that collie bitch that had six pups and all of them male. What about that? Huh? Was that a fluke too? No wonder Carmelita and Melissa left. This place is poison for women."

Especially bitches, Cooper thought, but wisely kept silent.

Bernie pushed his hands through his coarse black hair. "I should have got a job at a bank or in a store. Then we'd still be a family and I wouldn't be in this mess." He hung his head low. "And neither would Rafael."

"Bernie," Cooper said patiently, "you couldn't get a job in a bank or in a store because you haven't got any training for it. You're trained to work in livestock. It's what you do and it's what you do well. When you're not going crazy."

"Of course I'm going crazy," Bernie shouted. "I just lost my wife because of your fucking curse!"

"Well, shut the fuck up about it!" Cooper shouted back. Sally Anderson was probably the only woman—certainly the only attractive woman—in a two hundred mile radius who had never heard of the Cooper Curse and Cooper wanted to keep it that way for as long as he could. "Miss Anderson is coming back any minute now. She's taken time out of her busy schedule to talk to you about your son and you're damn well going to straighten out and be civil to her."

Cooper didn't know if Sally Anderson really had a busy schedule or not—most people in Simpson didn't have a whole lot to do—but Bernie didn't have to know that.

Bernie tried to focus on Cooper, head wobbling. He finally got Cooper in his sights. His eyes glittered an unholy red. "Make me," he growled.

He was spoiling for a fight. The last thing Cooper wanted was for Sally Anderson to walk in on a brawl. "Stop this shit, Bernie."

"No." Bernie stood up, swayed, then went into a fighting stance, which was ridiculous. He could barely stand on his feet.

"Fuck this." Cooper raised his eyes towards the ceiling. "We both know you can't take me in hand-to-hand. I'm trained and you're not. I've got six inches and forty pounds on you. Now cut this out."

Bernie was slowly circling him. "Make me."

"Bernie," Cooper said through gritted teeth. "You're hung over. You're probably seeing double. I'm not going to fight you and that's that. I'd take you down in a New York minute. It'd be as easy as a mule breaking wind."

Cooper was expecting Bernie to smile at one of his father's favorite expressions, but Bernie just set his jaw and swung heavily.

Cooper dodged the blow without moving his feet. This was going to be worse than he thought. Bernie swung again, so slowly Cooper could have finished reading his biography of Eisenhower and still have time to catch Bernie's fist in his hand. Cooper let Bernie wrench his hand free and said, "Don't be a fool, Bernie, you can't take me down and you know it."

"Oh, yeah?" Bernie was breathing heavily. He tried to sweep Cooper's legs from under him. It didn't work, but Cooper caught a sharp blow to the shin. "Damn it, Bernie! That fucking hurt."

Bernie showed his teeth. "It was meant to." He dropped to a crouch and started circling Cooper. Cooper backed up.

"Bernie, if you don't stop this shit right this minute—" Bernie lunged. Cooper moved. Bernie banged first his fist and then his head against the fieldstone hearth. Cooper winced at the sound. Bernie turned around, blood flowing from a cut above his eyebrow and lifted his fists. The knuckles of one hand were bleeding. Cooper sighed and lifted his.

The door opened.

Sally Anderson stopped on the threshold, wide-eyed, briefcase in hand. The two men, one bleeding, one seriously annoyed, turned their heads and stared at her with surly expressions.

"I guess this is male bonding, huh?" she asked.

Chapter Five

"Ouch!" Bernaldo Martinez tried to jerk his head away.

"Don't be a wuss." Julia caught his bristly chin and dragged his head back to continue cleaning the small raw-looking laceration on his forehead. It had almost stopped bleeding. "I thought cowboys were supposed to be such tough guys."

"I'm no cowboy," he complained as Julia finished cleaning the wound. "I'm just a poor *cholo* from the barrio who took courses in animal husbandry 'cause it meant cheap college credits." But he was smiling as he sat at the enormous kitchen table, letting Julia fuss over him. Cooper was smiling too...sort of.

Men! Julia thought in exasperation. A quarter of an hour ago they'd been doing their level best to beat each other's brains out, looking exactly like two of her more rambunctious seven year olds in a fight and now look at them.

Julia picked up Martinez's hand and looked at the knuckles. She met Cooper's dark eyes.

"When was the last time that room was cleaned?"

"It's clean." Cooper frowned, affronted. "My men take the cleaning in four-man details on a rota basis. They muck out the stables and then they muck out...er...they clean the house. Bernie's not going to get an infection from that scratch, believe me. And anyway...he's immune to everything, including common sense."

"If you say so." Julia looked at the cuts dubiously. "Still...I'd feel better if I put some disinfectant on it. Is your first aid kit still in the magic pickup?"

Cooper pursed his lips. "You'd be better off putting an antibiotic ointment we use for the horses on it. It's in a bowl in the refrigerator."

Julia stared at Cooper for a minute to find out if he was joking but he looked perfectly serious and she didn't know if he even could joke, so she walked over to the huge, industrial-size refrigerator, opened the enormous steel door and simply stared inside.

She had girlfriends in Boston with condos smaller than the inside of this refrigerator.

"Who does the cooking around here?" She looked over her shoulder. "Paul Bunyan?"

"The men take it…"

"In turns. Right." Julia turned back and examined the contents of the refrigerator. "So where is this horse ointment?"

"In a bowl."

"There are two bowls here, Cooper."

"The green one."

Julia checked the other one and her eyes widened. "And what's in the red one?"

Cooper shrugged. "Lunch?"

"No way," Julia said firmly. She backed out of the refrigerator with the green bowl in her hands and closed the heavy door with her hip, thinking there should be a biohazard sticker on the door. "No way is that stuff food. A mutant life form, perhaps. An experiment gone bad, maybe—but definitely not lunch." She drew in a deep breath and coughed. The stuff in the green bowl was either going to cure Rafael's father or kill him.

"I hope you're ready for this, Mr. Martinez."

"Bernie."

"Okay, Bernie. Time to separate the men from the boys. Ready or not, here it comes." She applied the smelly ointment to his forehead and knuckles. "I can't believe you two actually fought. Like seven year olds. Didn't anyone ever teach you that violence is no way to settle an argument? It's absolutely reprehensible behavior for two adults." Julia warmed to her topic. The use of violence was a subject of some poignancy to her at the moment. Her voice rose. "Violence is for barbarians. I mean, really. Engaging in fisticuffs. What on earth did you two hope to accomplish? You should be ashamed of yourselves."

"Yes, ma'am," both men replied in unison.

Julia laughed when she realized that she'd been shaking her forefinger at them like she did with her second graders when they misbehaved.

"I guess I was sounding an awful lot like a grade school teacher, wasn't I? Speaking of which..." Julia tried hard not to think about how terribly unqualified she was to say what she was going to say. "Um, speaking of which, Mr...Bernie, I brought along some of Rafael's homework to show you. He's really an exceptional pupil and his grades have been very good, but for the past two weeks, his work has just degenerated. He's not paying attention in class and quite frankly, I've caught him crying more times than I can count."

Bernie sighed. "You're quite right, Miss Anderson..."

"Sally," Julia said, hating the name all over again. Though again, now that she thought of it, a Sally Anderson could conceivably find herself out on an isolated ranch bandaging a damaged foreman. Julia Devaux certainly couldn't.

"Okay, Sally. The story is this. My wife and I have been...had been..." Bernie started breathing heavily. "We...we weren't..." Bernie stopped, unable to continue.

"Getting along?" Julia supplied gently.

Bernie nodded miserably.

"I gathered as much. And Rafael was suffering, wasn't he?"

Bernie nodded again and Julia's heart went out to him.

She hadn't had any experience personally with divorce, but she imagined that it would be horribly painful.

Then her eyes slid to Cooper. His wife had left him, too. Had he been in this much pain? He didn't look it. He didn't look like he felt much of anything. That sharp-angled face might as well have been carved out of a rock, the only sign of life those dark, glittering eyes. And yet, it took Julia an effort to wrench her eyes away from him.

"Bernie." Julia firmly fixed her attention back on the father of her pupil, which was exactly where it should be, and not on some rancher with an amazing resemblance to a rock. "I think someone should oversee Rafael's homework, maybe spend a couple of afternoons with him, making sure he gets back into the habit of doing his homework, bring him back up to speed. It wouldn't take long; he's such a bright little boy."

Bernie looked up, puzzled. Then light dawned on his face. "You're right," he breathed. He reached over and grabbed Julia's hand in gratitude. "You're absolutely right."

He pumped Julia's hand enthusiastically, then saw Cooper's scowl and hastily dropped it. "Why didn't I think of that? What a wonderful idea. Thank you, Sally. Thank you so much.'

"Oh no," Julia said in dismay. "I didn't mean that I..."

"That's just what Rafael needs." Bernie ran his hands through his already disheveled hair and blew a sigh of relief. "A tudor."

"Tutor," Julia said automatically.

"Tutor. This is great, just great."

"No, really..." Julia began.

"A woman's touch," Bernie mused. "Softness, gentleness but discipline, too. An iron hand in a velvet fist..."

"Glove," Julia said.

"Glove." Bernie nodded. "That's just what Rafael needs."

"Ahm, Bernie, I don't really think..."

"Someone to pay attention to him. Actually..." Bernie grimaced, "Carmelita wasn't really very good at that. No one would have given her the Mom of the Year award, that's for sure. But you, Sally, you're just what Rafael needs. He adores you. He's always talking about 'Miss Anderson this' and 'Miss Anderson that'."

"Listen—"

Bernie looked at Julia gratefully. "I can't begin to tell you how much this means to me, and to Rafael, too, of course…"

"Look, Bernie…"

"What a lifesaver," he said simply. "Thank you."

"Okay." Julia lifted her hands and gave up with a shake of her head. "If that's what you want."

All things considered, she didn't really mind all that much. What else did she have to do in the afternoons, anyway, besides freak out? Maybe it would help keep her mind off her troubles.

Bernie reached into his back pocket. "So, how much would you like for the lessons?"

"Put your wallet away." Julia narrowed her eyes and tapped her lip, considering. She turned to Cooper. "How good is Rafael with animals?"

"Very," Cooper replied. "He wants to be a vet when he grows up."

"Well," Julia turned back to Bernie, "that's my price. I want Rafael to help me clean up my dog, Fred." *My dog*, she thought, in surprise. It sounded so weird. "I want him washed and combed and…" dirty, matted fur crossed her mind, "…deloused. In exchange, Rafael can come over a couple of afternoons after school this week and I'll get him back up to speed." A thought suddenly occurred to her and she turned to Cooper with wide frightened eyes. "But someone will have to come pick Rafael up and drive him back here. I couldn't possibly…there's no way…"

"Well, I could—" Bernie began.

"I'll do it," Cooper's deep voice interrupted.

* * * * *

Sally Anderson and Bernie stared at him as if he'd grown two heads.

Sally Anderson probably because she didn't want a man who got a hard-on when he looked at her to show up in the afternoons.

Bernie because he knew damn well Cooper didn't have the time to drive into Simpson a couple of afternoons next week. And he didn't. It was his cock making plans for him and he was running along behind it, trying to catch up.

"I'll pick him up in the afternoons," Cooper said. Bernie opened his mouth, looked at Cooper and closed it again. "And you haven't stated your full price yet."

Sally's mouth curved. He stared at her mouth, fascinated. Her lips were soft and naturally pink, slightly upturned at the corners in a perpetual smile. Warm, welcoming lips...

She tilted her head and observed Cooper. "I haven't?"

"What?" Cooper tried to concentrate. "No."

"What's the rest of my price?"

"Your boiler needs first aid, the second step on your porch needs replacing and that's just for starters."

"You're right." Julia smiled dazzlingly at him and he forgot to breathe. "So tell me. How good a handyman is Rafael?"

"Rafael's a better handyman than his father, that's for sure." Cooper smiled at her, then was taken aback. He was *flirting* with her. The sensation was so novel, he lost track of what they were saying.

Flirting with a beautiful woman. In the Cooper kitchen. Impossible.

For as long as he could remember, his kitchen had been a cold and impersonal space where men refueled quickly then left for work as soon as possible, and that certainly included the grim period of his marriage.

But with Sally sitting there, gently bantering with him and Bernie, the kitchen became almost...cozy.

"Coop?" Bernie was looking at him. "You want me to fix her plumbing?"

"No," Cooper answered, the thought of a hammer in Bernie's hands snapping him back to reality. "I will. You're hopeless with tools or with anything that doesn't move or eat hay. I..."

"Dad! Dad!" Rafael ran full tilt into the kitchen and was in his father's arms before the kitchen door had swung shut. "Dad, Southern Star had a colt, and he's a beaut! He's got a star on his nose just like his dam, and you should just see the way he moves. You can tell he's gonna be a champ. You just wait till Coop trains him—he's gonna win every prize in sight!"

The little boy was hopping up and down with excitement.

"That so?" Bernie smiled down at his son, and hugged him. "Well, it looks like you're going to be a very busy little boy from now on, what with looking after the new colt and going over your lessons a couple of afternoons with Miss Anderson."

Rafael's head turned sharply and his eyes widened. "I am?"

"Yes," Sally smiled. "If that's okay with you. Of course, you're going to have to help me groom my dog in exchange."

"A dog?" Rafael's face lit up. "Neato! What breed is he?"

Sally looked over at Cooper. "Cooper? What breed is Fred?"

"Mixed."

"Mixed. Yes. I guess that about sums it up. Well." She rubbed her hands together. "I guess I should be..."

"Dad? What's for lunch?" Rafael rubbed his tummy. "I'm starving."

Bernie fingered his bristly chin and shot Cooper a wry look. "I haven't been doing much shopping lately, Coop. Who's on kitchen detail today?"

"Larry should have been," Cooper answered, "but he had to run into Rupert for some baling wire."

"Well then, who's gonna do the cookin'?" Rafael asked plaintively.

As if pulled by an invisible string, three male faces and three pairs of dark eyes turned to Julia with pathetic expressions, looking so much like Fred had last night that she had to bite her cheeks to keep from smiling. "Would the three of you like me to cook something for lunch?"

The two adults hesitated politely, but Rafael was too small to worry about anything as trivial as manners. "Awesome! I'll bet you cook real good, Miss Anderson."

"Well…" Julia replied. "Actually, I'm not a bad cook, if I have something to work with." Her eyes slid to Cooper. "Just not what was in that bowl, though. And I peeked in your vegetable bin. It's disgusting."

"You peeked in my *what*?" Cooper asked and Julia sighed.

"Never mind." She stood up, feeling unaccountably cheerful at the thought of having lunch with Bernie and Rafael. And, well, Cooper too. The idea of going back to her cold and lonely house was totally unappealing. "I'm sure you have a well-stocked freezer. I can't imagine anybody living out in the middle of nowhere without a freezer. Where is it?"

"Don't have much in it," Cooper replied.

"No?" That stopped her. She tried to imagine turning something, anything, she had seen in that refrigerator into food, and failed.

"No." Cooper walked over to her and Julia looked up and met his dark brown eyes. There was a faint smile lurking in the depths. "But we do have a locker."

* * * * *

Information is power and, ultimately, information is money. The more secret the information, the more powerful it is and the more money it's worth. The main law of modern economics, courtesy of Stanford.

So, the professional thought. I don't have Julia Devaux's whereabouts. Yet. But I do have the addresses and new identities of two people under the Witness Security Program. That information is useless to Dominic Santana, but surely, there would be someone, somewhere who would be willing to pay good money for the information.

All of a sudden, the professional was pulled up short by a thought. A brilliant one.

It was time to get out of the business. Of that, the professional had no doubt. With a good twenty highly successful hits under the belt, the professional had earned a brilliant reputation, but time was on the side of the police. Sooner or later, despite the most meticulous preparations, a slip-up would come. It was mathematically inevitable. It was definitely time to go.

With Julia Devaux's head, that made three million dollars for early retirement in a warm climate in the luxurious beach house. But three million dollars didn't go as far as it used to. Granted, a million and a half were already in a decent mutual fund—invested in low risk bonds. Life was risky enough as it was and money was serious business.

But relocating and purchasing the beachfront property would put a dent in the savings, which in turn would cut down on the income accruing.

More money was necessary.

The going price for an actual physical hit was $200,000 and up but there was a limit to the numbers of hits possible in a year and it was time to get out of the game anyway.

But the information leading to a hit—the location, say, of a former employee turned state's witness—well, that would be worth money. Serious money. With a decent computer and a modem, the information could be obtained from anywhere in the world, including a Caribbean island, and sent anywhere in the world, without any danger. And the sky was the limit as far as the number of info-hits was concerned.

No matter how many firewalls the DOJ set up, the professional could slice right through them.

The perfect business, the professional thought. Virtual hits, at, say, $50,000 a pop. Forever. With no risk.

Stanford would be proud.

* * * * *

"That was delicious," Rafael said, mopping up his plate with the last biscuit. "Thanks, Miss Anderson."

"Well, you guys are sure easy to please," she smiled. "Broil a few steaks, nuke some potatoes, then just sit back and rake in the compliments."

It was a bit more elaborate than that, Cooper thought. Sally had walked around the locker in wonderment, cracking jokes about its size and making an inventory of the contents. Then she'd managed to marinate the steaks, whip up some garlic butter for the baked potatoes and make a side dish of sautéed ham and peas in no time. She'd even made some biscuits from scratch.

She was a fabulous cook. Everything she prepared was delicious, but above all, she made it easy on everyone. While she moved comfortably around the kitchen, she had kept up a lighthearted conversation in a soft, gentle voice.

Bernie lost that haunted look he'd had lately and Rafael laughed and scampered like the seven year old he was instead of moping around, looking as if he had all the cares of the world resting on his slender shoulders.

They were eating a delicious lunch in an easy and relaxed atmosphere.

In the Cooper kitchen.

With a woman.

Impossible.

The Cooper Curse had been lifted for a few hours. Lunches with Melissa had been anything but lighthearted. And Cooper thankfully had no idea what mealtimes with Carmelita were like, since he had avoided her as carefully, and for the same reason, as he would have avoided a tarantula.

While Sally was busy turning his kitchen into a human-friendly place, Cooper was doing his very best to keep his mind out of the gutter.

He tried very hard not to notice Sally's breasts and ass and tried even harder not to imagine her under him, slender thighs hugging his hips. Tried not to think of what it would be like entering her — she'd be small and tight, he was sure — and above all, he tried not to think about fucking her as hard as he'd like because he'd probably kill her, the way he was feeling.

The carapace of ice that had enclosed him for as long as he could remember was thawing, which was good, of course, in the long run. In the short run, it meant clenching his fists to keep from throwing Sally onto the kitchen floor, stripping her and fucking her hard, for hours.

This was not the kind of thing he should be thinking about when a very beautiful and very kind grade school teacher was going out of her way to help his best friend's son and was even now turning his kitchen into a warm and relaxed place, a first in over four generations of Coopers.

So Cooper sat and watched and listened, sketching a smile when the others laughed, eating the delicious food, enjoying Rafael's smiles, scowling when Bernie flirted.

All the time thinking of Sally naked under him or — God! — over him. He couldn't get that picture out of his head, Sally riding him, smiling down at him as he pumped up into her. His cock swelled painfully against his jeans at the thought and he shifted in his chair, grateful that the table hid the hard-on.

If she was on top, he could watch that beautiful face while he fucked her. Find out how she liked it. Hard and fast or slow and easy. It probably didn't make any difference how she liked it, because right now he couldn't imagine fucking her any way but frantically and for about a week straight.

He usually had a lot of self-control during sex, able to use the strokes the woman wanted. He wasn't good at communicating with words but he had body language down pat. A woman didn't need to tell him what she wanted, he could read it in the way she moved her hips when he entered her, in the way her hands clutched at him, in the way she breathed.

Sally Anderson probably liked it slow and gentle and romantic. She just had that kind of face. Everything about her was so delicate. She would want wooing, lots of kisses, being undressed slowly, plenty of foreplay. She'd probably want him to enter her slowly, by degrees. He was big so he'd have to be careful. And once he was inside her, she'd probably want long slow strokes. She'd probably expect him to be a gentleman and not press his cock in fully but keep his strokes shallow.

Not an option.

He felt exactly like Grayhawk, his prize black stallion, mating with Leyla, a lovely Arabian filly. Horses coupled violently; it's how nature designed them. Cooper usually kept the owners from seeing it, because they all had romantic visions about their stallions, attributing to them a nobility and courtliness stallions simply didn't possess. Grayhawk was 1,300 pounds of pure male, pound for pound one of the strongest animals on the face of the earth. While mating, Greyhawk had bitten Leyla's neck so hard he'd drawn blood and his sharp hooves had nicked her flanks.

If Cooper wasn't careful, that's exactly how he'd mount Sally Anderson. From behind, using his strength to pound into her, holding her down with his hands and biting her neck.

The idea horrified him and he tried to direct his thoughts away from the image, tried to ignore the prickling hot feelings that image sparked. Tried to remember that, unlike Grayhawk, he was supposed to be civilized.

Cooper did his damnedest not to notice that Sally Anderson's breasts were small and high and round. His cupped hand was probably larger than her breasts. He'd always thought of himself as a breast man, the bigger the better, but what he'd been was an asshole. All of a sudden he could see that the old saying—a woman's breast should fit into a champagne glass— was absolutely true. And here he'd gone for women whose breasts would fit into the ice bucket.

She was wearing a sweater and if he looked carefully— while trying to hide just how carefully he was looking—he could see the faint outline of her nipple. It was small and delicate and probably tasted like a tiny cherry.

And her ass—Jesus, he couldn't tear his eyes away from it when she bent to check the biscuits in the oven. Slender but round. Perfect.

He had big hands that would fit perfectly over each cheek to hold her still while he was thrusting into her…

"What do you think, Coop?" Rafael's childish voice asked.

I think fucking Sally Anderson is the best idea I've ever had.

Cooper blinked, horrified.

Had he said that aloud? If so, he'd just have to go outside and shoot himself. He looked around frantically.

Maybe he hadn't blurted it out because no one was openmouthed with disgust. They were all looking at him expectantly. What the fuck had they been talking about? It sounded like a yes or no question, so Cooper took a shot at answering. He had a 50 percent chance of getting it right.

"Yes," he said.

Rafael shot his fist in the air, "Yesss!"

Bernie looked pleased and Sally was smiling. Cooper wondered if he'd just agreed to something irrevocable, like signing away the Double C to some cult.

It couldn't have been earth-shattering, though. Everyone continued sitting around the table smiling and eating. The food was delicious and they finished every bite. There wasn't a crumb left when Sally stood.

"Leave that," Cooper said suddenly, when she made to gather up the dishes. "You've done more than enough. My men will take care of it."

"Okay." She dusted her hands. "I'm sure glad the two of you have patched things up."

Patched things up? Cooper and Bernie exchanged blank looks. "Patched what up?" Cooper asked.

Sally rolled her eyes in exasperation. "Well, far be it from me to raise painful memories, but the two of you were at each other's throats a little while ago."

"Oh, that," Cooper said, with a shrug. "Didn't mean anything."

"Just getting rid of a little stress," Bernie agreed.

"Men." Sally shook her head. "When I want to relieve stress I do something relaxing, like taking a walk or reading a good book instead of bashing someone's head in. Speaking of which —" She turned to Cooper. "I wanted to ask you something."

"About bashing people's heads in?" Cooper was startled. He hadn't put her down as a violent woman.

"No. Reading." She propped her chin on her hand and directed the full force of that turquoise gaze at him. "I need to ask you something."

"Anything," Cooper replied immediately, then saw Bernie grin like a fool and swivel his head back and forth between the two of them. Unfortunately, Bernie was too far away for a kick under the table. "We owe it to you," he added, looking at Bernie pointedly.

"Your books," Sally said.

"My what?" Cooper asked, surprised.

"Books," she sighed. "There isn't anyplace in Simpson to buy books and I've seen that you have a lot of them. Where do you get your books from?"

"Rupert," he said and saw her wince. "Something wrong? Have you been to Rupert?"

"Well..." Sally sighed. "Yes and no. It was my first weekend here and I thought I'd sort of...explore a bit." She closed her eyes and shuddered. "And someone mentioned that Rupert was a nice town and that it was thataway, and they just pointed me down this road that went on and on and I started driving, not really knowing if I was going in the right direction or not..." She opened her eyes and glared at Cooper. "Did you know that there are no signposts to Rupert?"

"Probably not," Cooper replied calmly. "Anyone born in Simpson can get to Rupert with his eyes closed."

"Well, I wasn't and I can't." Sally swallowed. "So, like I said, I just drove on and on and there was nobody on the road and for all I knew I was driving to China, and every time there was a fork in the road, I wondered where I was and it was just so...so empty. My car's old and I kept thinking that if I had a flat tire or if the car broke down I would stay there forever and then the snows would come and I would freeze to death and they wouldn't find my body until the spring thaw. And by the time I saw a few houses and this big 'Welcome to Rupert' sign, it was getting dark and I was drenched in sweat, so I just turned around and drove straight back." She looked at Cooper with her heart in her eyes. "Is it a nice bookstore?"

"It's okay." Cooper drained his coffee. "Bob's got a good selection. And he'll order anything you want he doesn't have in stock. Takes about a week." Cooper stood up. "It's getting late and we've taken up enough of your time. I'll drive you back. Er...by the way, would you like to come with me to Rupert next Saturday? I've got some business there."

"You do?" She perked up. Oh God, just the thought of an hour in a bookshop..."

"You do?" Bernie asked. "I thought we were going to drive over to—" Then he saw Cooper's glare and slapped himself on the head. Something Cooper would have liked to have done. Only harder. "Oh, that's right. You've got that—that important business to take care of. In Rupert. Riiiiight. You just go off to Rupert on Saturday and stay as long as you want." Bernie winked. "All night, if necessary."

Cooper took Sally's elbow and reminded himself when he came back to give Bernie a few pointers in discretion.

With a cattle prod.

* * * * *

Something was missing, Julia thought as she looked out of the window so she wouldn't look at Cooper.

But she didn't have to look at him. He exerted this gravitational pull so she was aware of him at all times. It had been the same in the kitchen. He had sat quietly in his chair, rarely talking, and yet everyone seemed to have revolved around him, as if she and Bernie and Rafael had been minor planets to his sun. Bernie deferred to him, Rafael plainly adored him and she — well, she had trouble keeping her eyes off him.

And she had felt...different all afternoon. What was it? It was such a hard feeling to pin down. It was something she'd felt before, she was sure, but a long time ago. Before her parent's death, in fact.

That was it.

The last time she had felt this way had been in Paris four years ago, on vacation with her parents. The Devaux family had lived in Paris between her tenth and fifteenth years and they had all had very fond memories of their life there. They visited the city as often as they could. They had stayed in a charming pension on Rue du Cherche-Midi and visited with old friends. Her mother had had her hair cut at Jean-David's elegant salon, just like old times. They'd laughed and shopped for her new move to Boston and she had felt lighthearted, carefree and...safe.

Then her parents had died in a car crash and she hadn't felt safe since. She was happy enough in Boston, but at odd moments she felt unsettled and lonely — cut adrift after her parents' deaths.

And for the last month, she'd mainly felt terror and an immense solitude. This afternoon, for the first time in a long while, the heavy weight of fear and utter solitude had lifted from her soul. She had spent a happy and carefree afternoon, thinking mainly about how Rafael was looking better, how odd that huge kitchen was and how it somehow seemed to suit Cooper.

Rafael had laughed and joked all afternoon. "Happy as a pig in slop" was the way Bernie had described it.

She'd tried to prepare a meal the three males would like, nothing too fancy, though they'd practically been salivating by the time she'd set the food on the table. Anything short of sawdust would have done.

She'd enjoyed bantering with Rafael and joking with Bernie, who'd shed his earlier truculence. Even Cooper's silence had been an…interesting kind of silence. She'd felt a lot of things this afternoon — relief that Rafael was going to be all right, amusement at the men's pathetic gratitude for a little cooking, excitement at the thought of making it to a bookstore, this crazy attraction to Cooper. But she hadn't felt loneliness and above all she hadn't felt fear — her constant companion this past month.

That was thanks to Cooper. She had no doubt about that. It was impossible to feel fear around him. He had sat in the kitchen, silently watching her out of dark eyes, large and still, an immensely reassuring presence. It was like having a huge guard dog watching over her.

She sneaked a look at him. He was squinting against the sun, large hands easy on the wheel, the tanned skin around his eyes lined and weather beaten, the line of that angular cheekbone oddly elegant in profile. The late afternoon sun picked out silver highlights in the jet-black mane.

Well, maybe not a guard dog so much as a battle-scarred wolf.

But he was here and she felt watched over, protected by his very presence.

He felt her gaze and flicked a glance her way. She gave him a dazzling smile.

The black Blazer swerved slightly. "What?" he asked.

"Just a smile, Cooper," Julia said, astonished at how safe and free she felt with him, as if she could do or say anything. "For no reason at all. I guess you don't smile much, do you?"

"Nope." But there was a half curve to his lips.

"Or talk much, either."

"Nope."

"That's okay," she said cheerfully. "I talk and smile enough for two so I guess it all evens itself out."

Julia looked back out the window and, for the first time, allowed herself to really see the countryside. The trip to Rupert had been such a nightmare. She hadn't seen anything at all of the landscape itself. All she had done was to crouch anxiously over the steering wheel, painfully aware of the fact that the long sweeps of prairie grass afforded a potential gunman a clear view through the crosshairs of a telescopic lens. The long, lonely stretches of road through pine forest had been almost designed for ambushes.

It had been easy enough to imagine a murderer lurking behind every tree. By the time she reached Rupert, she had been bathed in sweat.

Now that she wasn't seeing the landscape through the prism of terror, she could see that the countryside had a kind of raw, untamed splendor. A strong wind sent light fluffy clouds scurrying across the deep blue sky. The scale of the landscape was so vast she could follow the shadows of the clouds as they raced across the grass.

"What are those?" Julia pointed to a stand of particularly handsome trees.

"Northern prickly ash." Cooper slowed the Blazer down as they approached the town limits. "But its popular name is the toothache tree."

"The toothache tree." Julia turned the name over in her mind. "Now how do you suppose it got that name?"

"Don't know," Cooper mused. "Never thought about it before. Maybe the taxonomist had a toothache the day he named the tree."

"Or else some trapper was hard up for food and boiled the bark and cracked a tooth." Julia could imagine all too well the brutal lives of the early settlers. "Or…or someone in a surveying party had a toothache the day they discovered the tree. Wait, here's a better one—someone had a hangover the day they discovered the tree and thought it looked like a tooth."

Cooper pulled up in front of Julia's house and braked to a stop. "I guess we'll never know for sure. Here we are."

"Well," Julia began, "thanks for driving me—"

But Cooper was already circling the Blazer. In an instant, he was at her door with a large, outstretched hand. It was a long step down from the cabin of the vehicle and she was grateful that she wore jeans and for the support of his hand. Once down, she lifted her eyes to his and again felt like falling towards him. He was safety and excitement and a host of other feelings she couldn't sort out. With the exception of fear. She felt no fear at all.

With a start, Julia realized that her hand was still in his. Almost reluctantly, she withdrew it.

"Would you, ahm…" Her throat was suddenly dry. "Would you like to come in for some coffee? Or try out one of the tea recipes I'll be giving Alice?"

"Yeah." The deep voice was soft. He answered immediately, which made her think he really did want to come inside with her, though she couldn't tell anything by his expression. He was totally unreadable to her.

The second porch stair creaked and Julia remembered Cooper had promised to fix it. Just the fact that she knew she'd be seeing him again made her feel better.

Fred was waiting for them at the top of the steps and slithered in, wriggling with happiness when she opened the door.

Inside her shabby little living room, Julia took off her coat and turned to Cooper. He was standing just inside the door, huge and broad, watching her. He wasn't moving, he didn't say anything and yet her heart pounded. She was drowning in those dark, dark eyes.

Something wet touching her hand made her start. "Oh!" She looked down to see Fred licking her hand.

Cooper crouched, stretching his jeans across his thighs. He held out his hand. "Here, boy," he murmured, and Fred limped over to him. Fred placed his muzzle on Cooper's thigh while Cooper patted his head. When Julia found herself envying Fred because he was able to rest his head on those amazing muscles, she knew it was time for tea.

Her hands trembled as she brewed Earl Grey in a teapot, adding vanilla beans. She placed the pot, two mugs, the sugar canister and two spoons on a tea tray. The familiar routine and the fragrant fumes calmed her a little. Cooper was sitting at the small table in her living room when she walked back in.

He'd taken his jacket off. Julia could see the massive muscles of his chest and biceps through the wool of his dark gray sweater. He stood immediately when she entered the room, a gesture of courtesy that had died out back east but which still survived out here, she'd noticed. He sat down again only after she'd taken her seat.

She had to work to keep her hands steady as she poured the tea, concentrating so hard she couldn't talk. They sipped in silence, gazes locked.

She found it impossible to make light conversation. To say anything at all.

Julia had never been so aware of absolutely everything in her environment as she was at this moment. All her senses were wide open. It had started sleeting again and little needles of ice made a light pinging noise against her windowpanes. Fred had fallen deeply asleep and was dreaming of hunting conquests, limbs quivering as he yipped gently in his sleep. The tea was strong; she could taste the underlying bergamot blending with the sweet vanilla. She could hear Cooper's breathing and her own.

She could hear her own heartbeat, thumping triple-time.

She couldn't talk. There was a huge lump of something in her throat that choked her words. A ball of emotions burned in her chest in a painful tangle. Fear, loneliness, despair. A desire so intense it blazed hot and strong throughout her body. She felt all of them. All of them hurt.

Cooper drained his cup and stood. He was leaving. Julia panicked.

Suddenly, she knew that she couldn't spend the night alone, shaking and lost, huddled in on herself for comfort in the dark. Simply couldn't. She needed Cooper like she needed air and sunlight. She had no idea whether she needed him for the sex or to keep the deep lonely darkness of the night at bay, or a combination of both. She only knew she couldn't be alone tonight and the only person she wanted was Cooper, no one else.

He was standing, looking down at her, unmoving, one big hand flat on the table.

Julia placed her hand over his. It flexed once, strongly, under hers, then stilled. His hand was warm, hard, powerful. Her eyes met his, sky to night.

"Please stay," she whispered.

Chapter Six

There is a man in Norway. The professional liked to imagine him as a little gray man in a little gray room, hunched over a little gray laptop, but the truth was, the professional had no inkling what the man looked like. No one knew what he looked like.

It was enough to know, as a choice few scattered throughout the world did, that the man in Norway had a service to offer. For a reasonable fee, the Norwegian would route any message to any person in the world, anonymity guaranteed. No one would ever, ever be able to trace the message back, either way.

The professional picked up the printout of the file hacked from the U.S. Marshal's office and looked at the first name that had come up: Richard M. Abt. Quickly, the professional scanned over the bare facts of the case and easily reconstructed the story.

Richard M. Abt, had been chief accountant for Ledbetter, Duncan & Terrance, a group of upscale lawyers who just happened to front for the mob. A few transactions sailing very close to the wind, then the illegalities, with Richard Abt's fingerprints all over them. The FBI investigation, then the arrest. It was all there. The professional understood quite well what had happened. It was clear that Richard Abt had been set up as a fall guy, looking at ten to twenty with no parole in the ultimate gated community—prison. Then last July, Richard Abt turned into a canary and sang a lovely, lovely tune, a siren song guaranteed to put the senior partners of Ledbetter, Duncan & Terrance behind bars for life. No doubt Ledbetter, Duncan or Terrance would be willing to pay good money to stop the canary from singing in court.

Lisa Marie Rice

It was two o'clock in the morning in Norway, but as far as the professional could ascertain, the Norwegian never slept.

The professional typed out the message to the Norwegian: MESSAGE TO SIMON LEDBETTER. INFORMATION RE LOCATION AND NEW IDENTITY OF RICHARD ABT AVAILABLE UPON RECEIPT OF NOTIFICATION OF DEPOSIT OF TWENTY THOUSAND US DOLLARS ON ACCOUNT N° GHQ 115 Y BANQUE SUISSE GENEVA HEAD OFFICE. HIT MUST LOOK LIKE ACCIDENT. And sat back to enjoy some smoked breast of pheasant and put on a CD of *La Bohème*.

Luciano Pavarotti's Rodolfo was to die for.

* * * * *

Stay.

Cooper had big hands, strong hands. Hands that could field strip an M16 in seven seconds, hands that could subdue an unbroken stallion, hands that could lift a 300-pound bale of hay. Sally Anderson's pale delicate hand was almost half the size of his. Her hand couldn't match his in strength in any way.

And yet, when she placed her hand over his, it was as if she'd driven a stake through it, spearing him in place. He couldn't move if his life depended on it.

As it had been the day before, her small hand was icy cold and trembled faintly.

He could understand the trembling because he felt shaky himself, but he wasn't icy cold. He was boiling hot.

All the sexual desire he hadn't felt in two years was geysering up in one huge flood of heat and sex. Every single cell of his body was swollen with hot, slick lust. His hard-on felt ten times bigger than it usually did. It pulsed painfully against his jeans.

She was looking up at him anxiously, obviously feeling she'd done something overly bold, wondering if he was going to refuse.

116

No. No, he wasn't going to refuse her.

There was no power on earth strong enough to peel him away from her, now.

Slowly, mindful of the massive hard-on that made moving painful, Cooper hunkered down until he was crouching in front of Sally, at eye level. Her eyes were amazing. Close-up, the irises were a stunning mixture of blues and greens that, at a distance, became turquoise. They were filled with anxiety, which he hated.

She withdrew her hand from his but he didn't dare touch her. Not yet, not while he had such a tenuous hold on his control. He gripped the corner of her chair with one hand and the edge of the table with the other. She was trapped between the table and him, in his embrace, though he wasn't touching her.

They watched each other in silence, Cooper trying to keep his breathing under control. He didn't know what moves he could make, what words he could say. So he remained immobile and silent. Sally's gaze dropped to his clenched hands. Her eyes widened when she saw the tight grip, the white knuckles, the effort he was making to keep his hands off her. Her gaze traveled upward, and stopped at his mouth.

A sign. Finally.

Cooper moved forward slowly, oh so slowly, and touched his mouth to hers. They both exhaled shakily.

Sally's mouth was everything he thought it would be. Soft, gentle, exciting as hell. Cooper's neck muscles ached with the effort of not pushing forward, not eating at her mouth, biting her.

He wanted his tongue in her, in that soft mouth. He wanted his cock there, too, but now wasn't the time to be thinking of that. He was way too excited as it was.

Cooper opened his mouth, just a little, heart pounding when she opened hers, too. He slanted his head for a better fit, licking the inside of her lower lip, angling his head again for a better, deeper taste of her. He nearly came in his pants when her tongue met his, shyly.

This was not going to turn out well when a simple kiss was turning him on so much he could hardly breathe. His hand gripped the chair harder as he opened his mouth over hers, tongue exploring. She tasted as wonderful as he imagined, her taste slightly sweet, either from the sugar in the tea or some innate Sally-like quality of sweetness.

Cooper released the edge of the table. Slowly, as if he were pushing his hand against a rushing powerful stream of water, he brought his hand to Sally's neck. Still kissing her, he ran the back of his forefinger along the soft skin of her neck, tracing the delicate line of her collarbone.

Sally's mouth softened at his touch and he nearly lost it, right there. She was so responsive he could feel her reaction to his touch in her mouth.

Touching her in two points was too much for him to take right now. His mouth lifted from hers. It took Sally a few seconds to register the loss of the kiss. Her eyes were still closed, mouth wet and slightly open. There was a slight rosy cast to the ivory and cream tones of her face. Her eyes fluttered open. They searched his, looking for something in his face. Something he didn't know how to give.

"Cooper?" she whispered.

He couldn't answer. His throat was closed tight; there was an iron band around his chest. He made a noise deep in his chest and even he didn't know what it meant. Every muscle he had was tight with sexual tension. He felt exactly like Grayhawk must have felt, with the smell of Leyla in his nostrils and every instinct screaming to get at her quickly and having a wooden wall in the way.

The wooden wall was the near-violence of his desire. Cooper was going to hurt this beautiful woman if he wasn't careful. He'd never in his life wanted to be as gentle as he wanted to be now, with Sally Anderson. He'd never in his life felt this bloodlust before, raging hot and nearly out of control. If he hurt her, in any way, he'd never forgive himself.

Carefully, Cooper opened his hand to cup it around her neck. The skin was soft, softer than the finest silk. He had rough, callused hands and almost expected the skin of his hands to catch on her skin, as it would on a fine material. He ran his hand up until his fingers caught in her short brown hair, feeling the delicate structure of her skull.

It was, perhaps, a good thing Sally wasn't a redhead. He loved red hair; it had always turned him on. Everything about her pleased him so much, if she had red hair, he'd probably come in his jeans.

Watching her eyes, Cooper ran his open hand back down, over the fragile bones of her shoulder, then around to the buttons of her sweater. It took every ounce of willpower not to rip her sweater open.

He could do it, too. She'd let him. He could see that in her eyes. She was a little hesitant, a little shy but she definitely wanted him.

She might even find it exciting if he ripped her clothes off. But if he started ripping, he'd tear a huge hole in his shaky self-control and the lust would come pouring out, like water punching through a cracked dam.

He wouldn't stop at ripping her sweater and bra and jeans and panties off. No, once he started down that slippery road and allowed instincts to swamp the tight clamp he held on himself, he'd simply drag her to the floor, open her with his fingers and shove his cock in, whether she was ready or not. Hold her legs so far apart she couldn't move. Start fucking her hard, pounding into her, grinding her into the floor...

She wasn't ready for a fast and furious fucking, might not ever be ready for that. Cooper would take whatever it was she was willing to give, but she had to give it willingly, when she was ready.

So instead of ripping her clothes to shreds, throwing her on the floor and mounting her, Cooper ran his forefinger around the neck of the sweater and fingered the top little pearl button, watching Sally carefully. Her expression didn't change. He slowly undid the button, his big hand a little clumsy.

When it opened, revealing an inch of creamy skin, her face relaxed. If he hadn't been watching so carefully he might not have seen it. It wasn't a smile; it was more subtle than that. Her tension dissipated a fraction, just enough to let him know they were moving in a direction she recognized. And welcomed.

At the animal level, Sally had sensed how violent his desire was. She could see the tension of his muscles, how tightly he held her chair. She was like a filly, prancing with unease while the stallion approached. Fillies knew that the mating would be wild, furious, brutal. And somehow Sally knew her own coupling with him could turn brutal, too.

The first steps towards sex — the restrained kiss and the slow opening of the button of her sweater — showed her that she could, after all, expect some control from him.

He hoped she was right.

Another button. Another and another. Cooper's trembling hand started to fumble. Luckily there were only six buttons in all. Sally's expression became more welcoming with each button coming undone. When he carefully opened the sweater and slid it off her shoulders, she let her breath out on a sigh.

Her white bra had a front catch, which Cooper was grateful for. If he had had to put his arms around her to undo her bra at the back, it might have set him off. Sally dropped her arms and the bra fell, caught between her waist and the chair back, on top of the sweater. She was naked from the waist up.

Sally gave him a tremulous smile, which he didn't return. He couldn't smile. What he was feeling was too big for a smile.

Still, a smile was good news. He was doing this right. So far, at least.

Cooper let out a shaky breath. Now he didn't have to watch her face so carefully. Now he could take a good look at what he'd uncovered.

He felt half dazed when he finally dropped his gaze. She was small, dainty, and utterly perfect. He was almost afraid to touch her, afraid he'd mar the milky pale skin so delicate it looked as if it would bruise if he breathed too hard on it.

He ran one long forefinger around her right breast, then cupped it carefully. He had been right. She fit neatly into his cupped hand. She felt like warm satin. He bent his head and brought his mouth to her breast, licking the small rosy nipple, sucking it. It tasted exactly as he'd imagined it would. Like a cherry. Both her nipples tasted like cherries. When he lifted his head, they were wet from his mouth, hard and deep pink.

Her breathing had sped up. He could see her heartbeat in her left breast, beating overly fast. Desire? Fear?

Cooper leaned forward again, brushing his mouth over hers. "Don't be afraid of me," he murmured. "I won't hurt you." He hoped to God that was true.

"No," Sally whispered. But the voice was soft, uncertain.

This was his cue to keep reassuring her with words, warm her up, soften her up. Sally Anderson was a teacher, a reader. Words would go a long way towards making her relax with him. If he found the right ones, words could even excite her. Cooper needed her to be excited, needed her little cunt to be wet and welcoming. Otherwise this wouldn't work at all.

It was just his stinking luck that Cooper didn't have any seductive and reassuring words in him, none at all. Not at the best of times, let alone now, when his brain was blasted with lust. It was a miracle he could even talk at all.

Cooper released his grip on her chair. He needed to get her naked, right now, and he needed both hands free for that. He unsnapped her jeans, pulled down the zipper and opened the jeans, nearly groaning as the backs of his fingers brushed against her soft, flat belly. Curling one arm around her back, Cooper lifted her easily, brushing jeans and panties down and off with his other hand, taking her cotton socks and shoes off with the rest of her clothes. Finally, she was naked.

Oh, shit.

Cooper eased Sally back onto the chair, keeping one hand on her upper thigh, staring at the glossy red curls next to his hand. He moved his head forward until his forehead met hers. "You're a redhead," he breathed.

Sally Anderson was a redhead and he was officially a dead man. Any hopes he had of keeping himself a little separate, not falling head over heels for her, were blown right out of the water.

She was stunningly beautiful, smart, kindhearted, warm. And a redhead. He was a goner.

"Yes. Yes, um…yes, I am." She took in a deep breath, lifting her head away to search his eyes. "Um…is that a problem?" Crazily, Sally looked frozen, uncertain, even a little scared. Did she think he was put off by red hair?

"No." Cooper cleared his throat. "I love red hair on a woman."

"Oh." It was more a soft exhalation of breath than a word. "That—that's good, then."

"Mmm." He couldn't answer. The noise in his head was too loud for that. He was too busy studying the contrast of his hand on her thigh, his rough dark skin against her soft pale skin. As if it weren't his, as if it had a mind of its own, his hand shifted, cupped her, right where he wanted to slide his cock in, just as soon as it was humanly possible.

Sally opened her legs, just a little, but enough to be a welcome. The hair covering her mound was soft rather than springy, not too thick. Cooper's fingers slid through the folds of her sex. They were both trembling now, as he tested her. As he'd suspected, she was tiny. But wet.

Wet was good. Enough of it and he was finally going to be able to sink his aching cock in her. Not now. Not yet. But very soon or he'd die.

He probed her, carefully spreading the wetness around the little opening, circling the clitoris.

It had surprised the hell out of him when a waitress had once said she loved being touched there by him. Apparently, most men poked and prodded, pressing hard, shaking and pumping their hand, as if the clit were a cock. Amazing what assholes men could be.

It was instinctive for him to touch a woman there carefully. They were so soft, it was so small. If you weren't paying attention, if you were ham-handed, you missed all the little signals a woman's body was sending you.

A woman's sex was like a horse's mouth. Before he hired a ranch hand, Cooper watched how the man used the bit. Horses might be big and rough but they had delicate mouths. Treat it badly and you hurt them. Treat it well and they were yours.

This was where a man's strength was no use whatsoever. He'd seen big strong tough stable hands fuck up with a horse's mouth. And big strong tough men fuck up with women.

Horses needed a delicate touch at times. Women were the same. How could you press and saw at flesh so tender and soft?

Sally's legs were open now. She was getting wetter by the second. Cooper probed with his finger, watching her carefully. Watching the flush rise from her breasts to her face. Watching her mouth fall slightly open to catch more air. Watching her breathing speeding up.

Cooper pressed his finger inside her, feeling the soft flesh open for him. He moved his finger carefully. Most women had a flashpoint, right there…

She moaned and opened her thighs for him more, the muscles in her belly tightening. Cooper stopped, frozen for a moment, his hand stilled. Inside his jeans, he could feel his cock weeping. He shook, a second from coming.

Sally brought a trembling hand to his face. Her hand was no longer icy cold. It felt like a brand against his skin. "Cooper?" She studied his eyes. "Do you — do you want to go to bed?"

"Like I want my next breath," he rasped. His throat was hot, scratchy. The words felt like stones in his throat, coming out painfully, one by one. "But once I have you on a bed and I get out of these jeans, I'm going to be inside you with my next heartbeat. I won't be able to stop for anything. So the only foreplay you're going to get is right now, right here. In this chair."

"Oh." Sally's beautiful mouth rounded into an O. He could almost see the wheels turning in her head as she processed what he said. She opened her mouth to speak again and his thumb circled her clitoris. Sally's breath left her lungs with an audible whoosh. He could feel her arousal in a long pull of her internal muscles against his finger and he could see it, in the increased heartbeat in her breast and neck. He gritted his teeth. If his cock swelled any more it would burst out of its skin.

He breathed harshly, in and out, in an effort at control.

"There's more," Cooper warned. This had to be said while he still had some blood in his head. "I only have one condom in my wallet. For sentimental reasons, I guess, because it's been over two years since I had sex. It's probably expired. And one rubber isn't going to be enough at all. The way I feel right now, ten won't be enough. I don't know how we're going to deal with that."

She flushed brightly, going from pale rose to bright pink in an instant. She smiled shakily and tugged at the hand inside her. Cooper let her pull his hand out and was astonished when she brought his hand to her mouth, brushing her lips across his knuckles. His finger and palm were slick with her juices.

"We're okay," she whispered. Her eyes were twin turquoise pools. So bright, so deep he felt as if he could drown in them. "I had irregular periods. My gynecologist put me on the pill. There's no need to —"

Whatever she was going to say was drowned in his mouth. Cooper rose with her in his arms, bearing her away.

Chapter Seven

It was like flying.

Julia had no sensation of gravity at all, of having a weight in this world. Cooper carried her so easily, it was as if she were airborne. What kept her anchored was the feel of his strong muscles holding her and his mouth on hers.

There was no hesitation, no fumbling, no checking rooms. As if he'd lived in the little house all his life, Cooper unerringly made for her bedroom. The door was partially closed and he kicked it open with his booted foot so hard it bounced off the wall. The sound was like the crack of a bullet in the silent night.

It was the first sign that his control was snapping, a sign that that iron grip he held on himself was cracking. If she weren't held in a net of fire, it would have chilled her. Though every muscle had been hard and tense as he'd kissed her, you wouldn't have been able to tell that he was massively aroused by the kisses. Sweet gentle kisses, actually. Sweeter than most she'd had.

Any other man would have gone straight for the goods after she'd said she was willing to sleep with him. Not Cooper. He'd kissed her carefully, touched her carefully, watched her carefully, waiting. If she hadn't seen and sensed his iron control, she'd have thought he was the kind of man who ignited slowly.

But the muscles of his face had been tightly drawn, nostrils flared like a stallion's. Though she hadn't dared to stare, she'd caught a glimpse of his massive erection through his jeans.

His control was so tight she'd thought she might get away with a gentle bout of lovemaking and she could cuddle afterwards. That was the part of sex she'd always liked best. The comfort of being held. But if Cooper was already kicking down doors, it was going to be rougher than she bargained for.

Cooper made a beeline for her bed and followed her down, still kissing her. When she was on the bed, he drew away.

The loss of his intense body heat chilled her. Lying on the bed, Julia was suddenly aware of the fact that she was stark naked. She reached for the coverlet to pull it over her.

"Don't," he growled. He shook his head, sharply. "Don't cover yourself."

"I'm cold," Julia whispered. She was. And a little frightened, too, though she couldn't say that. She'd started this, after all. She had no business being reticent. She'd invited Sam Cooper into her bed and there was no turning back now.

But there was something a little scary about Cooper as he undressed in hasty jerky motions, that male grace she'd so admired completely gone. He seemed even larger and more powerful than ever, thick deep muscles flexing and rippling as he stripped. The light from the living room through the open bedroom door allowed her to see Cooper as he jerked off sweater and tee shirt and sent them flying. A few swipes of his hands and he was naked, his large penis jutting out from a dense nest of black pubic hair.

Julia suddenly shivered at seeing what the clothes had masked.

She'd seen buff bodies before, of course, at her gym and in photographs. But they had nothing whatsoever to do with the powerful being standing naked by her bed. Cooper's body didn't look like a cover-boy type of male body at all. It was stronger, harder, tougher than that. His chest was covered in a mat of thick black hair, black hairs on his forearms and legs, too. His muscles were sculpted by something other than gym equipment. By life, by battle. His body was broad, hard, scarred. A warrior's body.

He was a warrior.

Julia had completely forgotten that, forgotten that he wasn't just a nice rancher who wasn't too good with words. He was, essentially, a trained killer. Probably just like the killers who were after her.

In one quick surge of panic, Julia realized that in her pain and loneliness she had broken Herbert Davis' cardinal rule — don't get involved with the locals. She wasn't supposed to let anyone get close to her. It was too dangerous, he'd said. She couldn't let anyone know she was in the Witness Security Program. Santana had a long reach and a million dollar bounty was enough to tempt anyone. Julia might well have signed her own death sentence in inviting Cooper into her bed.

In more ways than one. He was the most powerful man she'd ever seen. He could snap her neck with one strong sinewy hand.

Cooper turned slightly towards her. His penis was enormous, long and broad, weeping from the tip.

Danger came from many sources. This was one.

Julia's heart was thumping so hard, she thought the whole house must surely shake from it. Panic and fear and excitement melded into one huge emotion almost too big for her to contain it.

Cooper kneeled on the bed, his heavy weight making the old mattress dip. Julia had to clench her muscles so she wouldn't roll into the valley he'd created.

As he bent over her, Cooper didn't look like a lover about to have sex. He looked like a warrior about to kill. The muscles in his chest and arms were corded, biceps flexing and bulging as he braced one long, strong arm over her to mount her, pulling her thighs apart with his other hand. He wasn't smiling. There was no softness at all in his face as he looked down at her. The skin over his high angular cheekbones was stretched taut and there was a grim cast to his mouth.

Even his penis was more like a weapon than an instrument of pleasure. It was thick, hard as a club and much larger than any male member she'd ever seen.

He was danger personified and she couldn't run away.

Her body closed in on itself in panic, but it was too late.

Cooper covered her. He was heavy, unyielding. For a second she couldn't breathe. One big hand reached between them as he opened the lips of her vagina. She could feel the broad hard head of his penis being fitted to her before she had a chance to relax her vaginal muscles to ease his passage. He thrust sharply with all the strength of his pelvis, hard and deep.

It hurt.

Cooper's penis was too large for her, she wasn't ready. It burned inside her, stretching her mercilessly.

Julia blinked away the sudden tears. She whimpered once, then bit her lip. She'd wanted this, had asked for it. If it was too much for her, it was her own damned fault.

Cooper pulled his head back and up, gasping for breath, as if cresting a wave. A thick strand of straight black hair fell over his forehead. His jaw muscles flexed. The tendons in his neck stood out in raised cords.

"Fuck," he gritted, gripping her hips hard. "You're not ready." He was sweating. A drop of perspiration fell on her cheekbone. "Can't stop. Can't. Sorry." His deep voice was strained. "Sorry."

"It's okay," she whispered.

With a groan, Cooper's chest lowered until he lay heavily on her, face buried in the pillow next to hers. His thighs flexed powerfully and he began thrusting, fast and hard, with the full strength of his body.

It was exactly like being caught in a wild storm, buffeted by the wind and the elements. Julia clung to Cooper's shoulders, not in a lover-like embrace, but as she would cling to a tree in a raging tempest.

The tempo of Cooper's thrusts increased until he was slamming into her, the bed thudding heavily against the wall, the springs creaking loudly in protest. It went on so long Julia lost track of the time, until it felt as if she had spent her entire life with Cooper's penis inside her, pistoning back and forth.

Suddenly, with no warning whatsoever, Julia surged into climax. She cried out as a wave hit her like an oncoming train, her entire lower body clenching in hard fast convulsions.

Usually, it took her a long time to climax. She'd start feeling little tendrils of pleasure, as if they were arriving from a long way off. Her thighs would start shaking and she would feel warmth in her lower belly. Her body was letting her know what was going to happen long before it actually did.

Not this time. This time it was as if a powerful switch had been suddenly thrown, hurtling her into the strongest orgasm she'd ever had, her vagina pulling tightly on Cooper's penis.

Cooper shouted into the pillow and she felt the vibrations of his deep voice against her arms, her chest. He groaned and growled, swelled even further inside her and climaxed, too. His thrusts stopped as he pressed into her, as deeply as he could go, jetting waves of semen into her.

Julia's climax tapered off. She was clinging tightly to Cooper's shoulders. The muscles in his back were rock-hard with tension, slick with sweat. She was slick all over, too, from Cooper's sweat and her own, and from his semen trickling out of her to wet her thighs. Julia suddenly realized how…how polite the sex she'd had before had been. Nice polite sex, with no sweating, like taking tea with a man, only more fun and naked.

This had been elemental, brutal, animal. Not nice. Not polite. Even the pleasure had been an…animal pleasure, the way eagles or cougars mated.

He was still iron-hard inside her. Cooper hadn't been joking when he said once wasn't going to be enough.

Once was quite enough for her.

Julia was exhausted, overwhelmed by the rough, lengthy sex and the explosive orgasm. Her muscles felt limp, rubbery. Cooper was so heavy she had to inflate her lungs forcefully to be able to breathe. Her thighs were held open to their maximum width, completely open to him. Julia was wondering when it would be okay to push at his shoulder, when Cooper's hips started moving again.

Oh God, not again. Already it had been the longest sex she'd ever had. And the most exciting. It was still exciting. Though her head told her enough was enough, her lower body wasn't listening at all.

Cooper's deep, heavy strokes were more exciting than before. She was thoroughly wet now, with her climax and the amount of semen he'd pumped into her. He moved slickly in and out of her and she was burning up with the pleasure.

Cooper lifted his head and stared down at her, the strong dark features hard and expressionless. They were engaged in the most intimate act two humans could perform and yet she couldn't tell in any way what he was thinking, what he was feeling.

He was thrusting heavily now, deep hard strokes filling her with raw heat. His hands came up to frame her face, thumbs on her cheeks. Julia was completely immobilized. She couldn't move her body in any direction, his heavy weight pinned her. She couldn't move her head. His gaze was so intense she couldn't even close her eyes.

Slowly, Cooper's head lowered until his mouth touched hers. To her astonishment, the kiss wasn't rough, possessive. He touched her mouth lightly, gently, with his, over and over. Light kisses feathered over her cheekbones and eyelids, as soft and as gentle as butterfly kisses. Cooper's mouth roamed over her forehead, lightly brushing her ear, along her jawline. His mouth was warm and soft. Achingly tender.

The contrast between the light, loving kisses and the raw almost violent sex of their lower bodies was electric, as if two different men were making love to her at the same time. For the first time in her life, Julia couldn't talk. Even if she'd known what to say, she found her mouth gently occupied every time she thought to speak.

Her hand crept up over Cooper's hard back muscles and she hooked her arms up over his shoulders, relishing the play of hard muscles as he worked her. He was so amazing to the touch. Like iron, only warm. Though the kisses were slow and languid, as if they had all the time in the world, as if he were a young man kissing a pretty girl for the first time in a meadow, his hips were slamming into her, faster and faster.

Cooper opened her mouth softly, gently with his. When his tongue touched hers, it was enough to set her off. With a cry lost in Cooper's mouth, Julia climaxed again, harder than before, great waves of heat rolling through her, her vagina clenching tightly then relaxing in time with Cooper's thrusts. It was so intense she felt like screaming, like crying. Her heart was pounding its way out of her chest. She was clinging to Cooper, tears leaking out of her eyes, running down her face on to the pillow.

Cooper was murmuring something, she didn't know what. She couldn't hear, couldn't think, could only feel.

He was still hard inside her—it felt like he could stay hard inside her the rest of her life—but his movements had stilled. The sex had stopped but the lovemaking continued, soft gentle kisses over her face, along her neck. Low murmurs, more a vibration in his chest than a sound.

Julia's arms tightened around him, and she hid her face in his neck. She had no words for him, nothing to say at all. All her defenses were down, broken through. If she opened her mouth now, all her secrets would come tumbling out.

So she clung, and burrowed, eyes tightly closed, overwhelmed with emotions, chest aching, waiting for her heart rate to slow. Her breathing calmed, heart steadied. Holding tightly onto Cooper, the only stable thing in her rocking world, Julia fell asleep.

* * * * *

There was so much blood.

The pale, skinny man lay on the tarmac, a river of blood flowing from his shattered head. It pooled thick and viscous on the ground. She backed away, horrified, slipping over the slick ground. The man with the gun turned slowly, his mouth opening into a cruel scimitar-shaped smile, his lips blood red. "Pretty lady," he growled, the red smile widening, the gun slowly rising. "Die."

"No!" she screamed, but no sound came out. The word echoed in her chest but the world was filled with a chill silence. She was on her knees now, scrabbling for something, anything, feeling her heart beating like a drum at the base of her throat, wondering if she would feel the moment when it stopped beating.

"Too late," the big man growled and his finger tightened and she prepared to die, there on the gravelly ground, kneeling in another man's blood.

* * * * *

Julia gasped and opened her eyes, trembling, disoriented, lost. She was paralyzed with fear, sweating with it. Where was she? What—?

A large figure stood by the bed, darker than the night. The scream never made it past her closed throat. It came out a tight choked whimper while she scrambled up against the headboard, trying to curl into a ball, hoping she wouldn't feel the bullet—

The broad figure crouched by the bed and took her trembling hand. "Sally," a deep voice said.

"Who?" Julia's head whirled as she struggled to transit from nightmare to reality. "Who's Sa—" A warning bell clanged loudly in her head. She bit her lips so hard she could taste blood. Tears sprang to her eyes.

Cooper held her hand tightly clasped between his. His hands felt warm and hard and safe. "Sally, honey, listen to me."

Julia blinked, trying to connect her thoughts but they flew into tiny brittle shards. The only thing holding her together was

Cooper's grasp. She clung to him. Cooper leaned towards her. She could feel his body heat in the cold black night.

"I have to go, honey." Cooper was fully dressed, down to his heavy black winter jacket. His face was mostly in shadow but she could see his jaw muscles flexing strongly as he bit his back teeth. "Me and five of my men are leaving at 4:30 this morning on horseback to check the line shacks in the hills. It'll take us at least thirty-six hours. Maybe more. We'll have to camp out overnight in one of the shacks. I won't be able to call you 'cause there's no cell phone service up there."

"All—all right." Julia's teeth were chattering. She could barely get the words out. Terrifying images from the nightmare still clung to her mind, like smoke after a fire. She hardly knew what he was talking about, had no idea what a line shack was. All she knew was that Cooper was leaving her. Was leaving her alone, in the dark, to fight her demons by herself.

He was frowning. He watched her for a moment or two. "You okay?" he asked finally, the deep voice quiet.

Julia knew what he meant. She'd felt all her muscles protest as she'd scrambled upright. Her thighs ached and she was sore and very sticky between them. The sex had been incredibly rough. Harder and deeper and longer than any sex she'd ever had before. Cooper hadn't been able to control himself and she somehow sensed he was appalled at that.

He was asking whether he'd hurt her.

He hadn't, not really. She was sore but most of the soreness was the burning intensity of her climaxes.

You okay?

No, actually, she wasn't okay. She was lost and scared and lonely. She desperately wanted Cooper to stay. She wanted to hold onto him, feel his strength around her. She wanted him to keep the fear and the loneliness at bay.

"Fine," she answered tightly. She opened her mouth in a big false smile, knowing he would be able to see only the whiteness of her teeth in the darkness, not the unnatural expression. "Just fine."

His clasp tightened and his jaw muscles jumped again. He knew she was lying.

Cooper opened his mouth, then closed it again. What he wanted to say was clearly something he couldn't say. "I have to go," he repeated.

Julia nodded carefully, moving her head slowly as if underwater, holding on to her emotions by only the thinnest of threads. She clamped her jaws shut. If she opened her mouth she'd start crying and begging Cooper to stay.

He couldn't.

Nobody could stay with her. She was completely alone.

Cooper watched her for long moments. Julia was naked and freezing cold. The only warm spot on her body, in her life, was her hand in Cooper's clasp. When he let go, she managed to stop from shuddering only by an almost violent act of self-control. She was chilled to the bone.

He stood, looming tall and broad above her, standing about a foot from the bed. It was hard to think that a short time ago he'd been naked, and in her. For the entire time they'd had sex, Julia had thought of nothing but his body in hers and the almost frighteningly explosive pleasure he was giving her. While they'd been having sex, she'd felt as connected to him as she'd ever felt to another human being. She hadn't felt lost or lonely at all.

Now he was separate, apart from her. Leaving her alone in the cold darkness of the night.

The small luminous display on her alarm clock showed 4 a.m. If he was to make it back to his ranch in time, he'd have to leave now.

Cooper took one step back and stopped. Julia could hear him breathing hard, could almost feel the vibrations of frustration coming off him. He shifted his weight from one booted foot to another, clearly unwilling to leave her.

"Go," she said softly.

Cooper exhaled and nodded. After a moment, without another word, he was gone. She heard the front door open and close and, a moment later, an engine starting up.

The silence pressed in on her, as dark and cold as the night. Julia dropped her forehead to her knees and let the tears come.

Chapter Eight

The room was still reverberating with Luciano's high C when the e-mail sign blinked.

TWENTY THOUSAND US DOLLARS DEPOSITED IN SWISS ACCOUNT. CAR ACCIDENT OKAY?

The professional checked the Geneva account, one of ten in Switzerland, blessing the Swiss banking authorities for allowing 24-hour depositing privileges. The $20,000 was there.

Mimi was putting on her muff, telling Rodolfo that it would warm her hands. She was dying. The professional's fingers strayed from the keyboard to savor the achingly glorious moment. This part was so moving, so tragic. The professional hummed softly along as Rodolfo gathered Mimi's lifeless form in his arms, singing his sorrow. When the music ended, it took a moment for composure to return, and then the professional posted the message to the Norwegian.

RICHARD M. ABT: RELOCATED TO ROCKVILLE, IDAHO, ADDRESS 102 CRESCENT DRIVE, UNDER ASSUMED NAME OF ROBERT LITTLEWOOD. CAR ACCIDENT FINE. GOOD LUCK.

Spurred by idle curiosity, the professional poked around a little into the purloined file, searching for Richard Abt's middle name. It was a little like rummaging around in an old room. The process was fast. There it was. Marion. Richard Abt's middle name was Marion. What kind of a name was that for a man? No wonder he went by an initial.

No matter, the man was history.

The professional smiled. Richard Marion Abt. Destroyed by word of mouse.

* * * * *

"Whoa, there!"

Monday evening, Julia smiled and wiped soap out of her eyes. It was so good to have another human being in the house. Sunday she'd rattled around alone in the house, feeling hemmed in by the four walls, lost and lonely, talking to Fred who could only woof back. Thank God for Mondays, and a classroom full of kids.

Rafael had come over after school and they had gone over his homework, but Fred clearly trumped the Civil War and phrasal verbs as a little boy's focus of interest.

Rafael had raced through the written work, mumbled the phrasal verbs by heart, then scampered off to tackle the fascinating task of grooming Fred.

Grooming Fred required the bathtub, half a bottle of rose-scented bubble bath and almost every towel in the house. A couple of days of food, rest and affection and Fred was already filling out. He barely had a limp now and was deep in the process of falling in love with Rafael. It was clearly mutual. Fred and Rafael had identical dopey grins on their faces.

Julia watched as Rafael dripped more bubble bath on Fred and started shampooing him.

"You still smell, buddy." Julia told Fred as she capped her bottle of bubble bath. "But at least there's this overlay of roses over the eau de dog." He yipped in response.

A heavy knock sounded at the door. She stood, heart racing. "Cooper." His voice was muffled by the door, but was unmistakably his. She hadn't heard from him since he'd left in the early morning darkness Sunday morning.

Wiping her hands on the last clean towel and trying to still her racing heart, Julia went to the door. There he was, tall and broad, dressed in black, holding a package wrapped in brown paper. She'd thought about him constantly yesterday and all day today. Even if she hadn't thought of him, her body would be reminded of him, in her sore muscles, in the ache between her thighs, as if he were still inside her.

He took off his big black cowboy hat as soon as he saw her.

"Sally."

Oh, God. That voice. He'd murmured things in her ear as he was making love to her, in that deep, deep voice. Hearing it now gave her an instant flashback to the dark bedroom and Cooper deeply inside her, moving hard and fast. Her knees trembled.

"Cooper." Her voice sounded breathless. She clung to the edge of the door. He stepped forward, so close she could smell him. Leather, rain, man.

From behind her in the bathroom, Rafael squealed with pleasure and Fred woofed. Cooper's head lifted a moment and when he looked back down at her she could almost read his thoughts. Rafael was busy in the bathroom with Fred. They were, for the moment, alone.

Julia had rehearsed so many different attitudes to take when she saw him again. She'd be friendly but distant. No, cool but amused. No, affectionate without being clingy. No, friendly but ironic...

There was no chance to be anything because Cooper took another step forward and kissed her. Deeply, passionately. The kiss was the equivalent of the sex they'd had, when his penis had possessed her completely.

Holding her close to him, he lifted her up and moved them, fast, into her bedroom. He closed the door and locked it, still kissing her. One big hand reached under her skirt to caress her hip. Oh, God, it felt so good to have his hands on her again. Eyes closed, on tiptoe, Julia opened her mouth more to him and caressed his tongue with hers.

Cooper shuddered. He moved his body back a moment, lifting her up against the wall, holding her with one arm, stripping her of pantyhose and panties and shoes. He pulled her legs up around his hips. His big hand brushed her sex as he unzipped himself and he shuddered again. He could feel how wet she was.

Amazing. Julia had always been so slow to warm up sexually. She liked long, languid foreplay, tender words, soft caresses. She'd had none of that and yet now she was primed for sex. Just seeing Cooper had done that, like a hamster associating pressing the bar with food pellets. Cooper equaled rough, exciting sex.

He opened his briefs and his penis sprang free. His hand guided him to her. He spread her with two fingers, worked the head in and thrust hard.

Julia was completely possessed by him. His mouth was eating at hers, his heavy weight kept her pinned against the wall, his hands held her thighs up and wide apart. The rough material of his jeans abraded her legs.

He leaned heavily into her, mouth lifting from hers. He looked down at her through half-lidded eyes. His face was so stark, so unyielding. "Been thinking about this for a day and a half," he muttered, eyes dark glittering pools.

Just like that, Julia started climaxing, sharp pulls which made his eyes widen and nostrils flare. He sucked in a deep breath and pulled halfway out to start thrusting.

"Miss Anderson? Miss Anderson? Where are you? Fred needs a hairdryer. Miss Anderson?"

"Fuck," Cooper whispered.

They both froze, Julia staring into Cooper's dark eyes. She was still climaxing, her body continuing its processes even though her mind screamed — *stop!*

She was shaking with the intensity of the climax, her body completely out of her control. Cooper's harsh breaths sounded loud in the room. He held himself stiff and still inside her.

"Miss Anderson?" Rafael's voice faded. He was going into the kitchen to look for her, where of course he wouldn't find her. There was only one other room in the house left. Sure enough, his footsteps were crossing the little living room.

The contractions were starting to fade, thank God. Shakily, Julia pushed at Cooper's shoulders. His eyes closed as if in pain, Cooper pulled out of her. She dropped her legs, hoping they would hold her up. She was trembling.

"Miss Anderson? Hey, where'd you go?" The doorknob rattled.

"Just—" her voice was so weak it didn't carry. Julia cleared her throat. "Just a minute. Don't come in, Rafael. I'll be out in a second."

"Okay. We need a hairdryer." Rafael whistled cheerfully as he went back to the bathroom and Fred.

Julia couldn't help but look down. Cooper's penis was dark, hugely swollen and slick with her juices. He was trying to fit that massive erection back into his jeans. The zipper caught. She winced as she met his gaze. "That's got to hurt."

"You have no idea," he rumbled.

"And you didn't, um—"

"Nope." His dark eyes pinned her. "I intend to, though. After I drive Rafael home, I intend to come back and stay inside you all night and then I will. A lot."

There was no air in her lungs, just heat. From what she'd seen—and felt—Cooper was capable of doing just that. "Oh," she said weakly. "Oh, um, okay."

He cupped a big hand around her neck and dropped a kiss on her lips. His thumb continued to caress her neck when he lifted his head. "Better get to Rafael. I'll come out in a minute."

Julia nodded and walked weakly to the door.

"Honey?" She turned back and looked at him quizzically. "Might want to put on some shoes and underwear before going out?"

"Right," Julia said, still dazed. His words barely penetrated. She was still feeling the aftereffects of her climax, the wet swollen tissues of her sex rubbing against each other as she moved. "Underwear."

Underwear, underwear. Where—oh. Her panties, pantyhose and shoes were in the corner. By the time she was decent, Cooper looked less wild, too, though she noticed he kept his jacket on. It reached to his thighs and covered his erection.

Julia pulled her hand dryer from the drawer and was walking to the door when she felt him right behind her, felt his body heat and the large presence that was Cooper.

"Miss Anderson?" Rafael's voice sounded faint from the bathroom.

"Coming!" Julia shouted and nearly jumped when she felt Cooper's large rough hand on her neck. He bent and kissed her on the nape, a light kiss over almost before it began.

"Coming?" he repeated in a low rumble right next to her ear, so that she heard him more by vibration than sound waves. "That's what I hope you'll be doing all night."

She stopped with her hand on the knob, a wave of heat nearly bringing her to her knees. Cooper shouldn't say things like that. Not when she was about to face a little boy. She was sure her face was flushed. Her thoughts were scrambled and her pulse raced. It took her two tries to turn the doorknob. She couldn't turn around. If she did, if she saw Cooper, she'd simply lock that door, turn around and throw her arms around his neck. So she kept her eyes resolutely turned forward as she opened the door and made her shaky way to the bathroom.

The bathroom was an incredible mess, the bathtub filled to the rim with soapy water sloshing onto the floor each time Fred moved.

She handed the dryer to Rafael, who barely looked up. "Oh, great, thanks Miss Anderson. Gotta get Fred dry, otherwise he might catch a cold. Come on, Fred, out." Rafael snapped his fingers and Fred leapt out of the bathtub taking half the water with him.

"Wait!" It was too late. Fred shook all over, sending sprays of soapy water flying. Julia held up her hands to ward off the worst of it, but Rafael was drenched. The bathroom was so wet, using a hairdryer would be dangerous. With a sigh, Julia took the hairdryer away from Rafael and plucked an old sheet from the closet and put it on the floor in the little pantry room. She plugged the dryer in. "In here, Rafael."

Dripping water, Rafael and Fred moved amiably into the pantry. She left when Rafael fired up the dryer.

Cooper was waiting for her in the living room, the big box he'd arrived with in his hands. He held it out. "For you," he said simply.

A present. Julia blinked. The box was wrapped in brown paper and twine. Brown paper and twine packaging was considered very chic back in Boston. Except the paper had to be handmade, undyed and rough-cut, the twine had to be hemp and it usually wrapped up something very expensive.

But this box had "Kellogg's Hardware Emporium" unevenly stamped on the paper.

Julia took the box and hefted it. It was surprisingly heavy. She lifted her eyes to Cooper, heart pounding. "Thank—thank you."

He nodded gravely.

Julia shook the box and something bulky shifted heavily inside. She had no clue what it could possibly be. Cooper's face gave absolutely no sign. Julia cut through the twine and paper and opened the box. She stared at the huge steel and brass contraption then looked up, bewildered, at Cooper.

"Deadbolt, "he said.

"Oh," she replied weakly. "A deadbolt. Um, thanks. Just what I always wanted."

"Got a real flimsy lock on that door." Cooper was frowning now, as if her lock was a special, personal affront to him.

"Do you know how—can you fit it?" Was fit the right verb? What did one do with deadbolts? Assemble? But it was already assembled, one big gleaming unit. Cooper seemed to know what she meant, though. His head moved back in surprise and his frown deepened.

"Sure," he said, as if she'd asked him whether he could walk or read.

Had she offended him? There was absolutely no way to tell. His expression was what it always was—impenetrable. A few minutes later, Cooper was digging into his toolbox and doing something manly and competent with her door and the deadbolt.

So she went to do something womanly and competent in the kitchen. By the time a semidry rose-scented Fred and a grinning Rafael made their way into the kitchen, Julia had tea and a lemon tart she'd baked Sunday for want of anything better to do on the table.

Cooper appeared a minute later. Through the kitchen door she could see the dead bolt, huge and shiny, suitable for protecting nuclear secrets, fitted to her door.

That was so sweet of him. Julia beamed at Cooper as he stood in the kitchen doorway, filling it. "Thanks, Cooper." He froze at her smile, but Julia was beginning to recognize the various gradations of his impassivity. Her smile widened. "Have some pie and tea."

Rafael had already scarfed down three slices, and she'd caught him surreptitiously sneaking bits to Fred. Julia cut a huge slice for Cooper and a much smaller slice for herself. She'd flavored the tea with dried orange peel and cinnamon sticks. Cooper sniffed experimentally and drank, gingerly at first, then with evident pleasure. She smiled as she watched him chew with enthusiasm after the first bite of her lemon tart.

"Good," he rumbled. "Tea, too."

Good? For a moment, Julia was incensed. He was calling her lemon tart *good*? It was her mother's recipe and it was famous on three continents. It wasn't good, it was fabulous. She was about ready to tell him off when she saw him slit his eyes with pleasure while he chewed, just like Fred had. She relaxed.

"Good" was clearly cowboy for fabulous.

Julia wrapped the rest of the lemon tart in tinfoil. "For Bernie," she said, though she suspected Rafael would get most of it.

Cooper stood and Rafael stood, too. "In the pickup, Rafael," Cooper said, without taking his eyes off her. "But first thank Miss Anderson."

"Yessir. Thank you, ma'am," Rafael said obediently, bent to hug Fred, then scampered off.

Cooper stood still, watching her. His dark eyes dropped to her mouth. "Not going to kiss you now," he said. He lifted his gaze and there was pure dark heat there. "Couldn't stop."

Julia nodded. The intensity of his expression took her breath away. Sex hormones filled the air. She kept herself from swaying into him only by exerting iron self-control.

Cooper picked his hat up from the coat rack, flattened his hair and put it on. "Be back later, soon as I can make it," he said, and walked out.

By this time, Julia was getting used to his abrupt leave-takings. Who knew? Maybe elaborate goodbyes were effete, city things. Still, without admitting to herself that she wanted one last look at him, she pushed open the screen door and watched as Cooper hoisted Rafael up onto the passenger seat. As always, Cooper's movements were precise, graceful, powerful.

Though his sweater and jeans looked perfectly clean, they also looked exactly like what he had been wearing on Saturday. He was climbing into a black minivan she hadn't seen before.

Julia wondered about a man who seemed to have more vehicles than clothes.

* * * * *

Foreplay, foreplay, foreplay.

Cooper repeated the words like a mantra to himself as he drove back to Simpson and to Sally after depositing Rafael at the ranch. Maybe he should smack his forehead against the steering wheel to keep some blood in his brain, so he could remember.

Foreplay, foreplay, foreplay.

He was not going to pick Sally up, strip her, pin her against a wall and shove his cock inside.

Not, not, *not*.

There was going to be some foreplay. There was. He tried to keep that thought in the forefront of his brain, while it was still functioning.

He'd had a hard-on for two days straight now, getting a lot of funny looks from his men as they made the rounds of the line shacks in the high country. His cock would go down for a little while and then he'd be hit—*wham!*—by a memory of something…Sally's nipple, say, and how it tasted, or that electric moment when his cock entered the tight tissues of her cunt, parting them—and there it would go up again, harder than before.

He hadn't slept last night, not even a few minutes. He hadn't even dozed. They'd been trained for that in the Teams, of course. Part of the training was staying awake several nights in a row in a shallow stream after having marched all day; an endurance test using a combination of fatigue, extreme discomfort and sleeplessness. He'd aced the training sessions by sheer willpower.

This was an entirely different species of sleeplessness, completely involuntary. It wasn't that he didn't want to go to sleep. It was just that every time he lay down, he could see—he could nearly feel—Sally's soft little body. Her legs around his hips, her small little breasts against his chest, her soft mouth brushing his ear. When he closed his eyes in a fruitless attempt to nod off, he could smell her skin, faintly rose-scented, a unique womanly Sally smell.

So he'd been two nights without sleep, though he wasn't tired at all. He was wired on testosterone.

There was nothing he could do, no mind games at all he could play, that could make his cock go down at night. In his normal life B.M.—Before Melissa—unsatisfied horniness wasn't anything he'd ever suffered from after having gotten into Lory Kendall's pants in his sophomore year of high school. Ever since then, if he felt horny, there was always a woman around, somewhere. You just had to know where to look. The only times women weren't available, he was either deep in training or up to his eyeballs in danger on a mission, so busy scrambling to keep his cock safe that there wasn't room for thoughts of actually doing something with that cock. And of course, during his marriage and for a year after the marriage went belly up, his cock had stayed neatly down between his legs, inside his jeans.

Now his cock just wouldn't stay down, particularly at night. Last night he'd lain awake in his sleeping bag, sweating despite the freezing cold floor, running through fucking Sally like a movie on a continuous loop in his head. He'd have jerked off, but then his men would know what he was doing.

Nothing wrong with that, ordinarily. The line shacks were as close to a barracks as it got in civilian life and men jerked off in barracks; that was just a rule of life. Soldiering was a dangerous and lonely business and if a man could find some solace in his fist, no one begrudged it to him.

But he and his men weren't in battle, hundreds of miles from a willing woman. There were all sorts of women available, if you were prepared to drive to Rupert or Dead Horse or Boise. Beating off wasn't really justified. It's just that his cock wanted Sally and only Sally. She wasn't there and it wanted to know why.

Fucking Sally once had barely whetted his appetite. Having his cock in her for maybe two minutes an hour ago didn't count. If anything, it inflamed him even more. He'd done a lot of hard things in his life, but pulling out when he'd just got it in had been the hardest. While she was coming, yet.

He deserved a fucking medal.

Cooper's heart rate speeded up as he rounded the corner and saw Sally's ramshackle little house. He wanted to park right in front and make a beeline for the door, but he took the time to drive past and park a block down and over. His van was going to stay there all night, though he'd have to leave before first light to make it back in time for the dawn training sessions.

It was a vain attempt to protect Sally's reputation, though most people in Simpson knew everyone else's business.

He'd heard that schoolteachers had something called a "moral turpitude" clause in their contracts. If they did something that went against community morals, they could be fired.

The only person who could fire her, though, was the head of the school board, Larry Janssen, who was his second cousin. And Larry sure wouldn't fire her for sleeping with him. Larry would be glad Cooper was finally getting laid.

Still, what he and Sally did together was no business but theirs.

Cooper's blood was beating heavily in his veins as he walked up the porch steps, wincing at the creak. Fixing that second step was next on his list of repairs. The door opened before he could knock and a smiling Sally stood framed in the doorway. Just as beautiful as he remembered, just as fragile, just as precious. She'd opened the door to him without knowing who was on the other side.

That chilled his hot blood. "You opened the door," he said with a disapproving frown.

Her smile slipped. She looked at him, at the door, then back at him. "Um, yes. Yes, I did."

"I didn't identify myself."

Sally rolled her eyes. "Cooper, I heard you coming up the walk. I was expecting you. Who else could it be?"

Scumbags, drug addicts, rapists, serial killers—anything was possible. Cooper had a sudden chilling vision of Sally hurt, maybe dead and it hit him in a blinding panicky flash just what would disappear from his life if anything happened to her.

Cooper had had several flashes of intuition in his life, acute sensory impressions of danger. Once he'd had a vision of himself at the bottom of a cliff face with a smashed hip and shattered femur. He'd seen himself, leg bent at an unnatural angle, had felt the searing pain of bones grinding together, watched his lifeblood pumping from a severed artery. He'd felt darkness descend as he bled out. It had unnerved him so much he'd checked his gear once again, and noticed a frayed belaying rope he'd somehow overlooked.

Another time, he'd had a sudden vision of himself and his men walking into an ambush in the dense hot jungle of an Indonesian island. He'd lifted his fist, the signal to stop, and his team had obediently frozen in place. They stayed hidden for over four hours, not moving, barely breathing, fingers on triggers. Just when Cooper was beginning to wonder whether his famous intuition had failed him, a signal was given and twenty Islamist insurgents rose up out of camouflaged holes. His team took them all down. If he hadn't stopped his men, they'd have walked straight into the ambush.

Cooper had learned the hard way to trust his instincts. It wasn't magic and he wasn't psychic. All his senses were keen and he was a trained observer. He picked up subtle danger signals, his subconscious put them together and sent the danger message to his head in the form of a vision.

And that was what he'd just had. A sudden searing vision of Sally lying in a pool of her own blood, limp, lifeless, gone from him forever. Something in his subconscious was signaling him that there was danger threatening Sally. She could be hurt. She could die.

Not while he lived.

Cooper stepped into the house, taking off his hat, moving so close to Sally she had to tilt her head back. He was crowding her personal space and he knew it, but he wanted this message to be burned into her brain.

"You do not open that door until you know who's on the other side, is that clear?" His voice was harsh, hard, the voice he used with his men. The human animal remembers lessons learned the hard way, especially ones associated with pain. It's the way we're hardwired. Sally had to remember what he was saying and he put cold command into his voice to make sure she did.

Sally's smile disappeared and he was sorry about that, but not sorry enough to stop driving his point home.

"Yes, Cooper," she whispered, searching his eyes. "You're right. That was really stupid of me."

"Tomorrow I'm going to install a peephole and another deadbolt on the back door. Put alarms on the windows."

"Yes, Cooper."

"I want you safe." The stark words fell out of his mouth, coming straight from deep in his chest, probably somewhere around where his heart would be located, if he had one.

Sally flinched and turned pale. Shit, he was scaring her. *Way to go, Cooper.* The most beautiful and desirable woman in the world, even willing to sleep with him, and he was scaring her.

Couldn't be helped.

"Promise me you won't ever do that again."

"I promise." It was a shaky whisper, those stunning turquoise eyes wide. She reached a hand up and laid it flat against his chest, over his heart. "Believe me, I promise."

Words jostled in Cooper's head, so many he couldn't get any of them out. And none of them could make their way around that searing image burned into his brain, of Sally hurt.

The image fired his blood and he realized he'd kill to keep her safe. His blood was up, along with everything else.

Cooper slid his hands into her hair to keep her head still and bent to kiss her. Her mouth was soft, welcoming, just like he knew her cunt would be. She was ready. Everything in her body told him that. The way she met his tongue eagerly, opening her mouth wider for a better taste of him. The way she twisted against him to touch him in as many places as possible. The way her hands clutched his shoulders.

Her little cunt would be warm and wet, just like it had been an hour ago. He knew that as surely as he knew his name.

The thought of that—of her already wet and soft, waiting for him—filled his head with a roar.

Cooper picked her up and headed for the bedroom. Just making it to a bed seemed like an insane act of self-control because what he really wanted to do was drop to the floor where they stood, open just enough clothes for him to shove his cock in her and start moving, hard and fast.

But the floor was cold and hard and he was heavy. They needed a bed. He moved them into the bedroom, stripping her sweater and bra off before following her down on the bed, mouth fused to hers. He was frantic now, hoping his hands weren't hurting her. Thank God she was wearing a skirt. He lifted it and ripped her panties and stockings off. The sharp ripping sound had hardly finished echoing in the shadowy room when it was followed by the heavy sound of his jeans unzipping. Cooper's tongue probed her mouth deeply as he ran one hand quickly up her thigh while opening her legs with his other hand.

She was wet and moaned into his mouth when he touched her cunt. Soft, warm and welcoming, just like her mouth.

Cooper groaned as he held her open with two fingers and felt her whole body jolt when he thrust hard into her.

Shit!

He held himself deeply within her and raised himself on his forearms. Their eyes met. Arousal and maybe shock enlarged her pupils until there was only a bright turquoise rim around them. Her mouth was wet and swollen from his.

"Foreplay," he gasped. He'd forgotten all about it.

Sally tugged at his stiff neck muscles until his mouth was touching hers.

"Later," she whispered, and kissed him.

Chapter Nine

"Here, honey," Loren Jensen, the grocer, said the next day to his wife, "you can start bagging these." He ticked off the items slowly, but Julia knew better than to fret.

If truth be told, she was even starting to sort of…well…enjoy the slower pace of Simpson. Good thing, too, because the Jensens had to be the most laid-back grocers in America.

Back in Boston, she would have been fidgeting and glancing pointedly at her watch if the grocery store owner had moved with Loren's slow deliberation.

It felt like a lifetime ago that she had drummed her fingers on the steering wheel during a red light, or tapped her foot in line at the bank. There was no reason for that at all in Simpson. Drumming her fingers and tapping her foot wasn't going to speed anything up, and anyway—what was the hurry? She wasn't going anywhere and neither was anyone else.

It reminded her of all the slow-paced places she and her parents had lived in while she was growing up. Later in her father's career, there'd been Paris and London, but before that there'd been a small township outside Dublin and a village close to Amsterdam. Most of her childhood had been lived at the rhythm and pace of small towns and she'd almost completely forgotten it. Until Simpson.

I'm a true Devaux, Julia thought wryly. Digging in. Trying to fit in as much as possible. Before moving on.

Shopping at Jensen's was becoming a pleasant ritual. Loren and Beth were delightful, a sort of mom and pop Laurel and Hardy. Loren was tall and thin and Beth was round and apple-cheeked. She looked a little like the farmer's wife in *Babe*.

Whenever Julia asked for something they didn't keep in stock—special wholegrain breads, Greek yogurt, pasta made from durum wheat—they would take note of it, and order it for her from a Rupert wholesaler.

"...yogurt, milk, eggs, bread—say, ever since you started ordering that oatmeal bread, I've got more and more people asking for it." Loren smiled at Julia and turned to his wife. "Isn't that right, honey?"

"You bet. We're going to try the supplier's bran-nut bread next week. And we sold out of that Greek yogurt you ordered, too. You're not our best customer—you don't eat enough to keep a bird alive, Sally—but you're sure our smartest customer." Beth Jensen smiled at her. "You sure you got everything you need?" She narrowed her eyes and tapped her lip as her eyes swept around the store.

Julia wondered if she was actually seeing her store for what it was, or if she'd been there so long it was invisible to her, like women who couldn't see their living rooms any longer—the faded drapes, scratched furniture and worn upholstery of a house where a young bride had watched her kids grow up and couldn't see that the house had aged right along as well.

The store was small, wider than it was deep, mainly storefront, with sun-faded displays Julia hadn't seen changed in the time she'd been in Simpson. As a matter of fact, the store looked as if nothing much had changed since the Eisenhower Administration.

There was a tinkle from behind and Julia turned. The mayor and owner of Kellogg's Hardware walked in. Glenn Kellogg was middle-aged and paunchy. He usually had a big smile and loud greeting for everyone. He was especially boisterous when he met Julia. Beth said it was because she was the first person to move to Simpson in five years and Glenn liked to think she was the first trickle of a flood of new arrivals. Julia enjoyed his blustering friendliness. He was essentially harmless, if you didn't count his bottomless store of truly awful jokes. She braced herself for one, then saw that he was looking pale and drawn.

"Hello, Glenn," she said.

Glenn nodded, lips compressed. Julia had the feeling that he barely recognized her.

Loren was writing down Julia's new orders for pita bread and plum tomatoes. He looked up with a smile. "Hey, Glenn."

"Hey, Loren." Glenn sketched a smile in return, but his voice was dull, with none of his usual ebullience.

"You okay?" Loren asked.

"Yeah, yeah. Just fine." Glenn didn't look fine. Julia could see his hand shake as he pulled a sheet of paper from his shirt pocket and slowly unfolded it. Even when he had opened it up, he continued to stare at it blankly, as if forgetting what he was reading.

"How's business?" Loren was looking at him curiously.

"Fine." Glenn let the paper drop onto the counter and looked around him, as if surprised to be where he was.

"And the kids? They doing okay in college?"

"Yeah, yeah," Glenn said hollowly. "They're doin' just fine."

"Idaho State, right?"

"Mmm." He absently rubbed his stomach.

"And your ulcer?"

"Fine." Glen pushed his hand through his hair, leaving it standing up. "Just fine."

Loren looked mystified, then bit his lip. "Well, then…you want to show me that list?"

"List?" Glenn looked down, surprised, at the paper curling on the linoleum counter. "Oh, yeah. Here." He thrust it at Loren.

"How's Maisie doing, Glenn?" Beth asked, her voice gentle.

"Oh…fine," Glenn answered. "She's—no." He blinked at Beth helplessly. "No. She's not fine. She's not fine at all. She can't…she won't—hell!" Glenn blew a breath in frustration and his eyes turned glossy.

"It's okay, Glenn. Just calm down now." Beth walked over and put a hand on his shoulder. "She can't what?"

"Anything." Glenn turned to Beth in misery. "She can't do anything anymore. Or won't. I can't tell which. All I know is half the time she won't even get out of bed in the morning. And if she does, she won't get dressed. She's been like that since our youngest started college this September. All she does is stare at the wall and say that nothing makes any difference any more."

"I was pretty depressed when our Karen got married." Beth put her hand on his shoulder. "It was awful. It was as if my life had just…stopped. Then I was put on anti-depression medication and it was a little better, but only because I was so zonked all the time. I didn't really care if I was sad or not."

"Depressed?" Glenn looked uneasily at Beth, then at Loren for help. "Is that what this is? Depression? But what does she have to be depressed about?" He included Julia in his gaze, his pale Simpson-blue eyes watery and pained. "What?" He spread his hands—blunt and calloused, the hands of a man who'd worked hard with them all his life—in supplication. "We have a wonderful marriage. I love Maisie; I've always loved her. We have two great kids. We're healthy, the kids are healthy. What else does she want? What else could she want?" He turned to Loren, then Beth, then Julia. "Huh?"

Loren shrugged his shoulders and evaded Glenn's eyes, clearly ill at ease with the questions and with the emotions coming off Glenn in waves.

Julia met Beth's gaze and the message that passed between them was as old as womankind. *Men. They haven't a clue.*

Julia moved back a step, letting Beth know that dealing with Glenn came well before serving her. Glenn looked as if he'd been blindsided by life.

Julia had met Maisie Kellogg several times. Now that she thought of it, it had been at least a week since she'd last seen Maisie around.

"Well, Glenn." Beth pursed her lips. "I'm not too sure life works that way."

"What way?" Glenn asked.

"Yeah." Loren looked at his wife curiously. "What way?"

"Here, honey. Take care of this, will you? I think Glenn needs a little talking to." Beth pushed Julia's groceries towards Loren. "You see, Glenn, the fact that you're fine and the kids are fine doesn't necessarily mean that Maisie's got to be fine."

"But — but there's nothing wrong." Glenn spread his hands, baffled.

"Glenn." Beth drew in a long breath and let it out slowly. "Do you remember back in '79 when your store burned down and Maisie was pregnant with Rosie?"

"Sure do," Glenn said, smiling faintly. "And Maisie was a rock. She set up a field kitchen and fed the firefighters, then the men who worked on rebuilding the store. And she just refused to go into labor until the store was finished." He shook his head in admiration. "Rosie was born twelve hours after the last nail was hammered."

"And that time you thought you were having a heart attack and the doctors found out it was only a hiatal hernia?"

"Sure." Glenn frowned. "And Maisie drove me to Boise through a snowstorm and didn't leave my side until the doctors told us I'd be fine." He blew out his breath in frustration. "But that's my point, Beth. Maisie and I have been through a lot together. Some bad times, some really rough patches. And she's always come through. What's wrong now?"

"I think," Beth said softly, "I think the problem is that no one needs her any more. The kids are grown. Word has it that you're planning on selling the business..." She looked at him quizzically

"That's right." Glenn looked guiltily at Beth, then Loren. The only hardware store in town closing would make life even harder for the citizens of Simpson. "Town seems to be shrinking and each year our revenue drops. And besides, our Lee doesn't have any intention of continuing the business. Wants to be a history teacher, of all things. It's a real shame. Kellogg's Hardware has been around since 1938. My granddad founded it. I'll keep going another year, maybe two, then if things don't pick up, I'll have to close." He shrugged. "Guess that's life."

"But in the meantime, you have your business. And your Rotary. Hunting in the fall." Beth looked disapprovingly at Glenn and Loren. "Friday night poker."

Both men shuffled uneasily.

"But what does Maisie have?" she continued. "Up until now, she had to look after you, 'cause you had the store. And the kids. But now—"

"I need her," Glenn protested. "I still need her."

"No, you don't." Beth's voice was soft. "You and the kids needed her before. But not now. Now she needs—needs to do something for herself."

"But what? You said you went through this. What did you do?"

"Started helping Loren in the shop." Beth threw a disgusted glance around. "Though to look at it, you wouldn't think that a woman worked here at all."

"Go to work in the shop?" Glenn fingered his chin thoughtfully, then shook his head. "Naah. Maisie hates hardware."

"Well, it doesn't really have to be hardware," Beth said. "Could be anything. What does she like to do?"

"I don't know, really. She never..." Glenn began. Then he brightened. "Cook. She likes to cook. She's a fantastic cook. Knows all about food and things. How about you and Loren—"

"Sorry, Glenn." Loren had finished filling a paper bag with the items on the list. "We're barely making ends meet ourselves.

You know what the local economy's been like for the past couple of years. We might end up closing too. Neither of our kids has any interest in running the business." He sighed. "Or staying in Simpson. None of the kids want to stay. Simpson's going be a ghost town in ten years, you mark my words. You'll just have to find Maisie a job somewhere else."

"Yeah, sure." Glenn's shoulders slumped. "As if there were any of those going around." He paid for his purchases and hefted the bag. "Thanks a lot for listening. Beth. Loren." He nodded to Julia. "Miss Anderson."

Beth accompanied him out the door and gave his shoulder a consolatory pat. "Give Maisie my love. Tell her to call me if she wants to talk." She watched him walk out then lifted her shoulders and turned around with a well-that's-done air.

"Thanks for being so patient," she said to Julia. "I'll ring up your things right away."

"That's okay," Julia said softly. "My mom had a bad depression when I was fifteen. It scared me." Julia didn't even know she was going to say that until she opened her mouth.

"That so?" Beth looked at her sympathetically. "My kids were scared, too, when I had mine, but I just couldn't help myself. And how did you mom finally get out of it?"

"She…" It had been when Julia was fifteen. Her father had suddenly been transferred from Paris to Riyadh. Her mother had loved Paris and had hated Saudi Arabia. She hated the demeaning restrictions on women, the dour, cultureless, male-dominated society. Then, one Saturday, Julia had come across her mother, the Ambassador's wife, the wife of the cultural attaché, and the wife of the rumored CIA officer driving around the huge Embassy compound since they weren't allowed to drive anywhere else, tipsy from drinking too much of the port the Ambassador's wife had smuggled into the country in the diplomatic pouch, singing "There is Nothing Like a Dame" at the top of their voices.

After that, Alexandra Devaux had settled down to make the best life she could for herself and her family in Riyadh. As she'd managed to do everywhere they had lived.

Julia blinked back tears. She wished she could tell Beth the story. She was sure Beth would love it. But Beth thought she was Sally Anderson, who had never been outside the country and whose mother was alive and living in Bend.

"Sally?" Beth was watching her, head cocked to one side. "What happened to your mom?"

Julia surreptitiously wiped her eye, her mind racing. "Oh, she—she signed up as a volunteer to help migrant workers' children learn to read English. Then she became an after-school tutor. She's still doing it." As lies went, it wasn't too bad. Particularly since it was a spur-of-the-moment one. And it was probably what her mother would have done if she'd been Laverne Anderson instead of Alexandra Devaux.

Beth sighed. "That's what Maisie needs too. You know what I think? I think she'd be a great cook. But who's going to hire a cook in Simpson?" Beth shook her head sadly and moved behind the counter. She started ticking off Julia's items. "Box of rice, canned tomato sauce, macaroni—no it's not called that nowadays, pasta—decaffeinated coffee. Well, that seems to be it. Oh!" She reached out and placed a six-pack of beer on top of Julia's groceries. "Almost forgot this."

"But—but—I don't want beer," Julia protested. She preferred wine, though one sip of Loren's jug wine had left what felt like a permanent hole in her stomach. She'd steered clear of it ever since. "I don't particularly like beer."

"It's not for you, dear," Beth said easily. "It's for Coop. His favorite brand."

"I…" Julia felt her face flame. "Oh, it's…um…" Words defeated her. Her tongue disconnected completely from her brain and flapped around uselessly in her mouth. "Okay, um, just…just add it to the bill."

"Nah," Loren said. "I owe Coop. He loaned me one of his pickups when our delivery van broke down. Tell him it's on the house."

"Well…thank you, then."

"Our pleasure." Loren handed over the two bags of groceries and put his arm around his wife's ample shoulders.

Beth beamed, rosy little apple cheeks gleaming. "We're just so glad Coop's finally getting laid," she said.

Chapter Ten

"Well?" Alice watched Julia expectantly Saturday morning, pale blue eyes unblinking.

Julia put another bite of the lemon tart in her mouth, just to make sure she hadn't made a mistake.

"What do you think?" Alice asked expectantly.

Wonderful, Julia thought. *If you like diabetic comas.* "Um, Alice," Julia began, not wanting to hurt the girl's feelings, "did you follow my recipe exactly?"

"Sure." Alice frowned. "I mean, I thought it was a little skimpy on the sugar, so I added some."

"Well, maybe it would be better to just stick to the original recipe," Julia said diplomatically.

"You bet." Alice grinned at her. "I'm going to follow your advice right down the line from now on. I've had three repeat customers for the tea and Karen Lindberger said that she was going to try to convince some of her friends in the Rupert Ladies' Association to have some meetings here. Can you imagine? Karen said she'd told the president of the Ladies' Association that she'd talk to the manager about it. She meant me." Alice splayed a hand across her chest and beamed. "The manager."

Julia winced and made a conscious effort not to look around her, at dingy walls and scuffed flooring. Manager. Warden was more like it.

"That's nice," she said, trying to be enthusiastic for Alice's sake. "I'll give you some more pie and cake recipes next week."

"Thanks." Alice poured Julia some tea and watched her face. "So what do you think about the tea?"

"This is excellent," Julia said between sips, and it was. "Congratulations."

Alice sat back, pleased. They had the diner to themselves. Contrary to Alice's rising expectations, it was still empty on a Saturday morning. Julia was there because it was Saturday and Saturday was coffee shop time. She was also there sort of waiting for Cooper who'd sort of offered to drive her to Rupert today.

But that had been a week ago and he hadn't mentioned it since. They hadn't actually...talked much since. Her evenings and nights had fallen into a pattern. Cooper came over in the late afternoon, and while she brought Rafael up to speed with his homework, Cooper worked on her house in silence. The boiler ran like a dream, nothing in the house leaked, the porch step didn't creak and above all, she seemed to have every safety device known to man.

He'd suddenly become obsessed with her safety, so each door had a gleaming new lock and safety chain, her doors and windows were alarmed and linked to the sheriff's office, there were peepholes front and back, and what Cooper called "safety lighting" outdoors but was actually floodlights fit for theater so she could see who was outside the house.

It was all a little over the top for Simpson but Julia needed safety and she had to admit it did make her feel very secure. Short of an axe cutting through her doors, she was protected.

Not to mention the fact that the greatest safety system of all was in her bed all night—Sam Cooper.

After working on her house and driving Rafael home, Cooper came right back, herded her into the bedroom, stripped her, stripped himself, dropped her on the bed and dropped right on top of her. A second after that, they were making love. Hard and fast.

It wasn't the stuff of romantic novels, but it was exciting as hell. Julia had had ten times more orgasms the past few evenings than in her entire lifetime. They didn't stop to talk, they didn't stop to eat, they didn't stop to sleep. Before Cooper, she had had no idea that it was physically possible to make love for hours, night after night.

Sometimes Cooper was still erect when he pulled out of her before dawn. He'd get dressed, leave with a kiss and Julia would sleep like the dead until seven-thirty. Though she was about fifty-two hours behind on sleep, she was revved, not tired at all. And between school, Rafael, Fred and Cooper, she was kept busy all the time. No time to think. There had been no nightmares. How could there be? Her nights were filled with heat and sex.

Maybe she should tell the guys at the Witness Security Program about hot sex to keep their protectees in line.

"So," said Alice casually. "You going to Rupert with Coop?"

Julia stared. "How on earth did you know—" Then she broke off. The small-town bush telegraph. "I don't know," she told Alice truthfully. "I mean Cooper mentioned it last Saturday, just sort of casually, but he hasn't spoken of it since." She shrugged. "So...I don't know. Maybe he forgot. Or maybe he's busy."

"Oh, if Coop said he'd do something, he'll do it," Alice assured her earnestly. "Coop's a man of his word."

"When he talks," Julia said. She could feel herself turning bright red. Talking was not what Cooper did best.

"Well, yeah." Alice was studying her face and Julia wondered what she was reading there. "Coop's not much of a talker. But he's a good man, y'know?"

"Yes." Julia blushed brighter.

"I mean he's, he's...kinda quiet. It sort of makes it easy to—well, to underestimate him. His wife sure did."

The curiosity that welled up was impossible to repress. Julia didn't even try. This isn't gossiping, she told herself primly. Just a healthy interest in human nature. And a healthy interest in the nature of a man who'd become her lover. She leaned forward and tried to keep her voice casual. "His wife? What was she like?"

"Who, Melissa?" Alice made to pour more tea, but Julia shook her head and placed her hand over her cup. "Melissa worked for Coop's stockbrokers in Seattle. You wouldn't know it from his lifestyle, but Coop is actually a very rich man and Melissa knew what he was worth. They did all their courting in Seattle and he just showed up one day with this woman he'd married." Alice wrinkled her nose. "We all made an effort, for Coop's sake, but she never really fit in."

"What a shame." Julia barely stopped herself from tsk-tsking.

"And another thing," Alice continued. "Melissa always made this big point about how she'd sacrificed an incredible professional career to come bury herself here and how an MBA was wasted in the backwoods of Idaho." Suddenly, a wicked grin crossed Alice's sweet face, startling Julia. "Then Matt, my brother—"

"I've met him," Julia murmured.

"Yeah?" Alice rolled her eyes. "Then you'll know what a pain in the butt he is. Actually, at the time, he was only a fledgling pain. But he got as sick of her moans and groans as the rest of us did, so he logged into the University of Washington records and discovered that dear Melissa hadn't actually, technically speaking, graduated. Then he logged on to the stockbroker's files and discovered that Melissa was only a secretary there. And all this time, Coop had been too of a gentleman to say anything."

Julia could see it. See where remaining silent would be not only the natural thing but also the gentlemanly thing for Cooper to do.

"After a while, Melissa was complaining to everyone about how boring Coop was." All of a sudden Alice skewered Julia with a sharp, pale-blue gaze. "You don't think Coop's boring, do you?"

Julia was startled. Cooper? Boring? She shifted in her seat and felt well-used muscles ache. It took her until midmorning to get over the stiffness in her thighs.

"No," she answered truthfully. "I think he's mysterious and fascinating and a little frustrating — but boring? Never."

"Okay." Alice blinked. A slow smile creased her pretty young face. "Okay. That's great. I had this feeling about you — "

"Ahm, Alice, look." Julia shifted uneasily. Did the whole town match-make? This…thing, whatever it was, with Cooper was temporary. Julia was shooting back to Boston just as soon as the mess with Santana was over. "If you're thinking what I think you're thinking — "

Alice stood up, not listening, clearing the table. "I knew it, I just knew it. This is great. 'Bout time Cooper got laid again. And you're much too smart to pay any attention to that stupid curse."

Julia froze. Curse? Had she missed something here? Some important conversational cue? "Alice? What curse?"

But Alice had disappeared into the kitchen.

"Alice? Alice?" Julia raised her voice, almost shouting. "What curse are you talking about?"

Alice stuck her head out from the kitchen. "The Cooper Curse, of course." Her eyes widened as she looked past Julia. "Hi, Coop. You're sure looking spiffy. You get all dressed up to get married or buried?"

* * * * *

"He's just upped the ante by another million." Aaron Barclay tossed an audio cassette at his boss.

Herbert Davis didn't bother lifting his eyes from the file he was reading. He simply reached out and plucked the cassette from the air. Davis glanced up to catch the look of surprise on his assistant's face and bit back a smile. His wind and his waistline might be gone, but there was nothing wrong with his eye-hand coordination. "Who?" he asked, "upped what?"

"Santana." Aaron Barclay grimaced in distaste. "It's all right there on the tape. His lieutenant just sent out word to the street from Santana that the price for Julia Devaux's head has been increased by another mil."

Davis stopped fingering the cassette and stared. "Fuck," he breathed. "Santana's offering—" Davis stopped for a minute, hardly believing his own words, "two million dollars for—for…"

"Julia Devaux's head." Barclay's voice was grim. "That part hasn't changed."

"But that—that's crazy." Davis caught himself. "Well…crazy. What does the word 'crazy' mean when applied to a psychopath like Santana? And what the hell does he care what he's spending? If Devaux's dead, he gets off and he's still got another 348 million in the bank. But still—this is…this is against the rules. This means we're going to have every two-bit wiseguy wannabe in the country wanting to make his bones and earn a fortune all at the same time. It's going to be a zoo out there. What brought this on? I thought S. T. Akers was doing a pretty good job of stalling."

Barclay perched a hip on Davis' desk. "Yeah, but Judge Bromfield has decided that pending the trial, Santana is to be remanded to Furrow Island. Judge Bromfield has this thing about mobsters and she's making a point, probably for the benefit of Akers. His boy wants to stall, she's going to make him pay for it." Barclay shuddered. "Tell you the truth, boss, if I had two million, I'd use it to stay out of The Furrow myself."

"Furrow Island." Davis had been to Furrow Island once, to take a deposition. It was an experience he wasn't eager to repeat. Bleak cinderblock buildings on a bleak, windswept island. Inside had reigned something as close to hell as he ever wanted to see on this earth, a sort of legal no man's land where the most violent and crazed prisoners were sent. The guardians locked the prisoners up and threw away the key, letting each man fend for himself. It was basically a dumpster for the deranged.

Davis knew that Santana was a tough man, with the violent makeup of the born criminal. But Santana had been a rich man for many, many years now and rich men grow soft over time. They become used to having other people do their dirty work for them and no matter what else it is, violence is dirty work.

Davis wondered how many years it had been since Santana had got his hands dirty—or his knuckles bloodied. He wondered if Santana remembered how. Well, if Santana was headed for The Furrow, it would doubtless come back to him. Fast.

In the meantime, the D of J was left with a problem.

"Pressure's really going to be on, now," Barclay mused.

"Yeah." Davis rolled his head. The muscles in his shoulders had suddenly seized up. "Not too many hotdoggers out there are going to turn down the possibility of two million bucks... *Shit*!"

He banged his fist on the desk in frustration, then lunged for the papers that began sliding off. He gathered the papers together, tapping the edges, more to give his hands something to do than anything else. Then he stared at Barclay. Barclay stared right back. They were thinking the same thing.

Barclay spoke first. "We could take her out of there."

"We could." Davis nodded. "But where? Where would be safer?"

"Can't take her out of the country, that's illegal," Barclay said with regret. He crossed his arms and looked up at the ceiling, considering. "So would putting her behind bars. Behind bars is about the only place we'd be sure of her."

Davis thought longingly of putting Julia Devaux in a Club Fed—some posh federal facility with saunas and tennis courts, but the law said you couldn't do that, more's the pity. You couldn't imprison a citizen whose only crime was being in the wrong place at the wrong time. So what was left?

"How many people we got in Boise?" Davis began running through the options in his head.

"Eight."

"That's ridiculous," Davis said indignantly. "Hell, any metropolitan service station worth its gas pump has more staffing than that."

"Budget cuts," Barclay answered laconically. "And they've been cutting deeper and deeper."

Davis drummed his fingers. "What are the resources in Boise?"

"Here." Barclay handed over the Boise station file and Davis rifled through it. There was no one from Boise who could be spared. As a matter of fact, he didn't know how they kept their Boise office open and running. He looked up at Barclay. "Could we take Grizzard and Martinez off the Krohn case?"

Barclay shook his head. "We've got a personal request from Senator Fillmore about that one. He wants it to be given 'maximum consideration'. His very words. And you know how much political interest there is in the Krohn case. Santana's just a crook. Big-time crook, admittedly, but his case is nothing compared to the Krohn case, where a conviction will be worth ten thousand votes. Elections are coming up. So...ix-nay. Politics always win out over crime around here, especially since..." Barclay jerked a thumb upwards, "took over."

Davis nodded wearily. "Can't put trainees on a case like this, that's for sure. Who's left?" He took off his glasses and pinched the bridge of his nose. "What about Pacini?"

Barclay crossed his arms, a small smile on his face. This was going to be fun. "Pacini's on...paternity leave," he said.

"What!" Davis rose out of his chair like a rocket then sank heavily back. He took in a deep breath then let it out slowly until he could make his voice neutral. He rolled his eyes. "Paternity leave. Oh, God, just what we need. I can't believe this. Paternity leave. What's next? Sick leave for hangnails? Compassionate leave when your dog buys it?"

"Come on, Herb. I've heard the Old Timer's Lament until it comes out my ears. How tough you guys were, how nothing stopped you."

"Damn straight." Davis nodded. "You got shot, you took two aspirin and reported for work the next day. In my day, when a kid was born, you got the afternoon off and a cigar. No exceptions." Davis knew he was sounding like a dinosaur. Hell, sometimes he felt like a dinosaur. Old and scaly and on the verge of extinction. "I missed two of my kids' deliveries."

"I didn't see my firstborn for a month." Barclay's voice was low with regret. "Maybe that's why my wife left me."

Davis looked at his assistant's bare left hand with the white line on the ring finger. The guy was having a tough time dealing with the divorce. Office scuttlebutt had it the wife was taking him to the cleaners, too.

There was an uneasy silence.

"So...enough of that." Davis changed gears and flipped through the Boise file once again. "Looks like we're not going to have any extra manpower available for another what—two, three months? By that time, Julia Devaux will either be testifying in court under oath or she'll be..." he hesitated.

"Toast," Barclay said.

Chapter Eleven

Julia started to settle into the pickup's roomy front seat when she froze. Her eyes widened. "C-Cooper?"

The pickup dipped to take Cooper's weight and he pulled the driver's door closed with a soft *whump*.

"Mmm?"

"Cooper." Her voice sank to a whisper as she leaned close to him. "There's a—a gun in here."

Cooper threw an indifferent glance behind him, then put the pickup in gear. "Nope," he said.

"No?" Julia asked, confused. The pickup shot forward and she hung onto the seatbelt.

"Not a gun."

Julia had been astounded at the difference the sleekly cut businessman's suit had made. It hadn't made him handsome—nothing could do that—but it had certainly made him look...imposing. Forbidding.

He had stood before her in Alice's shabby little diner in his elegant suit, tall and large and powerful, face cold and hard and remote and for just a fraction of a second, Julia had had a panicked jolt of fear at the thought of driving out alone into the wilderness with this man who looked so forbidding. It was a flash of feeling, gone in an instant.

Cooper wasn't dangerous to her. She knew that. After all, she'd been sleeping with the man this past week. But it was very easy to separate the man who warmed her bed at night from this powerful, dangerous-looking man.

Then Alice had shoved a slice of that awful diabetic's nightmare of a pie in his hand and Cooper had gamely eaten it.

Julia had watched him and their eyes had met for a moment, and she could tell they were thinking the same thing—*isn't it awful?* But he had praised the pie in a low gentle voice, and smiled faintly when Alice beamed at him, though the smile had faltered when Alice had cut him a second slice, "on the house". And, to his everlasting credit, he had choked that down, too.

Julia could imagine a lot of things—it was one of her many failings—but she couldn't imagine a violent man choking down a second slice of that pie for friendship's sake. And when he had looked up at her, all she could see in his dark-brown eyes was kindness and maybe some loneliness. A little like Fred's.

But here she was, driving off into the wild blue yonder with a man who had a gun, right in the cab of the pickup, in touching distance, and her imagination started overheating again. Then Cooper started doing that sexy business with his thighs and something else started overheating. Julia looked away for a moment, then brought her eyes back and fixed them determinedly on Cooper's face. "You're trying to tell me that that—" she jerked her chin, not wanting to touch the wretched thing " —isn't a gun?"

"No," Cooper said, "it's a Springfield. Good hunting rifle."

"Oh." Julia was silent for a moment then twisted in her seat. Sure enough, there it was still, long and gleaming and deadly. She had never shared a space with a gun—a rifle—in her life. She didn't think even think she'd ever shared a space with a person who shared a space with a gun. Or rifle.

"You planning on shooting anyone in Rupert today?"

Cooper thought. "Well, now that you mention it, I wasn't too happy with the quality of the feed Davis Walker sold me last week—" He turned at her gasp. "That was a joke, Sally."

"Oh." The panic subsided but the worry didn't. "That's good. That's very good. So what do you need—" she jerked her chin backwards again, " —that for?"

"Actually, it's not mine. Bernie's the one who usually uses this pickup and that Springfield is his. I prefer shotguns myself."

"And what does Bernie use a gun—a rifle for?"

"Varmints."

Outside of old reruns of *Bonanza*, and a zillion B westerns, Julia had never heard the term used in real life. "Varmints? Like what—cattle rustlers?"

Cooper was still doing that little dance with the clutch and brake pedal, accompanied on the gearshift, and she was trying not to stare in fascination, so she missed his expression but she did hear what sounded a lot like a chuckle. From Cooper?

"What?" They were moving out towards the highway now and his legs stayed put and Julia could relax. She looked at him and thought she could detect a smile.

"Not many cattle rustlers left and we don't have cattle anyway. Bernie shoots at muskrats and jackrabbits, mostly. In hunting season, he might bag a deer or two. We're all partial to venison." He glanced at her and frowned. "Does the gun bother you, Sally? Do you want me to stow it in the back? Though it's safer in the gun rack. And I promise you it's unloaded. Ammo's in the glove compartment."

Julia was reminded again of all the reasons why she lived in the city. The city was where you went to a restaurant with nice waiters who put on your plate things people who lived in the country had to shoot and skin.

"N-no, that's okay." She didn't want him to think of her as some kind of wimp. This was the West after all. Kids probably cut their teeth on bullets out here. "I was just taken aback for a minute. I mean after all," she said, trying to reassure herself, "of course, you do know how to use it."

"Sure I do," Cooper said and pressed on the accelerator as he came to an open stretch. He flicked a glance at her. "But I'm even better with a knife."

* * * * *

Two million dollars for Julia Devaux's head.

The professional snorted in disdain at the message on the screen. Santana was definitely out of control.

The whole world was out of control.

It wasn't like the old days when the known world was divided up among twelve, maybe fifteen strong men. Men who ruled with iron and blood, merciless and resolute and who were never, never out of control. Men who could be counted on to follow the rules. Men who would never be sending these pitiful messages from jail, clear signs of weakness.

A million dollars for a hit was already outrageous, against all the rules.

Hits went for a hundred thou — two tops. Offering more wasn't going to get the job done any better — all it would do would be to smoke out the bolos who lived under the bridges and in the basement tenements and inflame them with hope. They would only get in the way of the pros and clutter up the territory. Offering another million dollars was insane. The Old Men would never have tolerated it for a moment, Furrow's Island or not. But apparently they were gone and the quiet deadly rules which had governed the world were shattered.

It was a sign that it was time to quit. No doubt about it. The two million of Santana's money would be put to good use. Money was wasted on thugs like Santana anyway. He hadn't the faintest idea what money was for. The Old Men had known that money was a precision tool — a scalpel, not a bludgeon.

The professional stared out through the floor to ceiling windows of the penthouse apartment, watching as storm clouds gathered. The view was excellent, as the real estate agent had pointed out. The real estate agent had happily walked away from the sale thinking the view had closed the deal. The pretty, young agent had never even dreamed that the sale had been made because — short of a sniper in a helicopter — the penthouse was out of the range of gunfire.

Sleety rain spattered the bulletproof glass. Winter was coming early. It was time to nail Julia Devaux and disappear to the Caribbean.

The professional exercised the sternest mental discipline when focused on a mission, but for just a moment it was easy to daydream a little about the beach house while the rain turned to hail and the sky grew dark. Lights started coming on early in the downtown office buildings in the distance. Ten stories below, people scurried for cover, the wind whipping at raincoats and jackets.

The house on St. Lucia sat on a bluff overlooking an unbroken stretch of sand as fine as face powder. The water was the same color as the sky and you could still see the bottom a mile out.

The professional was under no illusions about the people on the island. The Caribbean was full of shady characters, tax exiles most of them, many of them businessmen who had sailed just a little too close to the wind. People who would probably pay very good money for tips on how to shift currencies around, no questions asked. It would be very pleasant—and lucrative—advising them. It was going to be nice dealing with people whose money didn't come in suitcases of small-denomination bills.

The wind could be heard through the thick leaded panes, which meant that it must be howling outside. Sheet lightning lit up the sky and the clouds piled up, gray on gray.

The professional poured two fingers of *Calvados* and contemplated a future of sandy beaches, eternal sunshine and a better class of criminal.

* * * * *

Cooper remembered reading somewhere that scientists had figured out why some people were considered beautiful. It was a trick played on the mind by geometry. Beauty was symmetry, it was as simple as that. If the two sides of the face were equal—bingo! Movie star or cover girl.

Cooper risked a glance at the woman sitting beside him. One front tooth was slightly crooked and her right eyebrow had a higher arch than the left. Most of the time her smile was lopsided. And yet she was stunning. He couldn't keep his eyes off her. Which just went to show that scientists didn't know shit from shinola.

Wherever Sally was, there was a vibrancy in the air, like around a hummingbird. There was a glow to her, as if she were lit from within. As if there were a gently banked fire and all he had to do was hold out his hands and the coldness he felt inside would dissipate.

It was a good thing he could drive to Rupert blindfolded because he was so easily distracted by the emotions which crossed her expressive face, everything upfront, in vivid Technicolor. Her coloring was so exquisite, from the pearly perfection of her skin with faint peach undertones, to the deep turquoise eyes and the finely arched auburn brows.

When he got up the courage, he was going to ask her to let her hair grow back out red. As a redhead, Sally would be utterly irresistible.

What an asshole he was. He couldn't even get up the courage to ask her to grow her hair out.

He'd probably fucked Sally more in this past week than he'd fucked his wife during the entire course of their marriage. It was true he hadn't yet explored her entire body. He hadn't gone down on her; hell, they'd never even made it beyond the missionary position. He'd never become sated enough to try something new. But he did know exactly what made her come and was eager—at some point in the future in which he wasn't crazy to be in her—to lazily explore new ways to make love. He did know how her nipples tasted, the sexy little moans she made when he fucked her hard—not that he'd ever fucked her any other way—the tight contractions around him when she came…

Shit. Another hard-on. Good thing he'd kept his suit jacket on. *Think about something else*, he ordered himself. But his thoughts kept wandering back to Sally. He felt closer to her than he'd ever felt to a woman. Much closer than he'd ever felt to Melissa, that's for sure.

Cooper wondered with deep unease whether she found his silences offensive or strange. Melissa had complained loudly and often about his silences, accusing him of ignoring her.

Sally was a talker. Ordinarily, that would irritate him. He was a loner by temperament and by inclination, but he found himself ineluctably drawn in by her gentle voice as she talked about her week. She was delightful to listen to—articulate and amusing.

Then as he listened to her, he grew more and more astounded as she described her dealings with the people in Simpson. Was it possible that there were two different towns with the same name? How could he have been in the same places at the same time as she had been and not notice what was going on? She told him all about the lives of people he'd known for years. How could she know all this stuff? And why didn't he know it?

He learned that there was something called an "empty nest syndrome" and that Maisie Kellogg was suffering from it and that Beth Jensen had had it as well and that Chuck Pedersen was still depressed over Carly's death. As he listened to her talk about the people he had grown up with, he was amazed and a little saddened. Why didn't anyone ever say anything to him?

Where had he been while all this was going on?

For a while there, as Cooper drove her through the wilderness, Julia thought he didn't talk to her much because she was a woman. She kept stealing quick glances at his hard, craggy face and finally decided that he was probably an equal-opportunity non-speaker.

It occurred to her, not for the first time, that she knew his body more intimately than what went on in his head. They'd had the most intense sex she'd ever had in her life, and she couldn't get him to open his mouth.

Ordinarily, she wouldn't press anyone to talk to her if they didn't want to. Well, all right, she'd rather talk than not any day, but still...you had to respect people's choices. Even if the choices were hard to understand—like not talking.

But she was out in the wild now, out in the open. Out where there were no people, only long sweeps of grass. And then, even worse, a few miles out of Simpson the landscape changed and they drove straight into the heart of first-growth forest where tall, frighteningly dark trees blotted out the sun.

The landscape was as empty as her soul—as her life.

Her life. Julia tried hard not to think about what would happen to her life. Later. After the trial, if she made it that far. She wouldn't really have a life to go back to.

If she got back.

She knew perfectly well that her job wouldn't be waiting for her when she got back. Oh, the company might keep her on, if the government made a fuss about it, but it would be some low-level paper-pushing job, not the real editing she'd finally moved up to.

* * * * *

In the corporate world, nobody's leaving left a hole. Corporations were like the ocean. Waves just washed over the empty spaces and you never knew that anyone had been there.

Federico Fellini was with another family now and as long as he was getting ample rations and no one bothered him, he was perfectly happy. Jean and Dora would think about her on Saturday mornings, but that was about it. There was no empty space in Boston that she could step back into. She hadn't been there long enough to put down roots. Actually, she had never been anywhere long enough to put down roots, Julia thought sadly.

For better or worse, her life in Simpson was her life now.

She shivered and barely noticed when Cooper bent to turn on the heating system. She wasn't cold outside, she was cold inside. Cold and miserable and lonely.

177

Who knew how many men were gunning for her? Herbert Davis kept trying to sound reassuring when she called, but she could tell he was worried. Worried about the case, worried about the testimony. Worried that she wouldn't make it.

Well, so was she.

Still, probably as long as she was in a moving vehicle with Cooper, she was safe. She didn't need to look across to the steering wheel to know that his hands were large and competent. That he was tall and strong. That he seemed to know how to do just about anything.

If they had a flat tire, he could probably hold the vehicle up with a rope held between his teeth and change the tire while fending off marauders. He was, after all, a trained soldier. And to top it all off, there was even a gun in the truck and Cooper had said that he knew how to use it.

Then again, he had also said he was better with a knife.

Julia shuddered at the direction her thoughts had taken. She felt completely lost and alone, out of her depth. What was she doing here? In a place where she was a stranger, in the most literal sense of the term. She wanted to drown her black, bleak thoughts but she didn't have anything to drown them in—not an old film, not a good book, not even some whisky.

All she had was Cooper. Cooper was very good for drowning bleak thoughts in sex at night. But now it was daytime and they couldn't have sex, not while he was driving. So he had to talk to her.

"Cooper?"

"Yeah?"

"Talk to me." Julia could hear the wistful note in her own voice.

"Talk to you?" Julia could hear the tension in Cooper's voice. "What do you want me to talk about?"

"Tell me—tell me about the Cooper Curse," she said.

"Fuck. Sorry." Cooper's knuckles turned white on the steering wheel. "Where did you hear about that?"

"Oh…" she stalled. "Just around."

"It's nothing." Cooper's voice was low and tight. "A silly legend."

"About what?" When he was silent for a long moment, she repeated the question in a soft voice. "A silly legend about what, Cooper?"

The silence stretched on until it was clear that he wasn't going to answer. She'd asked twice. To ask again would be impolite. She was formulating a comment about something neutral, something Cooper would perceive as non-threatening, possibly something inanimate, when she heard his low growl. "What do you want to know?"

He wasn't happy about it. But he was talking to her and that was better than silence.

"Well…what is it? I mean, obviously it's a curse and it affects your family if it's a Cooper Curse — as opposed to a Smith Curse or a Jones Curse. It must be fascinating to have a family curse," she said earnestly. "They have such an impeccable literary pedigree. Like *The Canterville Ghost*." She turned to Cooper and smiled. "Think of it as being part of a longstanding literary tradition."

She thought she heard a little sigh. "Er…" he said, and stopped.

"Cooper?" She waited a full minute. "You still there?"

"Yeah." There were little groupings of houses now. They were approaching Rupert. "I told you about my great-great grandfather, didn't I?"

"The twelfth of twelve?" Julia nodded. "The guy who built the original Biosphere."

"Right." They were in the outskirts of Rupert now. Julia hadn't made it this far before turning around. She was surprised to see how attractive it was. "He came out West in 1899 and was granted the statutory hundred and thirty acres. Once he proved his claim, he got himself a mail-order bride."

"Well, that was strange."

"It wasn't strange in those days, it was sheer survival. Men outnumbered women by about a hundred to one. If you wanted a bride and a shot at a family, you had to import her, like you imported whisky and guns."

"Only with whisky and guns you could specify the brand, presumably." Her voice was tart.

Cooper shot her an odd glance. "That's right. And he…imported the wrong brand."

"What was wrong with her? Was she defective? Short shelf-life?" Cooper winced as he heard the sarcasm in her voice. "Not up to spec? Though I suppose in those days it must have been hard to send items back to the factory."

"He fell in love with her," Cooper said flatly. "She was Irish, like him. Her parents had taken the family over to America during the potato famine, but then they were both taken ill with influenza. This was before antibiotics. She was left on her own at sixteen, which is when she saw the ad in a newspaper. It was either marry a man she'd never met before or starve. She wrote my great-great grandfather and sent him a daguerreotype. My great-great-grandfather burned it later, when she left him, but they say she was a great beauty. He sent her the money and she traveled west. The problems began almost immediately. It seems that my great-great grandfather was a difficult man. A…taciturn man."

You don't say, Julia thought. "Well…" she said kindly, "a glib tongue isn't everything."

Cooper shot her a questioning glance. "No, I suppose not. Still, the people in Simpson could tell that things were going badly."

"Simpson existed even back then?" Julia found it hard to imagine that Simpson was what? Over a hundred years old.

"Yeah. It was just a hole in the wall back then."

As opposed to the bustling metropolis it is today, Julia thought. After a moment or two of silence, she gave him a verbal nudge. "So...we have your great-great grandfather, who wasn't much of a talker, and his beautiful wife. They're not getting on. They have a child. A boy."

Cooper's head jerked around. "You already know the story," he said accusingly.

"Nope." She sent him a smug smile. "You told me that much. Besides, if they hadn't had a child, a male child, to carry on the Cooper name, you wouldn't be here now, telling me all about it, would you?"

"No, I guess not." Cooper's thighs and forearms started dancing again as traffic thickened. If she hadn't been so interested in the story, Julia would have become completely distracted. "Anyway, to cut a long story short, she stayed just long enough to wean Ethan —"

"Your great grandfather."

Cooper nodded. "My great grandfather. Just long enough to wean him and ensure that he would survive. He was two when my great grandmother ran off. She just up and went one day, nobody knows where."

"Didn't he try to track her down?"

"No. They say he never spoke again."

"Wow." Julia was busy trying to fit all these details into the image she had of Cooper. "Did he ever remarry?"

"No. He just kept working the farm and making a little more money each year. Then he decided to import some stallions. That was the beginning of the stud farm."

"So you're a fifth-generation breeder." And a fifth generation non-talker. Maybe he was genetically hardwired for non-communication.

"Yeah." Cooper allowed himself a small smile. "We're fairly well-known."

That was an understatement. Loren Jensen had told her that the Cooper stud farm was one of the best in the country. "So what happened next?"

Cooper frowned. "What do you mean?"

"Cooper." Julia threw him a reproachful glance. "One bad marriage does not a Curse make. Any curse worth its name needs some bells and whistles. So what happened? Did your great-great grandmother die and haunt the property or something? Or maybe—let's see—"

Cooper shook his head. "Nope, it was just an old-fashioned bolt. She never came back. Either in the flesh or in the spirit."

"So then what happened?"

Cooper sighed. "Then my great-grandfather grew up and inherited the farm and imported more horses. He was the one who really started breeding scientifically. He was one of the first in this country to apply Mendelian genetics to horse breeding. He imported three Arabians in 1937…"

"Cooper…" Julia said in exasperation, "the Curse."

"Oh." He pursed his lips. "Yeah. Well, my great-grandmother had my grandfather and, after five years of marriage, she ran away with the Singer man." He thought for a moment. "She took the sewing machine with her."

"And your grandmother?"

Cooper swerved into a parking place. "Ran off with the foreman."

"And your mother died when you were small," Julia said slowly. "And…and your wife left you. That's all very sad. But where is the Curse in all of this?"

He was at the passenger door. "Well…" Cooper was looking very unhappy. He helped her down. "I guess people started putting two and two together and coming up with five. The legend is that that no woman—no female—can live on the Double C. That the Double C is cursed to be womanless. By some fluke, we also breed more colts than fillies." He put a hand to her back and they started walking.

Julia was silent as they crossed the street. On the other side, she looked up at him, disappointed. "That's it? That's the curse?"

"That's the curse."

"You didn't leave anything out? No wailing ghosts, no clanking chains?"

"Nope."

"Just Cooper women who run away from Cooper men?"

Cooper winced. "That's about the size of it."

Julia turned it all over in her mind. "Well..." she said consideringly and watched Cooper tense. "I think that's ridiculous. I can't believe the things people make up."

"You—what?" Cooper stared.

"I was expecting something more exciting. A curse. A proper one. I mean all you've told me is that there have been some troubled marriages in your family. So what? What's the big deal? That's not a curse. That's life."

He stopped suddenly, right in the middle of the sidewalk. "Do you mean that?"

"Sure I do." She blinked and smiled. "A curse," she said, waving her hand dismissively. "I think that's the silliest thing I ever heard."

"Me, too," he said, and she could hear the relief in his voice. "Let's get going, then. You'll want some time in the bookshop. Then I know a great place for lunch."

* * * * *

Richard Abt, a.k.a. Robert Littlewood, stepped off the curb in Rockville, Idaho. He wasn't particularly looking where he was going because there was little need to do so. Rockville was a quiet little town and he was in the residential district. Few cars were to be seen on Crescent Drive, which was a quiet, leafy road.

Abt was lost in thought. He was due to testify in five months' time, at which point he could go back to his former life, but the thought had little appeal. He wasn't married and there wasn't anyone waiting for him. Besides, there was a crying need for accountants in this part of the world. He could settle in nicely here in a private practice.

Abt was happily immersed in thoughts of setting up a practice of his own—he could quietly put the word around at the next Lion's Club meeting—when a car suddenly pulled out from the curb.

He didn't have a chance.

By the time the low growl of the engine registered on his startled senses, he was already flying over the hood like a limp, boneless rag.

* * * * *

"Good story, isn't it?" Cooper asked quietly. "Just shows what the human spirit can endure."

Julia looked up, confused. She had to wrench her attention back to the here and now. She had been totally immersed in Song Li's story, transported to Vietnam in the early '60s. It was a riveting book already in the first few pages. The back blurb promised the history of the Vietnamese conflict as seen through the eyes of a young girl growing up during the war.

Julia knew she was definitely going to buy it. "Have you read it?"

Cooper nodded.

Julia closed the paperback and tapped the cover. *Salted Earth*. "Is it as good as they say it is?" She'd read the reviews when it had been published and had been intrigued, but had never gotten around to reading it.

"Better." Cooper put down the pile of books he was carrying and picked it up. "I read it when it first came out. What a hellhole it was over there. It's a wonder the woman survived in any shape to tell the tale." His face was remote, unsmiling as if he were remembering something horrible.

"Oh, Cooper," Julia breathed. She hadn't thought...and yet she'd seen a thousand made-for-TV movies. And now a lot of things about Cooper made sense. She stepped closer and put a hand on his arm. It was like touching iron. Warm iron. "Was it—was it bad?"

Cooper looked down at her hand. "Was what bad?"

"The war, of course. But that's stupid of me. Of course it was bad. Dear God, it must have been sheer hell."

"Are you talking about the Vietnam War, Sally?" he asked.

"Well, of course," she said, confused.

"I was five when Saigon fell," he said gently. He thought for a moment. "I wasn't in the Korean War, either. Or World War II."

Julia added and subtracted and felt foolish. "Oh. Right." She shook her head and her hand dropped. "I watch way too many old films. Sorry about that. I always get dates wrong. But—" Julia tilted her head and looked at Cooper. His longish black hair was brushed back. His suit was either an Italian design or from an excellent tailor. It was beautifully cut. His tie was silk and echoed the silk square in his jacket pocket. Today, he looked like what he was—a prosperous businessman—except for his hands, which weren't the smooth, pampered hands of a businessman. They were large and rough—hands used to a lot of manual labor. Despite the elegant suit and the polished loafers, however, he still looked every inch a warrior. "Chuck Pedersen said you won a medal. What was it for, then? Desert Storm?"

"Nope. Joined the Navy in '92. And I quit in 2002 'cause my dad died, so I missed the Iraq war the second time around, too."

"So, what was it? What war were you in?" Had she missed a war somewhere between New York and Boston?

"No war." Cooper pulled in a deep breath. "Flight 101," he said grimly.

"Cooper!" Julia was stunned. Wars were remote events, played out somewhere far away. Flight 101 had been hijacked on American soil—at JFK, not ten miles from where she had just started her studies at Columbia. She had watched the tragedy of Flight 101 unfold on CNN. The whole country had remained glued to their TV sets for four days and four nights, praying for the hostages. Everyone had followed the terrifying sequence of events live—the terrorists' demands, the stalled negotiations and the horrifying sight of seven of the hostages being shot from the open cockpit, their bodies dropped on the tarmac one by one. "That little girl." The memory of it had Julia's stomach clenching. "Were you there when—when—" She couldn't say it.

"Yeah, I was there. We'd been called in immediately. We had orders to wait for negotiations to pan out. We waited and we waited. When the little girl was—" Cooper looked away and his jaw muscles worked. "That's when we decided to move."

She remembered the men in black ski masks who had swarmed into the plane on the runway. Two of them had died, she remembered. "That's what you got the medal for," Julia said.

"Mmm-hmm." Cooper looked around. "You about ready to go?"

"Yes, I think so." Julia was still struggling with what he had told her. It was one thing to know a man who had been to war. It was quite another to have seen him on TV doing it. Of course, he had been wearing a ski mask at the time. And of course, she hadn't known him then.

At the time, Julia suddenly remembered, she had been dating Henry Borsello, a history major. He had been charming, chatty, shallow and unreliable. All in all, very, very un-Cooperish. For a moment, Julia tried to imagine Henry in a ski mask, rappelling down a plane. Taking out terrorists with machine guns. Or even fixing her plumbing. She failed miserably.

"Let's go have lunch then, Cooper," she said. "It's not every day a girl gets to have lunch with a real live hero." She beamed at him. "My treat."

Cooper looked shocked at the idea and frowned as he took her arm. "Absolutely not."

Chapter Twelve

"Talk to me, Cooper," Julia said before taking another bite of her chiliburger. She thought of sighing with delight but didn't, out of respect for Alice.

"Ahm…" Cooper signaled for another cup of coffee. Probably to gain time while he thought of something to say. Julia was going to have to work on that with him. His eyes lit when he thought of something. "You like it here?"

Julia put her cup down carefully and looked around The Brewery. It had stained hardwood floors. Against one wall was a working fireplace and the merrily burning logs added coziness and warmth. It was haphazardly—and charmingly—decorated with old copper pots as planters and a wagon wheel as a chandelier. Pewter serving dishes were arranged on a trestle table decorated with earthenware vases full of what were essentially weeds—Bishop's Weed, vetch and water mint. A large wicker basket held dried pampas grass and bulrushes. The kitchen area was open, divided only by a huge old-fashioned marble-topped chest that served as a counter. She brought her attention back to Cooper.

"It's great," she said softly, watching him expectantly. "Your turn now."

His jaws worked as he mulled over something to say. "Er…nice day, isn't it?"

They were sitting by the large window and had a good view of the deteriorating weather outside. Grey clouds were dimming the already weak late afternoon sun. A sudden gust of wind rattled the shutters loudly. Julia laughed and after a moment, Cooper did, too.

"I guess you're not too good at this talking thing," she said.

"Nope." He leaned back so the waitress could clear the dirty dishes from the table. He drank the last of his coffee and eyed her warily.

"How come it's so nice here?" Julia asked.

Cooper blinked. "Beg your pardon? Nice where?"

"Here. In Rupert." Julia waved her arm, encompassing the warm café and the town outside. "This place is great. The food is wonderful. The decor is authentic. It's a truly great little café. Bob's Corner Bookstore was wonderful, too. It had a good selection and Bob was nice. It was a perfect small town bookstore. We walked down two perfect small town streets to get here and they were planted with larch and geraniums. The plants were well-tended and there wasn't a pothole in sight. Rupert could be in a guidebook. *Great Small Towns of the West*." She folded her hands under her chin. "So what went wrong with Simpson?"

Julia could almost see the wheels turning in Cooper's head as he turned the question over in his mind. "Well...maybe towns are like people. Some are hardy and some aren't. Some withstand hardship better than others. Horses are like that, too," he added after a moment.

It was one way of looking at it. "So...when did Simpson start to...ah..." Julia tried to find a word that wouldn't be too strong, or reek too much of must and decay, "decline?" she finished delicately.

Cooper paused to consider. "Guess maybe the death-knell was when the new interstate ran forty miles west of Simpson. That was back in '84."

"You mean surveyors draw a line in the map for a road and a town goes down the drain—" Julia snapped her fingers, " — like that?" It was a novel concept, and she realized that her time in Simpson was the first time in her life she'd lived anywhere that wasn't old and picturesque and in a guidebook. It was odd to think that she was living somewhere that might just drop off the map in a few years.

"Yeah. But then that's how most towns in the West were founded anyway, so I suppose it's poetic justice."

"What do you mean?"

Cooper visibly relaxed. The history of the West was something he knew a lot about, judging from the history books she'd seen in his library.

Cooper leaned to one side as the waitress deposited two servings of dessert and two steaming cups of coffee in front of them.

"Most of the towns out here were founded on a whim—where a miner happened to pitch a tent, then another miner joined him—or where a settler was buried, or where there was groundwater. In Montana and Wyoming, it was even more arbitrary. The railway engineers just took a pencil and a compass and marked off fifty-mile lengths along the tracks for where the trains needed to load up with water and that's where they founded the railway towns. Likely as not, the towns were named after the engineer's mother or wife or daughter. Lotta towns named Clarissa and Lorraine out there. Not more than a shack or two sometimes. Some grew, some didn't. Simpson was luckier than most—for a while, anyway. There's a lot of underground water around Simpson and there'd been a vein of gold that ran out around 1920. Then for a while there was cattle, and that was profitable until the railway changed its route. Since then there's been a slow decline. It'll become a ghost town soon."

"That's so sad." Julia thought of that. Of a whole town dying. Simpson, wiped off the map. If it had ever been on a map.

"You grew up near a ghost town yourself."

"I did?" Julia was startled out of her thoughts.

"Shanako." Cooper looked at her expectantly.

Julia blinked. "Shanawhat?"

Cooper cut into his cheesecake. "Shanako. Largest sheep exporter in the world until the Australian market opened up in the 1860s, then it just dropped off the map. Went from 40,000 people to zero in a year. Don't tell me you've never been there. It can't be more than seventy miles from Bend."

She smiled politely, as if Cooper had suddenly, inexplicably lapsed into Urdu. Cooper frowned. "Didn't Chuck say you came from Bend, Oregon?"

Where had she heard that name—Bend...Of course! Her cover. Julia had been so intent on talking with Cooper, finding him so intriguing and impenetrable all at the same time that there wasn't room for anything else. Her brain stalled and cogs whirled emptily.

"Sally?" Cooper was looking at her strangely.

"Who?" she said. Then—"Oh!"

She shook herself and tried to replay in her head the last few minutes of conversation. "No, I--I've never been to...Shanako. We moved to Bend when I was—" her mind raced, "in junior high then I went to college in--" Where would an Oregonian go to college?

"Portland?" Cooper was watching her with his head tilted to one side.

"Right," Julia said, relieved. "Portland." The only Portland she'd ever been to was in Maine.

This was such a strain. Why hadn't Herbert Davis issued her an Instruction Manual for Being Undercover? "So I guess I haven't explored as much around Bend as I should have." Cooper was watching her with a too-intent gaze. Those dark eyes had the ability to throw her into a tailspin. She shifted the focus of the conversation. "So what about Simpson? You said the interstate was moved, and I suppose it makes sense that that would have an impact on Simpson. There'd be less traffic going through town. Anything else?"

"Yeah." Cooper finished off the bite on his fork and chewed slowly and swallowed. He lifted up another forkful of the fluffy cheesecake and nodded. "I'm probably eating another reason for Simpson's decline."

Julia sighed. "You mean Alice's cooking?" She wasn't surprised. Alice's cooking was bad enough to cause the demise of a town, all by itself.

"Yeah. Not Alice specifically, but the fact is there isn't anyplace decent in town to eat. Carly was a lousy cook, too, but people went there, anyway. Just like I used to buy my feed from Erroll Newton even though he used to charge me about 5 cents more per pound. I was really glad when Erroll closed down in '94. Everyone used to make an effort to shop locally. But the younger generation doesn't seem to have that kind of loyalty. It doesn't help that the high school closed down and the kids have to be bussed to Dead Horse. Kids who grow up in Simpson now just take it for granted that they'll go away when they grow up. No one wants to take over family businesses any more."

"Mmm." Julia sipped her coffee and wasn't surprised to find that it was one of the best cups of coffee she'd ever had. The Brewery was truly a fantastic café. Poor Alice. "Lee Kellogg isn't going to take over Glenn's hardware store. He wants to be a history teacher, instead. Glenn is thinking of selling in a few years. Particularly since Maisie isn't interested in helping out in the store."

Cooper gaped. "Where do you get this stuff?"

"I talk to people, Cooper. Amazing what you learn when you do that." Julia finished her carrot cake. "Actually, what Maisie would really like to do is be a cook. But who could hire a cook in Simpson?"

"Not Alice." Cooper signaled the waitress for the check. "She's barely keeping her head above water. Like the other businesses in Simpson."

"The Broken Window theory," Julia said thoughtfully.

"The what?" Cooper's hand stilled.

"Broken Window theory. I read about it in a magazine." In another life, she thought.

She remembered clearly where she'd been when she'd read the article. Sipping coffee in a café as charming as The Brewery, clucking her head over the troubles of the world. Little realizing that the world would soon come crashing down around her ears. "They did this study on slums and housing projects. Some are kept up by the residents and some become a wasteland and the researchers wanted to find out why some escaped desolation and others didn't. And they discovered that everyone who lives in a place has to care about it. All it takes in a housing project is one broken window for the place to degenerate. It's like a symbol that no one cares. A license for everyone to trash the place."

"Yeah." Cooper nodded thoughtfully. "I guess Simpson's a bit like that. No one has done anything up in a long time. Shops have been closing for ten years and no one's investing in the place. Town's not going to last long if someone doesn't do something. Places need attention, just like people."

Places need attention, Julia thought with a sudden pang. Cooper's words echoed in her head. She was guilty of neglect, herself. She had lived for a whole month now in her little house and she hadn't done anything to make it nicer or more comfortable. It was unheard of for a Devaux. She was in Simpson under duress, it was true. Yet her mom had been in Riyadh under duress. And their house there had been her mother's decorating triumph.

I haven't done anything at all to make my new life into something better, she thought. Her mother would have been ashamed of her.

"Cooper, do you think you could—" She broke off.

"Do I think I could what?"

"No—" Julia waved a hand. He'd done her too many favors already. "Never mind."

"Tell me."

"Forget it, Cooper." She shrugged her shoulders. "Just a silly thought."

Cooper was watching her steadily, dark eyes deep and impenetrable. The waitress came bustling up with the check, and

Cooper waved her away. Then, to Julia's surprise, Cooper leaned back and crossed his arms. "We're not leaving until you finish that sentence."

Julia bit her lip and looked at Cooper. His face was set and he looked as hard as iron. She could almost feel the force of his willpower from across the table and gave up.

"Okay," she said softly. "Cooper, is there a decorating store around here?"

"A…decorating store?" he said carefully, uncrossing his arms and leaning forward.

"Yes, you know. Paint, wallpaper, stencils, fabrics. Well, the usual—a decorating store."

"Paint, wallpaper, fabric…" Cooper thought it over. "I guess Schwab's would be a good place."

Julia felt so guilty. He was fixing up her house. He'd accompanied her to Rupert, the bookstore and now to lunch, on him. "Do you have time to stop in a store, Cooper? Or do you have a lot of things to do today?"

He signaled the waitress. She brought the check and Cooper paid. When she left, he leaned forward across the table. "I'm not too sure you have the situation straight here, Sally," he said, his deep voice low and soft. "There isn't anything you can't ask me. I'd do anything for you, anything at all." His dark eyes stared straight into hers. "I'd kill for you. Stopping by a store doesn't really count."

* * * * *

Cooper kept waiting for Sally to turn to him and say, "Talk to me," on the ride back. And when she did, he would. He already had a few opening gambits which he practiced silently. He was ready. All she had to do was ask.

But she wasn't asking. Actually, she wasn't doing much of anything on the other side of the truck's cab, besides looking out the window lost in thought.

Silence was Cooper's constant companion, something he was familiar with, something he could handle. But somehow silence and Sally Anderson were two things that didn't seem to go together at all. He found himself craving her attention. He missed her turning to him, big turquoise eyes wide and focused on him, telling him to talk to her, then drinking in his every word. He wanted her to stop looking out that damned window at nothing and turn her attention to him.

It was crazy. He felt like a twelve-year-old wanting to do handstands to impress the pretty new girl in school.

She wasn't talking to him at all. She was staring out the window at the landscape. Damned if he could figure out what was so fascinating out there. It was already dark anyway.

Cooper realized just how far gone he was when he caught himself craving her smile. When she smiled at him as if he were the most fascinating man on earth, he felt something in his chest loosen, something that had been tightly wound for a long, long time. All his life, in fact.

He had to think hard about that one. About what she meant to him and about how he was treating her.

Sally Anderson was undoubtedly the most important women in his life, ever, and here he'd been fucking her like there was no tomorrow. Like she was there only for his personal sexual release, after a very long dry spell.

He winced when he thought about it. After driving Rafael home in the late afternoons, he headed straight back to Sally's house. Two minutes after she opened the door to him, he had her naked and on her back. The first time he fucked her was always frantic. The second and third times, too, for that matter. There never seemed to be time for anything but that.

He was still frantic for her, still gripping her hips tightly, still fucking her hard, in the early morning hours, when it was time to go.

He'd given her nothing. Not sweet words, not gentle caresses. Not even foreplay.

When he made it back to the Double C at dawn every day, he was immediately taken up with backed up chores, most of them outdoors with all his men around. He found it impossible even to call her. So basically, he fucked her all night, then disappeared at dawn. There was a name for men like that.

Today's lunch at The Brewery was the first time he was even able to offer Sally anything. Just beer and a chiliburger instead of a nice dinner out, and here she'd wanted to pay for it! She'd shocked him with that one.

Sally deserved expensive, elegant restaurants. Not that there were any in Simpson, but he could have offered to take her to Boise. It's just that he didn't have the time, but maybe he should make the effort. Melissa had insisted on several expensive evenings out a month while they were married and wanted to go out all the time when they were engaged.

Hell, he'd treated Melissa better than Sally, and Melissa was a bitch.

When you found a woman who meant a lot to you—and who was beautiful and warmhearted to boot—you courted her. You treated her…well, like the lady she was. You brought her nice presents—deadbolts and window alarm systems didn't count—and you took her out in the evening to nice places.

You didn't fuck her near to death, then disappear in the morning. Over and over and over again.

It was a real pity that sex got in the way. He desired her so much it took his breath away. When he walked into her little house, it was like a wind picked him up and blew him away. Lust blasted his mind and all he could think about was putting his cock in her as soon as it was humanly possible. And staying there for as long as he could. And since he was so behind on sex, he stayed in her until he had to leave in the morning.

This was not good, Cooper thought, as he turned into Sally's street.

Tonight was going to be different. He was going to be gentle. It was going to be making love, not fucking like there was no tomorrow.

Cooper had to leave really early in the morning for Boise airport. He had three connecting flights to make it to Lexington, Kentucky by evening. He had to attend the opening of the annual meeting of the Horse Breeder's Association, which was when he did his buying of six-month-old colts, and networked like crazy. This annual trip was the backbone of his business and he usually enjoyed it.

Not this year, though. He would be gone at least four days, maybe five. He had to let Sally know that he wasn't disappearing from her life. That they would pick up as soon as he got back.

He had to let her know that he would miss her, though "miss" was too tame a word for that wrenching ache in his chest when she wasn't around. The thought of a Sally-less week filled him with a scary, empty feeling.

Cooper drove on to her street and parked two blocks down, though by now all of Simpson, all of Dead Horse and most of Rupert were probably aware of the fact that they were lovers.

He looked over at Sally. She was being unusually quiet for an unusually long time and now he saw why. She was leaning against the window, fast asleep.

"Sally," he said softly. When she didn't move, he reached out with a forefinger to stroke her cheek. Every time he touched her, he was amazed at how soft her skin was. "Wake up, honey."

There was movement behind her lids, she was coming up out of it. For the first time, Cooper realized how exhausted she must be. He wasn't letting her sleep at night and she worked all day.

Maybe he should be a gentleman. Maybe he should escort her to her door and leave her with a kiss and a promise to see her in a week's time.

Sally's eyelids fluttered and opened, the color so vivid even in the darkness, it was like a little piece of summer sky in the shadowy cab. She looked bewildered for a moment, then recognized him. "Cooper," she breathed. And smiled.

His chest clenched.

Driving away was not an option.

Cooper cupped her neck and kissed her. As always, her mouth opened immediately, soft and warm and welcoming. Her first reaction always electrified him, plunging him straight into a panicky lust, as if she'd dissipate like smoke if he didn't nail her with his cock.

This time his reaction was just as intense, but different. Her warm, sleepy skin, the faint rose scent that clung to her, the soft small hand caressing his cheek lulled him with a hazy drugged pleasure, like falling into a sea of warm rose petals.

They turned towards each other, at the same time. Sally threw her arms around his neck. His hand opened her coat and slipped up under her sweater, nudging aside her bra.

God, he loved her breasts. So soft and round. When his finger circled her nipple, she moaned into his mouth. He felt her nipple rise against his palm, firm and hard. Exactly the same thing was happening with his cock.

Cooper was determined to make this time different. He pulled away from her. It always took Sally a moment to recover from his kisses. Her eyelids slowly fluttered open and her eyes met his in question.

"I want to do this right." The words came out stark and harsh. "I *need* to do this right."

Sally's eyes searched his. It was as if she could walk around inside his head and read everything he was feeling. He was sure she understood what he was feeling better than he did himself. Her face softened.

"Oh, Cooper." She leaned forward and pressed her lips to his. It wasn't a kiss, it was a reassurance. "You *are* doing it right. You always do it right."

They needed to be in the house, in the bed, naked. Right. Now. Cooper couldn't wait. It was as if there was a direct electric line between his heart and his cock and someone had just thrown the switch bringing them both to full roaring life.

In a minute, he'd collected her purchases — shopping bags full of material in colors he'd never heard of but Harlan Schwab sure had — helped her down and rushed her down the street.

Inside her door, Cooper let all the packages drop to the floor and picked Sally up.

It wasn't a romantic gesture, it was simply the quickest way to get her to the bedroom. He stopped next to the bed and let her slide down him. She had to feel his erection. It was pulsing so hard it was likely that the entire town of Simpson could feel his hard-on. He was probably interrupting radio reception with it.

Holding the back of her head while he kissed her, Cooper undressed her with his other hand, trying very, very hard not to rip anything. Coat, blouse, bra. Ahhh, there she was, in his hand once again. So soft.

Cooper left her breast reluctantly and only because getting the bottom half of her naked was necessary. When she was naked, she stepped fully into his arms and he could swear he could feel her bare skin through his jacket, shirt and pants. He cupped her ass with his hands, lifting her up into his hard-on and tortured himself with the feel of her.

He lifted his mouth from hers. "Undress me," he gasped. Someone had to do it and his hands were full of her.

"Okay." She smiled up at him and unbuttoned his shirt and pushed it and his suit coat off his shoulders so that they drifted to the floor, kissing his chest all the way down, through the undershirt. "Lift your arms." She wasn't tall enough to lift the undershirt away, so he held his arms out straight while she slipped it up over his head and off. She flung it over her shoulder and moved into his embrace, skin to skin. Her mouth opened under his, tongue tangling with his. He moved to take them to the bed when she said, "Wait."

Cooper stopped and tried not to quiver with impatience.

Smiling up at him, Sally unbuttoned his dress pants and slowly unzipped him, fingers brushing against his hard-on. She pushed down his trousers and briefs, slowly. Kneeling, Sally slipped his shoes and his socks off and he lifted his feet obediently as she got him naked. Sally looked up and smiled when she saw his cock, rigidly erect just for her. She grasped it loosely, fingers light, touch delicate.

It wasn't enough pressure. The only pressure that could possibly be enough would be to part the tight tissues of her little cunt.

"Bed," he growled, lifting her up then pushing her gently on to her back. He eased his weight on to her, closing his eyes briefly at the sheer mind-blowing pleasure of having her under him once again. Knowing even more mind-blowing pleasure was coming.

God, just the smell of her was enough to make him come. Cooper pressed his face against her neck and inhaled deeply, hoping he wasn't behaving like Fred when he met a new human.

The skin of Sally's neck was incredibly smooth and soft, smelling faintly of roses and her. His sense of smell was keen. He was so attuned to her smell, he could find her in the dark by scent alone. Her pulse was beating wildly against his lips and he licked her there, where her blood was beating just beneath the skin. Sally shuddered and arched against him. Her arms tightened around his back.

She was so responsive, her warm, soft, fragrant little body writhing against his. Cooper bit her earlobe lightly and licked the rim. Her neck arched back, her hips rose.

Cooper opened her thighs and touched her. She was, as always, soft and welcoming there. He slid a forefinger around her, being careful of the soft, tender flesh. He had thick, rough calluses on his fingers and he had just enough presence of mind to keep his touch light.

He settled fully on her, running his hands down the backs of Sally's thighs. He gently pushed her legs up and out, groaning at the feel of her opening for him.

One day he was going to take a tour of her body with his lips and his hands. Not now, though. Now he needed to be in her like he needed to breathe.

Cooper slid into her, feeling Sally open to him. Her entire body told him how much she desired him, arms holding him tightly, slender legs hugging his hips, cunt wet and welcoming. Every cell of his body felt welcome, encased in warm softness.

He pressed into her, into the slippery heat of her, feeling as if he'd come home after a long, long time away in a cold foreign land.

Cooper pressed his cock deep, holding himself still, savoring the tightness. He rotated his hips, settling himself more deeply inside her and *wham!* Sally came. Hard strong little tugs of her cunt, writhing underneath him, moaning and gasping. It blew his mind.

Cooper felt a prickle rush down his spine, felt his balls contract, and he too came, his whole body shuddering as he poured himself into her in a sudden electric rush of excitement.

Sally turned her head slightly and kissed his ear.

His grip on her legs tightened and all thoughts of taking it slow and easy vanished from his mind like smoke as he started pounding into her. She was soft and slick with his come, the warmest softest thing in the world, made just for him.

As always, he lost track of time, of himself, when he was in her. He stopped for a moment, panting, and turned his head to wipe the sweat off his face on the sheet. He could have used his hand but that would mean letting go of Sally.

Cooper's eyes lit on Sally's alarm clock. The phosphorescent hands glowed in an impossible configuration. Two-fifteen, the hands read. How could that be? Stunned, Cooper checked his wristwatch. Two-fifteen.

Oh, *fuck*.

He had to leave from the Double C by 3 a.m. at the very latest, and he still had to pack and get his documents together. Actually, he always went into Boise the day before so he could easily make the 6 a.m. flight. He'd decided to leave early in the morning instead of last night, so he could gouge a little more time with Sally out of his tight schedule.

Cooper had to leave now. He couldn't miss that flight. If he did, there was no way he could make it to Lexington by evening, where he was going to be presented with the "Breeder of the Year" award. He simply had to be there.

Cooper loosened his hard grip on Sally and pulled out of her. She was holding on to him tightly with her arms and legs. Even her cunt was holding on tightly to his cock, giving him up with difficulty as he slid out.

If he'd known how to, Cooper would have wept at the feeling of coldness that assailed his wet cock. There was distance between his chest and her breasts now, for the first time in probably four hours. He'd become so used to feeling her breasts against him that it felt strange, unnatural for a moment, to feel the chill night air on his sweat-covered chest instead of Sally's soft, fragrant skin. Sally's hands still clung to his shoulders. Her grip tightened.

"Cooper?"

With regret, Cooper lifted his hand and gently loosened her grasp. Sally's hands fell and he missed their warmth.

Cooper bent and kissed her cheek, her mouth. "Gotta go, honey. Sorry. I have to make it to—"

"Tomorrow's Sunday," she interrupted quickly, her voice lost and small. "Can't you stay? At least tonight?"

Stay.

That magic word had started it all. For a split second, Cooper was violently tempted to do just that—stay. Fuck the annual meeting. Fuck the award. It was just a lousy plaque, after all. Twenty dollars' worth of brass and wood. There was nothing in Lexington that could even remotely compete with remaining in Sally's arms, with being inside her warmth and softness.

Hell, why not just sell the Double C and move in with Sally? Fix her house up all day and fuck her all night. If he sold the spread, he could live very comfortably the rest of his life on the income. Actually, he already had a good income from his investments that he was plowing back into the spread. So Coop didn't have to work. He could retire tomorrow. Why not?

Because he had a responsibility, that was why not. Forty men and their families depended on the Double C. The Double C's business was what kept Simpson alive and was vitally important to a lot of the businesses in Rupert and Dead Horse.

He'd loved the Navy, but when his dad died, he knew he had to go back. America was full of brave young men with good eyesight, steady hands, a strong back and guts. There was only one Cooper who could take over the Cooper spread and keep it alive.

Duty and desire warred powerfully in him for an instant. But Cooper was hardwired for duty.

"Can't stay, honey." Could she hear the rough regret in his voice? Why the hell hadn't he told her before he had to leave? Because his entire brain had been blasted by lust, that was why. "Gotta go. Out of town, actually. To Kentucky. Should be back Friday."

She sat up quickly, the sheets rustling. "You're leaving town?" Her eyes were wide as she looked up at him. He could see the dismay even in the dark room, lit only by the dirty streetlamp on the street corner. "Do you — do you have to?"

He shrugged on his jacket. Damn, but the time was tight. He had to leave now. "Yeah. I have to. Business, you know?"

Sally nodded slowly, wide-eyed. He could hear her swallow. "Yes…um…business. Okay."

Shitshitshit! Cooper hated to leave her like this. He bent and gave her a swift kiss. He had to say the next part. "I won't be able to call, honey. It'll be a real…intense week."

She was looking more and more lost. "Intense," she said weakly. "Okay."

Cooper stood. Christ, he hated this. He should be able to stay with her, make love to her some more, then finally stay the night, holding her tightly. He should be able to spend Sunday with her, in bed, maybe going for a walk in the afternoon.

But this was the week that could make or break the Double C. He was bringing it back to life after years of neglect. Each year the bloodlines were better. Everything depended on the foals he chose on this yearly trip to Kentucky and on the contacts he made.

Duty called.

Cooper answered.

Two thirty-five.

"Gotta go now, honey." He backed away reluctantly.

"I'll—I'll miss you Cooper," Sally said softly.

There were no words for how he felt.

"Yeah," he said, and left.

Chapter Thirteen

The purloined file had had three names in it, all with a three digit code. Two of the witnesses had been relocated to Idaho. Chances were Julia Devaux had been, as well. The professional accessed the database of a geological surveying company and acquired maps of Idaho.

There were a little over 2000 people in the Witness Security Program. Logically, that meant about forty people per state. They would be as widely scattered as possible, so you wouldn't have people on the run tripping over each other. But it made sense that the files would be kept geographically, so that there could be a case officer running three or four cases in the same geographical area. Abt had been in Rockville, Davidson in Ellis. The professional consulted the survey map, as accurate as laser technology could make it, and ran a finger over the counties. Some of the towns were so small they were kept in a separate data file. Empty country. The professional said the old-fashioned names aloud, tracking them with a finger on the map—Jefferson, Clearwater, Butte. Somewhere in there was Julia Devaux and two million dollars.

The professional picked up the phone and booked a one-way business class ticket to Boise, Idaho.

* * * * *

Blood and brains, a shattered head. A small pale body crumpled on the greasy tarmac. The smell of cordite. The big man with the ferociously cruel face lifted the gun. His head turned slowly, mechanically, like a robot's, towards her.

Something stirred at the edge of her vision—a tall, black shape promising safety and shelter. Cooper! She tried to stand, to go to him, but there was blood all around her, thick and ropy. Her feet scrabbled uselessly for purchase.

Cooper stared at her for several heartbeats, eyes black and unreadable, then he moved in slow motion, wide shoulders turning. He was leaving! She could see his broad back, the long legs taking him away from her in giant strides, moving so quickly she barely had time to scream at him. Cooper! Come back! Help me!

She screamed until her lungs ached, but no sound came. Cooper kept on walking and in the time it took to stretch out her hand to him, he was gone. She stared at the cold empty space where he had been.

A low cruel chuckle sounded from behind her and she whipped around, dread pooling in her stomach. Santana's smile had stretched unnaturally, his entire mouth blood-red as he raised the large black gun. Red and black. The world had turned the colors of blood and death. He raised the gun and she braced. "Die, bitch," *he growled and pulled the trigger.*

* * * * *

Julia bolted up in bed, trembling and sweaty. The dream was different this time. She couldn't put her finger on it, but there had been a different feel to it, an urgency, as if something were closing in on her.

Lightning crackled and thunder roared across the sky. It sounded as if it were an inch above the roof and Julia realized that it was the crack of thunder that had roused her and not a bullet to the brain. Something wet touched her hand and she screamed, one hand at her throat, the other frantically reaching for something she could use as a weapon. Something about the quality of the wetness had her snapping on the lamp on the bedside table.

Fred sat on his haunches, big brown eyes warily watching her. He whined softly without opening his muzzle and Julia remembered that he had been mistreated. She had been thrashing about on the bed in the throes of the nightmare and had frightened him.

Well, she'd frightened herself. Julia patted the bed and Fred immediately jumped to her side, curling into a warm hairy ball, his weight causing the already sagging mattress to dip even further. At least he didn't smell anymore.

Julia leaned her head back wearily against the cheap imitation brass bedstead and tried to fight the waves of despair. But even despair was better than what was lurking behind it — fear.

Someone — probably several someones — was gunning for her and every day she spent here was a day he — or they — could crawl closer to her hiding place.

Davis wasn't any great help in reassuring her, either. He had sounded impatient the last few times she had called. The calls depressed her so much, she'd started calling less frequently. She was supposed to call from pay phones, not her home phone. They always had the same conversation, anyway.

Any news?

No.

Do you know what's going to happen?

No.

How long will this go on?

I don't know.

There were very few variations and Davis tended to turn testy when she tried to prolong the conversation. Julia didn't even like Davis that much, but he was all that was standing between herself and the abyss. Or Santana, which was the same thing.

Fred laid his muzzle on her knee and she patted his head with a trembling hand. She found that spot behind his ear that made his eyes slit with contentment, and wondered how it was that easy for dogs. No amount of scratching behind her ears would make the fear and loneliness flooding her soul go away.

Julia pulled up the blanket tenting her knees. Like most other things in the house, it was cheap and threadbare, the colors faded from many washings. A far cry from the down-filled pure raw silk comforter in gemstone colors her mother had sent her from Paris for her twenty-fourth birthday.

It had arrived after her parents' funeral.

Julia dropped her head to her knees and struggled to keep the tears back. Tears wouldn't help anything, and she should be all cried out, anyway. But apparently she wasn't because a few renegade drops seeped out. Julia lifted a hand to her cold cheeks and shivered as a gust of rain rattled the windows. Had the heating somehow gone off? She was too tired and too depressed — too scared — to get up and check.

Maybe Cooper — Julia stopped herself. She shouldn't get used to leaning on Cooper. Cooper had gone.

That was the other part of her nightmare. Cooper leaving. Turning his back on her and walking away. In life as in the nightmare.

Well, of course he had left her.

He was a businessman with a business to run. He had things to tend to and wasn't responsible for a forlorn Eastern lady who had had the bad luck to be in the wrong place at the wrong time.

Cooper and she were lovers, sure. But who knew what Cooper was thinking or feeling? What she meant to him. He showed up, they had sex for hours, and then he left again.

Repeat cycle.

A friend of hers in New York had had a married lover like that and she had called him The Bat. Cooper seemed to care, but he sure wasn't talking. And now he'd left her for a whole week.

Julia bit her lips. A week without Cooper in her bed seemed almost impossible to bear. She had no fear when he was around. And all that backed up fear was flooding in now. She wanted to call him back, tell him he needed to stay with her.

Which was nuts, of course. What was she to him besides a good lay?

What was she to anyone?

For the first time in her life, Julia took stock. She had moved all over the world with her parents and it had been wonderful, but she had never thought to look over her shoulder, to see what had been left behind. All she had ever seen was what lay ahead. It had been so exciting, each move a new country, a new city, new people to meet.

For the first time in her life, Julia wished she belonged to a community. People she could turn to for help. A community of people who lived in one place, and had done so for generations, not expatriates who lived in far-flung places.

There were new friends here, of course. Alice, Beth. But they thought the women they had befriended was Sally Anderson, a perfectly normal grade school teacher.

Not Julia Devaux, woman on the run.

* * * * *

Nothing, but nothing, was as satisfactory as surfing cyberspace. It was like being invisible and all-powerful. Nothing was safe from the prowling intelligence. People would be astounded at just how much could be learned if you knew what you were doing. You could find out a man's hat size, his favorite reading material, what trinkets he bought his mistress and whether he was on pain medication for his hernia and he wouldn't even know he'd been investigated.

Of course the Department of Justice's files were harder to access than most. The D of J's firewalls were thick and high and studded with protective devices. But it was all about as useful as a Lego fence if the right person wanted in. *And I'm the right person*, the professional thought. It wasn't a question of whether Julia Devaux's file could be found, but when.

Time to tighten the timeline. Accessing the D of J's computer system could be done anywhere from a laptop with a modem. That was the easy bit. The next step required intelligence.

The professional's ruminations were interrupted by the TV newscaster stating that the weather forecasters were predicting a cold winter. There would be snowstorms around Thanksgiving.

I want to be in St. Lucia by Thanksgiving, the professional thought. Sunshine and crab instead of snow and turkey.

* * * * *

"We've got a man down."

Herbert Davis looked up blankly from the circular letter written by the new broom upstairs who was so determined to sweep clean. The circular was the umpteenth reminder that terms derogatory to women and minorities were forbidden by amendment blah-blah-blah to ruling number blah-blah-blah. *We're law enforcement officers, damn you!* He sent the sizzling thought upstairs. *We can't make the world better. Just safer.*

How the fuck were they supposed to do that on a diminishing budget while tiptoeing around mincing words? Barclay coughed and Davis remembered that he'd said something. "What?"

"We've got a man down." Barclay grabbed a nearby chair, turned it around and straddled it. Barclay looked like shit and smelled bad, too. He looked uncomfortably like a bum. The divorce was dragging him down.

Davis shook his head morosely. The world really was going to the dogs. "Who?"

"Guy named Richard Abt. Remember him? We relocated him as Robert Littlewood."

Davis looked to the ceiling as if going through a mental Rolodex, but the truth was there wasn't a chance he could remember. The Marshall's Office ran over 2000 witnesses in the Witness Security Program and Davis found that he could no longer keep track of them all. He tapped his lip. "That was the..." Davis paused.

"Accountant." Barclay was reading from the file.

"Accountant," Davis said wisely. "Right. Uh-huh. And he was going to testify in the...the..."

"Ledbetter, Duncan and Terrance case." Davis nodded as Barclay read out the particulars of the case, then flipped the thick file closed. "Abt was due to testify in court on the 14th of November." Barclay tapped the file and sighed. "Looks like those creeps at Ledbetter, Duncan and Terrance are going to be let off the hook, after all. Abt was the only one willing to testify. All that trouble we went through and there won't even be a break in their tan line."

Davis took a pen and started taking notes. It wasn't his case, but losing a witness was something that shook the entire service from stem to stern. It was a rare event and when it happened, heads rolled. Davis wanted to be ready to cover his ass if any of the shit hitting the fan blew his way.

"We know who the perps were?" Davis gave a snort of mirthless laughter. "Besides the obvious—stooges for Leadbutt, Dunce and Torrid."

"Well, that's just it, boss." Barclay shifted uncomfortably. "Looks like...looks like it was an accident."

"A what? An accident? Who bought that crap? The local cops?" Davis looked pityingly at Barclay. "Where did we put Abt, anyway?"

"In Idaho. Little town named Rockville."

Davis snorted. "Local cops probably couldn't find their butts with a stick and a map."

"Nah, it wasn't the local cops who closed the case, it was us." Barclay rubbed his bloodshot eyes with the knuckles of his index fingers. "Our people say it really did look like an accident. A hit and run."

"A real one?" Davis frowned.

"Sure looks that way. If it's a hit, the wiseguys make sure everyone knows about it. Real clear message to anyone else who might have any bright ideas about testifying. Sort of a warning. Like shark repellant."

It was true. Still…Davis shook his head sorrowfully. "Can't believe that poor bastard's bad luck. Here Abt danced his way out of—" Davis checked the file again, "—a sure conviction on three felony counts, looking at twenty-five to thirty, easy. Decides to go state's witness and gets a whole new identity and a new job." Davis ran quickly through the info. "Looks like he was doing pretty well in his new identity, too. And it all goes kerblooey because of a drive-by—"

"Ain't that the way." Barclay picked at a dirty fingernail. Davis noted uneasily that his hand trembled. "Sometimes you're the windshield and sometimes you're the bug."

* * * * *

The professional scrolled through the facts on Sydney Davidson, the second name in the file hacked from the U.S. Marshal's Office. A real Doctor Feelgood, our Sydney, the professional thought.

A brilliant biochemist, Dr. Davidson had been hired by Sunshine Pharmaceuticals, a Virginia-based drug company, right out of college. But the good doctor's knowledge wasn't limited to aspirin and antibiotics.

The professional remembered clearly when the Sunshine Pharmaceuticals scandal hit, in the midst of a hotly contested Senate election campaign. A number of members of the company's board of directors had been involved in an extremely lucrative sideline—providing highly sophisticated designer drugs to the professional elite of the Southeast Seaboard.

The photographs of Sunshine's CEO being led to the courtroom in handcuffs and shackles helped the underdog candidate—an aspiring young district attorney running on a law and order platform—to a landslide victory. After a warrant had been issued to the entire board of directors, Sydney Davidson had turned state's witness on a dime.

The professional didn't care much about drugs either way—to each his own poison. Personally, the professional preferred *Veuve Clicquot*.

The professional checked the organization chart. No use contacting the CEO or any other of the board members. Only the head of security would do.

The professional typed the posting to the Norwegian: MESSAGE FOR RON LASLETT, HEAD OF SECURITY, SUNSHINE PHARMACEUTICALS. INFORMATION RE LOCATION AND NEW IDENTITY OF DR. SYDNEY DAVIDSON AVAILABLE UPON RECEIPT OF NOTIFICATION OF DEPOSIT OF ONE HUNDRED THOUSAND US DOLLARS ON ACCOUNT N° GHQ 115 Y BANQUE SUISSE GENEVA HEAD OFFICE. DEATH MUST APPEAR TO BE ACCIDENTAL. NO CAR ACCIDENT.

After two hours, the computer finally beeped and the professional blinked and sat up. There wasn't much do to in Idaho except doze.

ONE HUNDRED THOUSAND US DOLLARS DEPOSITED IN YOUR ACCOUNT N° GHQ 115 Y C/O BANQUE SUISSE GENEVA BRANCH PENDING ACCEPTANCE OF MODE OF TERMINATION. ACCIDENTAL ELECTROCUTION WHILE TAKING BATH PREFERRED MODE. PLEASE SIGNAL ACCEPTANCE SOONEST.

The professional's response was immediate.

ELECTROCUTION FINE. MUST LOOK LIKE ACCIDENT FOR AT LEAST 56 HOURS. NEW LOCATION OF DR. DAVIDSON AND IDENTITY: GRANT PATTERSON, 90 JUNIPER STREET, ELLIS, IDAHO. GOOD LUCK.

* * * * *

"An' then, an' then the Power Rangers morphed into Megazords 'cause they had…The Power!" Rafael said excitedly, pumping his little fist in the air and scattering a few spice cake crumbs. "An' then, an' then they were powerful beings like…like mastodons an' sour-toothed tigers 'cause they had to fight the evil Lord Zedd, but he was too strong for them, and he was going to take over the world, so then the Power Rangers morphed into Ninjetis!" He shouted the last word out, pumping the air again and grinning.

It was Wednesday afternoon and Julia had decided to reward Rafael for his renewed interest in his studies—and for turning Fred into a handsome mutt with glossy fur—by buying him hot chocolate and cake at Carly's, hoping as well to stimulate a little teatime rush hour traffic for Alice. Rafael was giving her a blow-by-blow account of "Power Rangers", but the plot kept escaping him and Julia had just about given up trying to follow it. She had her sketchpad out and was idly doodling.

"See—the Power Rangers had to help Zordan, an interchocolate being—"

"Galactic, squirt." Matt had come over with another slice of cake, Rafael's third. He slid it in front of Rafael. "Intergalactic being."

"Galatic," Rafael repeated obediently. He thought it over, then scrunched up his face at Matt. "What's 'galatic', Matt?"

"Galactic. As in galaxy." Matt tried to sound impatient and superior, but he was fighting a grin. Alice had obviously taken Cooper's advice and had involved Matt in the diner. He was taking his new job so seriously he even dressed up to the point of having a shirt on. "From outer space."

"Oh," Rafael said seriously. "Outer space." He was clearly thinking that over as he pulled the plate of spice cake closer.

Julia looked around, expecting Bernie to come pick Rafael up at any moment. Bernie had taken Cooper's place the past few days in picking Rafael up. It wasn't the same.

The diner was as crowded as she'd ever seen it. Apart from herself and Rafael, Matt and Alice, there were three ranchers sitting in a corner quietly discussing stock prices. Ruddy, weather-beaten men in faded flannel shirts, whitened jeans and scuffed boots, sipping tea. It was rush hour, but still. Tall oaks from little acorns grow, she reminded herself.

Rafael dug into his third slice with enthusiasm, continuing the ongoing saga of the Power Rangers. "And then the Power

Rangers had to fight Ivan Ooze 'cause he covered the world in purple slime and made all the parents want to kill themselves. And Ivan Ooze transformed into a giant robot and then the Power Rangers, they all transformed into a giant robot and they fought in outer space and Ivan Ooze got offed by a comet!" Rafael's young face glowed. "Awesome!"

As a plot synopsis, it needed a little work.

"Kids." Matt, all of seventeen himself, shook his head indulgently. He looked over at Julia, all business. "Will there be anything else, Miss Anderson? Freshen your tea for you?" He pulled a pencil from behind his ear and waited expectantly. Julia tried to look as serious as he did, but it wasn't easy. Matt was trying to be so adult and professional. He'd even removed his eyebrow ring.

Don't grow up too fast, Julia wanted to say to him. It's scary out there.

"Not for me, Matt." Julia shook her head. "And the name's Sally."

She had to give Alice points. The place was as dusty and as dingy as ever, but with Matt fairly quivering to attention and a few people around, it was a little less desolate. The tea had been excellent and judging from Rafael's appetite, so was the spice cake. Then again, Rafael was guaranteed to love anything with starch, sugar and fat in copious quantities.

Julia smiled up at Matt. "If you don't mind, we'll just wait for Bernie to come pick up Rafael."

"Sure, Miss Anderson—ah, Sally." Matt grinned. "Take your time. So…I guess Coop's not coming in this afternoon."

"Cooper's away," Julia said between her teeth. She watched a palm tree in a large terra cotta pot grow on the sheet of graph paper in front of her. It had come from her subconscious, but it looked good. Inspired, she added a palm leaf stencil on the wall. "On business." She bent her head and concentrated on her drawing. "'Till Friday," she added. She bore down hard on the paper and the point of the pencil snapped.

"Oh, that's right. To Kentucky." Matt nodded. "The annual trip. Coop's been planning that trip for months. Dad said that Bernie said that Coop was on the phone all afternoon the other day, trying to call the trip off, but he couldn't." He angled his head curiously, trying to catch a peek at the sheet of paper. "Can I see what you're drawing?"

"He wanted to what?" Julia whipped her head up.

"Cancel his trip." Matt leaned forward, nose ring twinkling in the harsh light of the overhead fluorescent strip. "Can I see what you're drawing?" he repeated.

"What I'm what?" Julia looked at him blankly, pencil still, mind racing. Cooper had wanted to back out of his trip? Surely not—not because of her? No, of course not. He knew they could pick up on the sex again once he got back. This bereft feeling was all her own, a compound of fear and anguish and loneliness. Cooper probably never felt afraid or anguished or—

"Sally?"

"Who?" Julia started and with an effort collected her wits, which seemed to dim whenever she thought about Cooper. "Oh. What were you saying, Matt?"

He looked at her curiously, then tugged her sheet of graph paper out from under her elbow and towards him. "What's this, Miss...Sally?"

"Oh...nothing. Just—" Taking a deep breath, Julia dragged her mind away from Cooper. "It's sort of a hobby of mine. I like decorating and I was just bouncing around a few ideas for the diner." She reached for the sheet, embarrassed. "It's nothing, Matt."

"No, hey, this is great." Matt took in the palm trees, the curvy aluminum counters, the gaudy jukebox, the neon lettering. His Simpson-blue eyes, so like his sister's, shone with excitement. "Really great." He looked around the diner, then back at the sheet of drawing paper. "This would really work here."

Despite herself, Julia was flattered. "You think so? I've always been partial to retro '50s funk, myself."

"Is that what this is? I just think it looks great."

"What looks great?" Alice wiped the crumbs off the table with a damp sponge, then sat down next to Julia and angled her head just as Matt had done. "What's this?"

Julia was suddenly struck by the resemblance between brother and sister, which had been hidden behind Matt's in-your-face trendoid dressing and body piercing. Now that she looked closer, Julia could see that Matt and Alice shared facial planes, coloring, gestures and expressions.

How long had it been since she had had a chance to observe families? Not since Singapore, her parents' last posting. Her mother had made friends with a whole clan of interrelated English families who had been expatriates for three generations. The Devauxs had made a game of trying to pinpoint genealogy by looks and mannerisms.

She'd lost all that when she'd lost her own family. In New York and Boston, she'd met individuals, but with no idea of their backgrounds. She hadn't the faintest idea whether her officemates resembled their siblings or even whether they had siblings. It had been so long since she'd had a taste of family life, even secondhand.

"Sally?" Alice was tugging lightly at the graph paper.

"It's nothing, Alice." Julia tried to hide her doodling with her elbow, but Alice pulled it towards her.

Julia cursed this habit of hers. Of course, Alice would think that it was a slur on the diner. The diner was dull and dingy, of course, but that was none of Julia's business. Trying to change her environment was such an ingrained part of herself, she'd started toying with ideas without really noticing what she was doing. It came from her mother, who could never leave a room alone until it was precisely as she'd imagined it. Julia had spent her whole life redecorating and it seemed that minor details like death threats and banishment weren't enough to break the habit.

"Don't pay any attention, Alice. I was just, ah, imagining what the diner would look like if it were…" …nice. Julia bit her lip at the last minute. "I mean, if —" She sighed and gave up.

"You mean if someone had done something to it in the last thirty years?" Alice said.

"I didn't mean to imply —" Julia began, then looked at Alice who was watching her steadily with a half-smile on her lips. Julia was beginning to know Alice well enough to realize that she was a straight-shooter. It was pointless to pussyfoot around the fact that the diner was as dismal a place as she'd ever seen. "Well…it could use a coat of paint."

"And a wrecker." Alice shook her head at Julia's automatic protest. "No, it's true. Mom never did anything to spruce the place up. She never made much money on the diner and then when maybe she could have afforded it, she got sick. Actually, I've been wanting to redecorate for a long time but…" Alice chewed her lower lip nervously. "I don't know much about redecorating. It's really not my thing. Like cooking."

"Oh, I don't know," Julia protested. "Rafael seems to be enjoying his cake. That's his third slice."

"It's not mine," Alice replied glumly. "I tried out that Sacher torte recipe you gave me. You know—the chocolate one?"

"And?" Julia prodded.

"And it was awful." Alice sighed heavily. "It came out flat. And gummy. So I gave the recipe to Maisie and it came out great. It's already gone. She made me the spice cake, too. Maybe if I redecorated, people wouldn't notice that I can't cook."

"Maybe," Julia said dubiously.

"So, Sally." Alice leaned over to look past Julia's sheltering arm. "What did you have in mind?"

Julia thought for a moment, then slid the sheet over to Alice. "Well, to tell you the truth, I was sort of thinking retro '50s funk."

Alice's smile turned glassy and Julia sighed. Maybe retro '50s funk wasn't quite what Alice had in mind. "What do you want, Alice? I mean if you could just wave a magic wand, what would you turn your diner into?"

Alice didn't hesitate a second. "A fern bar," she said, in exactly the same tone of voice she might have said "heaven".

"A...fern bar?" Julia frowned. "Isn't that kind of—you know—kind of '80s?"

"Mmm?" Alice was looking a little dreamy as she glanced around the diner. "You mean old-fashioned? Maybe, but Simpson hasn't ever had a fern bar before. I don't think Rupert has ever had one either."

With good reason, Julia thought and shuddered at the prospect of the '80s finally rolling over Simpson, the streets infested with suspendered yuppies sporting Adidas and women in power suits with big shoulder pads. "I don't know, Alice. Do you really—" Then Julia took one look at Alice's face, at the yearning and the stars in her eyes and shut up. She looked around Carly's Diner, at the Early Gulag decor and winced. Even a fern bar would be better.

Julia shifted fabrics and color schemes in her head. It could be done.

She quickly flipped through the line drawings she'd made of her vision of Carly's Diner until she came to the blank pages. Her ideas had been fun but this was Alice's dream, after all. Julia determined to do her best to help Alice achieve it.

Decorating was something Julia could do in her sleep. Actually had. Once, right after the Devauxs had moved to Rome, she had woken up one morning in her empty bedroom with a complete decorating scheme in her head, down to the exact shade of royal blue on the ribbon trim of the curtain tiebacks.

Julia's pencil hovered over the paper. "So." She looked up at Alice. "Let 'er rip, and I'll see if I can keep up with you."

"Let 'er...rip?" Alice looked at her, puzzled. "What do you mean?"

"Well," Julia said reasonably, "you're going to need a floor plan and a color scheme for your fern bar. We'll walk our way around it, and I'll just sketch the plans for you. I've done this hundreds of times for friends. Where were you planning on putting the bar?" Julia doodled for a moment, then drew the outside walls. As the silence lengthened, she looked up. "Alice?"

"Hmm?" Alice had spilled some salt from the cracked glass saltcellar and was drawing rings in the granules with her forefinger. Her cheeks were pink.

Julia put her pencil down and tried to think of the right words. "Alice," she said gently, "you do have some idea of what you want your fern bar to look like, don't you?"

"Er…" Alice looked out the plate glass window. It was smudged and greasy. The street outside was empty. "Sort of."

Julia felt as if she had walked into a minefield. "Alice," she asked carefully, "have you ever actually, ahm, been in a fern bar?"

"Well…not actually inside one," Alice explained earnestly. "I mean we used to go by what a friend of Daddy's said was a fern bar on our way to the hospital in Boise when Mom was sick. It was so—so pretty. The hospital was horrible, and then we'd all drive back home in silence and the diner was closed and dusty and dirty and just so—depressing. And then a week later we'd drive back to the hospital for the chemotherapy and that was so depressing and in between, we'd pass by this wonderful place called The Trattoria and it was just so fresh and clean and—and cool. And everyone inside looked so ace and—" Alice bit her lip and shrugged. "I don't know. Everyone in there looked so…happy and we were out there, looking in…and Mom…" Alice shrugged again and looked away.

"I see," Julia said. And she did.

Well, if Alice wanted her fern bar, then by God she'd do everything in her power to see that Alice got it.

"Right, then." Julia kept her voice brisk. "So, let's bounce a few ideas around, why don't we? Now, we could put the bar right inside the entrance to the left." She stopped and narrowed her eyes as she thought of something. "Alice, can you get a liquor license?"

Alice drew herself up indignantly. "I'm twenty-five," she said with dignity. "Of course I can get a license. And anyway, my cousin Newton is mayor, and Coop's head of the town council. Newton and Coop meet a couple of times a year for town business then go over to Rupert for a beer. I hadn't thought of it that way, but it would save them a lot of miles if I could sell liquor."

"Nothing like friends in high places," Julia said dryly. "Okay—the bar could be here. That could be built cheaply, just a waist-high brick wall with ceramic tiles on the sides and a wooden top for a counter. That's where customers wait until they can be seated and that's usually where the yuppies get pie-eyed on about fifty *Kir Royales* and the health freaks wash out their kidneys with gallons of Perrier and a twist of lime. We'll probably have cowboys and beer. No matter." Julia's pencil flew as she talked. She flipped a page. "Now in the central area, we can have the tables. Any kind of table will do, as long as it's round. Even cheap plastic ones. We'll just sew up some fabric to cover the legs. We can rag-roll the walls in either pale blue and cream or peach and cream. And we can marbleize the doors. We'll need big planters, something like—" Julia stuck out her lower lip as she drew. "This. Something large and deep, if we want ferns. Can't have a fern bar without ferns." She looked up as a shadow fell across the table. "Hi, Bernie."

"Sally." Bernie nodded his head. "Alice. Hey, Sport." Bernie put his hand on Rafael's shoulder.

"Dad!" Rafael's grin showed delight and a good deal of his last bite of spice cake. "Miss Anderson bought me some cake."

"I can see that," Bernie said indulgently, ruffling his son's hair. "I can see a little too much of it, as a matter of fact. Remember what I told you about chewing with your mouth closed?"

Rafael obediently closed his mouth and went on chewing.

Bernie took in his son's delighted grin and turned to Julia. "Thanks, Sally. How did the lesson go?"

"Fine," Julia smiled, crossing her fingers under the table. Rafael had barely looked at his books before heading for the backyard and Fred. "We managed to comb Fred, too."

"Glad to hear it." Bernie hesitated for a long moment, turning his Stetson around in his work-roughened hands and shifting from one booted foot to another. "And—and how's he doin' in school?" he asked finally. "He'd been having problems, you said, and I wanted to know if maybe…things were going better." Bernie shot his son a glance, but Rafael was busy chasing crumbs around his plate with a fork. "Are they? Going better, I mean?"

Julia looked at Bernie's tense face. He'd stopped fidgeting and was standing straight now, as if facing an inspection by a court-martial. Julia wondered if he'd been in the armed services like Cooper. If he had been, he'd certainly pass muster now. He was clean-shaven and his clothes, though well-worn, were clean and pressed. The whites around his dark eyes were clear, instead of traffic light red.

"Rafael seems to be doing just fine, Bernie," Julia said gently. "I don't think you need worry any more. His grades have shot up and he's adjusting well to…" Julia hesitated. How to delicately describe a runaway mom? "…to the new situation," she finished lamely.

Bernie let out his pent-up breath. "That's good. That's very good." He turned to his son. "You want to wait for me in the pickup, son? I'll be out in just a minute."

"Okay, dad."

Bernie waited until Rafael was out of the room, then turned back to Julia. "So…you're sure he's okay?"

"Well," Julia smiled. "I'm no child psychologist, and he might yet grow up to be Jack the Ripper or the CEO of a major polluting company. But for the moment, Rafael seems like he's gone back to being a perfectly normal seven-year-old boy."

Bernie let out a long sigh of relief. "I'm back on track now, too. It was...hard, for a while."

"I imagine it was." Julia's voice was steady. She remembered the wreck of a man she'd met. Not at all the sober, hard-working cowboy standing in front of her.

"I think we can stop bothering you now."

"Oh—" Julia waved her hand. Truth was, now that Cooper was gone, Rafael kept her company, kept the darkness at bay. When Bernie stopped by to pick Rafael up, only Fred was left for company. "Rafael doesn't bother me. Not at all—"

"And anyway, he needs to catch up on his chores. It's time for us to get into our new routine now. Get our lives together. But I couldn't have got to this point without you. I can't thank you enough." Bernie's dark eyes met hers. "I owe you. Rafael means the world to me. I'm ashamed that I let him down like that. If you hadn't picked up the pieces, I don't know what would have happened."

"Oh, no." Bernie was being much too hard on himself. "Nothing would have happened. Rafael's a good little boy. And you're obviously a loving father. You just had a rough time. It all turned out okay."

"Thanks to you," Bernie persisted. "I just can't thank you enough." He flattened his hair with the palm of his hand and put his Stetson back on. "If you ever need anything, all you have to do is ask. Thanks again and—" He stopped, suddenly noticing the drawing on the table. "What's that?'"

"Nothing," Julia said swiftly.

"What do you mean, nothing?" Alice asked indignantly. She pushed the paper around so Bernie could get a better look. "Sally's got these ideas for redecorating. Doesn't it look great? We're going to turn the diner into a fern bar."

"Yeah?" Bernie examined Julia's drawing with care, then looked around the dusty diner as if seeing it for the first time. "I'm no expert," Bernie said. "But it sure looks like it'll be nice."

"Yeah, it will," Alice said proudly. "Only we can't decide what to put the ferns in."

Bernie reflected. "Coop has some old horse troughs. We could sand 'em and hose 'em down. We could bring them over with a truck when you're ready. And as for the work itself— well, I'm not much, but Coop's real handy with a saw and a hammer. He'll be back soon. We'll help."

"That's awfully nice of you. Thanks." Julia looked at Alice's rapt face. She felt caught up in a river flowing towards an unknown destination. "And thank Cooper, too."

"No thanks necessary. I reckon Coop'd do just about anything for you. And so would I." Bernie tugged at his Stetson in a sort of cowboy salute. "Sally. Alice."

He walked away, leaving Julia with her head whirling.

Alice wasn't paying any attention. "Golly, Sally," she breathed. She was studying the drawings the way some women study the latest issue of *Vogue*. "These are great." She looked up and shook her head in wonderment. "You've really got talent."

"It's just a knack," Julia said modestly, wrenching her attention back to the fern bar. When Bernie mentioned Cooper's name, her heart had given a huge lurch in her chest. "Now, I was thinking that the kitchen area would be over here—" Julia stopped and thought about the kitchen and about how kitchens were where food was prepared for human consumption and about how the person preparing that food for human consumption would be Alice.

Alice was obviously thinking the same thing. "The kitchen area," she said unenthusiastically.

"You know, Alice," Julia put her pencil down and leaned forward. "I was thinking. If your café—your fern bar—takes off, and people start coming from, oh, Rupert and Dead Horse, well then, you'd want to concentrate on hostessing and not have to be involved in the kitchen area."

"Hostessing." Alice smiled. "I like that."

"So," Julia continued, "I was thinking that maybe you might want to hire someone...someone who could—well, look after that aspect for you."

"You mean like a—a cook?" Alice frowned.

"Well, yes. I was thinking that maybe Maisie Kellogg might give you a helping hand. Her kids are out of the house now and I think she'd enjoy a part-time job."

Alice blinked. "Maisie Kellogg?"

"Yes."

"As the cook?"

"Uh-huh."

Alice turned the idea over in her mind. "Well, one thing's for sure—Maisie's a great cook. We all fought over who was going to get her chocolate cake at the church bazaar when we were kids. But I don't know, Sally," Alice shifted in her seat in embarrassment, "the diner doesn't really bring in all that much money. I couldn't afford to pay anyone a salary."

"Well, why don't you try talking to Maisie about that?" Julia nodded at the phone. "Give her a call and talk it over. Maybe the two of you could come to an arrangement, say share in the extra profits or something."

"Now?" Alice asked.

"No time like the present."

Alice walked slowly over to the phone and dialed a number. Julia watched Alice lean against the wall, the cord wrapped around one finger like the teenager she had been such a short while ago, and listened to the one-sided conversation.

"Hi, Glenn, it's me, Alice. Just fine and you? And how's Maisie? Oh, I'm sorry to hear that." Alice's distressed eyes looked over to Julia who shook her head and mouthed—"*Go on*". Alice drew in a sharp breath and turned back to the phone. "Uhm, do you think I could talk to her for a minute, anyway? Uhm, business. I think. Tell her...oh, okay, I'll wait... Hi, Maisie. This is Alice. Listen, I'm here with Sally Anderson—you know, the new grade school teacher? And we're, uhm, sort of talking about redoing the diner, nothing definite, just bouncing a few ideas around...uh-huh...and—and I was thinking I'd need someone to help out in the kitchen, but I can't afford—oh. Well—sure, okay. See you soon, then." Alice hung up the phone, dazed and looked over at a smugly smiling Julia. "She said she'd be right over."

"There," Julia said. "You see? That wasn't so bad, was it? Now, let's get back to our stuff before Maisie arrives. The two of you will want to talk over the business side of things without me around." Julia finished a sketch of the room from the back wall, and added some troughs, filling them in with plants. "So," she said casually, concentrating on sketching the leafy fronds of the ferns, "you think Cooper might help us—you out?"

"Oh, yeah." Alice tilted her head curiously. "God, if you're around, Coop'll be around, no doubt about that. Say, Sally, where do you think we're going to get all those plants? The closest flower shop is in Dead Horse and anyway ferns don't come cheap."

Julia finished the last sketch and held it up admiringly. Carly's Diner would never look like that, but still. "Alice, it seems to me that between Simpson and Rupert there's nothing but ferns and trees."

"You mean we should steal some ferns?"

"I prefer to think of it as relocating them," Julia replied primly. "The State of Idaho has a gazillion ferns, anyway. It'll never miss a few. We'll just have to make sure we get all the roots."

"Steal them," Alice said admiringly. "I never would have thought of that. You've really got a good imagination. How do you do it?"

"Guile," Julia said on a sigh.

* * * * *

The hotel room was the best available, but it wasn't much. The professional had become used to the very finest over the years. Once, on a job in San Diego to take out the head of the longshoreman's union, the professional had stayed at the Hotel del Coronado and had celebrated the hit in the majestic Coronet Room with a deliciously dry local champagne.

Water gurgled in the hotel pipes as the tepid heating system kicked in and the professional sighed. It was a far cry from the Coronado.

It was raining and the room was cold and damp. The professional couldn't wait to finish the job and fly out. It was all carefully planned with three different identities. The trip out of Sea-Tac to Hawaii. From Hawaii on a new passport to Mexico City, and from Mexico City to Kingston on another one. Once inside the Caribbean, it was going to be easy to disappear. The Caribbean was full of "disappeared" people, anyway. "Pulling an 876" it was called in the trade, when you disappeared into the mass of tiny sunny islands; 876 was Kingston's telephone area code.

The professional froze.

It couldn't be that easy. It couldn't, could it?

Feverishly, the professional dug out the local phonebook. It was on the plastic board with a thin scratched veneer of cheap pine which served as a desk. Next to it was a plastic bowl with a bag of peanuts that had expired in September.

A quick perusal of the counties and the telephone area codes brought the answer.

There was an area code 248 in Idaho and it more or less corresponded to Cook county. An area of 2,347 square miles.

The professional consulted the laptop and the powerful database map hacked from the U.S. Geological Survey Department. There were three medium-sized cities, four small towns and a handful of hamlets in the county. They would have put Julia Devaux in one of the smaller towns. Ruling out the area around Rockville and Ellis left a triangle created by Dead Horse, Rupert and Simpson.

Well, well, well.

The professional's eyes narrowed. *I know where you are, Julia Devaux. Now all I need to know is* who *you are.*

* * * * *

"What do you think, Sally?" Alice asked anxiously Saturday morning, holding up some color samples. Peach and sky-blue and taupe.

Alice had begged her to accompany her to Rupert. Julia had reluctantly agreed and then had surprised herself by having a wonderful time.

Alice's chatter had kept her amused during the ride and she had discovered that the third time was the charm. Instead of feeling oppressed and frightened by the landscape between Simpson and Rupert, she found it imposing and majestic.

When they had walked into Harlan Schwab's store, Harlan had greeted them cordially. At first he had been disappointed that Julia wasn't with Cooper.

In his second sentence, he asked Julia whether she was married and for a moment she was taken aback. Was that some rule out West she didn't know about? You had to be married to buy dry goods? Then she realized that, like everyone else, Schwab was matchmaking. There were only three channels and no cable in the area. Matchmaking was obviously what people did instead of watch TV. It took Julia a good ten minutes to get Schwab back on track and focused on Alice's project.

"Well…" Julia stepped back three paces to get a better look. She put a finger to her cheek and watched Alice more than the color samples. Alice fairly hummed with excitement, her light blue eyes alive with the thrill of planning her new diner—or fern bar. She looked about twelve and as happy as it was possible for a human to be. Julia bit back a smile as she pretended to consider. But it wasn't even close. The sky blue exactly matched Alice's eyes. "I'd go with the blue and we can rag-roll it with cream. Harlan? What do you think?"

"Good choice." Harlan Schwab said, beaming at them both. "Well, ladies, I think you're all set now. You've got—" he ticked off the packages around the cash register, " — your paint, your fabric, your leaf stencils, a set each of coffee cups and tea cups. You're all ready to go."

Mindful of Cooper's comments about shopping locally, Julia had convinced Alice to buy as much as she could from Glenn and they had made the trip into Rupert only to buy what Glenn didn't carry. Harlan had seemed to understand that instinctively.

Alice paid and Julia started gathering up the packages when Harlan stopped them with a wave of his hand. "No, no, ladies, we can't have that. Just let me know where the car is, and when you plan on driving back and I'll have my son there with the packages."

"Harlan, you really don't need to — " Alice began.

"Oh, yes I do." Harlan was already beckoning to a sturdily built teenager and smiling at Julia. "Coop'd never forgive me if I didn't give his lady a helping hand."

Cooper's lady?

What do I have, Julia thought, *a sign on my forehead?*

* * * * *

"I know I said I wanted to be back early, but would you mind if we stopped at the bookstore?" Alice asked as they strolled back to the car. "I want to look at some decorating books, just for a few ideas, and I want to see if the new Mary Higgins Clark is in."

"Oh, yeah," Julia replied. She had nothing else to do, besides recolor her hair that evening. She'd been putting it off. She hated having brown hair. "I've always loved bookstores."

"I can't believe how incredibly nice you've been." Alice hooked a companionable arm through Julia's as they walked down Rupert's pretty streets. "I'm really excited about what we're doing. And I just love coming to Rupert. It's a pity Simpson doesn't have any — *Oh my God*!"

"What?" Alice's shocked tone had Julia whirling around, heart pounding, wondering from what direction this new danger was coming from and what form the danger would take. She stared narrow-eyed down the street but all she saw was clean empty pavement and neatly boxed geraniums. "What?"

"Look at that," Alice breathed. She was pointing, wide-eyed, at a purple and blue jumpsuit with a wide white belt in a shop window. It was made out of some kind of shiny polyester and it jostled for position with a sequined biker's outfit. "Can't you just see me in that? I can see myself in that. God, isn't it gorgeous? How do you think I'd look?" She had her nose pressed against the shop window and her breath was fogging it up.

Like a Power Ranger, Julia thought. "Alice," she said carefully, "don't you think you should be saving your money for the redecorating?"

"Oh." Alice blinked as reality rushed in and she heaved a huge sigh. She detached her nose from the window with an almost audible plop. "Yeah, you're probably right," she said reluctantly as Julia led her away, like a child being led away from a candy store. Alice swiveled her head for one last wistful look at the shop window.

"Come on, Alice," Julia coaxed. "Let's go look at some of the decorating magazines. I wonder if Bob's got the new *Metropolitan Home* in." She had a firm grip on Alice's elbow and kept her distracted with chatter and by the time they walked into Bob's Corner Bookshop, Alice seemed to have herself under control. She went straight to the home decoration section.

Julia stood still for a moment, breathing in the heady smell of books. She'd been to the bookstore less than a week ago, but she was used to dipping in and out of bookstores the way other people dipped into the cookie jar. Bookstores usually had twice-weekly deliveries, she knew, so there would probably be a whole new set of books in since last Saturday. And, to tell the truth, last Saturday she'd been so distracted by Cooper's overwhelming presence that she hadn't browsed as much as she'd have liked. Alice was a very nice girl, but she certainly didn't make her blood bubble hotly under her skin the way Cooper did.

Humming quietly, Julia dove into the bookshelves.

Half an hour later, she woke up from her trance, arms full of books, having thoroughly examined Bob's stock. It was a well-run little bookshop, for its size. Even if it had been in Boston, it would have been one of Julia's favorites. Now that the drive to Rupert didn't terrify her, Julia knew her stay in Simpson—however long that would be—would be more bearable.

And Simpson wasn't even as bad as she sometimes made it out to be in her darkest moments. Alice was turning into a good friend and the redecorating project was sure to keep her happily busy for a while. And, of course, there was Cooper, who kept her warm at night and gave her more orgasms than there were trees in Idaho. And who was coming home on Friday.

Julia looked around for Alice and spotted her in the magazine section, talking with a young blonde woman. Alice caught Julia's eye and waved, grinning. Julia walked over.

"Hey, Julia." Alice shifted her magazines to free an arm. "Meet Mary Ferguson. She's new to the area, too. She lives in Dead Horse. Mary, this is Sally Anderson, our new grade school teacher in Simpson. That's about 20 miles away."

"Hi, Mary." Julia shook her hand. "Nice to meet you." Mary Ferguson looked to be Alice's age, or maybe a year or two older. She shared Alice's blonde, wholesome looks.

"Hi, Sally." The young blonde smiled. "It's sure nice to meet another newcomer. It seems not too many people move out here. So you live in Simpson too. What's Simpson like?"

Julia thought that over. "Quiet."

"Oh." Mary looked downcast. "That's not too good. No lawsuits, no divorces?"

"Ahm..." Julia bit back a smile. "Not lately. You on the lookout for lawsuits and divorces?"

"I sure am." Mary grinned and pressed a card in Julia's hand. "If you need legal advice, I'm your woman." Julia noticed that Alice held a similar card in her hand.

Curious, Julia looked it over. It was cheap cardboard and had Mary Ferguson, Attorney-at-Law printed on it. "There's no address," Julia said. "Just a telephone number."

"It's an answering service in Dead Horse. I'll get an office just as soon as I get a client or two. In the meantime, I'm living in a rented room. I just passed the state bar exam this summer and I didn't want to work with my father's law firm. He's got a big one in Boise and he always just assumed...well, I guess he thought that I would automatically want to work for him. But if I start out with him, I'll never know if I'm any good or not. So I decided to open my own practice. But my graduating class was the largest class of law graduates ever and there are no openings at all in the Boise area. So I decided to take the scientific approach and studied the lawyer-to-population ratio in the whole state and this part of the state has the lowest. But," she added sadly, "I'm beginning to see why."

"Well, that's—" Julia hardly knew what to say, "that's a—a novel approach."

"Those are my dad's very words," Mary said glumly, "only he used 'stupid' instead of 'novel'."

"I'm starting a new business, too," Alice said. "Only I don't have business cards." She caught Julia's eye and grinned. "Yet."

"Oh, yeah?" Mary turned friendly eyes onto Alice. "What kind of business?"

"A fern bar," Alice said proudly. "And sometime soon, I'll have an inauguration. Maybe at the next meeting of the Rupert Ladies' Association."

"There's a Rupert Ladies' Association?" Mary brightened and took an enormous planner out of her purse. She pulled the pen from its slot and laboriously filled in a page. "Rupert Ladies' Association," she said as she wrote, then looked up. "That's great. I'll join immediately. Who knows if there's an unhappy wife who wants to file for divorce? Or someone got run over and wants to sue. Do you know when the next meeting will be held?"

"Oh," Alice said airily, "sometime in the next ten days."

"Okay. I think I could fit it in." Mary started flipping importantly through her planner. Julia was amused to see that most of the pages were blank. Mary's pen hovered. "Who should I contact?"

"Karen Lindberger. She's in the Rupert phonebook."

Mary was diligently writing the name down, then looked up at Alice. "And what's the name of your new fern bar?"

"Carly's—no." Alice bit her lip and looked pleadingly at Julia. "I don't want it to have the same name. What will we call it?"

"Well, that's not a problem," Julia said. "It seems rather obvious to me what it should be called." She hummed the first few bars of "Alice's Restaurant", and looked expectantly at Alice and Mary.

They looked blankly back.

Julia knew she didn't have much of a voice. She hummed the bars again and sighed when the two girls' smiles starting looking strained. They stared at her, looking for all the world like two very confused blonde puppies. Well, they were younger than she was and they didn't share her penchant for '70s movies. Of course they didn't recognize the song. Julia suddenly felt ancient.

"Ohhh-kaaay," she breathed. "How about...how about the 'Out to Lunch'?"

"Out to Lunch." Alice's eyes were gleaming. "Oh, that's wonderful!" She all but clasped her hands over her heart. "Oh, Sally, you're so smart. However do you think of these things?"

"It's a knack," Julia said.

* * * * *

The gun wasn't important, the camera was.

You didn't need a Dirty Harry .44 Magnum to take out Julia Devaux. Any Saturday night special would do. As it happened, the professional had purchased, perfectly legally, a Model 60 Smith and Wesson two hours after landing at Boise airport. It was snubby, with a 2-inch barrel, and it only carried five shots, but that was fine. Two shots would do it.

The gun had been purchased with one of the professional's deeper identities. The bullets would go to the ballistics lab, the gun would be tracked down and a trace put on the identity. The professional had created a character three layers deep, with cross-referenced credit ratings, an impressive educational background and even a few awards for public service from two local Chambers of Commerce in two different states. The professional had had a lot of fun with the wording of the citations.

The cops would go crazy.

And by the time the first underpaid lab assistant examined the bullets, the professional would be lifting an ice-cold margarita on the sundeck of the beach house.

No, the gun wasn't of any importance whatsoever. What was important was the camera. After much hard deliberation, the professional had settled on a Hasselblad 35 mm that automatically stamped the date and the time on the film. That was important.

Santana was an animal and when he'd specified Julia Devaux's head, he meant exactly that. The professional could just imagine Santana in some garage, recently sprung from prison, gloating over Julia Devaux's head. He would probably have it mounted.

But there was no way on earth that the professional could travel across the country with a human head. Thus, something else was necessary to convince Santana that the job was done.

The professional had it all planned, down to the finest detail. First the incapacitating shot to the shoulder, taking timed pictures, then putting the camera on automatic as the professional put the gun to Julia Devaux's head and pulled the trigger. And the final photograph.

A headshot of a head shot, the professional thought with satisfaction. *I like it.*

* * * * *

Cooper was seriously annoyed by the time he made it to Carly's late Sunday afternoon. It had been a harrowing week.

Sure, he got a lot of business done and had bought fifteen very promising foals, but he hadn't had a spare minute. He was up before dawn each day to watch the training sessions, busy all day with the annual conference, out to dinner talking business until very late every evening. The only time he had free to call Sally was very early in the morning but that was 3 a.m. her time.

Then a freak storm in Lexington had delayed his flight out until Sunday morning. Cooper spent the day grimly battling his way across the country from airport to airport with only one thought in mind — getting back home and getting back to Sally.

He'd missed her fiercely. The nights had been the worst part. He'd spent every night with an iron hard-on thinking of her, wishing with every cell of his being that he was back in bed with her.

Bernie had kept him informed via e-mail about what was going on in Simpson. How Sally was helping Alice redecorate the diner and how Sally, Alice, Chuck, Matt, Glenn and Maisie were working on the diner over the weekend. Cooper had e-mailed back, directing Bernie and as many of the men who could be spared to give a hand. He'd ordered all the old horse troughs to be taken out, cleaned with steam hoses, sanded and brought to the diner.

But he'd been champing at the bit the whole time, frustrated that he wasn't there to help. Frustrated that he wasn't with Sally.

Cooper finally made it to the ranch by five in the afternoon, quickly showered and changed into work clothes. He broke the speed limit into Simpson. It didn't matter because there wasn't anyone around to arrest him. Chuck was at the diner.

It was after six by the time he walked into Carly's.

And there she was.

Cooper's eyes were immediately drawn to the tall stepladder in the corner. Sally was precariously perched on the top rung, arms outstretched to reach the top corner. She was doing something complicated with a roller. Cooper couldn't tell what, but the effect sure was pretty. The walls looked mottled, pale blue and white, like the inside of a robin's egg. Around the top of the wall near the ceiling was a pretty light green leaf stenciling. If it had been explained to him in words, he wouldn't have understood it. But it was very attractive.

Sally had haunted his thoughts and even his dreams while he was in Kentucky and it wasn't just sexual obsession. Whatever it was, it was real because his heart picked up speed when he saw her. She was dressed in work clothes—faded jeans and an old shirt, but they couldn't disguise the slender, elegant lines of her body. He wanted her with ferocious intensity, but there was more to it than that.

He was a horse breeder and he knew all about the sexual pull the female has on the male of any species, horse or human. It had been over two years since he'd felt the pull, but it was as strong as any he'd seen in his stallions. So it was sex, sure, but also something more. Much more.

He wanted to fuck her, but it went further than that. He wanted her around, all the time. He wanted to tell her about his week. He wanted her to redecorate his house—hell, redecorate his *life*—like she was redecorating Alice's diner.

Something about the atmosphere in the diner was already different. The sad air of despair was gone. It was a miracle. The dusty old diner that he'd known for as long as he could remember was gone forever.

And good riddance. He could hardly count the number of heartburns he'd had thanks to Carly and Alice. And if Maisie Kellogg was handling the cooking end of it, they'd all be fine and not risk ptomaine poisoning.

Alice was flitting about like a hummingbird, looking focused and happy. Chuck was busily hammering nails into a two by four held by a serious-looking Matt. Loren and Beth were wiping plates. Cooper was satisfied to see that Bernie and his men were being useful. Rafael and Fred were scampering around happily, getting in everyone's way.

Glenn and Maisie were there, too, Maisie dressed in her cleaning clothes with a red bandanna around her hair. They all looked transformed and energized. Alice, Chuck, Matt, Glenn, Maisie. Even Bernie and Rafael were looking happier than two weeks before.

And all because of Sally.

Cooper watched her up on the stepladder, stirred to the bottom of his soul because he knew that he was being transformed by Sally, too. Turned into someone better and happier just like she was turning the diner into a better and happier place.

Cooper stood a moment, trying to get a grip on all the unfamiliar emotions washing through him. They were clean and powerful and brand-new. He was brand-new.

She had fixed his broken window.

Chapter Fifteen

When Julia tired of painting, all she had to do was think of Cooper and she'd get new energy in her painting arm by picturing slapping the paint all over him.

She'd missed Cooper with a ferocity that shocked her.

The nights were the worst. To her amazement, she missed the sex. Julia had never thought of herself as a particularly sensual woman, but a few nights with Cooper proved that she had had no idea of how quickly you could get addicted to good sex.

Not even good sex, really. Cooper wasn't much on foreplay, preferring instead to get straight down to business. No matter. Her body didn't care at all. The instant he started moving in her, she started moving towards orgasm. It was like reaching some erotic zone, where she would just have orgasm after orgasm. Santana, the danger she was in, Simpson—all her problems just fled her mind in an explosion of climaxes.

When she was with Cooper, there was no thought of anything but the wild, heart-stopping pleasure he gave her.

These past nights without him had been terrifying. She'd spent the evenings rattling around alone in the little house, unable to settle down to anything, waiting until it was time to go to bed, dreading it. Bed time was when the horror started.

She'd had a nightmare every single night. Around three every morning, she'd wake up, heart pounding, disoriented, dry-mouthed and terrified. It was getting so she was scared to fall asleep, because that's when the monsters came for her. Terrifying dark shapes, waiting…

That's when she missed Cooper with an intensity which was almost as terrifying as the nightmares. It was scary to want someone that much.

Be back Friday, he'd said. Hah! she thought, pushing down violently on the paint roller, easing up again when she saw she was spattering.

She'd started waiting for Cooper with a deep sense of anticipation already early Friday afternoon, when she and Alice and Maisie had started going over the plans. She'd look up expectantly every time the diner door opened, only to be disappointed. Bernie, Chuck, Glenn, Loren, Matt, even Fred had all crossed the threshold and each time a man approached, her heart leapt into her throat. And then sunk back to her heels.

All day Saturday while they'd worked on the diner, she'd been in a state of expectant tension, making excuses for him in her head.

The flight was delayed. He's tied up at the ranch. He's been kidnapped by aliens.

A hundred times, she'd turned to Bernie, the question burning on the tip of her tongue: where's Cooper? But she was embarrassed and anyway, she didn't want to hear the answer. What if it was—Coop's back at the ranch, but too busy to make it into town?

And what was so special about Cooper, anyway? Why should she care about him? He wasn't handsome and he certainly wasn't charming. He was —

"Cooper?" she whispered. She was reaching for the last bit in the corner to stencil the wainscoting when there he was at the bottom of the ladder—as if her thinking of him had suddenly conjured him up out of thin air.

He was looking stern, as always. With his dark skin, high cheekbones and midnight-black hair he looked a little like an Incan god. She stared at him for a moment, taking in his impassive features.

All the paint was dripping, destroying an afternoon's work. She lunged to catch the pale blue drops and overbalanced. The stepladder tilted and she felt herself falling.

"Cooper!" she screamed.

"Right here." His voice was low and deep and calm as he stretched up and caught her by the waist. His grip was gentle but strong. Julia let the roller drop to the floor as she instinctively braced her hands on his broad shoulders. As easily as if he were lifting a can of coffee down from the shelf, he lifted her off the ladder and let her slide slowly down the length of his body.

Julia could feel his strength permeate her entire being. It was as if the world — the universe — suddenly stilled and she and Cooper were the only people left on the planet. His face above her filled her entire field of vision. Julia reluctantly dropped her hands from his shoulders as her feet touched the floor and aligned her arms along his as he held her waist. Her hands clutched his rock-hard biceps for balance.

Everything suddenly came into alignment, as if that missing piece from the heart of her world had suddenly slotted into place. He was inscrutable and impassive and silent and she had been impatiently waiting for eight days for him to show up. With an almost painful jolt, she realized that she was falling in love with Cooper.

"You're back," she said breathlessly, stupidly.

"Yeah."

She tried to read his face, but couldn't. All she could see was that he was in the grip of some strong emotion, but she couldn't begin to decipher which one. His eyes glittered and the skin was stretched tautly over his sharp cheekbones.

"When did you get back?"

"'Bout an hour ago."

"I thought — I thought you said you were coming back on Friday." Julia knew that she should release Cooper's biceps and step back but she couldn't make herself do it.

"Had a meeting. Flight was delayed. Had a hard time getting back."

"Well, I'm…glad you're back."

His jaw tightened. "Glad to be back."

"We're redecorating here, did you know?"

"Heard that. E-mailed Bernie."

Julia was finally able to smile. She'd almost forgotten his laconic way of speaking. "I guess you left all your pronouns back in Kentucky," she said.

"Guess so." One side of Cooper's hard mouth kicked up in a smile. Funny, Julia had never really noticed what a beautiful mouth he had. His large hands tightened on her and he stared at her for long moments, his gaze roving over her face, finally settling on her mouth. Then he slowly bent his head.

Julia could feel his body heat all over, she could feel his arms under her hands, his long thighs aligned with hers. Julia's eyes started to close and she rose on tiptoe.

"Oof!" Julia was knocked sideways as Fred launched himself at Cooper and only Cooper's quick reactions kept her on her feet. Fred was wriggling with happiness, woofing and trying to lick them both.

Half a dozen people were watching them with interest. At Cooper's glare, Chuck coughed into his fist and turned away and the others drifted off, like spectators after the show.

"Maybe you should brand her, Coop," Bernie said to Cooper with a grin. "That way there'd be no mistake." He lifted his hands at Cooper's snarl. "Just a thought, boss. Just a thought."

"Come on, dearie," Maisie said kindly to a dazed Julia. "What you need is a good cup of coffee and my special double chocolate brownies." She led Julia to the kitchen and Julia followed her on rubber legs, knowing she needed a sugar infusion to get the blood flowing back to her head.

* * * * *

Sydney Davidson dipped a finger into the tepid water in the old, stained bathtub and rolled his eyes with a groan. He shivered. Damn but it was cold out here in Idaho! He thought with longing of his house in Virginia and its brand-new Jacuzzi.

Of course, dead men don't need Jacuzzis, he reminded himself.

Not for the first time, Sydney Davidson was sorry. Sorry he'd been tempted by the money, sorry he'd misused his training as a biochemist. Sorry he'd gotten his life so far off track.

Even now, he could hardly believe how easy the slide downhill had been. A few insignificant favors—say, a little recreational pharmacology for a party or two, in exchange for the use of a condo in Vail a few weeks a year. More favors— more substantial this time—but a brand-new Lexus in return. And soon he was spending more time on his…extracurricular activities than on the job, while the money just rolled in. And then it had all started spinning out of control, and here he was, running for his life.

Still, all in all, an old bathtub was better than a new coffin.

This was his second chance. By God he was going to do this right.

When this mess was all over and he'd testified, he would…he would dedicate his life to good works.

Not entirely sure exactly what good works entailed, Davidson reflected on how he could turn over a new leaf. The only thing that sprang to mind was the Red Cross. Yes! he thought excitedly. Red Cross workers were dedicated souls, combing the planet for lives to save. Surely that was stressful work. Surely they'd need a little help in coping with all those floods and earthquakes and famines and guerrilla wars.

Let's see now, he thought, *I could fix them up with a nice little cocktail to make them feel better. A few milligrams of desapramine and phenylethylamine for the stress, add a dash of serotonin-uptake inhibitors to feel better and forget all that ugliness. That would do the trick.*

He turned the hot water tap a little further to the right.

While Davidson was happily thinking of better living through chemistry, a tiny sensor, only a few angstroms thick and undetectable except under an electron microscope, caused a semiconductor to become a conductor instead of an insulator. A live wire that been so carefully frayed not even the keenest microscope could detect that it had been done deliberately, plunged straight into the boiler.

When Sydney Davidson finally sank into his tub of warmish water, the surge of current stopped his heart, brought the blood in his veins to a boil and fried one of the finest pharmacological brains of this century.

* * * * *

"Well," Beth said an hour later, fisting her hands on her ample hips. "This is something else." She looked around approvingly at the changes that the past forty-eight hours had brought to Carly's Diner. Now, officially, the Out to Lunch.

Julia looked around, too, though most of the attention in her head was taken up with Cooper. Every time she turned around he seemed to be there, handing her a brush, mixing her paint for her, generally driving her crazy with desire. He'd managed to hold her hand, touch the back of her neck, run a hand along her back until she seemed to be sensitized, almost magnetized to his presence. She could feel his presence by the way the hairs stood up at the back of her neck.

"Hmm," she answered dreamily. Cooper was standing slightly behind her and she could feel his body heat. Julia was trying to act nonchalant but she trembled with the effort it took not to lean into him.

Beth gently nudged Julia's ribs with an elbow. "So, what do you think, Sally?"

"Who?" Her brain seemed to be mired in molasses. "What?"

"The diner—or rather the fern bar," Beth said patiently. "What do you think?"

"I—" Julia looked around and tried to focus. Most of the work was done. The walls were painted, the counters sanded, the ferns planted. Everything looked and smelled fresh and new. It was easy to overlook the uneven rag rolling and the tables that were slightly askew. Alice had gone overboard with the ferns and Julia thought that prospective customers were going to have to come equipped with machetes.

Still, all in all, it had a sort of tacky charm.

"It's great," she said.

"Nice." Cooper's voice rumbled at her back and set up vibrations in her stomach that reverberated throughout her body. Julia took a deep breath to try to calm herself down.

"Do you think you could do something with our store?" Beth asked Julia.

"Your...store?" Julia asked, her senses quivering. Cooper had stepped even nearer. He put a large hand on her shoulder and her pulse went wild.

"Yeah. You know—make it modern or something." Beth waved her hand. "This is so pretty."

Julia could see in Beth's eyes the same look Alice had had and despite the fact that Cooper was distracting her, she found herself interested. "Well..."

"Yes?" Beth said eagerly. "What do you think?"

"I'm not too sure you should go modern. Maybe you should turn your store into one of those pretty, old-fashioned emporiums, like you see in the movies. You could repaint that long counter and put glass panes in to show the merchandise. And you could have the goods in barrels and canisters. And then—"

"Hey, everyone!" Chuck clapped his hands loudly. "You can put down picks and shovels. It's time to get out of the salt-mines. Maisie's cooked us all a real spread."

There was a scramble to see who could get to the trestle tables set up against the walls first. Julia found herself pushed towards one, then Glenn thrust a plate into her hands. She picked up a drumstick.

"Oh, God," she said and closed her eyes. Pleasure just didn't get any better.

"Good, huh?" Glenn asked proudly.

"Wonderful," she said reverently, and bit into the cold curried chicken again. "If this is any example of Maisie's cooking skills, then the fern bar's going to be a success."

"It's already a success, as far as I'm concerned," Glenn said, smiling. "It got Maisie out of bed and interested in something again. If the fern bar doesn't have any customers, then I'll buy forty meals a day just to keep them in business. It's worth it to me to see her smiling again."

"Yeah." Julia watched Maisie as she happily ladled out food from the buffet.

"I've got you to thank for this," Glenn said quietly.

"No, you don't," Julia said, surprised. "I didn't cook anything. It was Maisie—"

"I don't mean that." Glenn waved his hand impatiently. "I mean you're the one who gave Alice the idea of redecorating and calling in Maisie. Both Chuck and I are more grateful than we can say. If you ever need anything—anything at all, count on us."

"Oh, no really." She could feel herself turning red. "I didn't do all that much..." Her voice trailed off.

Cooper filled the doorway. One of his workmen, a tall lanky man named Sandy, had called him out. There were problems in hanging up the sign and Cooper had disappeared. Now here he was again, larger than life, peeling off his big leather work gloves, his dark eyes scanning the room until he found her. Their eyes met. Julia felt a deep tingle of excitement set up inside herself and her body tightened with anticipation.

Cooper started crossing the diner and Glenn caught the glass that fell out of Julia's nerveless fingers. Poker-faced, he set it on the table. "I—ah, have to go talk to someone," Glenn said. "About something. See you."

"What?" Julia turned to him blindly. "Oh, okay. Sure, that's fine."

He's magnificent, was all Julia could think as Cooper approached her slowly, broad shoulders blocking out the rest of the room. Moisture—condensation? rain?—clung to his inky hair and Julia's hands itched to run her fingers through the thick dark pelt. His expression was stern as always. She wanted to touch his face, see if she could make the frown lines go away, trace that hard, beautiful mouth with her finger.

Cooper came up so close to her that she had to tilt her head. He looked down at her and his face had never seemed more harsh, more angular.

"Come with me," he said. "Now."

"Yes, Cooper," Julia whispered, and put her curried drumstick down on the tablecloth, missing her plate by a good ten inches.

Cooper grabbed her hand and dragged her through the door and towards a black pickup.

"Where are we going?" Julia cried.

Cooper practically threw her into the cab, got in and pulled away with a squeal of tires. "To your house," he said tightly. "This time we're going to get it right. We're going to fuck all night."

Chapter Sixteen

"That's another one down." Aaron Barclay slammed down the phone and turned to his boss.

"Another what?" Davis took a hefty bite out of the stone-cold takeout pizza. The canteen was closed on Sundays, and anyway, it was past 11 p.m. Staffing reductions had cut hard and deep. He and Barclay had been forced into doing major overtime.

"Witness. In Idaho."

"Jesus." Davis swallowed the big bite he had in his mouth and felt the pepperoni slide down heavily and greasily. He absently rubbed his palm over his paunch. "That makes two."

"In two days," Barclay agreed.

"Who was it?"

"Dunno. Let's see." Barclay pulled up a file on his computer and quickly keyed in some data. "Here we go. Guy's name was Sydney Davidson. Used to work for Sunshine Pharmaceuticals. We'd relocated him as Grant Patterson. In a place called Ellis. Ellis, Idaho."

"A hit?"

"Accident."

Davis snorted.

"Well..." Barclay grimaced. "That's the thing. Our Boise people went over to—" He checked the screen again, "Ellis. The local police said it was an accident but our people were loaded for bear. Losing two in two is no joke. But apparently it really was an accident. Faulty wiring in the house. Short circuit drove the current straight into his bathtub. Killed him instantly. Locals and feds went over it again and again but they couldn't find anything wrong with it. Neither could we."

"Well, have our people go over everything again with a fine-tooth comb. Losing two witnesses like that." Davis angrily rubbed at a grease spot on his tie with a napkin. "We're beginning to look like Fort Fumble around here. Say..." Davis looked up suddenly. "How far away is Ellis from where we put Julia Devaux?" Devaux was far and away WitSec's most valuable protectee.

"Not far."

"Same area code?"

"Yeah." Barclay sounded resigned. Both of them had fought the decision to organize files according to area code. "Just goes to show."

The hairs on Davis' forearms rose. "Pull her out," he said quietly. "Pull her out now."

"But...boss." Barclay shifted uncomfortably and pointed to the new regulation booklet. He tapped its green and gray cover. "Regulation 5. 'No unnecessary expenditures'. It costs over fifty thousand dollars to relocate a witness and we have to justify that. If our own people testify there's no danger to Devaux and we pull her out anyway, we're in deep shit."

"Damn it!" Davis pounded the regulation booklet in frustration. "Somehow someone got the file! They must have. When we were switching over to CD-ROM a couple weeks ago, maybe. Remember that? We had some kind of glitch. Well, someone must have hacked into our system. And he's taking out everyone who was in that file! We've got to get Devaux out of there."

"Boss, let me play devil's advocate here. God knows she will." Barclay's eyes rolled to the ceiling and they both knew he was thinking of the 31st floor and the new director. He lifted a fist. Davis couldn't help noticing how grubby it was. "One," Barclay said, raising a dirty index finger. The nail was nibbled to the quick. "However improbable it seems, the police, the feds and our own people have ruled both deaths accidental."

"Oh, puh-leeze —"

"Wait. Two." Another finger. "There is a two million dollar bounty on Julia Devaux's head. News of that kind of money has crossed the country three or four times. Who knows how many hit man wannabes and real deals are out beating the bushes? Do you honestly think that some guy who is smart enough to penetrate our firewalls and discover where we've got Devaux is out there right now, taking out the people in that file one by one in — what? Alphabetical order? Taking out Abt and Davidson might be worth a hundred thou, tops. Do you think he'd leave Julia Devaux and two mil for last? Does that make sense?"

Put like that it didn't.

"And anyway," Barclay continued persuasively, "all our files have been recoded with 240-bit encryption. Nobody's getting in, boss."

Davis pursed his lips, thinking furiously. He usually trusted Aaron Barclay's instincts.

But Barclay wasn't looking good these days. He had bags under his eyes so big they could be checked in at the airline counter. Davis watched as Barclay's fingers drummed nervously on the booklet.

Barclay's hands shook and there was a distinct whiff of the unwashed about him. He was in bad shape. "It's your call, boss," Barclay said.

"Yeah, it is." Davis sighed, mentally saying goodbye to a peaceful Thanksgiving holiday. He was going to take a lot of flak on this one. He picked up the phone. "I'm going with my gut on this one. We're pulling her out."

* * * * *

She was trembling. Cooper could almost feel the air vibrate on the other side of the pickup's cabin. Shit. He was behaving like an animal.

He'd left Sally for a week without even a phone call. Then he'd come back to grab her and drag her off to bed.

He had to be real careful, here. Attractive women had a long history of leaving Cooper men for much less than this. She was already a fucking miracle. He needed to hold on to her. No matter that he was burning up to be in her now, he had to behave better than this.

Cooper leaned over in the dark cab and kissed her, holding on tightly to the steering wheel so he wouldn't be tempted to touch her. It was a light, gentle kiss. Sixteen-year-old-boy-out-on-first-date-with-school-cheerleader kind of kiss. Her lips curved under his and her small hand cupped his cheek.

"Let's go in," he whispered against her mouth.

"Okay," she sighed. He hadn't had his tongue in her yet, his lips had just brushed hers, but he could smell the dark chocolate brownies Maisie had fed her on Sally's breath. It was intoxicating.

Cooper's jaw clenched when he helped her down and saw her shiver. She only had a shirt on in this subzero weather. He'd dragged her away so fast she hadn't had time to grab her coat. He quickly unzipped his thick heavy parka and draped it over her shoulders.

She smiled up at him as if he'd showered her with rubies. "Thanks."

Jesus. She was thanking him, instead of complaining about what an asshole he was. He cleared his throat as he put his arm around her. "No problem. Let's get you inside; it's freezing out here."

Snow was falling, light flakes settling over the land like a gentle white blanket, muffling all sounds. Everyone in Simpson was in the diner. Her street was dark and silent. They could have been alone in the town, in the state, in the world.

Inside the door, Sally switched on the light and looked up at him. "Do you like it?" she asked as she shook the snow from his jacket.

Cooper was confused. Did he like her? What the hell did that mean? Hell, yes — then he followed her eyes and his own widened.

The sad, shabby little house was transformed. She'd painted the walls cream, made pretty cream and pink curtains and used the same material to make a tablecloth. The ugly cabbage rose sofa and armchairs were covered up with pale yellow lengths of cloth artistically knotted at the sides. A big glass bowl held quartz pebbles. Cooper recognized some of the stuff she'd bought at Schwab's, but he never imagined they could make such a dramatic change to a room.

"This is really nice." He tightened his arm around her shoulders. "You're a magician."

He could feel her sigh more than hear it, a light lifting of shoulders under his arm. "No. I just like making the best of things."

From his angle, Cooper could see long lashes, a delicate cheekbone, creamy skin. She took his breath away. She wasn't a magician, she was a witch and she'd cast a powerful spell on him.

Suddenly, the past week spent alone, far from Sally, seemed like the worst hardship he'd ever undergone. Worse than Hell Week. He couldn't stand it one second more.

"We need to get to bed." His voice was thick. "Now."

She smiled up at him. "Now?"

He nodded.

"I guess it's going to be one of those times," she said softly.

One of those times in which he was going to strip her and enter her as quickly as was humanly possible. "Yeah."

She smiled and stretched up towards him. He bent and took her mouth. It was as softly warm as he remembered. She turned fully into him, lacing her arms around his neck. He didn't want to change anything about their position, so he simply wrapped his arms around her, lifted her, and walked them into her bedroom. He put her down on her feet next to the bed and, without leaving her mouth, slipped his parka off her. It fell with a heavy thud. He didn't want to stop kissing her but he had to if he wanted her naked.

His hands moved fast as he bent. Flannel shirt, bra, jeans, panties, shoes, socks, ah...here she was. Naked. A pale glimmering angel. Watching her face carefully, Cooper stood back up, turned his hand and cupped her. She wasn't very wet yet. He slipped a finger in and caressed the smooth heat of her. Moisture rose up out of her very core, like a little miracle. It wasn't enough yet. He was as swollen as one of his stallions and she had to be very wet to take him, but they were getting there.

He bent again to her, kissing her deeply while his finger stroked inside her. Sally's fingers were digging into his shoulders, her breath coming out in a little shudder as he probed her softness. "Cooper," she breathed, then—"Oh!" when his thumb circled her clitoris. She shook and he shook, too.

He'd never known a woman he could take from zero to a thousand miles an hour so quickly.

He gritted his teeth, because though she was getting softer and wetter by the second, it wasn't enough. He was going to fuck her hard once he got into her and she needed to be ready.

"On the bed," he whispered against her mouth.

"Okay." Her lips curved in a smile against his. She recognized that tone, he could tell. The one where he was inches from losing control.

Cooper eased her down onto the bed with his free arm, then eased himself down next to her hip. His finger was still inside her, moving gently. He shifted his palm and she obediently opened her legs. She had lovely legs, long and sleek. His hand brushed the inside of her thighs and it felt like warm velvet.

Cooper watched her for a moment. It was dark in her bedroom but her body glowed palely in the light of the streetlamp outside like a woman-shaped pearl. Though he was itching to be inside her, he took a moment to savor every detail of her. The delicate collarbones, the small, upright breasts with their pale pink nipples, the smooth soft belly, the soft thatch of fiery hair between her thighs. Everything about her was elegant and perfect.

Her legs moved restlessly on the blanket while he let his finger imitate his cock. Only his cock had never been this gentle, he'd always pumped hard and fast in her. Maybe he always would. Maybe the only slow fucking she'd ever get from him would be from his hand.

There was complete silence except for his breathing and the wet sounds as his finger moved in and out of her.

He watched his hand moving between her legs. His finger was slick now with her juices. When his thumb caressed her clitoris again, her little cunt pulled at him. Her belly muscles rippled and her thighs trembled.

"Do you like this?" he asked quietly, finally raising his eyes to her face. She'd been watching him watching her.

Sally's hand caressed his arm. "I like everything you do to me, Cooper," she said simply.

His eyes closed, as if in pain. Impossibly, his cock surged, lengthening and hardening even more, rapping against the stiff denim of his jeans as if against a door.

He started unbuttoning his shirt, then stopped, astonished.

His hand was trembling.

His hand never trembled. He was an excellent shot and — as he'd told her — was even better with a knife. You don't shoot true and hit your mark a hundred times out of a hundred with a knife if you were the kind of man whose hand shook under pressure.

The only other time in his life in which his hand trembled had been the first time with her.

Sally Anderson was slowly undoing him. Then putting him back together. A better man.

He finished unbuttoning his shirt one-handedly. To take it all the way off, his right hand had to leave the warmth and softness of Sally's body and for a moment, he was tempted to just leave his shirt on.

But he loved the feel of her skin against his. When they made love, she rubbed herself against him like a little cat and he savored every inch of skin contact.

Reluctantly, Cooper pulled his hand out of her to slip off his shirt and tee shirt. He unlaced his work boots, toed them off and took his socks off. All he had on was his jeans and briefs.

He lay down next to her, running his hand down her torso. He leaned down and kissed her jawline, her neck, then nipped her earlobe. She shuddered and clung to him. "Missed you," he growled in her ear.

"Oh, Cooper, I missed you, too." One hand ran through his hair and she turned her head to kiss his neck. "So much. You have no idea."

Fuck *yes*, he had an idea.

"Thought about you every night." He licked her neck and kissed his way down to her breast. His hand settled over her mound. She lifted a leg and curled it around his thigh, opening herself to him.

"Aren't you going to take those jeans off?"

"Not just yet," he growled. "The second I do, I'll be in you."

He could feel her smile against his neck. "Sort of like a denim chastity belt, huh?"

"Yeah." Two fingers were fitting into her now. Good thing, because he was starting to lose control. Two fingers weren't as big as his cock, but she was softening up. He worked his fingers in and out of her, gradually spreading them, while he licked her nipples. Her fingernails were digging into his back and she was making those throaty little sounds he loved. The ones she made just before coming.

He bit a nipple lightly while thrusting deeply and she stiffened, breath held. He shook as her cunt tightened around his fingers and she surged into climax.

Nownownow!

Cooper kissed her deeply, shaking as he unzipped his jeans and pushed them and his briefs down. He wanted complete freedom of movement, so he didn't just pull them down his thighs enough to free himself. He wanted them all the way off. In a second, he was naked and rolling on top of her.

Sally was still coming, panting lightly. He pulled her legs further apart and thrust inside, feeling the sharp little tugs as he entered her. It was mind-blowing. Sally came with her whole body. Arms and legs clutching him, hips grinding upwards to take as much of him as she could, mouth open against his. Every cell of her body welcomed him.

His cock was super-sensitized, as if a layer of skin had been removed. He'd been in a state of arousal eight nights in a row and jerking off in his hotel room hadn't helped at all. He was primed and when his cock parted those soft tissues tightly milking him, he lost it.

Cooper groaned against her mouth, held her hips hard and pumped in short, hard strokes, moving upwards into her. He was beginning to know her so well. The fast upward strokes moved him against her clitoris and kept her climax going. He made a humming sound of contentment deep in his chest as he felt her move seamlessly into another climax, the pulses harder and stronger this time.

The warm, hard contractions finished him off. He groaned and came in hot spurts of seed, shaking and sweating and pumping. His senses—usually so keen—disappeared, wiped out by the intensity of his climax. He didn't hear the bed creaking, or Sally's cries of pleasure, couldn't see anything but the square inch of Sally's skin right in front of his slitted eyes. Everything in him spiraled inward, ferociously concentrated on his cock bursting with joy inside her.

With an enormous shudder, Cooper settled his full weight on Sally, face turned towards hers on the pillow, panting and trembling with aftershocks.

He was still hard. He'd barely taken the roughest edge of desire off. As soon as he caught his breath, he'd start again and it would be even better. She'd be softer and wetter, now that they'd come. Some nights he came four or five times inside her and, towards the end, she was so slick with her juices and his, he moved inside her like a dream.

But right now that orgasm had been more intense than usual. He had no desire to start up right away. They had all night. Right now all he wanted to do was savor the pulsing pleasure as sensation returned to his body. It had been so intense his head rang.

As he slowly came back to himself, Cooper realized it wasn't his head ringing, it was the phone.

Fuck it. Whoever was calling could go take a flying jump.

"Don't answer that," Cooper murmured. His nose was right up against the soft rose-scented skin under her ear. He kissed it.

"Answer what?" Sally said dreamily.

"The phone."

"Oh." She sighed. "I thought it was my head ringing."

He smiled in the darkness and nuzzled the skin of her neck. The damned thing kept ringing, but Cooper tuned it out.

Sally suddenly stiffened. "The phone. The phone. Oh, God, the *phone*." Her voice was sharp now, as if she'd suddenly woken up. She pushed his shoulder. "I have to answer it."

Cooper lifted his head in surprise.

"Please, Cooper, let me up. I really have to answer that."

Cooper frowned as he looked down at her. She was shaking. Her usually pale skin now looked bloodless.

"Cooper, please." She pushed at his shoulder again. He was about ninety or a hundred pounds heavier than her. No way could she get him off her if he didn't want to. And he didn't want to. He was fine, right where he was, with his cock deeply buried inside her, her body under his, thighs hugging his hips. "Cooper, please. Please," she whispered. The phone continued ringing.

Her voice trembled.

Scowling, Cooper pulled out of her and rolled off. She scrambled out from under him, a pale shadow in the dark room as she hurried into the living room.

Cooper was overheated and sweating from the lovemaking and climax, but he felt a deep chill run through his system as he thought about the expression on her face.

It was one he'd seen all too many times on his men under fire.

Fear.

Something had frightened her badly. Fuck this. Nothing and no one was going to frighten his woman. Grim-faced, Cooper got to his feet and followed her.

* * * * *

Julia was shaking as she slid out from under Cooper. She checked her watch and winced. 10 p.m. It couldn't be anyone from Simpson calling. Everyone went to bed at 9 p.m. It could only be one person.

Herbert Davis. And if he was calling at this late hour, it wasn't good news.

She stood for just a second by the bed until she was certain her legs would hold. She'd just finished climaxing and her system was still in overdrive. When she stood, she could feel wetness trickling down her thighs. She dried herself with a quick swipe from the sheet and grabbed a dressing gown from the chair as she went into the living room, the cotton whipping through the air as she struggled into it while lunging for the phone.

"Hello?" Her voice was still husky from sex and she cleared her throat. "Hello?"

"Julia? Julia Devaux?" Julia's heart gave a great thump as she heard her real name spoken for the first time in six weeks.

"Mr. Davis," she breathed. Clearly, the old rules were out. He was using her real name and he didn't complain that she was using his. Something was very, very wrong.

"Yeah, that's right. Herbert Davis. Now, I want you to listen carefully, Julia. We think your identity has been compromised. We're not absolutely certain, but we're going to play it safe. From this moment on, I don't want you to leave your house. I don't want you to talk to anyone; I don't want you to contact anyone. No one at all, do you understand me? You can't trust anyone. You might be in danger and we're coming to get you. Now this is what I want you to do—"

The phone clattered heavily on the table, falling from Julia's nerveless fingers. She could hear Herbert Davis' voice squawking from the receiver, a tinny remote sound. "Julia? Julia! Answer me! What the hell is going on? Julia?"

"Who was that?" a deep, raspy voice asked.

Julia gasped and swiveled. Cooper stood in the doorway, one powerful arm braced against the frame. *I don't want you to talk to anyone. I don't want you to trust anyone*, Davis had said.

Well, though Cooper didn't talk much, having sex with him was probably included in Herbert Davis' list of things not to do.

"No one," she said breathlessly. She reached down blindly and slammed the still-squawking phone back on the hook. It bounced and the receiver lay askew over the keys. "No one at all. It was...just a wrong number." Her dressing gown was gaping open. It was crazy, she and Cooper had just made love, but she pulled the gown around her tightly. Cooper moved forward and Julia took an instinctive step backwards.

"Sally?" Cooper frowned. "What's wrong?" He walked towards her as she backed away, until she hit the wall. Julia clutched the wall at her back, as if it could protect her. As if anything could protect her against Cooper.

He was so powerful it frightened her. She hadn't often seen him naked in full light. He was fearsome. His shoulders and arms were heavily roped with muscle, massively powerful. It would be useless struggling against him if he chose to attack her. If he wanted to, Cooper could overpower her in one second, snap her neck the next and never break the rhythm of his breathing.

Julia could remember reading somewhere that the soldiers of Sparta had fought naked, to terrify the enemy.

Well, it worked. She was terrified.

Cooper stopped in front of her, arms braced on either side of her head. She was trapped.

She stared straight ahead at the black chest hairs, at the indentation where his pectorals met, then slowly brought her gaze up. His face was tight, expressionless. A stranger's face. Her lover's face.

Trust no one.

She brought a trembling hand to cup his cheek. She could feel his jaw muscles working under her fingers. He hadn't shaved recently. His skin was warm, and his heavy beard rasped against her fingertips.

Trust no one.

"Cooper," she whispered. A tear welled over and slipped down her face. She shook her head slowly, her eyes on his. "God help me, if I can't trust you...I don't want to live."

Cooper didn't answer. He just opened his arms. Julia rushed straight into them.

After holding her for several long minutes, Cooper carried her to the sofa and sat them down. Julia wound her arms around his neck and cried. It was totally unstoppable. She cried out her rage and despair and fear, holding on to him tightly. He didn't say anything. He just sat and held her until she calmed down.

It occurred to Julia that this would be the last time she ever saw Cooper. She had such strong feelings for him, stronger than she'd ever had for any man, and now she'd lose him just when she'd found him.

In an hour, maybe two, U.S. Marshals would be coming for her and she would be relocated. Whisked away in the heart of the night.

It was clear to her that she had to cut off all ties to her previous life. Lives, at this point. So she'd leave Simpson forever and end up in North Dakota or Florida or New Mexico, with a new name and a new identity. Santana's trial would probably be in the spring, Davis had been saying. Maybe later. And it could last for months. Afterwards, she had to stay in the program until all appeals ran out. It would be at least a year, probably two, before she was free to go where she wanted.

Would what she had found with Cooper last through maybe a couple of years' absence? It was all so fresh, so new. They'd only been lovers for two weeks and he'd been gone for a week of that. They hadn't really even talked that much. Most of their time alone was taken up with the sex. Maybe that's all it was, sex.

Still, she'd be forever grateful to Cooper for the time they'd had together. He had kept her sane, especially during the nights. She had a sudden flash of herself in her new life. In some small, anonymous town somewhere, completely alone—and realized in a rush of warmth what Cooper meant to her.

She was sitting on his lap. He was still naked. She could feel his erection under her thighs, but he wasn't pushing at her with it. Her face was buried against his neck and his chin rested on top of her head. She kissed his neck. It was strong and warm, wet with her tears.

"I have some things to tell you," she said quietly, drying her eyes on his shoulder.

"Yeah." She could feel Cooper's nod. "I'm listening."

"I'm not—I'm not what you think I am." Julia sat up a little straighter, but kept her head on his shoulder. His broad, strong shoulder. She wouldn't be able to lean on it for very much longer. She'd tell Cooper the truth, then she'd have to start packing. In a few hours' time, she'd disappear from his life. Maybe forever. Julia closed her eyes for a moment.

Her heart was thudding. This was so hard.

Right now, right this instant, was the last second in her life in which she was Sally Anderson. Sam Cooper's woman. Friend to Alice Pedersen, and Maisie and Beth and all the others. Mother to Fred. Maybe Cooper would keep Fred for her.

Maybe not.

Maybe Cooper would be so disgusted that she'd been living a lie, telling him lies, that he would just tip her out of his lap, out of his life, and walk out the door.

"My name—" Her voice wavered. She bit her lip and waited until she was sure her voice was steady. "My name isn't Sally Anderson, Cooper. I'm not from Bend. I'm not a grade school teacher." He didn't move in any way, except to tighten his arms around her. "My real name is Julia Devaux and I live— used to live in Boston. I'm an editor. Or rather, I was. Now I don't know what I am anymore. Except scared."

Julia tilted her head on his shoulder so she could see his face. He was expressionless, as usual. His black eyes watched her steadily, patiently.

Now came the hard part.

"I—I saw something terrible," she said finally. "In September. I was taking a photography course and was wandering around the docks in Boston on a photo shoot, looking for gritty realism. I came across this abandoned warehouse. The gate had been removed, so I walked in. I had one of those automatic cameras like fashion photographers have, and I just walked around, shooting picture after picture. Finally, I walked into this inner courtyard and—" She bit her lip and tried to control the deep tremors in her body as she remembered. She could see it all again—the gray industrial landscape, the small terrified man, the black gun to his head, the massively built killer with the cruel face, the death shot.

"I witnessed a murder, and it's all on film," she said simply and heard Cooper suck in a deep breath. All his muscles tightened. She stared at the place where his neck muscles met his shoulder. Even that part of his body was beautiful. "It was some gangland slaying. I—I was able to identify the murderer, a man named Dominic Santana, in a lineup. Apparently he's some big mafia boss the FBI has been trying to get for years. I'm supposed to testify at the trial and I'm told he has put out a-a contract on me. A big one, apparently. A million dollars. In the meantime, pending the trial, I've been put into the Witness Security Program. Something's gone wrong with the security—"

"Those fucking bastards!"

Cooper lifted her off his lap and surged to his feet. Julia stared up in astonishment at his face, suddenly not impassive and not impenetrable. Cooper was enraged, every line of his big body tense with anger. Julia felt a little flutter of something beneath her breastbone. Not fear, of course. She wasn't afraid of him...not exactly.

But something was going to happen and it was out of her hands now. In some remote corner of her being she'd wanted to dump her problems into Cooper's lap and now she had. Quite literally. But mixed with the relief was trepidation because Cooper suddenly seemed charged. A huge, terrifying figure of a man. An uncontrollable force of nature.

A warrior.

"Cooper?"

But he wasn't listening. He strode to the telephone, pressed his finger on the hook, lifted it again and angrily punched *69.

When he heard someone say "Herbert Davis" on the other end of the line, he snarled, "Who the fuck are you, Davis?"

Cooper heard a sharp intake of breath, then a cautious voice asked, "Who is this speaking?"

Cooper tightened his grip on the phone, reminding himself to tighten his grip on his temper, too. "This is Sam Cooper. I'm speaking from Simpson, Idaho, from the phone of—" he shot a glance at Sally—no, Julia—curled up on the sofa. She was deathly pale, her wide turquoise eyes fixed on him. She looked as small and as vulnerable as a child. The tactile memory of her soft, delicate frame still lingered in his hands and the very thought of anyone hurting her made him half insane. He turned slightly, so he wouldn't be distracted. "I'm speaking from Julia Devaux's phone. Now I'm going to ask this just one more time— who the fuck are you?"

"I'm not authorized to disclose that information." The man's voice was distant, impersonal.

It was a wonder his hand wasn't crushing the plastic receiver. "You listen to me, you son of a bitch. If you're from the U.S. Marshal's Office, then you guys running WitSec are worse bunglers than I thought. I'd heard the rumors about the Office going downhill, but this is beyond bungling. You can't send an innocent woman with killers on her trail out here without even an agent to watch out for her. What the hell kind of protection is that?"

"Ah...er..." Cooper could hear the indecision in the man's voice. "We've been having some budget cuts and our Boise office—"

"The hell with budget cuts!" Cooper roared. "What's the matter with you people? You can't just dump a witness and hope she'll be safe. She's got a contract out on her head. She needs the protection you're not providing. Starting now."

"Well, starting now, she's no concern of yours. We've got a leak in our security and we're pulling her out."

"The hell you are," Cooper said, his voice suddenly soft with menace. "You just try it."

"Cooper?" Julia's voice was faint as she touched his elbow. Cooper turned. "Cooper, what's he saying?"

A muscle tightened in Cooper's jaw.

"Cooper?"

He placed his palm over the receiver. "He says they want to pull you out."

"Yes, I know. When are they coming?" She rested her forehead against his shoulder for a moment, swiping at the tears with the heel of her hand. She looked small and frightened and confused. Cooper felt that harsh squeezing in his chest again. He clutched the receiver until the dark skin of his knuckles turned white.

"You're not leaving here," he said bluntly.

"What? I don't understand—"

He hated the sound of her voice like this—lost and dazed. "You're not going anywhere. You're staying here. With me."

This shouldn't be happening to her. This shouldn't be happening to them. Right now, they should be in her bedroom, still fucking. He was always so frantic the first time, but he hadn't worried too much about it. He knew he'd settle down some, in time. He thought they'd have all the time in the world.

And now their time was up.

"Cooper?"

He looked down at her upturned face, pale and confused, and in it saw the future he'd only dared start hoping for begin to recede. With Sally—no, Julia, dammit!—he felt more alive than he'd ever remembered feeling. Before she had arrived he had been losing himself, sinking more and more often into his bleak thoughts, as if he were on an ice floe that had broken off from the continent, drifting slowly away from the mainland.

She had changed all that, her very presence had been a lifeline thrown to him at the last minute before he disappeared over the horizon. She had brought him back to life. She was bringing Simpson back to life.

Damned if he'd let her go!

"Cooper, they're coming for me. I have to get ready, pack—"

"Honey, listen to me. You're not going anywhere. You're staying right here, where I can protect you."

"But—" Julia looked around, as if the men from the U.S. Marshal's office were coming any minute. "They want to pull me out. It's over, Cooper."

"No, it's not over." Only the fear underlying the stubbornness in her pale, pretty face kept him from shaking her. "It's not over at all, honey. Don't you see? The Marshal's Office is just going to give you another identity and put you somewhere else. But their security has been compromised. If that happens once, it can happen again. So hush. Let me deal with this."

He lifted his hand from the receiver. "Talk to me," he growled.

"Well, Mr.—ah, Cooper," Herbert Davis began.

"That's Senior Chief Cooper."

"Oh." There was a long silence at the other end of the line. "Navy."

"SEAL." Cooper never tried to impress anyone with the fact that he'd been a SEAL. But right now he needed Herbert Davis' attention and the best way to do that was to let Davis know who he was dealing with. "And for the record, you're not taking Julia Devaux anywhere. She's staying here. She'll be under the care and protection of the Sheriff, Charles Pedersen. And me."

There was a small shocked sound. "Absolutely not! Why I've never heard anything as outrageous as that in my entire—"

Cooper made his voice soft and deadly. "There's no way in hell I'm letting you take her out of here. Not with the kind of protection you've been offering. So let the sheriff and me take care of it."

"I'm afraid that's impos—"

"You'd damned well better do it or I'm taking this straight to the Justice Department. Right after I contact my very good friend Rob Manson at the *Washington Post*. You've read his byline. He's the one who wrote the series of articles on how the Marshals botched the Warren affair. He'll love this one. Federal witnesses with no protection put out as bait. I can see the headlines now."

"I—ah—I wouldn't do that if I were you Mr.—"

"Cooper. And I've got Manson's number right in front of me." Cooper was so convincing that he saw Julia look, startled, at his empty hands, expecting to see an address book. He didn't need an address book for Rob's number. "Manson works late Sundays while the newspaper is put to bed. He's still at his desk. You're going to notify the sheriff here, Charles Pedersen, and we're all going to come up with a plan to keep Julia Devaux safe until the trial or I'm calling Rob and then Justice. And I mean right now. Rob might be in time to have the story in tomorrow's paper."

"Look, Mr. Cooper, surely you realize that I can't trust you. How do I know who you are? You're complaining that we're not protecting Miss Devaux adequately. But we'd be reckless if I just entrusted her to the first man who calls me up."

He was making sense, damn him. Cooper stared at the wall, thinking furiously. "Okay," he said finally. "This is what you're going to do. You're going to call a number I'm going to give you. It's Josh Creason's private cell phone number. You ask him who I am. Tell him I have Harry and Mac Boyce with me and that none of us have lost our edge. I'll hold the line."

"This Joshua Creason," Herbert Davis hedged, "would that be General Joshua Creason? Chairman of the Joint Chiefs of Staff?"

"No." Cooper raised his eyes to be ceiling. "That's Joshua Creason, the opera singer. Of course it's General Creason, you—" Cooper bit his tongue. He wanted the man's cooperation, not his antagonism. "You're wasting time. Check me out with Josh. And tell him he still owes me ten bucks and that he'd better have improved his poker game."

Cooper was put on hold. He leaned against the table, preparing to wait it out. Sally—Julia—watched his face, her own white and strained. They didn't speak. He just pulled her into his arms and held her close, his cheek against the top of her head.

After a quarter of an hour, the voice came back "Mr. Cooper."

"Yeah." Cooper straightened and Julia looked up at him tensely.

"This is—this is highly unusual." Davis blew out a breath. Stress reliever. Cooper just bet that this son of a bitch was under stress. His fumbling had almost cost a witness her life.

"Yeah." Cooper wasn't about to give him any slack. He waited.

"I, ah, I consulted with General Creason, who gave me a number of reassurances about yourself and Sanderson and Boyce. And we checked Sheriff Pedersen out."

This was stuff Cooper already knew. He was silent.

"After, ah, after consulting with my colleagues, we have decided that if you come up with a feasible plan, we can keep Ms. Devaux in place. You will coordinate with our Boise office."

"Roger that."

"You'll give me status reports on a regular basis."

"Yeah. And I want more information on the case right now."

The hairs on the back of Cooper's neck rose as Davis recounted, as blandly as an accountant discussing the new tax code, how they suspected a security breach. And how the word on the street was that the price on his Julia's head was now two million dollars.

"So…I'm placing Ms. Devaux in the hands of your sheriff and yourself. Her safety is your direct responsibility now. You're okay with that?"

"Absolutely."

"Okay. Call me tomorrow afternoon and we'll go over the details."

"Will do. I'll call you at thirteen hundred hours with a detailed security plan. And you plug those leaks, you hear?"

Cooper heard another little puff of air and Davis hung up. When Julia timidly touched his shoulder he whirled to gather her in his arms, holding her tightly.

"So that's that. You're staying here," Cooper said finally. Every muscle was stiff with tension and battle-readiness. "The only way anyone will ever get to you will be over my dead body."

Julia drew in a long breath. "In that case, Cooper," she said faintly into his shoulder, "maybe you better put some clothes on."

Chapter Seventeen

At Stanford, Professor Jerzy Stanislaus had perfected a computer model he'd called Matrix Architecture Topography, or MAT. The whole idea of MAT was that the best way to navigate a computer's database was three-dimensionally. Stanislaus' concept was that a computer was like a house, and like any house, it had a door and a key to the door. Then the Professor had gone on to explain how three-dimensionality was a key itself to the door. The professional had been fascinated by the symbolic logic MAT represented.

There wasn't a student in the room who hadn't hacked from time to time. And there wasn't a student in the room who hadn't immediately grasped the very real uses of MAT as a literal key to enter locked rooms.

Occasionally in the professional's forays into cyberspace, there had been traces left behind by someone who had clearly used MAT to penetrate the firewalls. The size of the key told the professional that it was one of Stanislaus' students. Usually, the professional symbolically closed the door quietly and tiptoed out with a silent salute.

The professional was going to use MAT to penetrate the Department of Justice's files and access Julia Devaux's location.

The Department of Justice's computer codes were now three levels deep and with a 240-bit encryption code. No more Yale locks and flimsy window casements. Their computers now had reinforced concrete doors and bulletproof windows. And no amount of rattling the doors and using a hairpin was going to open them. But a door was a door was a door—in other words, a way in.

The professional carefully made a salami attack into a powerful array computer in Madison; it belonged to a company that foolishly left its magnificent machine unoccupied during the night. The machine had immense number-crunching potential — the mother of all motherboards, the professional thought wryly.

Julia Devaux, compute your prayers.

The professional began the search for the key. It was an enormously long string of numbers that stretched even this computer's abilities.

While the laptop in Idaho communed with the computer in Wisconsin, the professional dined — very badly — on saltines and Diet Coke. No caviar and champagne out in the boondocks. Thank God this business would soon be over.

The professional checked the time. The company's computer could only be used for short bursts of less than half an hour, otherwise the engineering department of the company the professional had hacked into would notice. Twenty minutes had elapsed.

Time to sign off.

The professional sighed and started the long delicate process of backing out. Cracking the Department of Justice's code would take another two nights — three at the most. The problem was what to do with the partially decoded key. It was too long and too complex to fit into the hard disk of the laptop. Where to leave it?

The professional suddenly smiled.

Where to leave the key? Why the answer was obvious. Under the MAT, of course.

* * * * *

"Cooper, no," Julia whispered, shocked. Then more loudly, "No!" Shaking with nervous tension, she jumped up and paced around her living room.

Cooper watched her with his usual impassive expression, but Chuck looked concerned, then pained, as he shifted uneasily on one of the broken springs of her couch.

Cooper had called Chuck immediately after hanging up. Chuck had made it to her house in less than ten minutes, huffing and puffing, which had given Julia enough time to put on her jeans and to pull a sweater over her head. Chuck walked into the house just as Cooper had come out of the bedroom buttoning his shirt, missing a few buttons as he worked his way up.

Despite the serious circumstances, Julia had felt a quick flush of embarrassment. Chuck would draw the obvious conclusions. But to his credit, Chuck didn't give the slightest indication that he thought she and Cooper had been doing anything more than sipping tea and discussing the weather.

Chuck had listened soberly as she told him about the murder that September day and what had happened since. Then both of them had listened as Cooper outlined his plan to keep her safe.

Julia grew more and more anxious as she listened to his low voice outline a plan that would have been banned by Amnesty International as cruel and unusual punishment.

Cooper's plan basically consisted of keeping her in a locked room with an armed guard outside the door for as long as it took the State to take its case to court. Julia felt her throat close at the thought.

"That's not a plan, that's a sentence." Julia wrapped her arms around her midriff, shaking with cold and tension. "You'll have to come up with some kind of alternative plan, Cooper. You can't keep me under lock and key like some prisoner. I'd go crazy."

Cooper watched her calmly, dark eyes steady. "You won't be anyone's prisoner. It's just that you'll be safe. As safe as I can keep you."

"That's not safety, Cooper. It's death." Julia shuddered. Over the past month and a half, having her Thursday and

Saturday coffee with Alice, planning the resuscitation of the diner, getting involved in the lives of the people of Simpson—all those things had kept her sane. She knew herself. Knew how swamped with terror she would be if she holed up in a room, cowering. She would feel like a frenzied moth, beating itself to death against the windowpane. "You can't do this to me, Cooper." Her hands clenched. "You just can't. I think—" She drew a shuddering breath, "I think I'd rather die."

Cooper's eyes honed in on her face, judging how serious she was. "So what are you suggesting?" he asked, frustrated. He pinched the bridge of his nose. "Walking around with a bull's-eye on your forehead? Taking out an ad in the *Pioneer*? Maybe with a map and an arrow. 'Attention all hired killers. Julia Devaux is here.'"

Julia bit her lips and willed herself not to let the threatening tears fall. "I want to be safe, Cooper. Of course I don't want to take any unnecessary risks. But I also don't want to be buried alive. Now what exactly did Herbert Davis tell you? Does he know for certain that Santana knows where I am?"

"No," Cooper said reluctantly. "But he strongly suspects it."

"On the basis of what?" Chuck asked.

Cooper turned gratefully to Chuck, clearly hoping Chuck would be more rational. "Julia's data was in an encrypted computer file together with two other cases. The other two witnesses were both relocated to Idaho, like Julia." Cooper clenched a big fist. "They're both dead."

The stark words hung there. Chuck looked thoughtful and Julia felt panic rise again, a dark fluttery winged thing which threatened to cut off her air.

"Dead...how?" she asked finally.

"Accident. Both of them." Cooper's jaw muscles clenched. "So they say."

The tight cold band around Julia's chest eased a little. "They who?"

"Police and Feds."

"Both the police and the FBI think they were accidents?" Chuck asked.

Cooper nodded tensely.

Chuck scratched his jaw. "Don't know, Coop," he said finally. "The police and the Feebs, they're not dummies, you know. They'd have investigated pretty thoroughly. Nobody likes to be caught with their pants down...beg your pardon, Sally."

Cooper's jaw muscles jumped.

"And surely—" Julia licked dry lips. She was finding it hard to think straight, but one fact was staring her in the face. "Surely, if someone knew where I was—he'd have come after me first, wouldn't he? I understand there's a million-dollar bounty on my head."

"Two million," Cooper said grimly. "It was upped."

Julia closed her eyes and shuddered. Santana was willing to pay two million dollars to see her dead. She'd never been on the receiving end of such hatred. Her mind raced as she tried to grope her way through the situation. "There's no hard evidence that my cover has been blown, is there?"

"No." Cooper spoke the word reluctantly. "But there's no guarantee that it hasn't."

Julia walked slowly to the window and looked out. The temperature had dropped and the ground had frozen. The light coating of snow gleamed a dull, sodden gray in the lamplight. The world looked cold and lifeless. Julia tried to imagine staring out this little window, hour after hour, day after day, frightened, lonely and trapped. Her heart turned as cold and as sodden as the ground at the thought.

Cooper walked up behind her and she could see his reflection in the dark window. She met his reflected gaze. "I can't do it, Cooper," she said softly. "I can't be locked up. Please don't make me."

He lifted his hands and put them on her shoulders. "You won't go anywhere without telling me." She turned around, hope flaring in her eyes.

"No." Her eyes searched his. "I won't."

"Promise."

"I promise."

"You'll go to school and back, and either Chuck or Bernie or Sandy or Mac or I will accompany you."

"Yes, Cooper."

"You'll carry a gun at all times. Except when you're teaching and Chuck will be right outside the school."

"I will?" Julia blinked, startled. "I've never used a gun in my life."

"You'll learn. I'll teach you. It's not rocket science."

"Okay." Julia tilted her head, considering. "And I want you to teach me the basics of self-defense."

"Good idea. Aikido."

"Ai...what?"

"Aikido," Cooper repeated. "It's a martial art. Doesn't require the bulk or strength of judo or karate."

"Yes, Cooper."

"You want to see one of your friends, Alice or Beth or Maisie, you let me know, and I'll accompany you. Either that or Chuck or Sandy or Mac or Bernie will. I've got to tell Loren and Glenn, too," Cooper went on, shooting a glance at Chuck. "And the other men in town. They won't have to know why. All they'll have to know is that she's never to be alone. Not for one minute."

Chuck nodded.

Julia wasn't too sure what she'd bargained herself into, but right now there was only one answer. "Yes, Cooper."

"You don't answer the phone. Ever. You let me answer."

"Yes, Coop—" Julia began, then stopped. "At all hours? How can you do that?"

"I'll be here as much as I can. I'm moving in with you."

"But, Cooper—" Julia's mind whirled. "If you move in with me—what about—I mean, what will people here think? It's not really..." She shrugged helplessly and turned to Chuck.

"That's okay, honey." Chuck patted her shoulder. "The very last thing you have to worry about is what people in Simpson will think. Everyone here likes you a whole lot. Hell, if anything, we're all really happy that Coop is finally getting laid."

* * * * *

I'm being protected to death, Julia thought a few days later. She pushed open the lavatory doors at school and stopped the janitor from following her in by slapping a hand on his chest.

"Not here, Jim," she said, exasperated.

"But—but Miss Anderson," Jim protested. His watery pale blue eyes widened with distress. "Chuck said that I wasn't supposed to let you out of my sight."

Julia curled her fist around the door's edge. "I'm sure Chuck didn't mean that you had to follow me into the ladies' room. I assure you, Jim, I'm going to be fine."

Without giving him a chance to say anything, she slid into the teacher's lavatory, closing the door behind her. Bracing two hands on the sink, she examined herself in the mirror.

And she'd thought her life had raced out of control after witnessing the murder. That was nothing compared to being protected by Sam Cooper. She looked around the small lavatory. It was the first time she'd been alone in three days. Cooper had spent the rest of Sunday night and early Monday morning on the phone with Herbert Davis and conferring with Chuck. They had drawn up elaborate plans, that she hadn't been able to follow, full of "clear lines of communication" and "fire zones" and "signal intelligence". Julia had fallen asleep on the couch to the sound of Cooper's deep voice discussing military strategy.

She now lived in an armored house. Everything that could open was alarmed. Her front and back doors were now made of reinforced steel. Two of Cooper's men had been sent to Boise, and on Monday night, motion detectors and tripwires were installed. Her phone was set up to record messages and had caller ID. Each room had a fire extinguisher.

From the moment she woke up in the morning to when she came back to her house in the evening, Julia was handed from man to man in an unbroken chain of stewardship.

After breakfast, Cooper waited until Chuck came over before leaving for the ranch. Chuck walked her to the school door and left her with Jerry Johnson, who walked her to her classroom door. After school, Chuck was waiting at the school entrance. The past two days, Chuck had accompanied her to Jensen's grocery store, where she and Beth pored over drawings and colors. Julia had promised to help Beth redecorate. Then Chuck or the lanky foreman called "Sandy" would walk her home. They would wait until Cooper arrived and make a solemn little ceremony about "handing her over".

Julia felt like the baton in a relay race.

She hadn't the faintest idea what story Cooper and Chuck told the men in Simpson, but it got results. Loren stood rigidly behind the counter, eyes scanning the street outside, while she and Beth happily planned the grocery store's rejuvenation. Julia had sketched sheet after sheet while Beth talked and Loren hadn't once taken his eyes off the door.

Once, when a lost and bewildered traveling salesman had walked in and asked for directions, Loren had pulled a walkie-talkie from under the counter and spoken into it quietly.

Chuck and Bernie had immediately materialized. Chuck's hand hovered over his pistol in its brand-new leather holster and Bernie carried a rifle. The traveling salesman had looked from one unsmiling, suspicious face to the other, bought a bag of apples, asked the way to Rupert and quickly exited. Julia could see him mop his brow outside the shop and run to his waiting car. Chuck and Loren and Bernie had moved to the entrance and watched until the car's taillights had disappeared from sight.

It was no way to increase tourism.

Julia was looking forward to the evening with Cooper. He had hooked up a DVD player to her TV set and had brought over enough films on disk to keep her busy for the next fifty years. To her astonishment, it turned out that Cooper was a film buff, too. The older the better, just like her. Their tastes ran along remarkably similar lines, though Julia had a slight preference for romantic comedies and Cooper leaned towards Hitchcock and Westerns. Tonight he'd promised to bring over *Casablanca*.

She shivered as she thought of what would come afterwards.

Except for when she was in school, Julia carried a gun, a small, powerful one. A Beretta Tomcat, that took .32 caliber bullets. Or "rounds", as Cooper called them.

Cooper had said that he didn't want her to have a "girl's gun". The Tomcat was small, but Julia was astonished at its kick, and at the damage it could do to the few tree trunks she was starting to hit.

She had a callus between the thumb and forefinger and had had to set aside special clothes for shooting practice because she came home reeking of cordite after a practice session. It took her an hour to get the powder out from under the fingernails of her right hand.

Cooper was an excellent instructor, patient and thorough. At first, he had walked her through the theory over and over again, until her head spun with "sighting planes", "trigger pulls" and "creeps". Then he had let her start target practice. The back of her legs still hurt from the improper stance she'd adopted at first. Cooper had made her lean forward in a slight crouch, steadying her hand with his until she got off the first shot of her life. She missed, but not by much.

Cooper made a big point of praising her aim, but Julia knew better. Still, a gun no longer felt like an alien metal lump in her hand. She doubted she'd ever have the nerve to actually fire at a human being, but it was astonishing how reassuring it was to have the gun near to hand at all times, which she was sure had been Cooper's intention all along.

A sharp rap startled her. "Miss Anderson?" Jim called anxiously. "You okay in there?"

She sighed. "Fine, Jim. I'm coming right out."

* * * * *

There it was!

The professional leaned forward eagerly as the computer beeped.

It was about time. This place was enough to give anyone the creeps. The bed sagged, the weather was lousy and the food was worse. But the long wait was over.

kdsjcnemowjsiwexnjskllspwieuhdksmclsldjkjhfd

kdiejduenbkclsjdjeudowjdiejdocmdksdldkjdjeiel

mpnwjcmsmwkcxosapewkrjhvgebsjckgfnghgdsj

Decryption 60% complete...70%...80%...90%...

Come on baby, we can make it to St. Lucia by

Thanksgiving.

Decryption completed.

Bingo!

The letters moved across the screen.

File: 248

Witness placed in Witness Security Program: Julia Devaux

Born: London, England, 03/06/77

Last domicile: 4677 Larchmont Street, Boston, MA

Case: Homicide, Joey Carpuzzo, 9/27/05. Last known address: Sitwell Hotel, Boston, MA.

Approximate cause of death: massive hemorrhaging from .38 caliber bullet wound in left anterior lobe of brain.

Accused: Dominic Santana.

Current address: Furrow's Island Correctional Facility

Come on, come on. The professional leaned forward, eyes riveted to the screen. *I know all that. Tell me something I don't know.*

Placed in Witness Security Program: 10/03/05

Area 248, Code 7gb608hx4y

Area 248. Well, we know where that is. Now for the rest of it. It was Mickey Mouse stuff. The information was already in the file, the only problem was how to tickle it out. Just a question of time, and patience.

Too bad there wasn't anything to while away the time with. Nothing at all, except staring at dusty green wallpaper with pink flamingoes and hunting down the cockroaches. The computer whirred silently.

Area 248, Code 7gb608hx4y: the cursor blinked in place for a quarter of an hour. The computer beeped just as the professional finished counting all the cracks in the ceiling.

Decryption 60% complete…70%…80%…90%…

Decryption completed.

Ahh! The thrill of the chase. Nothing like it.

The letters started scrolling.

Julia Devaux. Relocated as: Sally Anderson

Current address: 150 East Valley Road, Simpson, Idaho

Well, well, well, the professional thought, sitting back. Sally Anderson.

That was it. In no time, the professional would be flying out of Seattle, two million dollars richer.

* * * * *

The following Monday afternoon, Julia stood at the door of Jensen's grocery shop and listened wistfully to the bursts of female laughter coming from the Out to Lunch.

Alice finally had the Rupert Ladies' Association over and it sounded like everyone was having a wonderful time in Simpson's brand-new fern bar.

Everyone except Julia.

She was under strict orders from Cooper to wait in the grocery store until he could come pick her up. Even Beth was over at the fern bar, probably gorging herself on Maisie's rum chocolate mousse, Julia thought resentfully.

To be honest, Beth had asked Julia if she'd mind. Julia had set her jaw and told Beth to go right ahead. But it wasn't fair that she had to miss out on all the fun.

It wasn't even as if she could look forward to popping in on the ladies' tea once Cooper had arrived, either.

No, sir.

Cooper had made it very clear that the Rupert Ladies' Association was strictly off limits to her. She'd argued and pleaded last night, to no avail. She'd tried seduction and that had worked. Very well, too. Not to change Cooper's mind, just to give her six or seven mind-blowing orgasms.

She might as well have argued with the walls. Cooper was unmovable. It was crazy to think that someone from the Rupert Ladies' Association could suddenly pull a submachine gun out of a flowered handbag.

Julia had watched the ladies arrive, one by one. Women in Rupert obviously didn't know that small handbags were in. To tell the truth, some of the handbags the women had been carrying *were* large enough to carry bazookas in.

Still, it was ridiculous of Cooper to be suspicious of anyone who belonged to the Rupert Ladies' Association. They'd all known each other forever. She'd tried to wheedle the reasons for his refusal out of him, but even there she'd come up against a solid brick wall. The only thing she had gathered was that he didn't trust anyone he hadn't known for his entire lifetime, childhood included, even if the person in question was seventy, female and arthritic.

Well, this wasn't living. What was the point of being alive when you couldn't even taste some of the best rum chocolate mousse in the world? Not to mention the best sour cream apple cake or chocolate Bavarian or brown betty. Maisie had outdone herself. Julia knew because she'd had a few preview samples. But now she wanted the real thing.

Another burst of laughter came from the fern bar and Julia gazed longingly down the street. It was empty, as usual. No crazed killers toting guns, no sinister figures, not even a stray dog. She was all alone, and everyone else in Simpson was at the party.

Except for Loren, who was out back, fussing with the supplies. Paint, varnish, nails, scaffolding, antique wooden barrels. Saturday was going to be the big day for Jensen's Groceries. The store was going to be redecorated according to the plans Julia and Beth had drawn up.

Julia could hear Loren muttering to himself and smiled. He wasn't familiar with hardware and paint and she'd seen how he had been a bit overwhelmed by the plans. It was only because Beth was so excited that he'd agreed to go along. He was probably shaking his head even now over all the things he'd had to buy.

He'll probably be busy for the next half hour, going over all the unfamiliar supplies, Julia thought. She checked the street again. Still empty. It was four thirty. Cooper said he wouldn't make it before five.

Four thirty-three. Julia checked again and ran her eyes up the empty street.

Why not? What could possibly happen? She could just nip into the "Out to Lunch", have a quick cup of tea, nibble on a few of Maisie's masterpieces, have a laugh or two, then run back before Cooper or Loren would even know she'd been gone. Just for a quarter of an hour.

Feeling daring, she gave one last glance behind her, then shot down the street. She pushed open the doors of "Out to Lunch" and smiled as she took in the smells of wonderful food and the familiar sounds of a hen party.

"Sally!" Alice bustled over, a wide smile on her face. She'd obviously foregone the Power Ranger look and was dressed in a simple black dress. She looked young and fresh and happy. "It's great to see you. But I thought Coop said—" She turned at a hand on her arm. "Yes, ma'am," she said to a stout matron dressed in a dreadful shade of orange-yellow, "it's in the back, to the left. Pink bow for the ladies. Blue bow for the gents. Here, I'll take you there." With a laughing glance back at Julia, Alice escorted the lady to the back of the room. They looked like an exclamation point and a pumpkin.

She'll do okay, Julia thought fondly, watching Alice. She looked around. Now that it was full of people, the fern bar looked a little less cheesy. As a matter of fact, with Maisie's mouthwatering spread out on a trestle table covered with a pale blue linen tablecloth and with pretty tea cups and saucers and several types of tea on offer, it actually looked…elegant.

Certainly, nobody was complaining. There must have been about thirty women in there and from the looks of them—and judging by the decibel level—they were all having a wonderful time. They were also devouring the food like locusts.

Julia narrowed her eyes at the solid row of backs around the table of food and gauged the terrain. She would have to make a beeline for the table. There wasn't much time and she wanted a taste of everything. Resolutely, Julia went forward, prepared to do battle.

"Hey." A young blonde stepped in her path with a plate full of everything going. "How you doing? Gee, it's nice to meet someone I know. Have you tasted this chocolate foamy thing? It's really great."

Julia studied the young girl. Something about her was familiar... "Mary," she said suddenly, remembering. "Mary..."

"Ferguson."

"That's it," Julia said politely, eyeing the table. There were three goblets of mousse left. "We met at the bookshop in Rupert, didn't we?"

"Yeah." The girl picked up a cruller and bit into it. "Wow." Her eyes rounded. "What are these things called?"

"Crullers," Julia said. A hand snaked out from the crowd and took a goblet of mousse. One down, two to go. "Basically, they're sweet fried dough. If you'll excuse me—"

The girl laid a hand on her arm. "You were right, you know."

"I was?" Another goblet disappeared and Julia gave an inward sigh. "About what?"

"I made a stupid move."

"You made a—oh, now I remember." Mary had talked about canvassing Eastern Idaho for clients for her law practice. "You mean you haven't found any clients yet?" The sour cream apple cake was history and it looked like the chocolate Bavarian was on its last legs.

"No, I've found a few clients, but..."

Julia was finding it hard to concentrate on the conversation, her mouth was watering so much. She watched jealously as Mary finished off the last cruller on her plate. Too bad she was a hostage to the good manners her mother had drilled into her. "But?"

Mary sighed. "I don't know. I got a divorce case and a personal injury." She shrugged. "But the divorce is really bitter and the husband and wife are using the kids as hostages. And the personal injury—" She leaned forward and whispered. "The guy's faking it. He's hoping to make a lot of money out of the insurance company."

"No." Julia tried to look suitably shocked.

"He is," Mary said solemnly. She pursed her lips. "I didn't think it would be like...this. I thought it would be like on *L.A. Law* or *Murder One*. You know, fighting for justice, getting an innocent client off."

"What kind of law does your father practice?" Julia asked.

"Real estate. I used to think it was boring, but now..." Mary sank a fork in the chocolate Bavarian and Julia watched as the fork moved to her mouth. She wanted to weep. "Now, I don't know. No deadbeat dads and no fake medical certificates in real estate."

"Maybe you should rethink your position—maybe your father's practice isn't so bad, after all."

"Yeah, maybe." Mary said. "Say. This is really good, too." She pointed with her fork at the Bavarian. "I was going to stick it out until Christmas, but you know what? I think I'll go home after Thanksgiving. It's only a few days away and Alice said the 'Out to Lunch' is going to have a real blowout for Thanksgiving. Then I think I'll just pack up and go back home to Boise. Dad's being real good about not saying 'I told you so'."

"Mmm," Julia answered politely, trying to sidle past her. The lone goblet of mousse just sat there, a sitting duck. It wasn't going to last long. "See you on Thanksgiving, then." A woman reached out for the mousse and Julia lunged to get there first. Suddenly, an iron hand clamped on her shoulder, and yanked her back.

"What the hell do you think you're doing?" A deep angry voice sounded from above and behind her.

Uh-oh, Julia thought.

Chapter Eighteen

"What the fuck was that about?" Cooper asked for the thousandth time. He had hustled her out of the fern bar without even allowing her to say goodbye and had frog-marched her to her house, his restless eyes searching up and down the street the entire time.

Over the last half hour, he had worn a hole in her threadbare carpet, pacing as he chewed her out. "I thought I told you—"

"Not to leave the store," Julia finished wearily. "Yes, you told me."

"You knew you weren't supposed to go to Alice's, didn't you?"

"Yes, Cooper." Julia's eyes were closed.

"You knew it was dangerous. We've gone over it a hundred times."

"Yes, Cooper."

She was usually so vibrant. Everything about her now seemed dull and subdued. Her eyes were firmly fixed on the floor as she struggled for control.

"I'm sorry," she said quietly, hauling in a long, calming breath and finally looking up. She raked a hand through her hair. "You're only trying to protect me and I behaved like a child. I apologize, Cooper."

Cooper was finally able to look through the haze of white-hot rage flashing through him when he'd seen her at Alice's, chatting with a blonde girl and eyeing the dessert table. He'd dragged her out of there so fast she hadn't had time to say goodbye to anyone, still clutching her dessert spoon. And all the while he had pulsed with rage.

But the anger had been better than the fear. And the fear had come first, when he'd entered Jensen's grocery store and found it empty. Fear such as he had never known had flooded through his system when an apologetic Loren had come in from the back room, wiping his hands on a floor-length apron, saying, "Sorry, Coop. I got carried away out back. Where's...?" and then Loren had looked around white-faced, horror dawning in his eyes.

Julia hadn't been there and Cooper had felt the bottom drop out of his life.

He'd watched Loren swivel his head, looking for her, knowing already that it was too late. "Oh, God, Coop—" Loren had whispered. "She's not here. *Ohmigod*, what have I—" But Loren had been speaking to empty air because Cooper had already shot into the street. He headed arrow-straight for the only place she could be, other than dead.

Alice's ladies' tea party.

No matter that they'd fought bitterly over her going, as they'd fought bitterly over the fact that she wanted to go to Maisie's Thanksgiving celebration at the Out to Lunch. No matter that she was under strictest orders not to go anywhere unless he or a handpicked man escorted her.

Though she knew in her head that someone was after her, Julia was completely out of her element. She wasn't wired for the chase. But he was. He'd hunted men and knew what a potent taste it was.

He'd forced Herbert Davis to e-mail him the entire Santana file and his worry and fear had streaked up into the stratosphere.

Santana wasn't just any smalltime thug. He was a major mobster with the savvy and cruelty to go with it. Cooper knew enough about law enforcement to realize that a bounty of two million dollars meant that all the terminators across the States would be angling for information on her whereabouts. Right now, the U.S. Marshal's Office stood between Julia and Santana, but two million was a lot of dead presidents.

"I'm sorry, Cooper," Julia said again softly and looked up at him. "I shouldn't have gone."

Cooper's rage and the fear behind it were starting to subside. He still didn't trust himself to touch her, so he tucked his hands in his jeans pockets and took a step back. "No, you shouldn't have."

"I shouldn't have disobeyed you."

"No." The stark word hung there heavily in the air.

"You were worried."

Worried was an understatement. Terrified was more like it. "Yes."

"Still—" Julia struggled to keep her voice light. "Still, it's hard to imagine a Rupert Lady in cahoots with Santana."

"You don't know anything about it," Cooper answered. He realized how harsh his voice sounded only when he saw her wince. She seemed to be retreating from him without moving a muscle and he didn't know how to hold onto her. "The danger can come from any quarter, at any minute and if you're not prepared—you're history in a heartbeat." He watched those beautiful eyes widen and he swore viciously at a fate which had made such a lovely, gentle woman a hunted creature. "I'm not going to let Santana get you, no matter what. You can take that to the bank."

"He already has." Her voice was quiet and it took a moment for what she said to sink in.

"What the hell do you mean by that?" Cooper knew his voice sounded hard as he checked her out, ceiling to basement. She didn't look hurt in any way. The very thought of it...he clenched his fists.

Julia lifted her head. Her turquoise eyes were wide and shadowed with sadness. "Santana's already won, Cooper. He's already taken my life away from me. My job is probably gone and I haven't seen my home in almost two months. Who knows when I'll see it again? All my plants will be dead. And my cat." She made a stab at a laugh, then angrily wiped at her eyes, promising herself that she wouldn't cry. "Federico Fellini. I named Fred after him." At the sound of his name, Fred lifted his muzzle from the floor and he gave a questioning thump of his tail. "Though God knows Fred's nothing like Federico. No hard feelings, Fred." As if he understood, Fred dropped his muzzle back onto his paws with a whine.

Her voice was desolate and empty. "Everything I had. Everything that's me…it's all gone. I don't have a life any more. He's already taken my life away."

It was true. That vivid aliveness that was such a hallmark was gone. She looked as if someone had dimmed the lights inside her. Santana had taken away her life, her core, her very essence.

Cooper could count the new lines in her face, the dark bruises under her eyes, the brand-new lines of tension bracketing her mouth.

She'd lit Simpson up, single-handedly. Simpson had been dying for a long time. But now, with the new eatery and Loren branching out, who knew? Maybe Simpson might survive after all.

Cooper didn't know too many people who could suffer the loss of a home, a job and a life, find themselves parachuted into a strange town, and yet make friends. He certainly couldn't have. If the same thing had happened to him, he wouldn't have had the courage to plunge into the life and soul of a town, make friends, turn people's lives around. He wouldn't have had the courage to start a love affair and give as much as she'd given him.

"Cooper?" He could see her anxiety rise as she watched him. "Are you still mad at me?"

"No." He let out his breath slowly and reached out to gather her close, grateful that she was there. Alive and in his arms. "Not mad. Just scared."

She clutched his back. "Me, too," she whispered.

Cooper pulled away a little. "Then why—" he began, then stopped. He knew why. She'd done all of the planning and a lot of the work in redecorating Carly's. The "Out to Lunch", now. Of course she wanted to join in the fun.

"I...care," he said finally, the words wrenched out of him from some place deep inside.

"I know, Cooper." Her eyes were as soft as her voice as she pulled away. Those wonderful, expressive eyes, sad and tired now, when they should have been sparkling with her triumph. It wasn't fair that it had been taken away from her. "And I made you worry because of my selfishness. I'm sorry. Will you forgive me?"

A stone would have been moved. And as often as Melissa had accused him of it, Cooper wasn't a stone. "Yeah," he said huskily. "I forgive you. It was my fault anyway. I shouldn't have been late."

"Don't, Cooper. Don't blame yourself." Julia reached up to touch his bristly cheek. He hadn't had time to shave this morning. "I'm the one to blame. It's just that I can't help myself. I can't live like you want me to. I'd have to be deaf and dumb and...not care about anyone, I guess. I wanted to see how Alice was doing."

Cooper drew in a long sigh and his mouth turned up in a half smile. "You wanted a taste of Maisie's chocolate glop, is more like it," he grumbled.

"Mousse," she smiled. "And, yes, that too. Though as it turns out, I didn't get my taste. Maisie'll bring some over to Beth's tomorrow, anyway, if I ask her. Cooper?"

"Hmm?" He looked down at her and she put a tentative hand on his arm.

"We just had our first fight."

He sighed. "Yeah."

"And we survived it."

"Yeah."

"Though, of course, you were impossibly pigheaded."

Cooper's lips thinned. "And you were unforgivably reckless."

"And you forgave me." She smiled sunnily at him. "Didn't you?"

"Yeah." Cooper reached out and pulled her into his arms. She lifted her mouth to his. Long moments later, she murmured, "I guess that means you really do care."

Cooper gave a rueful smile. "I guess it does."

* * * * *

"Ooof!" Cooper rolled onto his left shoulder two evenings later. He was grateful for the mats he'd insisted Julia install in the living room for her daily Aikido lesson. Instantly, Julia was on him, straddling his chest.

"I did it!" Julia crowed. She punched the air in delight. "I did it! I threw you!" She got up and did a little war dance, knocking ferocious punches to imaginary enemies.

"You sure did," Cooper grinned as he stood up. He loved watching her happy and triumphant. He loved it when her cheeks turned that luscious pale peach instead of chalk white. When her mouth curved naturally into its normal expression, a smile.

It wasn't easy throwing yourself, but it was worth it to see what a boost it gave to her self-confidence.

She had learned some basic holds, and he was beginning to be confident that she could fend off an untrained attacker. A very weak, untrained attacker. But he wanted her to have the feel of a throw in her hands, to know what it was like.

So he'd thrown himself.

Julia was humming the *Rocky* theme, jabbing the air like a heavyweight champ. She feinted a jab to his chin. "You're not so tough, big guy," she said, and laughed.

Cooper smiled "Guess not. It's a humbling thought."

"I want a prize for winning." She shuffled around him, shadowboxing. "Otherwise I'll clean your clock."

"You've got me running scared." He couldn't resist her when she was in this mood. "Okay. Name it. Anything you want."

Julia stopped and looked up at him. "Do you mean it?"

He smiled at the thought of giving her something. "Sure do. Anything you want. You want a horse?" he asked eagerly. "I've got a beautiful little sorrel with the sweetest mouth. You'd love her."

Julia shook her head. Okay, horse was out. "Jewelry?"

She shook her head.

"Fur coat?" She shook her head again.

Nope, not that, either. "Well, what do you want?" If it was at all possible for him to get it for her, he would.

"I want to go to Alice's Thanksgiving blowout."

The smile was wiped from his face instantly. "No," he said. "Absolutely not."

She lost her smile, too. "You said I could have anything I wanted. I want to be there when Alice and Maisie see how successful they're going to be."

"No." Cooper set his jaw. "Anything but that. You can have diamonds or pearls. You can have my best stud horse. But I don't want you in a Thanksgiving crowd. And that's final."

The air filled with tension. Julia stopped her clowning and stood very straight and very still. "I worked days and days to renovate the diner. Alice is my friend." She swallowed. Her voice was strained. "If I can't have friends, if I can't watch a friend's triumph, if I can't make plans, then I might as well not exist, Cooper. I might just as well be dead. I'm asking you as a favor. I want to share at least a part of that day with Alice. Just for a little while." Her eyes searched his. "Please, Cooper."

"Damn!" Cooper wanted to punch something. A wall. Dominic Santana. Herbert Davis. He knew exactly what she was asking. The danger it represented. It was crazy, foolhardy. And he also knew how much she deserved it. How right it would be for her to be in the diner on Thanksgiving. What it would mean to her and to Alice and Maisie. It wasn't right that she not share in Alice's moment.

The hell of it was, she didn't plead her case any further. She just left it up to his sense of fairness. He held still a moment while the clang of opposing ideas fought it out in his head. It was foolhardy taking any kind of risk. And yet she deserved to be there. Finally, the clanging stopped as he came to a decision.

I don't want to do this, he thought. *I don't want to say it*. But he did.

"Okay." The word came out reluctantly and he felt a granite boulder press in on his chest.

"Oh, Cooper!" It was almost worth that sinking feeling that he'd made the biggest mistake of his life to see her face light up. "Oh, Cooper, thank you." Julia hugged him, then danced away. "Oh, I've been looking forward to it so much, I know how hard Maisie worked on the menu and it's going to be—" She stopped and eyed him warily. "You did say I wasn't to be anywhere near strangers."

"I know what I said."

"I mean, you were freaking out at the thought of the Rupert Ladies' Association."

He set his jaw. "Yeah."

"So this is a big concession on your part," she said.

"Yeah."

"This is our second fight."

"Yeah."

"And you gave in."

"Er..."

"It'll only be an afternoon, Cooper," Julia said coaxingly. "Just a few hours. And maybe you could be there, too."

"Of course I'll be there." Cooper stared at her. How could she think otherwise? He'd be there — and armed. As would be Bernie, Sandy, Mac and Chuck. It was going to be as safe as he could make it.

"Well, I'm glad you changed your mind." She smiled up at him. He reached out and pulled her firmly back into his arms. She lifted her mouth to his. Long moments later, she murmured, "It's nice to know that you're not always pigheaded."

"Thanks." He tried to smile for her. "I think."

* * * * *

Like many in the trade, the professional had the gift of invisibility.

Of average height and weight, the professional could slide in and out of places, probe for information, and afterwards nobody could give a clear-cut description. It went with the territory, so to speak. Part of a good hit was information, and you couldn't get information if you were going to stand out.

It had been impossible to locate a map of Simpson, but 150 East Valley Road had been easy enough to find. There were perhaps six roads in the whole town and the professional hadn't even had to ask. Just walking inconspicuously around had been enough to pinpoint Julia Devaux's house.

It was a small one-story cottage, with fading paint and a tiny, forlorn front garden. One of the columns on the front porch had an inch-wide crack. All in all, a far cry from where she used to live back in Boston. 4677 Larchmont Street was a building of yuppie condos, each condo worth at least $250,000.

You've come down in the world, Julia Devaux, the professional thought.

But it looked like she'd been busy during her time in Simpson. She seemed to be involved with some cowboy, a Sam

Cooper. And, annoyingly, she also seemed to be surrounded by people all day long. From the moment she left that little dump of a house in the morning to the time she got back in the evening with Sam Cooper, who stayed the night, Julia Devaux was with someone. If Sam Cooper wasn't around, three of his hired hands were. The professional had heard the townfolk call them Sandy, Mac, and Bernie.

There had been a brief window of opportunity during a stupid hen party at the local diner, but then that blasted cowboy had shown up.

Ordinarily, all of this wouldn't have presented any difficulties. The professional knew how to handle a sniperscope and one shot from a rooftop as Julia Devaux was crossing the street would have been enough. But there were two problems. Big ones.

First, the men in Simpson seemed to be a suspicious lot, starting with Sam Cooper, whose eyes swept everything along the horizon as he walked. And the sheriff, too, displayed unusual vigilance, his hand never straying far from the gun in its holster. It was not at all certain that the professional could slip away in the confusion after the hit, and the professional liked certainty.

But most of all, Santana needed to know exactly who it was who'd taken Julia Devaux out, otherwise the professional could kiss the money goodbye. Julia Devaux dead meant nothing to the professional unless it could be proved to Santana who'd done it, so the professional could pocket the two million.

It was all so well prepared. Everything was in place, good to go. The small-gauge gun, the camera with timed film…it was really too bad things seemed to be slipping off schedule. The professional had arranged to take possession of the beach house on Sunday the thirtieth and these unexpected difficulties were throwing the schedule off.

Damn Sam Cooper.

Bored and annoyed, the professional called up Cooper's file, expecting to read all the stupid details of a cowboy's life. The facts concerning Sam Cooper came on the screen. There was a symbol indicating distinguished military service and the professional sat up straight.

A former soldier. Now this was bad news.

With a sinking feeling, the professional hacked into the Department of Defense data.

Very bad news.

Sam Cooper was not a simple cowboy, after all. He was a former SEAL. A brown belt who was also skilled in several other martial arts. The professional's eye scrolled down Cooper's military file, warning signs going off. Not only was the man an ex-commando, he was, according to his file, a gifted military strategist. Several men under his command had followed him to his ranch, including two highly decorated snipers called Harry Sanderson and Mackenzie Boyce. Sandy and Mac. It didn't take much imagination to put two and two together.

Very, very bad news.

There wasn't a Bernie amongst the men in Cooper's team, but the professional would take even money that this Bernie knew his way around a gun, too.

It wasn't a coincidence, then, that Julia Devaux was never alone.

The professional suddenly felt a surge of rage. It was supposed to have been so fucking easy. So neat. So precise. It would have been painless—a surgical strike. And now all that planning down the toilet.

Thanksgiving. It would have to be Thanksgiving, when people were distracted. When everybody would be celebrating by overeating, slowed down by all that food and drink. A well-planned strategy, no false moves. A clean in and out job. Nothing messy.

The professional detested violence.

* * * * *

"Cooper, talk to me," Julia whispered into Cooper's neck.

She tightened her arms around his shoulders and her legs around his waist. They'd just spent the past several hours making love.

Something about her predicament changed Cooper's lovemaking. Whereas before, it was like a wild wind picked her up and hurled her into orgasm, he now insisted on foreplay so long, she ended up shaking and begging him to enter her.

Nothing could hurt her while Cooper was in her. It was time out of time.

He was collapsed on her, his heavy weight bearing her into the mattress. She was sticky with sweat and semen.

She turned her head to kiss his neck. "Talk to me," she said again.

Cooper's eyes suddenly popped open. He'd been falling asleep.

"That's not very fair of me is it, Cooper?" Julia said softly. She caressed the back of his head, her body sated and replete, her mind ricocheting off the walls.

She seemed to be doing that a lot, lately. Her emotions swung wildly from one extreme to the other. Fear so great at times it paralyzed her. Mind-numbing pleasure. Anxiety. Contentment. Sadness. Joy.

She sighed. "I just can't get my mind to stop sometimes, you know? It just whirrs on and on and I don't know how to—"

"I love you." Cooper's quiet voice dropped the little bombshell into the still night.

Julia's heart stuttered then stopped.

"I don't—" Her mind flailed about for a response while her body, entirely of its own accord, reacted to Cooper's large hands holding her hips as his penis surged and lengthened inside her. "I don't seem to have a response for that."

"That's okay." His deep voice was even. "I imagine you don't. You're all tangled up now with what's happening to you. And I have no business telling you something like that, especially now, except that I wanted you to know in case—" Cooper hesitated. "Just…in case," he said finally.

"Cooper, I…" A long forefinger was placed against her lips.

"No. You don't need to answer me. Things are too crazy now for you to know your own feelings. Mine are enough."

Unbearably moved, Julia kissed his chin. "When did you get to be so wise?"

Cooper lifted his head and smiled ruefully. His hips started thrusting gently. "I may not be the most sensitive man in the world, but I'm not made of stone."

"No, you're not. Except for one part of you." She rubbed her lips over the tendon in his neck and cupped his shoulder. She loved the feel of him, the strength, the sureness.

Her legs curled around his backside, heels riding him as he thrust in and out. His movements were lazy at first, languid and slow. Her eyes closed as she concentrated everything she was on the spiral of electric pleasure in her loins. Cooper's tempo gradually increased until she hung, shaking, on the sharpest edge.

A few short, hard movements and she tipped over. With a wild cry, Julia climaxed in sharp contractions that set him off, too. Cooper held her tightly as his penis swelled inside her and he came in long jets. She was already incredibly wet with his previous climaxes. Every night she slept with him, she had to change the bottom sheet.

She didn't mind.

She held him through the shudders of his climax until he finally stilled, easing his full weight on her.

She loved everything about Cooper's lovemaking, but this moment was special. When they'd both found intense pleasure but turned quiet, still connected in every way a man and a woman could be connected. Loins and hearts and minds.

She shifted along his long, solid length. Cooper. Her Cooper. However strong he was, he wasn't a man of steel. He wasn't Superman. She'd seen him tired and worried and anxious. There were several new lines in his face and they looked permanent. She knew that she was the cause of most of them, but he had never once indicated in any way that he resented her intrusion into his life.

She tried to read her wristwatch in the darkness. She couldn't see the dial face, but it must have been close to eleven. Ranchers kept healthy hours. She hadn't had such early bedtimes since she'd been a child.

It was a starless night, the sky blanketed with clouds heavy with the snowstorm all the forecasters were predicting. There was no sound at all outside the house. All the animals had hunkered down in expectation of snow, Cooper had said. She and Cooper could have been the only people in the world.

It was all so utterly unlike Boston. Back home, Larchmont Street would still be alive with people spilling out of the theaters and cafès at eleven. Life never stopped in the heart of Boston. It went on around the clock. The late-night revelers on their way home would meet the sanitation trucks and the office workers trying to get an early jump on the day.

Outside her backyard here in Simpson was wilderness unbroken for fifty miles.

Such an odd place to find love.

Love. Cooper had said he loved her. She loved him, too. Or at least it certainly felt like love. But surely love required a sense of a future together? Some sense of where they were headed? It was a problem that Julia couldn't see into her future at all. Every time she tried to get a handle on her life, plan a little, a dark curtain descended in her mind. There was no future for her that she could see, only the now with its terror and with Cooper by her side.

Suddenly, she needed for Cooper to know that she cared. She lifted her head to tell him, but he pressed a finger to her lips.

"Sleep now, sweetheart," he whispered. "Tomorrow's Thanksgiving."

Chapter Nineteen

"Hey, Davis, Yuletide greetings from the FBI." The junior assistant's voice echoed in the empty offices of the Department of Justice.

"It's Thanksgiving, you dork," Herbert Davis answered grumpily as he bit into his turkey sandwich. It was 9 p.m. and he was doing overtime. *Again.* On a major holiday. "Yuletide is Christmas."

"Whatever," the assistant answered cheerfully, bending over and depositing a package on his desk. "'Tis the season to be merry." Davis caught a whiff of too many beers and rolled his eyes. In his day, any hint of drinking on the job would have been enough to get you fired or so severely reprimanded you picked yourself up off the floor.

Well, times changed.

Davis picked up the vacuum-packed, sealed package marked RUSH. He felt through the plastic seal. An audio cassette. He ripped it open, then noticed the time stamp. "Hey!" he yelled at the back of the departing assistant. "This says seventeen hundred hours, November 28th. That's twenty-four hours ago. It's marked RUSH. What the—"

The assistant turned and waggled his fingers merrily. "Mail clerks," he said. "On a go slow. Sorry, gotta run."

Davis sighed and pulled out the slip of paper in the sealed container. He was tired and out of sorts. Maybe he was coming down with the flu Aaron had caught. Aaron had been home sick for two days now and Davis was feeling the pinch.

He unfurled the FBI message. It took a moment for it to penetrate his tired brain. The FBI had been bugging S.T. Aker's private phone line on an unrelated drug case and the agent in charge had sent him the tape, thinking he might find it of interest.

Davis walked down the long, empty hall to where the audiovisual equipment was kept and inserted the tape, curiosity getting the better of his tiredness. He'd been doing overtime for too long. For a moment, even the prospect of Thanksgiving with his in-laws seemed better than being here.

He shook himself. He knew better. It was just that he was so tired. Again, Davis wished Aaron hadn't fallen ill. He pressed "play".

The sound was a little scratchy, and it took him a minute to realize what was being said and who was saying it. When it clicked, the hairs rose on the back of his neck. He punched the pause button, then rewound.

His finger hovered over the "play" button for a moment, knowing that he would never feel the same way about his job again. He pressed it.

There was the sound of a phone ringing, then an impatient voice. "Yes? Akers here."

"Mr. Akers?"

"Yes, yes, who is speaking?"

"A friend of yours, Mr. Akers. Or rather, a friend of Dominic Santana's."

"I'm listening."

"I know where Julia Devaux is —"

"Now wait a minute. You know I can't receive information like this. It would be in total contravention of the law."

"Well how —"

"But let's imagine a hypothetical situation. Let's imagine that I hang up now and put my answering service on. I'll be out of the room when you leave your message, so I won't know what's being said. And let's imagine — hypothetically speaking, you understand — that I take the tape recorder to visit my client in jail. Let's further imagine that I had to play another part of the tape for him. I won't know what's in your message until it's already been played and it's too late. Do you understand me?"

"Sure."

"Then as soon as I hang up, I'm leaving my office for a quarter of an hour. Will that be enough time?"

"Yeah, it's just an address. But I want money. I want half the reward. I want a million dollars—"

"I don't know what you're talking about. But if you have any requests, put them on the tape."

There was the click of the phone being put down and Davis pushed the off button. He didn't need to hear any more. He sat with his head bowed and let the sadness wash through him. There were a million things that needed doing. Time was tight, but he allowed himself this minute of mourning.

The man who'd sold the information on Julia Devaux was going to be prosecuted to the fullest extent of the law. He would lose his job, his pension, his friends and his freedom. Breach of security for personal profit carried a mandatory 25-year sentence. The man had already lost his family.

Herbert Davis had just listened to a man commit suicide. And not just any man. His best friend for twenty years.

For the man who had betrayed Julia Devaux to a killer was Aaron Barclay.

* * * * *

"Happy Thanksgiving, Coop, Sally," Alice said happily. It was late in the afternoon and the first flakes of the snowstorm that had been threatening all day were finally beginning to fall. Cooper put a hand to Julia's back, and stepped over the threshold of the "Out to Lunch", dread pooling in his gut.

He didn't like this, not one bit.

"Come on." An excited Alice tugged at Julia's hand. "You've just got to see how we arranged the vegetable platters, you'll love it. And Maisie made this amazing sherry bread dressing. To die for."

God, I hope not, Cooper thought sourly as he relinquished his hold on Julia. He was reluctant to have her out of touching distance, even if it was to follow a chattering Alice into the kitchen. He nodded to Bernie, who got up and followed the two women through the swinging doors. Sandy remained where he was, at a window seat, his eyes sweeping the room, then tracking the street outside. Good men, both of them.

Cooper looked around. For the first time that day, he blessed the lousy weather. Very few people he didn't know had made it in for Thanksgiving. A proudly beaming Glenn sat with Matt at a table near the kitchen. At another table were three Simpson families seated as a party, the Rogers, the Lees and the Munros and two couples Cooper recognized from Rupert, though he didn't know their names. Then there was an elderly couple he didn't know stuffing their faces with a selection of Maisie's desserts, but both were in their seventies, and Cooper managed to fight down the temptation to walk over and ask for identification.

He eyed a man he'd never seen before. He looked like a traveling salesmen. Cooper stared unblinkingly at the man. After a few uncomfortable moments, the man looked around and met Sandy's hard, hostile gaze. The man fidgeted in his chair for a few minutes, put his fork down and got up, searching his pockets for money. A few minutes later, the elderly couple followed him out.

Cooper saw the young blonde girl Julia had been talking to when he'd grabbed Julia and dragged her away by the hair. He wondered if he should walk over to the girl and apologize for his behavior the other day, but then decided against it. The hell with manners.

Cooper whirled, narrow-eyed, at the commotion from the door. He had his hand halfway to the shoulder holster before he realized it was Roy Munro's boisterous voice congratulating Alice and Maisie. He drew in a long, calming breath.

He'd deliberately timed it so that they would arrive as the last of the customers would be leaving. He felt reasonably sure that there would be no dinner guests. Storm warnings had been going out all day. Only a madman or a fool would venture out in such isolated country during a snowstorm after dark.

Cooper seated himself at the table Alice had reserved for them and waited with resignation for Julia to emerge from the kitchen. He pulled at his shirt collar. The "Out to Lunch" was overheated and he cursed the shoulder holster that forced him to keep his jacket on.

For the thousandth time that day, Cooper regretted his impulsive decision to allow Julia to celebrate Thanksgiving here and hoped it would be over soon.

This was the last time he was going to let her out in a public place before the trial, whenever it was. And then Cooper realized that Christmas was coming. He gave an inward groan. No way could he stop Julia from celebrating Christmas with her friends. Julia struck him as the kind of woman who would consider not celebrating Christmas unconstitutional.

He didn't give a fuck. His past two Christmases had been normal workdays just like any other.

Horses didn't observe Sundays or Labor Days or Thanksgivings or Christmases. They needed to be fed and watered and exercised every day, without exception. Cooper had well over twenty-five million dollars in horseflesh at the Double C.

Actually, it was becoming a problem trying to juggle everything. Cooper didn't know how much longer he could manage. If only he could convince her to stay with him…a slow smile spread across his features, his first in a week.

Oh, yeah. That would solve all his problems. If he could convince Julia to stay over at the ranch, everything would be so much easier. He allowed himself a moment's daydreaming. She'd make the ranch house less bleak, that was for sure. Maybe he could coax her into doing a little decorating for him, like she'd done for Alice and Beth. Warm the place up. Maybe he could coax her into staying on. Maybe, if he played his cards right, he could convince her to make the arrangement permanent...

"Well, it's sure nice to see you smiling," Julia said as she slipped into the seat next to him, adjusting her waist pouch. "I was beginning to think those frown lines were tattooed on."

Alice placed two enormous plates in front of them. "A little bit of everything," she informed Cooper. "Eat up." Cooper didn't recognize most of what was on his plate. Thanksgiving was turkey, yams, cranberry sauce and pumpkin pie. Period.

But Julia seemed to know what everything was. "Mmm," she sighed, closing her eyes and breathing in the smells. "Sweet potato soufflé. Corn pudding. Turkey with raspberry coulis. Maisie's outdone herself."

Alice fairly wriggled with happiness. "Yeah, she's great, isn't she? Try that raspberry sauce. I mean coulis. We had the editor of *The Rupert Pioneer* in here and he went wild. He said he would do a write-up." Alice looked around. "But it's a good thing not that many people made it in today. We haven't got all the problems ironed out yet. We ordered too many turkeys and not enough vegetables. Also, we're running out of coffee and pies. Still—" she shrugged her shoulders, "things'll be on track by Christmas. We're not doing too badly for beginners."

Cooper dug in, though he had no appetite whatsoever. He chewed slowly, then with more interest. No, they weren't doing too badly at all. He had two full bites before his pleasure ended abruptly.

His cell phone rang. When he looked at the display, he froze. It was Davis' number.

Bad things were coming.

* * * * *

Julia watched Cooper eat, secretly amused. Cooper obviously liked good food and he had just as obviously not had too much of it in his life. He thought she was a great cook. She wasn't bad, but nothing like in Maisie's league. She took a bite of Maisie's stuffing and tried not to close her eyes in delight.

She'd been right to come. She needed this. She'd known that Cooper would want to be with her and he needed this, too. A moment out of time.

Cooper needed to let his guard down. He needed a little relaxation. She knew — though he hadn't said a word — that he was neglecting his work. He was turning himself inside out, trying to keep up the ranch and look after her.

Maybe she should offer to stay out at the ranch with him.

Though the idea would have horrified her only a short while ago, now it held a crazy sort of appeal. She could try her hand at redecorating his Addams family house, have fun rattling around his seven-acre kitchen, watch those beautiful horses being put through their paces.

But most of all, she'd have more time with Cooper. She could imagine them in the evenings, cuddled up around the hearth. There were probably hundreds of fireplaces in his house and they could try making love in front of each one.

Julia put another delicious bite in her mouth, fantasizing about fireplaces and Cooper when she started. "What's that?" she asked.

Cooper put down his fork and reached into his pants pocket for his cellular phone. His jacket shifted and Julia caught sight of something dull gray and metallic under his armpit. He flipped the phone open and frowned when he looked at the display.

"Cooper."

He listened, his hand white on the phone. Julia watched with growing dread as he clenched his jaw. His eyes went hard and opaque.

"Cooper," she said softly. He turned his head to her, but he looked right through her. She could hear the tinny sound of someone talking in the receiver but couldn't make out any words. Cooper shifted the phone into his left hand and reached across with his right and withdrew a gun from his left side. "Cooper?" she whispered, scared now.

He cut off the connection, his face tight. "Sandy," he said. His voice was low but the answer came immediately.

"Yo."

"Mac."

"Yeah."

"Bernie."

"Yeah."

"Get Chuck."

"Right, boss." Sandy disappeared into the swirling darkness. Bernie and Mac took one look at Cooper's face and came over.

"Bernie." Cooper didn't look at up. "Get the Springfield and the .38 from the pickup. Make sure you have plenty of ammo."

"Cooper." Julia tugged at Cooper's jacket. Her hand was trembling. "Tell me what's going on, for God's sake. What happened? Who was that on the phone?"

Cooper turned to her. "That was Herbert Davis," he said, his voice flat and cold. "Santana found out where you are twenty-four hours ago. His men are probably already here."

* * * * *

Everything seemed to happen all at once.

Chuck burst in, shaking the snow off his sheepskin jacket, carrying what looked like an arsenal. Bernie and Mac went out for a moment and came back in carrying several weapons. They both looked grim.

It was all happening so fast. Julia reached out a hand for Cooper, but he was already halfway across the room, talking to Glenn. Julia watched him for a moment, as if he were a stranger. The men had formed a ring around him and he was addressing them in a low voice.

"Sally?" Mary Ferguson's frightened voice made her turn around. "Sally, what's going on? What's all the commotion about?" Mary was white-faced and trembling. Julia put an arm around her. "It's a long story, Mary, and not a very pleasant one. I'm so sorry you're caught in the middle of it." Over Mary's shoulder Julia could see Maisie come out from the kitchen, wiping her hands on her apron. She went over immediately to Glenn.

"Sally?" Alice had followed Maisie out of the kitchen. "What's going on?"

Julia turned to Alice. She reached out and patted Alice's shoulder reassuringly, though she herself felt anything but reassured. "It's okay, honey."

"It's not okay." Cooper's deep voice from behind her made her jump. "Alice, there are some men on their way to Simpson. They're hired killers and they're out to get..." He hesitated a moment.

"Julia." She took a deep breath. What was the point of keeping secrets any more? "Alice, my real name isn't Sally Anderson. It's Julia. Julia Devaux. And those men are after me."

"Are they now?" Alice said calmly. "Well, they're not going to get you. You can take that to the bank and use it as collateral." Alice looked up at Cooper. "Coop, what do you want us to do?"

Cooper looked around the refurbished café, taking in all the details. His features were pulled tight with tension but his voice was as calm as Alice's. *I guess Westerners don't have panic genes,* Julia thought.

"Okay," Cooper said, "here's the drill. I want you to lock all the doors and dim the lights. Keep everyone in the center, away from the windows. Clear away all breakables. Anything that's glass or ceramic or pottery. The last thing we need is people getting cut. I'm leaving Bernie, Sandy and Mac here and—"

"And me." Glenn stood straight under Cooper's scrutiny. "I can handle a gun, Coop. You know I can. You can count on me. We're in this together."

"Yeah," Loren echoed.

Cooper just nodded his head. "Right. Get a weapon from Chuck. Post yourself by the back door and Bernie will be by the front door. Sandy and Mac will cover the windows. I don't expect any trouble here, they'll be gunning for Julia at her house, but you never know."

Julia watched as Chuck handed out weapons and Glenn, Bernie, Sandy and Mac took up their stations. Cooper put some objects she didn't recognize into a leather satchel and then, oddly enough, stuffed in two tea towels he'd taken from the kitchen.

There seemed to be no question that Chuck would be going out with Cooper. Chuck was overweight and over fifty, but Julia knew better than to question his decision. She also knew that Cooper had deliberately left his best men with her.

He'd be facing hired killers essentially alone.

Julia's throat tightened as she looked around. The women were busy clearing away dishes and shifting tables. The men checked their weapons. No one said anything to her.

It was her problem and everyone could have simply looked after their own skins and let her fend for herself. Cooper would have defended her—after all, she was his woman. Chuck was the law. But Glenn, Loren, Bernie, Sandy, Mac, Beth, Alice, Maisie—it wasn't their fight, it was hers.

Tears stung behind her eyelids. The people of Simpson were laying their lives on the line for her, without question. Julia felt a touch from behind and whirled to find herself in Cooper's arms.

She tightened her arms and breathed in Cooper's scent, pine and leather and man, trying to hold him so hard she could imprint him on her skin. A heavy ball of tears and terror settled in her chest. "Cooper," she whispered. "Be careful."

"Yeah." Cooper peeled her away, holding her at arm's length. "We'll be okay." He searched her face. "How about you?"

Every gutsy movie heroine Julia had ever seen flashed across her mind and she did her best to give Cooper a Greer Garson-Katherine Hepburn-Vivien Leigh smile. "Yeah." She forced the sound out from a tight throat. "Yeah, I'll be fine."

"Get out your gun."

"Oh." Crazily, Julia had forgotten all about it. She pulled out the deadly little snub-nosed weapon, hefting it in the palm of her hand. Wondering if she'd ever be able to use it.

"Now you remember what I told you about trigger pull."

"Yes, Cooper." Julia blinked back tears.

"Present as small a target as you can. Lean your upper body forward. Pull don't jerk. You have extra rounds?"

Julia pressed her pouch and nodded.

Cooper gave her a brief, fierce kiss and was walking out the door with Chuck before the first hot tear fell.

"Dad?" Matt's voice cracked on the word. Chuck stopped at the threshold and looked back.

"Yeah, son?"

"I'll need a weapon, too."

Julia could see the struggle play itself across Chuck's face. Surprise. Fear. Pride.

Pride won.

Chuck went to the side table where Bernie had stacked the weapons and picked out a rifle. He clutched it tightly, then walked over to his son.

Julia couldn't stand it. It was one thing to have Cooper and Chuck and his men defending her. But Matt was a child. "No, Chuck," she pleaded. "This is my fight. I can't have a boy getting shot because of—"

Chuck quelled her with a look. "You're one of us now, Julia, and we look after our own. Matt started learning to shoot when he was six. Taught him myself. I guess I didn't realize it before, but he's all grown up now." Solemnly, Chuck held the weapon out to Matt, and just as solemnly Matt took it. "Look after the women, son," Chuck said gravely.

Julia didn't know whether to laugh or cry. Matt's face looked suddenly grownup, the crazy haircut and earrings and nose rings a mere mask over features forged by generations of pioneers living in a country where the boys grew into men fast.

"I will, Dad." Matt's voice was low and didn't crack.

Chuck nodded once, then followed Cooper out the door.

As soon as they were gone, a grin split Matt's face. "Hot damn!" he cried happily as he took up position next to the front window. With one hand he held the gun close to his ear, just like on TV, and with the other he punched the air. "From zero to hero!"

* * * * *

The snow was falling in great gusting sheets of white. Already, a few inches covered the ground, softening footsteps, deadening sounds. Snow could be a deadly foe and Cooper knew he had to make the snow work for him and not against him. The temperature was a few degrees below zero and falling rapidly. He was glad that this wasn't an outdoor job. He'd risked frostbite before and it wasn't fun.

Cooper crouched and made his silent way from door to door along Main, followed by an equally silent Chuck. Cooper's mind was racing. The timeline. The timeline was all-important. Davis had obviously felt guilty as hell that one of his own had betrayed Julia. He had worked hard to give Cooper as accurate a timeline as possible. Cooper reviewed what he knew as he flattened himself against the side wall of Glenn's hardware store.

S. T. Akers had called on Santana after visiting hours at Furrows Island, citing a medical emergency. No phone calls had been allowed to prisoners on the island until seven this morning, when the records showed Santana placing a call to one of his minions in Boston.

Davis had checked all the flights. Even assuming that a hit team had been assembled and ready to go, the very earliest the killers could have made it to Boise would have been by two this afternoon. All flights out of Logan had been delayed for four hours because of the weather. It was a three hour drive from the Boise airport to Simpson under fair conditions and assuming you knew the road. For men unfamiliar with the territory and in a snowstorm, it would take at least four hours.

Cooper checked his wristwatch under a streetlamp. Five-thirty. He had about half an hour to set things up.

Cooper jerked and cursed when his cell phone went off. Before the second ring, he had it open and had cupped his hand around the receiver. "Cooper." His voice was low as his eyes scanned Main Street.

"Davis here. We've got news on this end."

Cooper closed his eyes and said a prayer. "Tell me the hunt is over and the dogs have been called off."

"Sorry." Davis sounded regretful. "I wish I could. What's happening over there?"

"I've secured Julia. She's safe, barring a mortar hit on the building she's in. Now the Sheriff and I proceeding to her house to prepare the welcoming committee."

"Well, good luck." Davis' voice sounded tinny. The snowstorm was dampening the sound. "Tell the bad guys they'd never have collected anyway."

A pickup turned slowly onto Main, the headlights cutting through the needles of sleeting snow and Cooper tensed until the pickup passed him and he recognized a man whose ranch bordered his. "What the hell does that mean?" he snarled into the phone.

"Santana's dead."

"What?" Cooper frowned. Had he heard right? He couldn't afford to make the slightest mistake. Not with Julia's life at stake. "Run that one by me again."

"Santana suffered a massive coronary around three." Not even the heavy static could hide the rich satisfaction in Davis' voice. "He was pronounced dead at 3:15 p.m. Eastern Standard. I just heard about it."

"Could he be faking it?"

"Not unless he's got a special arrangement with God. Santana's guts are spread out on an autopsy table right now. The pathologist says he drank too much and his liver is a mess. So — if you catch these guys, it's all over."

"Save a piece of Santana's hide for me," Cooper growled, "I want to nail it to my wall." He pressed the "off" button, and put Davis' news in a far corner of his mind. He had to focus his entire attention on the mission at hand.

"Who was that?" Chuck's voice was the merest breath in his ear.

"Later." Cooper's voice was just as low. He pointed to Julia's corner house and rotated his fist. *We're going in the back.* Chuck nodded that he understood. They made their way silently around the house and Cooper let himself in with his key. He slipped into the house and closed the door after Chuck. Moving quietly, efficiently, he pulled a pinpoint flashlight from his pocket and pulled a flashbang and a tripwire from the satchel. He pulled out the towels he'd stuffed into his satchel and gave one to Chuck.

"Dry off," he whispered. "Can't leave any tracks." Chuck nodded and dried off while Cooper fixed the flashbangs to the front and back door handles.

It took forty-five seconds to set it up. Cooper grunted with satisfaction and moved quickly into the bedroom.

He was stuffing some of Julia's clothes under the blanket to make it look as if she were taking a nap in case someone checked through her windows when he felt Chuck's hand on his shoulder. He nodded. He'd heard it, too. A car, coming down East Valley Road.

Cooper checked out the window. The car was traveling without headlights. It came to a gliding stop about fifty yards away and two figures got out without the inside lights coming on. They closed the car doors quietly. It was impossible to see their features, but the stealthy way they moved showed Cooper that they were pros.

Cooper pushed Chuck into the closet and pulled the door closed. That should protect them from the worst of the stun blast.

Cooper checked his watch. The men were fifteen minutes early on Davis' earliest estimate. These guys were fast and they were good.

But he was better.

* * * * *

Julia heard the explosion from three blocks away. The windowpanes of the "Out to Lunch" rattled briefly, then there was utter silence, echoed by the sudden void in her chest.

Julia looked around and saw shocked faces, except for Sandy, Mac and Bernie. Their faces were grim, their weapons held at the shoulder and cocked.

"No," Julia whispered. Alice stared at the floor and Maisie moved forward to put her arms around Julia's shoulders. Julia pushed her and her sympathy away with stiff arms. "No," she said, louder.

No one said anything.

With numb fingers, Julia checked the tip up barrel of her gun for the thousandth time and snapped it back in place. She realized suddenly that if anything had happened to Cooper, she'd have the nerve to use it. She clicked the safety off and bolted out the door so quickly she got past Cooper's men.

"Hey!" she heard Bernie yell, "Coop said—"

But by then she was out on the street. She didn't want to hear from Bernie what Cooper had said. She wanted to hear it directly from Cooper. She wanted Cooper himself, in the flesh, to scold her and complain about her lack of obedience. She wanted Cooper to chew her out, tell her she'd put herself in danger, and that he wasn't going to tolerate it. She wanted Cooper…she wanted Cooper.

Alive.

Julia ran towards her house, wiping tears and snow out of her eyes, slipping a little because she didn't have the right shoes for bad weather. The snow reached almost to her ankles, but it could have reached her chest and she wouldn't have noticed or cared. All she wanted was to get to Cooper.

She slid the last few feet before her gate, stopping her slide by a hand to the gatepost, then tore up the rickety steps and slammed the door open, standing wildly panting and wide-eyed in her gunman's crouch as she took in the scene.

Two sullen handcuffed men were sitting on the floor with their backs to her living room wall and Chuck was reading them their rights in a monotone. Cooper walked in from the bathroom sucking his reddened knuckles, a heavy scowl on his face.

Julia's heart gave a great lurch and her voice tried to make its way through her throat. Shaking, she put the safety back on and put the Tomcat down on the coffee table. "Cooper—" Nothing came out and she tried again. "Cooper." It was thready and weak, but he heard.

He turned, still frowning, and frowned even more when he saw her. "What the—" he began, then looked past her. "Bernie, I thought I told you to keep her safe."

Bernie opened his mouth to answer, but he was out of breath. It didn't make any difference, anyway, because Julia had launched herself into Cooper's arms with a cry of joy. "Oh God, Cooper, when I heard the explosion, I thought—I thought—"

"I know." Cooper hugged her tightly. "Listen, I thought I told you to stay put."

Julia couldn't talk. She simply nodded into his shoulder.

"I told you to stay put at the 'Out to Lunch', didn't I? That wasn't asking too much, was it? You were supposed to stay right where you were until I came back to get you."

Julia nodded, shook her head, nodded then laughed. She pulled her head back from his shoulder. "I'm glad to see you, too."

It was so wonderful to feel him, his strength, his solidness, even his scratchy jacket smelling of wet wool. She stilled and stared at the two men slumped against her wall. Disengaging herself from Cooper, she walked over and looked down.

"What happened to their faces?" she asked.

"Walked into a door," Cooper said.

"Resisted arrest," Chuck said.

Julia studied the battered faces of the enemy. One man was blondish, with a long, dirty ponytail and the other was dark, with a crewcut and three earrings. But no matter the superficial differences, they shared a look. The same look Santana had had. That kind of face was etched into her memory forever. Cold, cruel, brutal. She knew with a sickening certainty that they would have killed her without a second thought.

And Santana still would.

She turned, the thought rousing in a heartbeat all the sheer terror she'd felt over the past seven weeks. "Cooper." She put a hand to the wall to steady herself. "Cooper, Santana knows where I am now. He can send others —"

"Santana's not going to be sending anyone anywhere," Cooper answered. "He's dead, honey. He died a few hours ago. Heart attack. The nightmare's over."

It took a second or two for the words to penetrate.

The nightmare is over. She let the words roll around in her head. The nightmare is over. They hardly made sense.

"Oh," she said inanely. "Oh, that's — that's good."

Cooper looked at her, frowning. "Sit down, sweetheart." When she shook her head, he walked her over to the armchair and exerted gentle pressure. "Sit down before you fall down."

She didn't want to obey him. It was just that her knees buckled.

Julia felt a deep tremor start from within and her fingers bit into the arms of the chair. Dots swam in front of her eyes and she tried to focus. Her mind was finding it hard to absorb what Cooper had just said.

The nightmare is over.

Weeks and weeks of agonizing fear, of a loneliness so deep she sometimes thought she would die of that alone. Weeks of isolation and exile. Of waking shuddering and sweating from sleep only to find that the waking terror was worse than the terror that stalked her in her dreams. Of teaching herself to live from minute to minute because she had no future.

The nightmare is over.

A great sob exploded from her chest, then another.

"Oh, God," she gasped, dazed. The enormity of it struck her all over again. She could hardly catch her breath, could hardly get her mind around the thought.

Cooper took her trembling hands in his and she stared blindly at their linked fingers. "It's over. I don't have to stay here anymore. I can do what I want. I can go home. Oh dear God, I can go home again. I can't wait. Oh, God, I can't wait. I want to go home now." Tears were leaking out of her eyes and her heart was thumping wildly in her chest. Julia barely noticed when Cooper released her.

She raked her trembling hands through her hair. Her head was filled with one thought—home.

The nightmare is over.

She looked around and focused on Cooper, watching him retreat. Chuck was retreating, too. Bernie had turned his back and was standing stiffly by the door.

All of a sudden, Julia remembered what she'd said and it struck her how Cooper would take it. He thought she meant that she wanted to go home and never come back. But she hadn't meant that—not at all. What she'd really meant was—she'd meant...she didn't know what she'd meant.

Julia tried to gather her thoughts but it didn't work. It only made her head hurt.

She realized now how far she'd come in understanding Cooper, how well she had learned to read his face, because all of a sudden she couldn't read anything at all. He stood before her, straight and tall and broad, his face an impenetrable mask.

Chuck was herding the two shackled prisoners out the door. Bernie had already left. Cooper had one hand on the doorjamb.

"You won't be bothered again." Cooper's voice was as remote as his face. "Davis said that he'll call you in for a deposition but it won't be anytime soon. I'll book you a flight out tomorrow. One of my men will take you to the airport."

"No, I—" Julia stretched out a hand. She couldn't stand to see that blank look on Cooper's face. But the emotions were washing through her in great roiling waves, so enormous she couldn't get a handle on any one. She bit her trembling lips and let her hand drop.

There was so much she wanted to say to Cooper, but it looked like she wasn't going to have the time because he was out the door and past her gate before she could get her leaden feet to stir.

Maybe it was better this way.

There was no way on this earth that she could explain anything to anyone, not tonight, certainly not right now.

Julia sank bank onto her couch. The horrendous little couch with the broken springs.

It struck her, for the first time, that she was going to miss that stupid couch. Her own couch in Boston was covered in an exquisite beige Sanderson chintz but this couch, ugly as it was, had...character.

There were a lot of things she was going to miss.

She was going home. For the first time, Julia allowed herself to savor that thought. Home.

Home.

But what did she have there? What was home now? What was waiting for her? Her job? Even if she managed to get her job back, she'd been starting to get dissatisfied with it. She'd even toyed with the idea of setting up as a freelance book doctor. Since the takeover, personnel were shuffled so often she never got a chance to deepen her ties with her colleagues or the authors. She was basically a faceless paper-pusher with a good degree.

She would see Jean and Dora again.

But Julia suddenly realized that all the time she'd been in Simpson, she hadn't wondered how they were getting on. She and Jean and Dora had got along reasonably well together at the office, read the same books and met on Saturdays for coffee and gossip. That was all.

It wasn't like here, where she was intimately involved in the daily lives of her friends. She wanted to know what Alice would be doing, if the "Out to Lunch" would be a success. She wanted to go on trying out Maisie's wonderful recipes. She wanted to help Beth redecorate. Matt had mentioned that he had written a hundred twenty pages of a science fiction epic and she wanted to read it.

She couldn't leave them.

Julia started at the wet muzzle laid adoringly on her knee. Federico, her sleek Siamese, had found another family to lord it over. Not like Fred. Fred needed her. She couldn't leave Fred.

She couldn't leave Cooper.

Not in a million years.

It had been the emotion and relief of the moment that had made her react that way, but the fog was beginning to clear. She wanted Cooper back—her Cooper who made her feel safe and excited all at once, who scolded her and repaired things for her. Cooper who was so exciting in bed she sometimes thought her heart would stop.

That great tidal wave of emotions was receding, leaving her calmer now and resolute.

She'd been foolish, but that was okay. Cooper would forgive her. He had to or she'd...she'd beat him up. They'd had a mock fight once, and he'd laughed so hard she'd managed to wrestle him to the floor.

Some martial arts expert.

Well, if he had his stupid pride, she didn't. Julia stood up, grateful her knees were finally steady.

She picked up the phone and stared at it. There was no dial tone. She shook it as if that would give her a signal. The phone rang, startling her and she dropped the receiver, frowning at it. It rang again and she realized that it was the doorbell ringing and not the phone.

Whoever it was would have to go away because she didn't want to talk to anyone right now but Cooper.

Julia opened the door. Mary Ferguson stood on her doorstep, shoulders covered in snow, clutching an overnight case. "Hi." Mary smiled timidly. "I'm leaving. Going back to Daddy. I guess he was right all along. I just wanted to say goodbye. Can I come in for a minute?"

Mary definitely wasn't Cooper. Julia wanted her to go away. Good manners warred briefly with her desire to run after Cooper and good manners won by a hair. She'd say goodbye to Mary and then go run after Cooper.

"Sure." Julia smiled wanly and stepped back. "Come on in."

"That was some excitement we had this afternoon," Mary said. She put her case on the floor. "I was scared to death."

"Yeah." Julia went into the kitchen to put some water on to boil and came back holding two mugs. "I'm glad the whole thing is over."

"Well, that's the thing, Julia," Mary said regretfully. "I'm afraid it isn't over at all."

Julia could barely hear the sound of the mugs shattering over the roaring in her ears.

Mary Ferguson was holding a gun, pointed right at her.

* * * * *

Cooper regretted leaving Julia almost as soon as he was out of town. His pickup bucked over a hillock of snow and he fought fiercely for control of the wheel. The wind was blowing the snow straight into his windshield, and the wipers could hardly keep up.

Even the wind wanted him to turn around and go back.

Pride was a funny thing, he mused. Cooper men had been choking on their pride for four generations. But pride didn't make you laugh or warm your bed at night. Pride made a very cold companion.

So she said she wanted to go home. Big deal. Of course she wanted to go home. Anyone would. He'd watched her blend in so well in Simpson that he'd forgotten that she hadn't been born here, that she'd left a life behind her.

He hadn't even given her a chance to say anything. He hadn't allowed for the aftermath of shock and fear. No, siree. He'd just coldly informed her that she'd be accompanied to the airport.

Cooper could imagine Julia now, forlorn and shaken from the day's events. He could just see her, curled up in a small ball on that ridiculous couch with the broken springs.

Tonight, of all nights, Julia shouldn't be left alone. He could kick himself for his behavior. He should be there now, comforting her, cooking a lousy meal for her, watching her choke it down and inventing outrageous compliments on his cooking.

The pickup bucked again and Cooper slowed. All of a sudden, he couldn't wait to get back to her. He didn't want Julia to spend one more second feeling lost and lonely. He tried to keep the pickup on the road with one hand while he fished for his cell phone with another to tell her that he was turning back. He switched it on and dialed her number. There was no answering ring.

He must have dialed a wrong number. Cooper stopped the pickup and punched Julia's number again, frowning. He tried three more times, then switched the phone off.

Fear such as he had never known before seized his innards.

You fucking asshole, he raged at himself. His pride had been hurt and he hadn't been thinking straight.

Nobody had said that Santana had only sent two killers. Another one could easily have been dropped off as a backup before arriving at the house. A killer could be in her house right now.

He had left Julia alone and defenseless.

While ice ran in his veins, Cooper wrenched the steering wheel of the pickup, backed into a snowbank and turned around. Cursing himself for a fool, he pressed the accelerator and sped through the swirling night.

* * * * *

"Uhm, Mary." Julia licked dry lips. "You want to be careful with that...that gun. It might be loaded."

"Of course it's loaded, you fool." Mary reached into her case and brought out a camera, setting it down on the coffee table. "And there's a bullet with your name on it that's been waiting for almost two months now." She eyed Julia critically, dispassionately. "Move against that wall over there. I need a white backdrop."

"Mary," Julia whispered. "What are you doing?"

"Doing?" Mary stared at her. "I'm earning two million dollars, darling, what do you think I'm doing?" She waved the gun. "Now move."

Julia shuffled in the direction Mary indicated, watching her. She sidled by the coffee table where her Tomcat was. As she got closer, Mary suddenly reached out.

"Unh-huh, Julia." Mary held the Tomcat up, flicked open the chamber and emptied it. "A Tomcat .32. Someone very smart has been advising you, Julia. Not that it's going to do you any good."

How had she ever thought that Mary was a young girl? The woman must be a genius with makeup. Now that she looked carefully, Julia could see the fine lines around the eyes, the crease from nose to mouth.

"Mary," she whispered. "Why are you doing this? What have I ever done to you? Please don't do this."

Mary laughed. "First of all, my name isn't Mary, not that I have any intention of telling you what my real name is. Secondly, of course I'm going to do kill you. I've been tracking you since October. You're going to buy me a charming beachfront villa and a handsome annuity. Or rather your head is."

Mary bent over to check the lens of the camera, then walked around the living room, turning on all the lights. The whole time, her gun was trained rock-steady on Julia. "The light has to be just right," Mary murmured.

"But—" Julia's mind whirled, trying to take in what was happening. "They took Santana's men away. He tried to get me, but it didn't work."

"Those goons?" Mary's face grew pinched and white and Julia realized that the emotion she'd seen in Mary's face in the café had been rage and not fear. "Two-bit hired guns. That's all they were. And to think they almost cheated me out of my money. But with these snapshots, Santana will know who he has to pay."

"He won't!" Julia almost sobbed with relief. Mary—or whatever her name was—obviously didn't know. "Santana won't pay you. He can't. Haven't you heard? Santana's dead. He died this afternoon."

"You're lying!" Mary snarled.

Startled, Julia looked into Mary's pale blue eyes. She didn't see the cold brutality of Santana or the two thugs who'd broken into her house. All she saw was the flat, blank stare of madness.

"You're lying, just to save your own skin. But it's not going to work." Mary's thin-lipped smile didn't reach her eyes. "I'm going to shoot you and send Santana the snapshots. And then he'll send me my money."

"But he can't! He can't send you any money." Julia tried desperately to get through to her. But Mary was impenetrable, utterly unreachable. The gun in Mary's hand began its slow trajectory upwards.

Time! Julia thought wildly. She needed more time. If only she could do something—delay Mary until someone could come for her. Surely Cooper…

But she'd sent Cooper away. Stupidly, stupidly, she'd sent Cooper away. Maybe she could distract Mary's attention. "You might as well turn around and go home, Mary, because you'll never collect your money. If you go away now, I won't tell anyone, I promise. No one will ever know. Just put down the gun and leave. Santana's dead."

The gun was aimed at her heart now, her wildly thudding heart. "Please," she whispered.

"Please what, Julia?" Mary mocked. "What on earth can you offer me that can top two million dollars? I'm going to buy myself a new life with that money. A new life in exchange for yours." She gave a short, harsh laugh. "Seems fair."

"No, you're not." Julia tried to keep a calm tone. "You can't buy yourself a new life with mine, Mary," she said reasonably. "You're not going to be able to get far in this snowstorm. They'll catch up with you. And all for nothing, Mary. All for nothing because there isn't anyone to give you the money. Santana's dead, Mary."

"You lie!" Mary screamed and pulled the trigger.

Julia was slammed against the wall and a fiery pain erupted in her shoulder. She stood, wavering, until her legs collapsed. She watched through a numb haze as Mary approached and squatted. A flare went off in her eyes and then another. It took her a moment to realize that it was the flashbulb of the camera.

Mary stood, her shoe slipping a little in the blood and a look of disgust crossed her face. "Blood," she grimaced. "I hate blood. Now just a few more shots, darling, and then the last shot—the head shot—and we'll be all done. Then I have to go. I've got a plane to catch."

Julia watched the front of her sweater turning red and realized dimly, as if the information were being faxed to her from a foreign country, that it was her blood turning her sweater red. Julia heard a low, vicious growl penetrating the fog clouding her mind.

"Damn it!" Mary kicked at Fred. He was standing in front of Julia, hackles raised. He snarled and snapped at Mary's hand as she tried to put the muzzle of the gun against Julia's temple. Fred bared his teeth and gave another hair-raising growl. "Call this stupid dog off," Mary hissed. "I've got to get out of here."

"Nice doggie," Julia murmured. "Good Fred." There was pain now. Waves of it. Starting from far away, but coming closer.

"Well, if you won't call him off, I'll just have to do it from here." Mary sighted down the barrel at Julia and closed one eye.

Julia's head felt as if it weighed a thousand pounds. She lifted it with difficulty and stared down the gun barrel pointed straight at her forehead.

She didn't want to die. She wanted to live. She wanted to live and marry Cooper, break the Cooper Curse and give him a houseful of redheaded girls who would drive him crazy. And she'd never even told Cooper she loved him.

Julia watched Mary's finger tighten and thought—this is it.

There was a loud noise and a red blossom flowered on Mary's forehead. Fred was barking and Cooper was kneeling beside her, tearing off his jacket and stuffing it against her shoulder, cradling her in his arms, shouting, "Julia, Julia!" She could feel his hands running over her, checking for injuries, then he pressed down strongly on the wound in her shoulder.

Pinwheels exploded behind her eyes and she wanted to tell him to cut it out, but the pain took her breath away.

"Julia." Cooper lifted her carefully. His deep voice cracked. "Don't die on me, Julia. I need you. Just hold on, I'll get you to Doc Adams in Rupert. Just hold on. Talk to me, Julia. You won't die, I won't let you. Talk to me, please."

Talk to me.

"Hey," Julia whispered. She reached out with a trembling hand and cupped his cheek. It was warm and rough and solid, just like Cooper. "That's my line."

Epilogue
Four years later

"THE END."

Julia sat back, contented, watching the blinking cursor on the screen for a moment or two. With a deep sigh of satisfaction, she saved the document, then turned the computer off and stretched, wincing. Her shoulder was hurting more than usual, which meant more snow. According to the weather reports, it was shaping up to be as big a snowstorm for Thanksgiving as had fallen four years ago.

That snowstorm had almost cost her her life. The doctors at the Rupert clinic had told her that her blood pressure had been fifty over nothing and falling when Cooper had carried her in. Though she had been barely conscious, Julia's nightmares were still colored white—snow, bandages, doctors and nurses in white, the light in the operating theater just before going under...

She was lucky to be alive and with only a barometer shoulder to show for being shot. If Cooper hadn't known how to apply a pressure bandage and if he hadn't battled his way through the storm to Rupert... Julia shuddered at the thought.

As soon as she had been able to sit up in bed, Cooper had brought in a Justice of the Peace to marry them. And it had been there, in a hospital room filled with the flowers Cooper had bought, surrounded by her friends from Simpson, that Julia had joined her life to his.

It had taken six months in a cast and another six months of rehabilitation to get the use of her shoulder back. And in all that time, Cooper had forbidden her to work. After that, of course, the birth of the twins had pretty much taken care of any free time she might have had for the next couple of years.

She'd broached the idea of children on their first trip to Boston, when she could move with a degree of ease. She'd closed down and sold her condo, shipped her belongings to Idaho and had had an emotional reunion with her friends. Everyone had a standing invitation to come visit her and several already had.

As decisions went, it hadn't been traumatic. After making love half the night in her old apartment, Julia had said quietly, into Cooper's shoulder, "I haven't gone back on the pill."

"Good," was all he said. And that was that.

Nobody expected rambunctious twin girls. For the first couple of years, work was unthinkable, but then Julia started getting restless. And now she'd begun her new career as a freelance editor — or as she called it, a book doctor. Fittingly enough, her first contract was Rob Manson's first novel.

Manson had won the Pulitzer Prize for his article on her — "The Town That Saved Julia".

Cooper had told him Julia's story. Intrigued, he had traveled to Simpson to research the story, had met Alice and had elected to stay on as managing editor of *The Rupert Pioneer*. His article had been picked up as a national news item and had swept the country. His exposé of the inefficiency of the Witness Security Program had led to a new director and new funding. "The Town That Saved Julia" had been featured on *Dateline*.

Rob often joked that Simpson was actually "The Town That Julia Saved". In the past couple of years, several new businesses had moved into town. Rob's brother, a software engineer in Cupertino, visited often and was thinking of establishing his new startup company in Simpson. Rob and Alice had married the year before and were expecting their first baby.

Julia got up to see what the girls and Cooper were doing. It took time to cross the huge room that served as her study. Cooper had refurbished the entire top floor of the house for her use and she had more floor space than the company she used to work for. It was a good thirty feet from her workstation to the door.

Julia had a work room, a library for her reference books, a room for her printer, a sitting room, and what Cooper called her "thinking room" — an airy, spacious corner room with a view of the front lawn so she could watch Cooper's men trying to keep the girls out of mischief.

Julia ran a hand over her stomach. If this morning's pregnancy test was anything to go by, there was going to be another Cooper girl come August. It was going to be a girl. She had no doubt about that. The Cooper curse had been shattered forever by the birth of Samantha and Dorothy. Fred had found a wife too, a lovely collie bitch, and they produced a litter of mostly female pups. Even the horses had started foaling fillies. Cooper was up to his eyeballs in females now.

Julia opened the massive door to her study and hung her "The Book Doctor is IN!" sign on the fist-sized brass doorknob. Just in time. The front door slammed shut and she could hear Cooper's deep voice and the treble babbling of the girls.

There was the pounding of boots and the clicking of dog nails on the hardwood stairs as Fred followed them up. Julia smiled fondly down at Cooper through the railing.

"Can we come up?" He had a two-year-old in each arm and he looked happy and frazzled — his usual expression since the birth of the twins.

"Sure." Julia smiled down at her family. "Come on in. I've got some news for you."

Cooper came up the last flight. "All done?" he asked. "How did it go?"

"The book?" Julia gave him a thumbs-up. "It's going to be a winner. But that's not—"

"Good." Cooper grinned. "Alice danced around me all morning when I stopped by for a cup of coffee. She didn't have the nerve to ask me what you thought of the novel. I finally put her out of her misery and said that you'd be finishing it soon."

"I'll deliver it to them personally. With my comments. All positive." Julia raised her face for a kiss. Cooper bent, smiling, then grimaced as Samantha pulled sharply on his hair. Cooper's once jet-black hair was quickly turning silver and the girls were responsible for every single white hair.

"Ouch! Sam, let go." He tried to gently disentangle Samantha's fingers from his hair. "Honey, let go." He winced as Samantha pulled harder, gurgling gleefully. "Please, Sweetie. Let Poppa go."

With a sharp sigh of disgust, Julia stood on tiptoe so she could meet Samantha's eyes and said sternly, "Samantha! Stop. Pulling. Your. Father's. Hair. NOW!" Turquoise eyes met black eyes and Samantha opened her chubby hand. She knew who was boss.

"How do you do that?" Cooper asked ruefully, rubbing at his scalp. "I can never get her to do what I say. Dot, either."

Julia rolled her eyes in exasperation. "Honestly, Cooper. You're bigger and stronger than the girls are. You're a martial arts expert. You're a former SEAL, for God's sake. If you can't convince them—use violence."

Julia bit her lip at Cooper's shocked expression. His sense of humor had gone straight down the toilet with the birth of the girls.

The girls were wriggling impatiently. Cooper bent and deposited the toddlers on the ground. Samantha and Dorothy stood miraculously still for a moment. They looked around, blinking, at the room that was normally off-limits, wondering what damage they could wreak.

Julia watched her two beautiful daughters, the love in her heart swelling until her chest ached. Sam and Dot kept her running too much for her to get weepy over the miracle of their existence but, for just a moment, as she watched them, Julia felt tears prick her eyes. Dot and Sam had her glossy red hair and

Cooper's black eyes. They were bright and absolutely fearless. *My daughters*, Julia thought, with an uncharacteristically sentimental pang.

Probably just hormones, she thought. From the new life growing in her. She leaned against Cooper and he absentmindedly put his arm around her as they watched the two toddlers go off in opposite directions.

Julia poked Cooper in the ribs.

"Ow," he complained mildly. "What was that for?"

"I've got something to tell you, but first I want you to kiss me."

"Is that all?" Cooper's dark eyes gleamed. "Why didn't you say so?"

Julia twined her arms around Cooper's neck and gave herself up to the magic they could still create after four years of marriage.

Before they could get lost in the kiss, Cooper opened a wary, paternal eye. His other eye opened in horror and he broke away.

"Dorothy!" He lunged and snatched the scissors from Dorothy's hand just in time. Fred was lying on his side, patiently allowing the little girl to cut the long yellow hairs on his belly. Dorothy was very close to ensuring that Fred would never sire another litter.

Cooper hunkered down. "Dot, honey, you mustn't do that. Poor Fred, you were about to —"

Dot burst into noisy tears and Cooper assumed that panicked expression he always had when his girls cried. "Aw, honey," he said helplessly. "Don't cry, it'll be all right —" He glanced up to see Julia laughing at him. "What?" he asked, aggrieved.

"It's your own fault, Cooper." Julia leaned against a bookcase. "If you and your men and Rafael and even Fred are going to roll over and play dead for the girls, of course they're going to ride roughshod all over you. Sam and Dot are growing up to think that anything with a Y chromosome is their servant."

But it was useless. Cooper had picked Dot up and was cooing at her, trying to get her to smile. Julia could almost see the little gears in Dot's head whirring as she tried to figure out how to use the situation to her advantage.

"There you go, love." Cooper put Dot back down again and gave her bottom a little pat.

"Coop?"

He looked up with a smile. "Yeah?"

"What I was trying to say was—"

"Oh, I forgot to tell you," Cooper interrupted excitedly. "Sandy put them on Southern Star. He says he can tell that Sam has the seat of a champion. Dot's seat is going to take some working on—"

"Cooper." Julia heaved a sigh. "The girls are two years old. It's way too early for Sandy to know whether they have a good seat or not. Let's get back to what I wanted to tell you—"

"It's not too early." Cooper frowned. "Pure Gold's new filly will be ready for riding in about two and a half years and the girls should get acquainted with her as soon as possible. Why just the other day—"

"Cooper, I'm trying to tell you something here—"

"Bernie was telling me that that new girl he was dating over in Dead Horse, you know—the pretty one who trains horses for the Hughes' spread? Well, he said she said—"

"Cooper—"

"—that she started training at two. Her father put her right up on a pony on her second birthday and she never looked back. Why I'll bet our girls—"

"Cooper—"

"—are going to be State Champions. Hell, they could probably go to the Olympics, if they wanted. Let's see, the earliest would probably be the Olympics of 2020 but if we start now, I'll bet we could—" He stopped as Julia placed two fingers against his lips.

"Cooper," she said lovingly. "Shut up."

Enjoy this excerpt from

Port of Paradise

© Copyright Lisa Marie Rice 2003

Bari, Italy

"Subjunctive mood," the young English teacher, Mark Harrington, said.

Captain Franco Rivera stirred uneasily in his seat and wondered about his own mood. He stretched his legs out in the aisle, paying scant attention to the earnest young man pacing in front of the cadet *carabinieri*, the elite police corps of Italy, and a few of his trusted lieutenants.

"This is a tricky mood to get right," the teacher intoned.

Rivera knew that his men were paying attention to the subjunctive, for he had made it clear to all that a good working knowledge of English was essential to the job and, above all, essential to a promotion. Police work nowadays was international, crossed too many frontiers. Rivera himself worked closely and often with Interpol, Europol, the FBI and the DEA. English was a must and his own was damned good.

So what was he doing wasting his time in a class? It wasn't even as if he had nothing better to do. His office desk was piled a foot high with files waiting to be read.

He shifted in his hard chair and told himself he was keeping his men company. Through the windows came the sounds of a crash and glass shattering. Imprecations floated up from the street below. An instant later, horns blasted as angry drivers discovered that they were stuck behind the scene of an accident.

Rivera suppressed a grin. Some poor sucker of a traffic cop was going to have a very difficult half hour.

"I wish she were here," Mark said, pushing up with a forefinger the wire-rimmed glasses which kept slipping down his nose. "That is the subjunctive as an expression of desire."

Desire, Rivera thought.

Okay.

That was why he was sitting in a hot classroom when he had better things to do. Desire. Desire for Hope Winston, a woman he hadn't yet managed to meet.

Six months ago, he'd met Kay Summers at a city-sponsored event and they'd become good friends immediately. Both of them realized right away that they were destined to be friends, not lovers.

Rivera had done what he could to help Kay, recommending the school to colleagues and acquaintances, fully aware of the weight a senior police officer's recommendation carried in this society.

And his word had ultimately cinched the city's contract with Kay's school to teach English to all city policemen. In return, Kay had offered him endless cups of weak coffee and a sympathetic ear when he needed to let off steam.

He'd been heartbroken over Kay's accident and visited her often in the hospital. She didn't know that he'd been moving heaven and earth to find the hit-and-run driver who'd almost taken her life.

So when Kay had asked him to look out for her best friend, Hope Winston, he had agreed, unhesitatingly. He was willing to do anything to make Kay's friend welcome.

But after one look at Hope, even from a distance, he'd realized that whatever help he could give, it wouldn't be purely for Kay's sake.

He'd been hooked the first time he saw Hope Winston. At the time, he didn't know who she was. All he knew was that she was tantalizing.

The woman was climbing the big marble steps of the English Language Center. He'd been walking to the corner bar to have a cappuccino before going into the school to introduce himself to Kay's friend when he stopped dead in his tracks to watch the woman who instantly mesmerized him.

Woman-watching was one of his favorite past-times, a hobby he shared with roughly 30 million other Italians – the entire male population. But there had been something truly compelling about the woman gracefully climbing the steep marble stairs.

A foreigner, she was clearly a foreigner. For one thing, she wasn't elegantly dressed. Old jeans hugging glorious hips and long, slender legs, tennis shoes and an old tee shirt. Clothes any self-respecting Italian woman wouldn't be caught dead in. But the giveaway was the hair, long, straight, thick and a stunning platinum blonde. Natural, he'd bet his badge on it. There wasn't a woman in Bari with hair like that.

So he'd stood on the street staring much longer than was usual, ashamed of his behavior - he wasn't fourteen and woman-starved, after all, he was thirty six and had more than enough sex, thank you very much. Just last night, in fact, he'd had a very satisfactory couple of hours in bed with Silvana Lucarini. So what was he doing, stopping and staring at a woman's back?

Then someone from street level called, and the woman turned and Franco caught his breath. *Gesù*, she was gorgeous. In a country of beautiful women, she was a knock-out. Pale, oval face, stunning features, eyes a pale silvery blue so intense the color was still startling from 50 feet away. It was Hope Winston, it had to be. There wasn't another woman like that in all of Apulia.

Helping Kay's friend had suddenly become his new top priority.

Like an idiot, he'd stood stunned in the street just long enough for her to turn back around and disappear into the building. It took him a minute to gather his wits and then he sprinted up the steps, cappuccino forgotten. He'd described her to an amused secretary, who confirmed that the person he'd seen was, indeed, the new director, Hope Winston. But *la Direttrice* Winston had just left the premises, two minutes ago.

That had been four days ago and it was always the same story. She'd just left or hadn't arrived yet. Franco had caught tantalizing glimpses of a platinum head disappearing around corners, slender curves in ugly clothes walking down a hallway and vanishing from sight and once--two days ago--he'd looked down out of a window at the school to see her looking up. Their eyes met, and held. She was breathtaking, so beautiful it was as if she'd come from another world. And maybe she had because she'd completely vanished by the time he'd run down the flight of stairs.

He couldn't get her face out of his head all that first day, and that night he'd had a wet dream for the first time in years. Silvana had called him the next day for a repeat performance and he found himself pleading overwork. *Cristo*, since when did he turn down sex?

It was insane, he needed to see her. He'd been walking around with a semi hard-on for four days now, that couldn't be healthy. And Kay was becoming more and more insistent that something dangerous was going on. All the more reason to corner the woman. Maybe he'd just knock on her door and introduce himself.

The soft knock startled him out of his reverie and stopped Mark Harrington in mid-sentence.

"Mark?" Hope Winston opened the door a crack and stuck her head in, the pale spill of hair catching the light from the open windows. She looked around the room, silver blue eyes wide and anxious. "Can I interrupt your class for a minute?"

Enjoy this excerpt from
Christmas Angel

Naples, Italy
Christmas Eve, 2003

'Guarda o' mare quant'è bello,
Spira tanto sentimento'

Look at the sea, how beautiful it is,
How it moves the heart

-Old Neapolitan Song, Torna a Sorrento

A full moon shone brightly over Mount Vesuvius, casting an exquisite shimmering veil of silver over the Bay of Naples. Cruise ships lit from stem to stern with bright twinkling lights made their stately way across the bay like floating Christmas trees. The moonlight reflected off the calm bay sketched a pearly-white path to forever.

It was the most beautiful sight Nicole Caron had ever seen, and she'd traveled the world and seen her share of them.

The terrace of the French Consulate in the 17th century Palazzo Loredana was right on the bay itself, affording a view of Vesuvius, the bustling brilliant glittering city of Naples and the isle of Capri, a distant glimmer strung out on the horizon like a necklace of diamonds.

It was heartbreakingly beautiful and exactly as Alessandro had described it a year ago in Amman.

She'd lie in bed with him, her head on his broad chest and listened to his deep rumbling voice as he described his Naples.

She hadn't been listening all that closely, to tell the truth. She'd just had the most explosive series of orgasms in her life and any kind of exertion other than breathing and smiling seemed insanely ambitious. Nonetheless, his deep voice was hypnotic and she listened to what he had to say.

Some.

Just enough to get an impression of a glittering city by the bay, beautiful and lively and sparkling.

At the time, Naples had been the last thing on her mind, or what passed for a mind in the time she'd come to think of as 'The Alessandro Period'. Like an art historical period studied in college. From the 17th of December 2002 to the 24th of December 2002.

As historical periods went, it was short. Only a week, but a week that had rocked her world. She'd fallen wildly in love and had been brutally abandoned, all in a week. Seven days.

There was even an Italian film on it. *'Sedotta e Abbandonata'*. *'Seduced and Abandoned'*. 1964, director Pietro Germi. She'd seen it during an art film festival in her sophomore year at Brown, when she'd fancied herself an intellectual, dressing entirely in black, with a dyed white Susan Sontagian streak in her dark hair.

At the time, she'd been so sure of herself. So certain that romantic love was dead, a figment of oppressed female imagination. Modern liberated women didn't *do* love; they did conversation and sex. She'd dated Howard Morgan, another intellectual, that year. They'd spent endless hours talking, going to the movies and having very bad sex.

The last she'd heard, Howard was curator of a major museum in Texas and was on his fourth marriage.

To her surprise, Nicole hadn't stayed in academia. On a whim she'd sat for the Foreign Service exam, aced it, and had found herself in the diplomatic corps at the age of 25. Postings in Haiti, Peru and Jordan had followed. All hard posts. Career makers. With hazardous duty pay and opportunities for advancement.

All in places where a single woman had to watch her step.

Turned out sex and the single girl were unspoken Foreign Service no-nos.

Taking a lover meant — always — a security concern. 'Locals' were generally off limits. Single female foreign service officers were prey — considered by all the other male foreign service officers in the tightly knit diplomatic community a highly prized fuck. A single female officer would never endanger her career by making a fuss over being treated badly and she would be gone in two years, anyway. Which made them targets for all the married scumbags in all the embassies in the entire world.

Sex had been more trouble than it was worth.

Nicole had safely negotiated the shoals of singledom in the Foreign Service, feeling smug about resisting temptation and concentrating on her career, which she wanted to crown with an ambassadorship in twenty years' time. So she'd kept her nose clean and very close to the grindstone.

Until Amman.

Until Alessandro.

About the author:

Lisa Marie Rice is eternally 30 years old and will never age. She is tall and willowy and beautiful. Men drop at her feet like ripe pears. She has won every major book prize in the world. She is a black belt with advanced degrees in archeology, nuclear physics, and Tibetan literature. She is a concert pianist. Did I mention the Nobel?

Of course, Lisa Marie Rice is a virtual woman and exists only at the keyboard when writing erotic romance. She disappears when the monitor winks off.

Lisa welcomes mail from readers. You can write to her c/o Ellora's Cave Publishing at 1056 Home Avenue, Akron OH 44310-3502.

Why an electronic book?

We live in the Information Age—an exciting time in the history of human civilization in which technology rules supreme and continues to progress in leaps and bounds every minute of every hour of every day. For a multitude of reasons, more and more avid literary fans are opting to purchase e-books instead of paperbacks. The question to those not yet initiated to the world of electronic reading is simply: *why?*

1. *Price.* An electronic title at Ellora's Cave Publishing runs anywhere from 40-75% less than the cover price of the <u>exact same title</u> in paperback format. Why? Cold mathematics. It is less expensive to publish an e-book than it is to publish a paperback, so the savings are passed along to the consumer.

2. *Space.* Running out of room to house your paperback books? That is one worry you will never have with electronic novels. For a low one-time cost, you can purchase a handheld computer designed specifically for e-reading purposes. Many e-readers are larger than the average handheld, giving you plenty of screen room. Better yet, hundreds of titles can be stored within your new library—a single microchip. (Please note that Ellora's Cave does not endorse any specific brands. You can check our website at www.ellorascave.com for customer recommendations we make available to new consumers.)

3. *Mobility.* Because your new library now consists of only a microchip, your entire cache of books can be taken with you wherever you go.

4. *Personal preferences are accounted for.* Are the words you are currently reading too small? Too large? Too...ANNOYING? Paperback books cannot be modified according to personal preferences, but e-books can.

5. *Innovation.* The way you read a book is not the only advancement the Information Age has gifted the literary community with. There is also the factor of what you can read. Ellora's Cave Publishing will be introducing a new line of interactive titles that are available in e-book format only.

6. *Instant gratification.* Is it the middle of the night and all the bookstores are closed? Are you tired of waiting days—sometimes weeks—for online and offline bookstores to ship the novels you bought? Ellora's Cave Publishing sells instantaneous downloads 24 hours a day, 7 days a week, 365 days a year. Our e-book delivery system is 100% automated, meaning your order is filled as soon as you pay for it.

Those are a few of the top reasons why electronic novels are displacing paperbacks for many an avid reader. As always, Ellora's Cave Publishing welcomes your questions and comments. We invite you to email us at service@ellorascave.com or write to us directly at: 1056 Home Avenue, Akron OH 44310-3502.

NEED A MORE EXCITING
WAY TO PLAN YOUR DAY?

ELLORA'S
CAVEMEN
2006 CALENDAR

COMING THIS FALL

Lady Jaided magazine is devoted to exploring the sexuality and sensuality of women. While there are many similarities between the sexual experiences of men and women, there are just as many if not more differences. Our focus is on the female experience and on giving voice and credence to it. Lady Jaided will include everything from trends, politics, science and history to gossip, humor and celebrity interviews, but our focus will remain on female sexuality and sensuality.

A Sneak Peek at Upcoming Stories

Clan of the Cave Woman
Women's sexuality throughout history.

The Sarandon Syndrome
What's behind the attraction between older women and younger men.

The Last Taboo
Why some women – even feminists – have bondage fantasies

Girls' Eyes for Queer Guys
An in-depth look at the attraction between straight women and gay men

Available Spring 2005

Lady *Jaided* Regular Features

Jaid's Tirade

Jaid Black's erotic romance novels sell throughout the world, and her publishing company Ellora's Cave is one of the largest and most successful e-book publishers in the world. What is less well known about Jaid Black, a.k.a. Tina Engler is her long record as a political activist. Whether she's discussing sex or politics (or both), expect to see her get up on her soapbox and do what she does best: offend the greedy, the holier-than-thous, and the apathetic! Don't miss out on her monthly column.

Devilish Dot's G-Spot

Married to the same man for 20 years, Dorothy Araiza still basks in a sex life to be envied. What Dot loves just as much as achieving the Big O is helping other women realize their full sexual potential. Dot gives talks and advice on everything from which sex toys to buy (or not to buy) to which positions give you the best climax.

On the Road with Lady K

Publisher, author, world traveler and Lady of Barrow, Kathryn Falk shares insider information on the most romantic places in the world.

Kandidly Kay

This Lois Lane cum Dave Barry is a domestic goddess by day and a hard-hitting sexual deviancy reporter by night. Adored for her stunning wit and knack for delivering one-liners, this Rodney Dangerfield of reporting will leave no stone unturned in her search for the bizarre truth.

A Model World

CJ Hollenbach returns to his roots. The blond heartthrob from Ohio has twice been seen in Playgirl magazine and countless other publications. He has appeared on several national TV shows including The Jerry Springer Show (God help him!) and has been interviewed for Entertainment Tonight, CNN and The Today Show. He has been involved in the romance industry for the past 12 years, appearing on dozens of romance novel covers and calendars. CJ's specialty is personal interviews, in which people have a tendency to tell him everything.

Hot Mama Cooks

Sex is her food, and food is her sex. Hot Mama gives aphrodisiac a whole new meaning. Join her every month for her latest sensual adventure -- with bonus recipe!

Empress on the Mount

Brash, outrageous, and undeniably irreverent, this advice columnist from down under will either leave you in stitches or recovering from hang-jaw as you gawk at her answers to reader questions on relationships and life.

Erotic Fiction from Ellora's Cave

The debut issue will feature part one of "Ferocious," a three-part erotic serial written especially for Lady Jaided by the popular Sherri L. King.

Discover for yourself why readers can't get enough of the multiple award-winning publisher Ellora's Cave. Whether you prefer e-books or paperbacks, be sure to visit EC on the web at www.ellorascave.com for an erotic reading experience that will leave you breathless.

www.ellorascave.com